PENGUIN BOOKS

LOVE IN THE LAND OF MIDAS

Kapka Kassabova was born in Sofia, Bulgaria, in 1973.
After a year of study in England, she moved to New
Zealand with her family eight years ago. She is the author
of one novel and two books of poetry. She lives in
Auckland.

GW00669748

'*Take me by the hand to show me the world.*'
'*I have no hands, there is no world.*'
NIKOS KAVADIAS

LOVE IN THE LAND OF MIDAS

Kapka Kassabova

PENGUIN BOOKS

PENGUIN BOOKS

Penguin Books (NZ) Ltd, cnr Airborne and Rosedale Roads, Albany,
Auckland 1310, New Zealand
Penguin Books Ltd, 27 Wrights Lane, London W8 5TZ, England
Penguin Putnam Inc, 375 Hudson Street, New York, NY 10014, United States
Penguin Books Australia Ltd, 487 Maroondah Highway,
Ringwood, Australia 3134
Penguin Books Canada Ltd, 10 Alcorn Avenue,
Toronto, Ontario, Canada M4V 3B2
Penguin Books (South Africa) Pty Ltd, 5 Watkins Street,
Denver Ext 4, 2094, South Africa
Penguin Books India (P) Ltd, 11, Community Centre, Panchsheel Park,
New Delhi 110 017, India

Penguin Books Ltd, Registered Offices: Harmondsworth, Middlesex, England

First published by Penguin Books (NZ) Ltd, 2000

1 3 5 7 9 10 8 6 4 2

Copyright © Kapka Kassabova, 2000

Designed by Mary Egan
Typeset by Egan-Reid Ltd
Printed in Australia by Australian Print Group, Maryborough

ISBN 0 14 029879 7 C format
ISBN 0 14 100012 0 B format

To the memory of my grandmother
Anastassia Bahchevandjieva-Atanassova

To her ideal world which exists, somewhere.

ACKNOWLEDGEMENTS

Above all, I am grateful to the fabulous and disquieting cities of Thessaloniki and Marseilles, for firing and feeding my imagination; to Ohrid, my grandmother's home-town, for breathing wonder into my childhood; to my Balkan birth and history, for the gifts of tragedy and paradox.

My affection goes to Kostas Papazachariou in Greece for tirelessly providing me with knowledge of local detail.

My gratitude to the following people for giving generously of their time, knowledge and books: Pavlos Voskopoulos in Greece, Alexander and Vasilka Popovski in Macedonia (FYROM) and Michael Harlow in New Zealand.

I also wish to thank Anne-Marie Soulié for her friendship and readership and for introducing me to the writing of Nikos Kavadias; and Collette Lehman for her unforgettable house and company in Marseilles; my agent Michael Gifkins for his faith and humour; and Bernice Beachman at Penguin Books (New Zealand) for her enthusiasm.

I wish to acknowledge the support of Creative New Zealand in the first half of 1999 and of the Sargeson Trust and Buddle Findlay in awarding me the Buddle Finlay Sargeson Fellowship in the second half of 1999.

I am grateful to these authors for their illuminating and inspiring books: *Salonica Terminus* by Fred Reed, *The Heroic Age* by Stratis Haviaras, *Vanishing Point* by Aristotelis Nikolaidis, *The Rape of Greece* by Peter Murtagh, *The Salonika Bay Murder* by Edmund Keeley, *The Flight of Ikaros* by Kevin Andrews, *Memories of a Mountain War* by Kenneth Matthews, *Mission Box* by Aris Alexandrou, *Eleni* by Nicholas Gage, *Les Kapétanios* by Dominique Eudes, *Xenia – A Memoir: Greece 1919–1949* by Mary Henderson, *The Struggle for Greece: 1945–1949* by C. M. Woodhouse, *The Marked Men* by Ares Fakinos, *Black Seed* by Tashko Georgievski, *The Macedonian Conflict: Ethnic Nationalism in a Transnational World* by Loring Danforth, *Alexander the Great, the Invisible Enemy* by John Maxwell O'Brien.

Grateful acknowledgement is also given to the following publishers for permission to use excerpts from published works: Princeton University Press for 'Mythistorema (9)'; 'Mythistorema (8)', 'The Mood of a Day' from *The Collected Poems of George Seferis*, translated by Edmund Keeley and Philip Sherrard; Adolf M. Hakkert for 'Esmeralda' and 'Letter from Marseilles' from *The Collected Poems of Nikos Kavadias*, translated by Gail Holst Warhaft; Domaine Étranger for quote from *Le quart* by Nikos Kavadias, quotation translated from French by Kapka Kassabova.

AUTHOR'S NOTE

During the Second World War Greece was occupied by Nazi Germany and Italy. There was a strong partisan resistance consisting of left-wing and right-wing factions which coexisted in increasing discomfort. At the end of the war, and under British pressure, the Varkiza Agreement was signed; according to this the remnants of the left-wing resistance still roaming the mountains were to be disarmed. The clause in the agreement whereby Nazi collaborators were to be punished was not observed. This and further repression against former resistance fighters polarised a society only just beginning to pick itself up after the occupation. In the devastating, three-year civil war that followed, Britain supported the right-wing government against the rebels until the United States of America took over. Its Greek policy was summed up in the Truman Doctrine of 1947, which vowed to crush the guerrilla movement at any cost. At the end of the Second World War the great powers had decided that Greece was to be in the Western sphere of influence.

The guerrillas, organised into the Democratic Army of Greece (DAG) whose stronghold was in Northern Greece, received logistical support from Tito's Yugoslavia and from other communist countries in Eastern Europe. A large fraction of the guerrillas were Slav

Macedonians living in Greece, whose ambition was to receive long-lost recognition as a legitimate minority and even possibly secede from Greece. The guerrillas believed that Stalin and Tito would ultimately help them win the war. The break-up between Stalin and Tito meant that the Democratic Army was left to its own devices and eventually crushed by the government army and the American mission in two large-scale battles in the summers of 1948 and 1949.

One hundred and fifty-eight thousand Greeks and Macedonians died in the civil war, and there were at least as many refugees. The country was in ruins. The rebel survivors found asylum in the 'people's democracies' and many later emigrated to Australia, Canada and the United States.

The bitter legacy of the civil war heavily influenced subsequent events in Greece. In 1967, a military coup by a group of army colonels turned the country into an American-supported ultra-right-wing dictatorship. Non-violent resistance against the junta became a *cause célèbre* throughout Europe although very few governments opposed the colonels officially. Many Greeks were tortured and jailed during what is today known in Greece as 'the seven miserable years'.

PROLOGUE

July 1998, Marseilles

'Tell me the story about the Ohrid lake.'
'I've told you that story before.'
'Tell me again.'
'The surface of the lake shimmers. Here's why. King Samuil sent his troops to seize Constantinople, but the Byzantine emperor Basil took them to task. He had the fifteen thousand prisoners blinded, except he left a single one-eyed man per hundred blinded men, to lead them back home. When King Samuil saw his returning army of blinded soldiers, he died of heartbreak.'

His voice was tangled like an old rope extracted from the sea, overgrown with algae. He longed to look at her but he was a dis-embodied voice. His voice talked while his eyes gazed at the fabulous green surface. His fingers held a cigarette that was burning fast in the wind. He felt like a raving tourist guide whose group had long since sailed away from the island, behind his back.

'But before he died, he sent back for the eyes to be collected, and had them placed in a golden casket which was dropped in the lake. That's why it shimmers.'

Not a sound came from her. It was as though, like Orpheus, he had been instructed not to look away, or behind, just keep going until he left the underworld and found her next to him, restored, corporeal. When he finally turned to her, she was looking at him from afar, from that hypothetical place which offered her a greater truth than these ruins – or greater than him at least. Euridice was gone and he couldn't even tell her this. No, the banality of myth couldn't do justice to how he felt. She was still in that breathless way she had when events surpassed her.

'Keep talking, Theo.' She barely opened her mouth. 'Please.'

June 1949, Grammos

When everyone appeared to be asleep except the crickets in the field below, Pascal and Daphne sat on the fringes of the camp under a dry, broken tree – the last salient growth before the precipice hardened into rock. The only human noise was the typewriter at the other end of the camp, the political co-ordinator's endless reports to HQ.

'I brought you some new boots.' Pascal took them out of his rucksack. 'I hope they fit.' Daphne stroked the expensive leather but didn't put them on. He felt the heat of her face as she turned to him.

'Pascal, why have you come back?'

'To tell you a story. You see, for the last four months, I lived alone in my father's house in Marseilles. It's called Villa Maldormé, which approximately means bad sleep. From the windows, you can see le Château d'If where the Count of Monte Cristo was locked up, thanks to Alexandre Dumas's imagination. It's a bit like the Aegean islands, bare white rock. It's actually not a castle but a prison. The Man with the . . . masque de fer, iron mask, spent some time there too. His cell is still there. He was the brother of le Roi Soleil, the Sun King Louis XIV, and he looked too much like him. The king had him locked up, and as if that wasn't enough, he had him wear an iron mask.'

'A bit like this war really.'

'How?'

'It's a fratricidal war. The two camps are too much alike, and so we try to wipe each other out. A son killing his father. A brother killing his brother. Because one happens to be in the government army, and the other happens to be one of us. Every time you fire, you might be firing at your own. Except me. I'm out of danger now.'

She scraped at the dry soil and took a handful which she crumbled in her dirty, broken-nailed fingers. He brushed the remaining soil from her palm, then folded her fingers, as if they enclosed an invisible key, and held her hand. The crickets creaked madly in an optimistic crescendo. The orphaned stars twinkled like the eyes of small frightened animals in the dark. There was no moon. He let her talk.

PART ONE

The
Disquieting
City

ONE

September 1997–March 1998, Thessaloniki

The faded plush curtains of the myth-making years parted. The Aegean light revealed a place she recognised in the way she would recognise a blurry face in the background of a forgotten photograph. The harbour of Thessaloniki from which the stink of sewage rose when the vardari, the northern wind, pierced the city. The warm-faced people dishevelled by the vardari. The now deserted, windswept, unbearable beaches of Halkidiki. Everywhere, she had to stop herself from looking for the tall, stooped, bald silhouette, carrying paper-cones darkly full of sunflower seeds. She found a chronically worn-out Thessaloniki, like a very slowly ageing woman whose astonishing beauty has absorbed hardship all her life – impossible to say whether the beauty or the hardship had taken over in the end.

In Kassandra, the first protrusion of the three-legged Halkidiki peninsula, she walked past closed restaurants with chairs and tables in a heap. She sat on cold, wet sand and saw him standing on top of a cliff, arms comically flapping, then jumping off, straight and precise, his hair transparent against the bright sun. Then splash. He waited for her in the water, daring her to jump. She was afraid of deep water. 'It's okay, see – I did it, so can you! Come on, show me you're brave!'

She felt the detestable warm trickle on the inside of her leg, but ignored it, shut her eyes tight and, her heart bursting through her mouth, leapt off to her death, screaming. After that, she wanted to jump all the time. He would swim and she would lie on his back, her hand on his already balding head, the bare patch of skin smooth and strokable. That's where she liked to kiss him most – perhaps because it was the most inaccessible part of him. But as she grew older, he started to object to that old habit. 'Attention!' he would say. 'Do not disturb the growth of the flora!'

When, at the age of five, she cut off her favourite doll's hair and didn't see it grow back, she confided this to her mother who said, 'Don't be silly, it won't grow back. It's a doll.'

She went to her father. He examined the doll gravely and said, 'Yes, it will grow back, but you cut it very nicely, so you wouldn't want it to grow back, would you? You'd be annoyed if it grew back, no?'

She would have been, in fact.

'So, if you keep an eye on it and decide that it won't grow, then it won't grow! It's all here.'

He knocked gently on her head as if there was someone shy and precious living inside. He was a real diplomat.

She bought indiscriminately and read avidly the poets she could remember him reading while they lived here – Seferis, Cavafi, Ritsos, Kavadias – looking for lines that would have struck him, shaking them like branches overgrown with the ripe fruit of his delight, hoping for something to tumble into her lap, something of his that she could still hold.

In the deserted morning cafés and in the quiet of her apartment she eased the nuts of Greek words out of the shell of her memory.

Twenty years before, her father had read these poems on a Halkidiki beach. He wore his striped blue togs. He had yellow sunglasses that made him look like someone else.

'Just listen how he puts it, there's all of Greece in here, all of the Greek pain.' He was serious in his sudden, implausible way.

Véronique lay, her head on his folded elbow, her mother's head on his chest. She didn't understand all of it. In fact she couldn't remember whether he read the poems in the original or in French translation. She soon got bored and her father's voice like a sun-swing rocked her to sleep.

The harbour is old, I can't wait any longer
for the friend who left for the island with the pine trees
for the friend who left for the island with the plane trees
for the friend who left for the open sea . . .

From her sun-swing, she heard a faraway voice – 'She'll burn.' And a light fabric landed on her legs like feathers from a giant fantastic bird, and the shade of the bird fell on her face as it passed over silently.

Keep reading, Dad, she implored silently. I'm not asleep, I'm listening. All of Greece is here, all of the Greek pain . . . She wanted to wail but her pain like a rusty nail scratched the inside of her body and not a sound came out of her raw throat. The apartment was a tomb tiled with silence. Across the narrow street the black three-legged dog that she occasionally fed crouched in the November chill by a rubbish container, precisely beneath the polished scythe of the moon, as if waiting for overdue slaughter.

She rented a car and drove to the airport along Via Egnatia, then back. On the way back, she tried to locate the place where the crash had taken place. Via Egnatia was a fairly straight road. Did he know it was over the moment he saw the dusty truck rushing desperately towards his taxi, trying to regain its lane? What was his last thought? Five more seconds and it could have never happened. He would have been dropped safely at his hotel and gone about his business. But nobody would have known how close he had been to a hideous death. Everyone, including her, would have gone about their business, ignorant of the horror that could have been, had time been set back by five seconds.

Véronique pulled over with unsafe abruptness as the traffic flashed past. She looked at the bare hills, unbelieving that she should be here, tracing the last moments of the one person in the world she loved completely. The hills nudged towards her. Dirty, ragged November clouds gathered like a firing squad before the lightning. She had turned into an impasse and there was no point in driving on along the Via Egnatia of death. All roads lead to the place where her father had gone.

Less than two months before, one late morning in Istanbul, Véronique had a phone-call from him. He was calling from Paris, on his way to Thessaloniki 'to look up a couple of things'.

'What things?'

'You know, the old story.'

'But Dad,' she had said, 'it *is* an old story. I mean, thirty years!'

'Oh, thirty years is nothing. Piss under the bridge.' In his bon-enfant tone, verging on clownish, which he used when unsure of himself. 'Thirty years go just like that. Look at you.'

'What are you hoping to find out anyway that you couldn't last time?'

'Oh, this and that. I've got something that might be interesting to follow up. And I've got to see an old friend of Father's. It's a long story. I'll tell you when I finish down there.'

She didn't insist. He asked about her, about Istanbul. She said he should drop in. He would. In any case, he would call her again soon, from Greece.

'And keep some baklava for your sugar-depleted father, will you? Don't eat it all!'

They both loved baklava and made themselves sick on it when they lived in Greece. They made each other swear they wouldn't touch the stuff again. 'Until next time,' her father would add. Her mother, who was on a permanent diet, was disgusted. 'I don't want to look!' – and she looked.

Next time the phone rang in her Istanbul apartment, less than twelve hours later, it was her mother's flat voice: 'Your father has been in a road accident in Thessaloniki.' She didn't say 'killed' but Véronique knew it from her voice. She still felt a chilly stillness inside her at the thought of that call. She had held the receiver with a hand that hadn't felt attached to her body. A new wasteland had suddenly spread all around her – the world without her father. Like a city blasted by a nuclear bomb, with her the only survivor, stumbling around in a daze, neither dead nor alive. A Hiroshima of the heart. For a moment she had forgotten how to move, what to do, how to be herself – or anyone at all. She had felt her mind vacating her. And the bottomless, anaesthetic sea of grief had pulled her under.

Now she sped along the dusty Egnatia like any demented driver of the Mediterranean variety and thought how easy it would be to just let go of the wheel. What stopped her? Not fear but the animalistic sensation of long-forgotten adrenaline flushing her body, an almost orgasmic rage, a raging pain that was also an inebriation, a dark hissing flame she wasn't prepared to snuff. Back in her apartment, she briefly contemplated drowning herself in the bath. But she had a punishingly cold shower instead, snorted some heroin and lay on top of the unmade bed. For a slow, slow eternity, she listened to the muffled, scuttling noises of the night.

Eternity was a hotel of long corridors with blood-red plush walls and glistening, pleasantly slimy floors. Down the corridors echoed the distant footsteps of many dwarfs running. They laughed with mouths like red vulvas – approaching, expanding, stretching into interesting vowels, ho-ho, he-he, hi-hi, and a long, rather obscene ha-ha-ha-ha, but when she peeped inside for the tongues, there were none; the dwarfs were mute. And even though the dwarfs had stopped running and collapsed into their own giant mouths, their footsteps were still echoing, and she realised they were her own footsteps – ever-approaching, golden-heeled, ring-ankled, exquisite-boned, coming from a place whence every good news came, ringing with the good news: her father was alive again! Not just alive, but alive again – now that was something. The accident had happened all right, but he had come back to life. Jubilation filled her to the rim and spilled over. Her whole being wept with ecstasy. Without surprise, she noticed that her body was in fact the hotel with plush-lined walls and her bloodstream was the slippery corridor of excellent news, and the excellent news was contained within, forever warm and true.

Véronique decided to go to Thessaloniki soon after her father's funeral in Paris, in August. She was strangely affected by the sight of her grandmother Pauline, who, like a rare species of bug surprised in amber, was caught in the astonishment of having lost her only child. Véronique could feel the amber hardening by the minute, and Pauline remaining forever imprisoned, contorted impossibly into this ultimate loss. Véronique's mother wept continuously, perhaps realising what she had lost by divorcing Alex and what she would never regain. Everybody was stunned. As if Greece was not already written in large black letters in the family chronicles. Véronique had to find somewhere to flee. Being in Paris was unbearable. And if she had nothing to do in Thessaloniki except grieve, she had nothing to do elsewhere either.

As soon as she made the decision, she went to her father's apartment. His girlfriend Nour and her daughter Justine were still there, though when Véronique stepped in she saw boxes stacked in the corridor. Nour was going back to Alexandria, the city of her birth. Nour and Véronique's father had been together for ten happy years. She had perhaps been the love of his life. Véronique had once said to them, 'It's just a shame that you two didn't meet earlier.' Her father had replied, 'Well, I've got a couple of years yet before I hit the geriatric phase.' Nour had laughed her throaty, erotic laugh. She had a ten-year-old girl from a disastrous marriage and was now in her early thirties – although Véronique's mother conveniently referred to her as 'that girl'. Having spent little time in Paris in the last decade, Véronique rarely saw them, but the few times when she did, the sight of the beautiful olive-skinned girl, the exotic Nour and her beaming, balding father stabbed her with the sadness of things utterly lost to her.

The two women stood in shocked silence for a moment at the door. Nour's skin had lost its glow and grief had sucked the health from her cheeks. But Véronique knew her own transformation was worse.

'Jesus, Véronique!' Nour said, looking up. 'Your hair . . .'

'I know.'

When they sat down in the lounge, Véronique told Nour about her pending trip. She asked to see the contents of her father's travel bag, especially any papers and addresses he was carrying. Nour shook her head.

'His address book perished in the crash; it was reduced to tatters. There isn't much else there.'

'He told me on the phone he was going to visit an old friend of his father's. Do you have any idea who that was?'

'If it's the same one, it must be a certain Michel . . . mmm, Michel something. An Italian name. I'll remember it in a moment. I'm not sure what the story is. Alex was rather vague about these things, you know.'

'He was.'

'But then I didn't prod too much either.'

'I didn't either.'

'He was excited about going. But then lately, he'd been quite listless. I think he needed something to focus on, a sense of meaning and direction. Don't we all . . .' Nour cleared her throat. 'What I'm saying is, I'm not sure how much of his excitement was grounded in fact and how much was just the old call of adventure.'

Her father had carried only one small bag. He had kept the bag at his feet in the taxi from the airport. The only surviving items were his clothes and his shaver. The small address book had been in the pocket of his shirt. Véronique fingered these humble objects that still belonged to him even though he no longer owned them. They carried the vanished imprint of his fingers and body after he had been reduced to a pile of ashes. She pressed a shirt to her face, a toiletry bag soaked and stinking with everything that had been inside. She wanted to lie among these objects and sleep, and wake up only when he was back from his trip. Nour had left the room, with the tact and grace so natural to her.

There was also a brown envelope with a letter typed in Greek, addressed to her father in Paris, from the Ministry of Internal Affairs of Greece. Her Greek was rusty and she had to concentrate hard to make out the sense of the two laconic sentences. 'Dear M. Loublier, Your . . . for copies of the records of the . . . has been . . . You are (requested?) to . . . them in the person, at the . . . address.'

Nour knew nothing about this, but she knew something else.

'Michel Franchitti! Michel Franchitti was the name of the man he was going to see in Greece.'

She rummaged through scraps of paper by the telephone while Véronique listened to the name which rang like a distant bell.

'I've got it! 62 Mavrodromion, Edessa.'

'Where is Edessa?'

'No idea.'

Justine emerged from her room where she had been packing her things.

'Hello, Justine.' They kissed. 'Are you looking forward to going to Alexandria?'

The girl shrugged her shoulders.

'I guess so.' She was subdued. 'I will miss Alex though. I would've liked him to come along too.'

Nour and Véronique stared at the interesting patterns in the Egyptian carpet. When she hugged Nour and Justine goodbye, she felt with a dull ache that Nour was making a quiet, discreet exit from her life in Paris. Her departure doubled Véronique's loss.

TWO

March 1998, Thessaloniki

The faded plush curtains of the myth-making years parted. The Aegean light revealed the unkempt glory of an ancient décor. Smaller than the idea of it, like all things we have longed for excessively. Smaller than the memory of it, like all giants of our childhood. A green Alexander the Great on the waterfront, elaborate houses with surprising corners. The incurable humanity of Thessaloniki, despite the dehumanising efforts of history.

The difficult Philipidis family lurked in the northern suburbs like a many-headed monster waiting to smother him in its loving embrace. He didn't tell them when he was coming. He didn't want to be caught in sticky intimacy from the first week. He wanted to come as the stranger he was.

Immediately, he fell under the spell of inexpressibly old-world pleasures. The central market with its narrow, dingy streets bristling with hanging dismembered carcasses, its stalls of colourful Orthodox and Hellenic kitsch, its cheeses, crumbling hot pastries and *koulouris*. Girls with smooth skins and prominent, tightly controlled bottoms.

He kept postponing the meeting with the Philipidis family. Not because he didn't like them. But he had a vague memory that nothing here was simple.

'Theo darling, Australia swallowed you up.' Dafina on the phone from Ohrid, deep-voiced in her imperturbable way.

He shuddered. Not because he didn't love Grandmother Dafina, but he couldn't face the bursts of shaky emotion that greeted the estranged son, although of course Dafina was too solemn for the vulgar swoons of reunion. The Philipidis family here had waited for him for years – and for anyone from the Australian half of the family. Dafina over the border was always waiting too. And the Pacific stretched across with unnerving permanence. He, the representative of the virtually unknown new Australian generation, had a duty towards them. It was energy-consuming, though, to overcome the inertia of not needing them. And he needed his energy for other things.

When Theo came with his father to meet the family in Thessaloniki for the first time, he was five. He was trying very hard to make a good impression. Uncle Panayotis was bigger and hairier than Theo's father, and yet he sobbed embarrassingly when he clasped his brother, then Theo. He lifted Theo up as if to examine him against the sun, saying through his tears, 'My boy, look at you.' Theo did not enjoy this. Everybody else was crying too, except his grandmother, Hrisoula, who simply couldn't, with her stony face, expressionless and etched with a kind of stylised resignation. Panayotis's wife Paraskevas had lavishly golden hair and an enthusiastic, mobile mouth, even when she cried. Theo's older first cousin was just as embarrassed by the adults' erratic behaviour and made a point of not being impressed by his Australian cousin.

It was on his second visit, at the age of twelve, that Theo asked the only question capable of imposing silence on the entire Philipidis family who were dining extensively and all speaking at once. This time his mother was here too.

'Why do we all live in different countries?'

In the ensuing silence, Theo's father looked at Theo's mother, then at his brother Panayotis who looked at his wife Paraskevas who looked at her mother-in-law Hrisoula who looked at Theo with her expressionless face. It was Panayotis who spoke in the end.

'When we were children – me, your father, and your Auntie Sophia – there was a civil war in Greece, a long and cruel war. Thousands of children from the north of Greece were sent abroad to be safe and to be fed. Some were taken by force. Your father and Auntie Sophia were among those children. They ended up in Tashkent, in the Soviet Union. I was the oldest, so I stayed here with my mother, because our father, your Grandfather Angelis, was in a prison camp on the island of Ikaria and . . .'

His father interrupted Panayotis. 'I've told you this already, Theo . . .'

'Let the boy ask. He should know everything,' Panayotis cut in. 'What you're asking is actually why your father and Sophia didn't return when the war ended.'

Theo nodded, just in case.

'Well, they didn't return because the Greek state didn't allow them back in. All those children who were sent to other countries were barred from coming back until, well, much later. That's why we haven't seen each other for . . . so long. We don't want to think how long.'

Theo's father sat, smoking in silence, playing with his used napkin. He was suffering visibly from a post-dinner attack of his ulcer. He reached out and held his brother's arm, as if Panayotis was about to fall off his chair. Panayotis blew his nose.

'In fact, your Dad never saw our father again, except after his death in '67. He saw him in his coffin, across the border with . . .'

'Panayoti,' Paraskevas implored, 'the boy doesn't have to know all this. It will traumatise him.'

'Traumatise him? On the contrary, he must know this. When we die, who will remember what happened?'

'I have actually told him this,' Theo's father lied, suddenly, and looked at Theo intently. Theo glanced at his father in surprise but didn't say anything.

'Good,' said Panayotis. 'You have told him how you came to the border and Mum was standing by the open coffin on the other side, not able to recognise you, so much you'd grown up since '48, you were a grown man in fact, and you had to shout, and how the guards looked on, but one of them, the young one, broke down . . .'

'Yes, I have,' Theo's father lied again. At least he was consistent. Grandmother Hrisoula was distant as ever, as if she hadn't taken part in these events.

'Your Uncle Panayotis wasn't there,' Theo's father said to him. 'He was in prison where your Grandfather Angelis actually died. They were together there . . .'

'I thought you'd told him this!' Paraskevas observed dangerously.

'Yes, of course. Just reminding him.'

And the issue was closed. When, later, Theo asked his father about it, he simply said, 'I haven't told you this, son, because some things are too terrible to tell. Perhaps I will one day. But not yet. Some things need time.' It had been twenty years since it happened, Theo wanted to point out, but he felt his father's ulcer in the pit of his own stomach. Over the years, he fell into the habit of not asking ulcer-inducing questions. More time was needed, always.

The monster of the Philipidis family now stirred its weighty body and mauled him affectionately. They were almost more offended that he hadn't come to them straight away than happy to see him, but only for a grumpy, proprietorial moment. Then they squeezed him, kissed him, clasped him; he lifted a child he hadn't seen before, five-year-old Hrisoula, his cousin's daughter, pretended to tickle delightedly a baby with the bitter face of an old man, answered vaguely a thousand vague questions. It struck him that people of the same blood can exist in different dimensions for many years, seemingly never missing each other, but when a reunion occurs, it is an event of almost mystical proportions. Theo was not sure if he felt excited or ill in this old apartment with its old views of the harbour, the old furniture, the faces that had aged. Just as the cheap excrescence of the new town tried to merge with the ruins of the ancient town, so Theo tried to merge his Australian self with his Greek family. The Philipidis family were the crack between the real Greece and the transplanted Greece, between battered, self-obsessed ancient Europe and the smug Antipodes. Theo suddenly stood at the lip of that crack, unprepared, feeling that, if he fell, he wouldn't be able to crawl out.

At dinner, Theo sat next to little Hrisoula, a doll with round black eyes. Uncle Panayotis got up, flushed from the wine.

'A toast!'

Everyone raised their glasses. Theo expected the worst.

'A toast to the young! May they travel the world and may we, the not-so-young, follow them to America, Australia, wherever they go!'

'And Albania!' yelled out a chiming voice. Hrisoula was glowing.

The red wine froze in the glasses. Theo laughed and his laughter sounded hollow. Then suddenly, everybody else laughed, a little tensely, but then with relief. Uncle Panayotis laughed too, doing chin-chin with the baffled Hrisoula.

'So here's to the young! And may they come to us more often!' Uncle Panayotis concluded without losing his dignity and took a sip, then grabbed Hrisoula under the arms and twirled her around. She shrieked with delight. They were saved. Sweat trickled down Theo's hairline.

Smoking on the balcony among pots and wood carvings of the Macedonian dynasty sunbursts – somebody's patriotic pastime – and breathing in the multiple stench of dull modern suburbia, Theo let himself be sucked into the black hole that was the idea of Thessaloniki. The city put on her tattered cloak for the night. She sprawled, ancient and oblivious. The daytime bustle was finally vanquished, wrapped in softly rustling carbon paper, its pulsing lights flickering in the south, and the sea darkly behind them.

The family had gone to bed, exhausted by the strains of eating and bonding. Little Hrisoula scuttled across the moonlit lounge. In her transparent nightdress and with flowing hair, the nymph appeared in the indigo night and disappeared in the direction of the toilet.

Theo leant back in the wicker chair and travelled back to his uncomfortable arrival in Athens, a week ago. A stony-faced officer studied his Australian passport, scrutinising his photo, then him.

'What is the purpose of your visit to Greece?' His voice screeched like cheap suitcase wheels across an airport lounge.

'Research. For a PhD.'

'What in?'

'Classics. Ancient history. Alexander the Great.' He should have offered only one of these.

'Are you a Greek citizen?'

'No. I was born in Australia . . .'

'Why not?'

Theo opened his mouth, then smiled, amused.

'You have a Greek name.'

'My father is Greek but he lost his citizenship when he left Greece during the war.'

The officer gazed into his eyes severely. 'So he isn't in fact Greek.'

'He is. But he is an Australian citizen.'

'You can stay for up to three months.'

'But I was told six months!'

'Three months.' The thump of a stamp on a virgin page.

'But . . .'

'Next!'

He waved Theo through with that trademark look of faint disgust at which airport officials excel.

Theo shivered in the night breeze and stubbed out his cigarette. Hrisoula startled him, appearing in the moon-struck lounge like a ghost. She was startled by him too. She retreated behind the arm-rest of a couch, twisting the hem of her nightie around her index finger, peeping over shyly. He walked inside, lifting the lace curtain and ducking under. In the musty room the smell of coffee and moussaka lingered still. The loud ticking of the veteran lounge clock took him back to his childhood summer here when he would wake up in the morning, pounded into consciousness by the grave tolling. Would it remind Hrisoula of her childhood one day, when she returned from a faraway country to what would be left of the Philipidis family? He slumped in an armchair, feeling heavy and aged.

'Do you want me to tell you a story?'

She wound her nightie with increased vigour and nodded.

'Okay then, come over.'

She took one step in his direction and stopped, unsure. His strangeness in her eyes was the measure of his strangeness here. Hrisoula crossed the lounge, carefully stepping over a moonbeam that cut the worn, old-fashioned printed carpet in two. He made room for her in the oversized armchair. She climbed in and sat beside him, looking straight ahead, pulling the white nylon over her knees. Sensing her cold, he took a chilly little hand with peeling painted nails, and covered it with his seemingly giant paw.

'Once, there was a city so beautiful that its creator called it Saloniki, after his wife who was a princess, the sister of Alexander the Great. No, hang on, I'll start again. Once, there was a princess called Saloniki, so beautiful that her husband built a city and called it after her. The city was in the kingdom of Macedonia, ruled by Philippos, father of Alexander the Great. Saloniki prospered, great ships came to its port. A lot of riches were brought into the city's port and the kingdom blossomed, as did the beauty of the princess. But because Saloniki was so rich and beautiful, many others coveted her. They all planned and schemed how to conquer her. Finally, many, many years later, the legions of a guy called Consul Aemilius Paulus, a large, brutal general from Rome, came to the city gates in their shining helmets and long spears.'

Hrisoula's cherry eyes were fixed on his face.

'The wealth of the city was so great that it took the invaders a whole day to carry it out. Then the new invaders built a road called Via Egnatia, a very important road which ran through the heart of the new Roman Empire. You walk along Egnatia every week. A few centuries later, a noble young man called Demetrius was thrown to the lions by an evil emperor called Galerius, and from then on, Demetrius became the patron of Saloniki.'

'What did the lions do to him?'

'Well, they . . . ate him.'

'But why?'

'Because he was a Christian, and the Roman emperor didn't like Christians.'

'Why?'

'Well, he was rich, fat and corrupt, and didn't want the people to believe in God. Or rather, he wanted the people to believe that he was God.'

Hrisoula seemed happy with the explanation.

'Then, the Byzantines came and Saloniki became peacock city, which means a Byzantine city. The peacock meant immortality. Then the Turks came. When they took the city, one of them marked their victory by climbing up to the top of the city walls and cutting off the head of one of the city's Venetian defenders, throwing it to the army below.'

Hrisoula's eyes glowed. This wasn't a story for children but it was too late. If he stopped now, he would lose face completely.

'For several hundred years, Saloniki was a city in the Turkish Empire. Several hundred years is a long time: if you imagine that you grow up and have kids, and your kids have kids, that's not even one hundred years. Can you imagine that?'

She threw her head back in the Greek way.

'Then, there was some trouble in the Turkish Empire. Some officers wanted to change things, and the sultan opposed them. The sultan was their king. Finally, the sultan was sent into exile to Saloniki, where people hated him and couldn't wait to take revenge on him for all the evil that the Turks had done. When he learnt that he was being sent there, he fainted in the arms of his favourite eunuch.'

He couldn't help smiling at this.

'What's a eunuch?'

'A eunuch? It's a . . . man, like a servant to the sultan, who is not a real man.'

'What is he then?'

'Mmm, he is a man with a high voice and can't be with a woman.'

'Because his voice is high?'

'Yes.'

Theo lost the thin thread of his story.

Hrisoula was settling more comfortably, lifting her legs to her chest and hugging them with her arms. 'So . . . Saloniki was liberated from the Turks and the Greeks took it, because they got here first. Saloniki became Thessaloniki. This is where we are now. And that's all that matters.' A lame ending. He was disappointed with himself.

'But what happened to the princess?'

'Oh, the princess . . . had a happy life and then . . . died. But she is immortal because her name lives through the city.'

Hrisoula sighed and leant her knees on his lap, taking his hand again. At least she still liked him, after all the bloodshed.

'Are you cold?'

She yawned and muttered something. He put a plump cushion beside her. He sat still, looking at the little silky head, and then out of the window over the flat roofs of apartment buildings, his heart soaked with melancholy like a piece of cork forgotten in wine. Leaning on him with the heaviness of sleep, Hrisoula was breathing evenly, her warm hand twitching slightly in his. He hoped she wouldn't have nightmares about severed heads. Like a typical adult, he had told her a story which was really for himself – to lull himself with myths of glory perhaps – because the wounded glory of Thessaloniki reflected on the ingloriously wounded Philipidis family, and remotely, sympathetically, on himself.

On her way to the kitchen in the early morning, grim Grand-mother Hrisoula found Uncle Theo slumped uncomfortably in an armchair, his head drooping, his legs sprawled across the floor, and little Hrisoula huddled beside him, her hand invisible in his.

THREE

September 1997, Athens / Thessaloniki

The professionally weary, walrus-mustachioed director of archives read the letter carefully and drummed his fingers on his desk.

'I see, I see,' he grumbled fruitlessly, before finally saying in elegant French, 'It's an unusual request. We don't normally give access to files to . . . outsiders.'

'But the request has been granted, according to this letter.'

'Mmm. It's up to us whether to honour it, of course.' He looked at her with a tobacco-stained smile that wasn't entirely free of suggestiveness. 'Mademoiselle.'

'My father was coming to collect these records. I have no idea why. Even so, I feel that I have to finish his unfinished business, whatever it was.' She hoped to come across as delightfully stupid.

'You see, Mademoiselle, after the big clean-up in 1981, only some records were kept for reasons of national security. You are lucky to have this letter. Very lucky. Your father was able to obtain it only through diplomatic channels. We won't speculate too much about that because we're . . . well disposed towards you. But my strong personal advice is, whatever your father was up to, with all due respect, forget about it. Don't worry your pretty head with it. It's

a non-starter. Now, what are you doing tonight? I know a fine
taverna . . .'

Despite her revulsion, she was impressed with his French. And
unimpressed with the five precious photocopies he handed to her,
his fingers lingering on hers to convey the importance of the
transaction. In exchange, she gave him the phone number of a taxi
company in Athens she had just used, saying she would expect
his call.

*Grigoriadis Maria, née Nikolau, b.1895, Edessa, executed 1947,
Thessaloniki.* No photograph.

*Grigoriadis Stavros, b.1886, Edessa, member of ELAS, KKE and DAG,
died 1948, Makronisos.* A middle-aged man with bags under his eyes.

Grigoriadis Alexis, b.1928, Edessa, member of DAG, died 1948. A
fiery-eyed, groomed bird-face with clenched jaws.

*Grigoriadis Ilias, b.1919, Edessa, member of ELAS, DAG and KKE,
died 1948.* A light-eyed, clean-shaved, handsome face, the kind that
would have an ironic smile.

*Grigoriadis Daphne, b.1924, Edessa, member of DAG, whereabouts
unknown, non-grata.* Long-haired, with a tense mouth and dark eyes,
resembling the younger brother.

Véronique made a trip to the library. ELAS was a left-wing organ
of the resistance movement during the Nazi occupation. DAG stood
for Democratic Army of Greece. KKE was Kommunistikon Komma
Ellados, the Communist Party of Greece. And that was where her
investigative genius stopped. Not only were four of these people dead
fifty years ago and the fifth either dead or untraceably alive, but she
couldn't think why they could have been of any interest to her father.

On the plane from Athens to Thessaloniki, she brooded about the
pointlessness of her effort with the weary director. These days the
slightest effort exhausted her.

She also tried to listen to the distant ringing of the bell that was
Michel Franchitti's name. Franchitti. Michel. Just as she was slipping
into a slumber, a Riviera summer flooded her with its listless heat,
buzzing of flies and distant thunder of traffic. Rocking in a chair . . .

She must have been around ten. Like most years, she was spending the summer in Nice, in her Grandmother Pauline's Villa des Marées. She had discovered the disturbing beginnings of breasts – as if it wasn't enough that she was alarmingly tall. People started saying to her, 'You are so gorgeous, you will become an actress or a fashion model when you grow up.' It sounded like a threat. Twenty years on, her aunt would say to her, 'You don't look after yourself when you're young and pretty. And not even that young any more!' It was the same threat: you had better make something of your looks or else.

Grandmother Pauline was nice to be with, although Véronique was sometimes bored in the big house. She would sit on the verandah, in the ever-scorching sun, playing with Diane the Alsatian, eating ice-cream that melted before it reached her mouth, feeding Diane with the melted ice-cream and reading *Le Comte de Monte Cristo*. The island of If where the unfortunate count was locked up was only a couple of hours away, off the coast of Marseilles, but she knew that the current one was a fake, and only the one in the book was real. She knew her Grandfather Pascal had had a house in Marseilles called Villa Maldormé, but she suspected that like him and the island of If, the house was a legend and therefore not subject to real-life inspection.

Sometimes the chauffeur dropped her off downtown and then picked her up. She wandered through the flower market, sat on the fringes of the crowded beach, tried to feed broken biscuits to the ever-hungry gulls, watched with incomprehension the vanity fair that strolled along the coast: women with sagging brown breasts, men with giant stomachs, and others with gleaming knotted torsos, poodles that left little heaps of dung on the Promenade. It was around this time that she began to apprehend the nature of the aloneness that would stay with her ever after.

Up at the castle walls by the sea, a mad old lady came every day to feed the gulls. She wore diamond rings and gumboots over her tight trousers. She reached into a slimy bucket and extracted stinking fish which she threw to the gulls, her head shaking uncontrollably, her greasy lipstick the colour of dead sunsets. 'Come on, my little ones,' she croaked to the giant birds, ugly and bloodthirsty like vultures, 'eat up, eat up.' Véronique stopped feeding biscuits to the gulls.

One particularly sultry afternoon, the maid announced that a certain Monsieur Franchitti was there. Véronique was on the balcony. Enter Monsieur Franchitti. He wore a long beige overcoat, like a detective or a musketeer hiding a sword. Pauline greeted him. They kissed on the cheek, once, twice. He looked vaguely familiar, like a character from a book, the way Count Monte Cristo would look if he turned up in the lounge. They sat down.

'Would you like some whisky?' Pauline asked.

'No thanks. I don't drink any more.'

'Congratulations.'

'Where is Véronique?' he said.

Watching them through the shutters, Véronique was startled to hear her name in the voice of this near-stranger.

'Véronique, mon trésor,' shouted Pauline, 'come say hello.'

Véronique went inside. Michel Franchitti had grey hair and bushy eyebrows weighed down by the beads of sweat that clustered over them. She thought that was hardly surprising, considering the overcoat. She instantly liked his overcoat and his eyebrows and his name, Michel Franchitti, quick and sonorous like the chin-chin of crystal glasses in an empty, candle-lit castle.

'Goodness me, you've grown all right!' he said, smiling at her, leaning back in surprise. She was overcome by a coquettish shyness. She felt self-conscious about the points of her someday-to-be-breasts poking through her T-shirt. 'Last time I saw you,' he said, 'you were this big.' And he held his hand at the level of her waist. She couldn't remember last time but stood in a polite sun-daze. Pauline was sitting with her freckled, jewelled hands on her knees, careful and focused, as if she too was trying to remember last time.

Véronique was free to go back to the verandah. Glued to the shutters outside, her hand on Diane's head to keep her quiet, she watched the striped scene.

'Did Alex tell you?'

'Yes.'

He handed something to Grandmother Pauline.

'They found nothing else?' Pauline said.

'Nothing else.'

Michel Franchitti moved over from the armchair to the divan where Pauline was sitting and put his hand on her shoulder, or was it on her knee? He kept muttering something but it didn't reach Véronique.

'Now what?' Pauline said. Véronique had never seen her grandmother so helpless.

'I don't know. I don't know. Alex will want to set up another inquiry, possibly spend some time there . . .'

'Where? In Greece? Go to Greece?'

'Yes. Possibly with the family.'

This was news for Véronique. When Michel Franchitti left, Pauline sat motionless, clutching the arm-rests, her eyes fixed on an invisible nightmare. Véronique sat next to her without a word, instinctively knowing her grandmother needed comforting. Pauline's stone-cold hand clutched hers convulsively for a long, eventful moment. She then retired to her bedroom and stayed there for several hours. Véronique fell asleep on the verandah and when she woke up, her face and shoulders were burnt. Pauline came out, wearing dark glasses.

Véronique didn't ask questions; she was used to living amidst the incomprehensible. The two of them sat on the verandah – Pauline in her dark glasses, Véronique in hers. They sipped lemonade. The sea glittered with gold. The pastel houses shimmered in the air. A siren went off. The dog was drowsing. Véronique felt she was on the verge of something.

'Véronique, mon trésor,' Grandmother Pauline said in her smoker's voice, the one she had when she had important things to announce, 'you must never fall in love. It's the biggest calamity. Remember this from your grandmother.'

'What's calamity?'

Pauline thought for a moment and said, 'Calamity is when the man you love leaves you. And he never returns. And you never find out why.'

'Like Grandfather Pascal?' Véronique suggested helpfully.

Pauline nodded – in fact it was more like a slump, her chin doubling, as if she was falling asleep.

'Calamity is when you have everything except what really matters,' she said.

Véronique was tempted to say 'You mean Grandfather Pascal?' but knew better and said instead, without much conviction, 'But you have François.' Somehow she sensed that François couldn't compare with Pascal. François was in Paris preparing for an election campaign. Pascal had disappeared. They were total opposites.

A tear quivered on Pauline's trembling chin and fell inside her freckled, scented bosom. A rustling, hollow sound came out of her chest, as if someone was unfolding a dusty paper accordion inside her.

'Remember this from your grandmother,' she said again. 'And something else, my treasure. If you do go to Greece with your mum and dad, be very careful. And remember your grandmother who will be waiting for you.'

Véronique knew that, technically, Grandfather Pascal was dead. When his passport was handed over by the Greek police, it was like handing over his remains. Technically, that was. But she could not shake off the impression that Pascal was the kind of man who could easily live without a passport, a face, or a country. She wished she could communicate all this to Pauline, who sat on the verandah, motionless and breathing like an accordion, for the rest of the afternoon. She was perhaps asleep, or crying so quietly that Véronique moved around her on tiptoe, and so did the dog. Soundlessly, restlessly they paced in the hot, padded cell of that never-ending Riviera afternoon.

FOUR

March–April 1998, Thessaloniki

The tall, peroxide-haired woman dipped in and out of his vision for weeks. He noticed her soon after he arrived. She moved slowly but without deliberation. Her absent movements tugged gently at the tattered edge of his disorientation. He saw her buying something at a yoghurt and cheese stall at the central market. People turned to look at her – and not just men. Everything about her was arresting. The crowd swallowed her but didn't digest her. She stood out as though she was standing alone against a backdrop. She was structurally incapable of merging – and it wasn't just her hair. He saw her sitting alone at the waterfront, at dusk, eating sunflower seeds out of a paper bag. He saw her reading a book at an outdoor table on his way to the Museum of the Struggle for Macedonia. She was eating a horiatiki salad, her weird white hair ruffled by the wind. She looked distantly familiar, like everything in this city, except she was even more distant than his most remote memory of Thessaloniki. She went a long, convoluted way into the recesses of his imagination.

He started looking out for her. He happened to find himself in the areas where she had appeared to him before. It was hard to tell whether she noticed him. Sometimes her strange amber eyes screened him placidly, with no sign of acknowledgement. Her face betrayed no emotion, her body no particular purpose. But whenever she crossed his day, in slow motion, she left a trace of light in her wake. His days began to bear the involuntary imprints of long, distracted limbs, a frazzled shock of bleached hair, an olive-green leather jacket. Sometimes she wore sunglasses. Was she Greek? There was something decisively foreign about her. Scandinavian? Her skin was too olive. Latin? The colour of her hair disturbed the balance. American? Too sophisticated, even in her negligence. Theo knew that American women had a certain literalness to their movements, which was not the same as simplicity. She had simplicity, but it was the simplicity of obliqueness.

Theo went out with a slightly horsy American-Italian girl in his second year at university. He was attracted to the breezy worldliness she seemed to exude, which turned out to be a simple lack of interest in anything other than her organic diet and her horoscope. He then dated an Australian woman who was a feminist and wouldn't have doors opened for her. When, one imprudent night, in a bar, he told her that European women were real women in a way Australian women didn't understand (and nor did he, of course), she slapped him on the face and told him it was over. Then came the Greek–Australian woman who was a painter of giant, blackly nihilistic oil compositions and demanded to be hit during sex. He was intrigued at first, then tired, then started avoiding sex with her altogether and they both realised there was nothing else worth hanging on for. He went out with a feisty Macedonian–Australian for a few months; they had unsophisticated but explosive sex and sophisticated but passionless conversations, until she fell in love with her lecturer. At one point, he developed a crush on a classics lecturer, several years older than himself, but she was already taken. Since then, he had been going through a stoical abstention period, despite being continuously sought after. Somehow, there were blank spaces in most women, but he wasn't sure what exactly should be there. Somehow, he was always talking and feeling past them rather than with and for them, like a blind man trying to hit a target. He wouldn't settle for a woman less than perfect.

The Museum of the Struggle for Macedonia was closed for reconstruction. And so was the Museum of Ancient History, which was essential to Theo's study. Everything from excavations in the region was there. The finds from Philip's tomb in Vergina: the gold leaf-crown, the quiver, the larnax with the Macedonian star of Vergina, sixteen-pointed; the tiny ivory heads, intricate and instantly recognisable – father and son. The mosaics of Pella. The mosaics of Dion.

After two days of frustrated effort, he managed to make an appointment with the assistant director of the Museum of Ancient History.

Mr Papadopoulos was a stubby, heavily perfumed man, carrying his importance like an expensive suit. Theo shook his small hand with a long nail on the little finger and showed his card from the Australian Archaeological Institute. He explained the nature of his research. Papadopoulos inspected the card.

'Who issued this authorisation?'

'I'm a member of the AAI. This entitles me to access all facilities in Thessaloniki.'

Papadopoulos sized him up and handed him the card back.

'So, you come from Australia. How's life in Australia?'

'All right.'

The man nodded repeatedly. 'And your parents are Greek?'

'My father is. My mother's Macedonian.' Theo wished he could swallow his words back the moment they came out.

Papadopoulos cocked his head interestedly. 'You mean she's Greek Macedonian.'

'No, she's Macedonian, from Macedonia.'

'Excuse me? You mean Greek Macedonia of course?' Papadopoulos placed his small palms on his desk and leant forward, preparing for his dramatic outburst.

'She's from Macedonia, for Christ's sake! She's not Greek. Now . . .' Theo really had no time for this.

'What Macedonia? What are you talking about? *I* am Macedonian! *This* is Macedonia, right here!' Papadopoulos struck his chest with a proud fist, rage rising towards his face in a red wave. 'You must learn ancient history, Philipidis, before you set foot in my office again! They don't teach you history in Australia? What, you've been hopping about with the kangaroos all this time?'

'Oh look, I know about all this stuff and I'm not interested, okay? I'm here for something else.'

'Something else?'

Papadopoulos deftly, almost graciously in fact, circumnavigated his desk and came forward, stabbing his hairy finger in Theo's chest. From the involuntary close-up, Theo was able to establish that his hair had been dyed.

'Something else, huh? I know the likes of you. You're a fake Greek! A Skopjan agent, and an Australian agent! Agent of the global conspiracy against my fatherland! Get out before I call the police! Researching Alexander! You come to twist my history, rape my heritage! I don't want to see you again in my museum!'

Dazed, Theo stepped out into the warm bright afternoon. He should complain. He would complain. He turned around, determined not to be bossed around by this homunculus with long nails on his little fingers, and walked back into the office. The assistant director was looking through some files. Theo cleared his throat.

'I'm going to make a complaint about this. This is against the law. I am Australian. I have the right . . .'

'Against the law?' Papadopoulos looked at him almost with compassion. 'What law? *I* am the law here, boy. Understand? Now go back to your kangaroos.' And he bent over his files again.

Theo slammed the door behind him. He walked past the closed Museum of the Struggle for Macedonia on shocked, unstable legs. It was of course silly to expect that all Greeks dealing with archaeology would be like Professor Vengos in Melbourne – gently sardonic, sighing at the absurdity of things . . . The museum would not open until June. And he was only allowed three months here.

For him, it all began during the double demonstrations of the Greek and Macedonian ethnic communities in Melbourne. The Macedonians shouted, 'Macedonia for the Macedonians!', waving the new flag of the Macedonian sunburst of Vergina. Some voices shouted,

'Get your hands off Alexander!' The Greeks held their own demonstrations against the new republic's name and flag. 'Greece is Macedonia,' shouted their banners, and 'The only Slavs in Greek Macedonia are tourists.' 'Well, I wonder why!' brooded Theo's mother, who was allergic to all things political otherwise. 'They slaughtered them in the civil war, and kicked out the rest, that's why.' His father regarded the protests as childish: 'Who cares anyway, whether the Vergina star is Greek or Macedonian and how many rays it has? Let the Greeks have eight rays of it, and the Macedonians the other eight, and everyone should be happy.' Theo was not politically inclined and to him it all looked like two school camps standing in their Alexander costumes, complete with helmets, spears and shields, shouting at each other in front of the amused cameras: 'Is mine!', 'Is not!', 'Is too!'

That was when, drifting and in need of a focus, a twenty-year-old Theo decided to become an expert on Greek and Macedonian ancient history. To show that the drama of ancient history transcended the petty yapping of modern nationalisms. To delve into the timeless extravagances of the human imagination. To show that Alexander's legacy was not the property of one single modern nation, but the heritage of all human civilisation. That some things were universal and beyond appropriation. Three years later, he wrote an outline for his thesis:

Alexander's Gods and Heroes: A Study of Cult and Deity in the Life of Alexander the Great.

1. *Achilles. The psychology of immortality. Alexander's heel.*
2. *Dionysius. The hidden enemy. Alexander's death.*
3. *The son of Ammon. The Alexander cult.*

Professor Vengos was impressed by Theo's ideas and stood behind him in his application for access to Thessaloniki's facilities. But he gave him a word of warning: 'Remember, Alexander is a Greek hero, above all. Make sure your abstract is more positive. Alexander can't be an alcoholic. You can't have this kind of irony in your thesis.'

'But that's ridiculous!' said Theo. 'Who cares about keeping Alexander's face?'

'Believe me, they care.'

'But this is not just a biography.'

'I know. It's a minefield.' Vengos sighed, but then he sighed often, even during his lectures, in the middle of sentences.

FIVE

Winter 1997–1998, Edessa/Thessaloniki

Like many northern Greek towns, Edessa was withholding something essential from the visitor. The bus drove in. Scooped houses watched from the slopes like a convention of tight-lipped women.

At the door of his whitewashed house, Michel Franchitti greeted her with the same warmth that had been in his voice on the phone.

'Ah, my dear Véronique, how you've grown! The last time I saw you, you were this tall.' He raised a hand to his chest. She smiled. Kisses on the cheek, one, two.

The bushy eyebrows were firmly in place, now completely white. The green eyes had an obliqueness both comforting and prohibitive. He had the face of a retired Balkan warlord, the way Véronique had seen them on the TV news – wild-haired, charismatic, with a degree in psychiatry. But above all, he wasn't the decrepit man he should have been; he appeared younger than the Michel Franchitti in the overcoat, in the striped scene of twenty years ago. A Greek woman, at least thirty years his junior, gracefully served olives, cheese, tomatoes, warm bread and meatballs but didn't sit down with them. She wore fluffy slippers on heels and tight jeans over her large bottom.

'My wife Eleftheria,' Michel said. The woman smiled inscrutably and shuffled out with the empty tray. Véronique had trouble distinguishing between wives and housemaids in this part of the world.

'I am very sorry about your father.' His French was touched by a Greek accent.

'Did you know him well?'

He hesitated. 'Yes, you could say that. At least in the past.'

There was a silence.

'Help yourself to some lunch. You are familiar with Kalamata olives, no doubt? The best in the world – after Nyons olives, of course!'

Véronique nodded vaguely and took an oily olive.

'I see that you've made Greece your home,' she glanced around. The lounge was a shrine to kitsch – statuettes of the Virgin, bucolic pastel drawings, lace over the furniture.

'That's right. I haven't been back to France for five years now.'

'Are your children there?'

'Yes, of course, but they're grown up, they have families, you know how it is.'

Véronique nodded vaguely.

'No, you don't, how could you know!' he exclaimed a little too abruptly, startling her in her hard wooden chair. 'You're young.' He glanced at her hair with polite curiosity. She was suddenly gripped by the timidity of twenty years ago. He poured some red wine, broke off some fresh bread and cut the feta cheese with his fork.

'So, tell me, what have you been up to?'

As if they were friends catching up. Véronique hesitated. She wasn't sure she liked this Michel as much as the one she remembered. But he was waiting. So she talked about Toronto, Cartagena, Istanbul. She avoided mentioning her father, keeping it for last. Michel listened, his mouth working away, his greedy green eyes on the table, hardly ever looking up at her. His scalp moved thoughtfully as he chewed. When the first silence set in, she took a sip of wine. He cleared his throat.

'Véronique, I haven't been able to sleep for the last two nights, since you called. This is a very strange visit indeed.'

She held her breath.

'Greece has been kind to me,' he went on. 'She is my home now. I've forgotten my previous life. I prefer it that way.'

Véronique was stabbed unpleasantly by this warning.

'Your call was like an echo from that previous life. The same happened when your father called, a couple of months ago.'

He was playing with the many stones of his eaten olives, arranging and rearranging them on his plate with a fork. He cocked his head to inspect the latest composition.

'Why did Dad call you? I gather he wanted to see you.'

Eleftheria shuffled in with aromatic coffee and baklava.

'I hadn't seen Alex for many years. I was fond of him. He was a remarkable boy. A remarkable boy.'

I don't know, I don't know. Michel shook his head and played with the rim of his glass thoughtfully. Véronique felt like a glass of wine about to be spilled. The green eyes looked up at her, as if for help.

'Did Alex tell you much about Pascal?' he asked.

'No, not much. But I didn't ask much either.'

He sipped his coffee and lit a cigarette. 'Everyone suffered from Pascal's disappearance in their own way, Véronique. Pauline, Alex, all his friends, including myself. But Pauline suffered the most. And now, when I look at events, it does seem like . . . like there is some sort of curse over the Loubliers, a kind of evil eye . . .'

The hand holding the cigarette shook.

'That's a very Greek thing to say.' Véronique tried to smile, but sensed a chill in her spine.

'Maybe. It's impossibly complicated. No, actually it's not. It's probably very simple. The problem is, nobody knows just how simple it is. The unknown is, by definition, complicated. But the unknowable can be promoted to mystery. Pauline was poisoned by this. It killed her. And of course it killed Alex.'

'Yes, I know,' Véronique heard herself say rather loudly.

Michel stubbed out his cigarette with the same melancholy attentiveness he seemed to apply to everything, from olives to memories. Véronique was shocked by a stray thought: he must be a wonderful lover. She pulled the photocopied sheets from her bag

and silently handed them to Michel. He craned his neck to look at
them but didn't touch them.

'Where on earth did you get these?'

'At the Ministry in Athens. Dad had a letter in his travel-bag. I
think he was intending to pick them up.'

She spread out the pages.

'Partisans Pascal could have known in the civil war?' he speculated.
'These records must be prodigiously hard to get hold of.'

'Was Dad trying to get hold of these people, do you think?'

'Well, they're dead.'

'I mean the one survivor.'

He looked at the photograph of the woman. 'This woman is
most likely not in Greece – if she is alive at all.' The green eyes were
screwed up.

'Was this the thing Dad had found and wanted to show you?'

Michel shook his head. 'I don't know, but I don't see why.'

'Can you guess why he wanted to see you?'

'I don't guess any more. Besides, does it matter now?' Michel put
the sheets together, aligning them into an excessively neat pile and
handed them back to her. He looked at something above her head.
Later, she realised it was the cuckoo clock.

'Look,' Véronique said softly, 'if there is anything else you think I
might not know . . . I want to make sense of why Dad made that last
trip here, if there is any sense to be made of it.'

Perhaps he knew nothing more after all. Perhaps he was a tired
old man who had no more answers. He motioned her to move over
to the sofa, like Grandmother Pauline . . . He sat in an armchair,
facing her, and lit another cigarette.

'I don't know if I should mention the manuscript. It might be
completely irrelevant.' He threw his large head back. 'Ah, where do I
start? Okay. When Pascal went to Greece that second time, in '67, he
wanted to write a book about the survivors of the civil war. I backed
him up. I was going to work on finding a publisher while he was
away. I believed in what he was doing . . .' Michel's voice was flat, as
if reciting a memorised piece of text. 'He was going to collect as
much information about the survivors as possible, in Greece and

around the Eastern Bloc – because that's where most of the survivors were.'

His cigarette was burning absently in his hand.

'Would you like a little cognac?'

It tasted like fire.

'For weeks we waited to hear from Pascal, until we smelled a rat. He became an officially missing person. An inquiry was set up. As you know, it didn't yield any results. It wasn't a good time for Greece, or for such inquiries to be set up, with the colonels' coup and all. It was the worst possible time, in fact.'

Michel paused and looked inside his glass. The silence stretched.

'What about that manuscript?'

'Right. In '76, a manuscript arrived for him at his Marseilles address. In Greek. There was a note attached to it, signed with a first name, saying that the author had died in jail and it was his son writing. There was no return address. We, I, didn't know about it for ages because the house in Marseilles was basically derelict, nobody collected the mail. When we saw it, we didn't know what to make of it. We had it translated. It was a memoir, basically, of a prisoner on the Aegean islands, during the civil war. It was . . . how shall I put it . . . harrowing. That's when Pauline had her second breakdown. She read parts of it and was beside herself thinking that he could be interned on such an island. I tried to reassure her that these camps didn't exist any more and besides why would they imprison a French writer . . . But she'd already snapped. We thought she'd never recover. That's when she burnt a whole lot of Pascal's papers.'

'Including the manuscript?'

'To the best of my knowledge.'

Michel leant back in the armchair and suddenly looked very aged. Véronique felt the way he looked.

'Who was the author, I hear you ask. But first let me tell you about the passport.'

'I actually remember the time you came to la Villa des Marées in Nice,' she said.

'Oh, do you! You were a very tall and serious little girl.'

'Well, I was surrounded by serious little adults, I suppose. But I

He was right, of course. At the door, Véronique thanked him
through a daze of despondency. He waved to her from the square of
the door, large-headed, almost leonine – but a tame lion. 'Come
again,' he shouted, 'we'll talk more.'

She nodded with false energy and quickened her pace as if she
had somewhere to get to. The tight-lipped houses watched her.
Waterfalls pounded the cold Edessa plain.

The contrivance of her 'inquiry' was embarrassingly plain. She
had imagined a door in the middle of an empty space. The door had
opened. She had stepped into the sudden Aegean light, the door
closed behind her. She was still in the same place because the door
had been imaginary. She was free from the burden of possibility now.

The night she returned from Edessa, she went into a bar in
Thessaloniki, drank a large amount of antiseptic ouzo as if swallowing
a medicine, and watched numbly the manic breaking of plates as the
music and dancing gathered speed and eventually became slurred
like the night, like her life. She briefly considered inviting an
attractive, fiery-eyed young man to her apartment – more out of a
tired reflex than desire – but then remembered the boy in Istanbul
and, disgusted with herself and the world, crashed on her bed and,
too disgusted even to cry or snort some powder, caved into uncon-
sciousness. When she woke up and remembered her whereabouts
and recent events, she saw, with blinding clarity, that she had nothing
to live for.

The winter weeks in Thessaloniki rolled by, gruff and prohibitive
like the old men at provincial *kafeneios* trudging along with their
bent sticks, muttering curses, spitting out phlegm. She began to float
in a vacuum of habitual grief so boundless that she needed to cling
to something, however insignificant and banal, and shape it into a
boundary within which she could find momentary respite. Miraculously, she got a job at the foreign language bookstore in Tsimiski
Street. Every other day she sat behind a desk on the second floor and
catalogued new arrivals and old ones that had been mislaid. Often,
she was called upon to deal with customers in French or English;
sometimes even her basic Italian was useful. The pleasant, mindless
absorption of this occupation provided her with a routine of fitful

forgetting. But she also chose to forget to change her clothes for a week or wash her hair. She didn't see the point. On her free days she took long strolls around the city, trying to take an interest in the Byzantine churches and historic vestiges scattered seductively around the modern platitude that Thessaloniki was striving to become. She climbed the streets of the old town, from her apartment to the highest lookout spot at the city walls, followed by a pack of faithfully homeless dogs.

One cold January afternoon, she stood at the walls and told herself: these are Theodossius's walls, built in the fourth century AD. Theodossius slaughtered thousands of civilians at today's International Fair grounds. Galerius slaughtered the Christians, the Normans from Sicily slaughtered the Salonicians, the Turks slaughtered the Christians, the Nazis slaughtered the Jews and the Greeks, the Greeks slaughtered each other . . . Was that the right order? Fathers and daughters were slaughtered together and separately. The prison of the Seven Towers, Eptapirgio, just beyond the walls, saw thousands of political prisoners tortured and killed in its embrace. How many fathers were lost there, wasted by starvation, their bodies and spirits crushed in ways uglier than a car crash?

But this only caused convulsive shivers to run down her body. Her nose numb with cold, her body shaking in the piercing vardari wind, she thought of one warm mountain afternoon.

After an arduous climb, she and her father stood on a Mount Olympus peak. For the first time then, she had the disquieting feeling of remembering something as it was taking place. Not quite a déjà-vu, but a head-on collision with an angular, disjointed time, awkward and faintly repellent, like touching a dislocated limb.

'Think that now we are where the gods were,' her father said, sweepingly describing the glorious peaks around.

'When did the gods die?' Véronique knew she was asking the wrong question.

'They didn't die. Gods don't die.'

'But you said they *were*.'

'Did I? Okay, I meant they *are*.'

'Where are they?'

'They're us. While we stand here, we can be the Greek gods, if you want.'

'Which ones?'

'Any one. All of them.'

Véronique didn't believe him but, for his sake, she closed her eyes and tried to imagine being the Greek gods, or at least one of them, a minor one perhaps, a little one . . .

'Which one is a little god?', she asked.

'There's no difference. They're all big. Or they're all little, doesn't matter.'

Véronique looked at her feet.

'You don't have to do anything to be the gods.' He saved the day. 'It's very simple. It means that while we stand here, we can live forever. That's what it means being the gods.'

'Do we have to stand here forever, to live forever?'

Her father thought for a moment. His frizzy fair hair glowed and trembled in the warm summer breeze.

'No, because in a sense, wherever we go from now on, we'll always be standing here. There's no end to our standing here, you see. No one can interfere with us standing here forever. I mean, do you see anyone rushing to interfere? Our forever is nobody else's forever. And in that sense, we are the gods.'

He took her hand in his and held it tight. Véronique knew happily that her father was telling the truth, even if it didn't make any sense. And whatever the story with the gods was, she would never be as close to anyone as to her father.

If her father wasn't mistaken, they must still be standing on Mount Olympus. It was – it is – 1979 forever. It is a moment that lasts forever, and so by definition has no beginning and no end – which is why she remembered it even then, as it was happening. Still, what was real was not Mount Olympus but this desolate damp wall overlooking a battered Thessaloniki, the city which engulfed her father and, before that, her grandfather. A city at once tiny and immense, ancient and modern, human and indifferent, real and unreal like a nightmare, with her standing at the top, fatherless, faithless. Because the gods had vanished with her father.

She knew that day that the loss of her father was not a wound that would close with time. The hole he had left was shaped like him and went as deep as her life would ever go. That hole would not change its shape or size with time. It was just a question of managing to stay on the edge without falling in.

Her father's abrupt disappearance from the familiar world made that world unfamiliar. Memories weren't the same any more. As though a desperate, vanquished army had cut off all the bridges and mined the fields in the wake of its retreat back to the country of shadows. That's the kind of metaphor Pascal Loublier would have used, Véronique reflected and, for about half a second, was surprised to have thought of him. Then anger flooded her. Pascal, the man who never died properly, turned her past into a graveyard. Pascal, for whom the word speculation was invented, had to disappear the year, perhaps even the month, when Véronique was born, branding her forever with the hateful 1967. Pascal, the man she never loved or knew, had taken from her the only man she loved completely. Pascal's phantom touch had petrified her.

SIX

Winter 1947–1948, Athens

In the faux splendour of the Grande Bretagne Hotel lobby, Michel Franchitti and Pascal Loublier clasped each other with great vigour.

'Mon vieux, look at you! What do they feed you here?' Pascal tapped his friend's absent stomach.

Michel just grinned. 'I'll tell you everything you need to know about this place and you'd better brace yourself for a long rant.'

They sat on the low couches, and the morose, hollow-cheeked waiter brought them whisky.

'How are Pauline and Alex?'

'Fine. Fine.'

There was a moment of silence.

'When you get back, keep an eye on them, will you? You know Pauline . . .'

'You needn't ask. I don't suppose she was thrilled to see you go.'

'Nope. It was awful actually. I almost stayed. Well, not really, but you know . . . I felt I should've stayed. She said I was dooming our only child to a life of an orphan, that sort of thing. At least you don't have that to deal with.'

Michel downed his whisky in one gulp and Pascal felt, ever so slightly, the stab of unspoken reproach. Pascal opened a fresh packet of Gauloises and offered them to Michel.

'How I've missed the things!'

'Why didn't you say? I would've sent you some!'

'Oh, you know. You get sucked into things, forget about your bodily needs.'

'Yes, you look every bit the Orthodox saint . . .'

They laughed. Pascal slapped Michel's thigh affectionately. 'So!'

'So. I'll start with what I know you're curious to hear: Ascent to the misty peaks, part one of "The UN Inquiry Commission's Search for the King of the Mountains", a political farce in three parts.'

Pascal smiled but the nervous knot in his stomach was not being dissolved by the whisky. He had just stepped into a minefield and Michel, his only trusted guide, was going to disappear over the hill in twenty-four hours and leave him to his own undeveloped devices.

'By the way, how's your Greek?' Michel asked.

'Etsi-ketsi.' They laughed.

'Right. Well, you know the basics already. It's old news anyway. There were the usual suspects, the eleven members of the Security Council all represented, plus twenty-four journalists, interpreters, secretaries, the whole merry bunch loaded onto jeeps and lorries, plus a taxi. A circus. Our guy was okay, a scholar in archaeology, probably the only one among the lot who really knows Greece. We climbed for two days, saw some grim things in the villages. The guerrillas reign over a desert. The idea is to starve them out of the war. There's close to two hundred thousand refugees as a result. That's the government taking care of its subjects, you see. But don't think this has gone into the UN Commission's report – we don't want to sully the Greek government, it's got *barba* Truman's seal of approval after all.'

'Uncle Truman?'

'That's the media's affectionate term for him since he announced his doctrine. Reminds me of the 250 million-dollar loan to France. They have a way of making friends . . .'

'Yeah, shutting us up with cash.'

'But the Greek case is different, you see. The Greek government and the king are actually getting exactly what they want, without having to make compromises. That's why the American aid is so sweet. This is no Marshall Plan. Which is why I'm pretty sure about the outcome.'

'You think the rebels are done for?'

'Well, let me put it this way, Pascal. There's a rift in the middle of the KKE. See, the General Secretary Zachariadis imposed this insane policy of non-mobilisation, against Markos's better judgement. Zachariadis has this lunatic idée fixe about revolution of the proletariat, and he's blind to the fact that there isn't enough proletariat in the cities and they should be betting on guerrilla warfare, not on bloody Stalinist orthodoxy. It's clear as day that the Central Committee, with Zachariadis at its head, is committing suicide. There are tens of thousands of potential recruits stranded in the cities with their hands tied by this policy of non-recruitment, and they get arrested en masse and shipped off to the islands to break rocks like slaves. And Zachariadis is denouncing those who enlist in the Democratic Army as cowards, as failing to support the urban unions, the people's resistance . . .'

'And naturally, in Paris the Parti Communiste Français welcomed him at the congress as a hero, the future leader of a free Greece. And frankly, I'd be quite misguided too if I wasn't following your write-ups.'

'Right. The PCF should come and see what's going on in those mountains.'

Pascal nodded. 'I'm impressed by your insights.' He wondered if he was being sarcastic.

'And do you know what the result is? Zachariadis is beginning to realise his mistake but it's too late, and instead of letting Markos get on with the military side of things and make some progress, he's looking for scapegoats, for "traitors", and he's having them expelled or executed. It's a mess.'

'And there isn't much help forthcoming from Stalin.'

'"Limit the extent of the guerrilla struggle", if we want to be precise.'

'I suppose Zachariadis will have to take notice now and stop fooling himself about the great Commintern saviours.'

Michel shook his head bitterly. He was on his second whisky.

'I think you can begin to appreciate why I'm quitting. I don't want to report the deaths of twenty thousand adolescents who are sent to the front lines like smoked meat. Because that's what's going to happen in a few months, I reckon, when the Americans have had time to spruce up the government army. And the Soviets aren't going to send their army in, and nor is Bulgaria or Hungary, or Czechoslovakia, or Albania. They're all loyal to Stalin. And Tito has his own agenda, of course.'

A handsome blond man flew in through the swingdoors of the hotel and approached Michel with a springy stride. Michel got up and shook his hand energetically.

'George,' he said, 'meet my friend and colleague Pascal Loublier, also from *Le Monde*. He's just arrived to take over from me. Pascal, this is George Polk, the Columbia Broadcasting correspondent.'

Pascal shook the large hand and took an instant liking to the radiant American, despite his superior height. Americans were irritatingly statuesque – it was a fact Pascal just had to live with. They exchanged a few words in broken Greek and English. Perhaps he should have brushed up his English, not tried to learn Greek . . .

'George knows how I feel,' Michel said in English. 'He feels the same and he is, er, vocal about it too. Somebody must tell the truth, no?'

'Right,' said George Polk, suddenly grave.

'George, you'll look after Pascal, show him how the things work around here, no?'

'Sure thing.'

After Polk was gone, Michel became mellow.

'There's nothing else to say really. Part two of the odyssey is Waiting for Markos, King of the Mountains, the man who might exist. When we reached the HQ of the Democratic Army, the Western camp was very impatient, whinging the whole time about the guerrilla sense of time and how he'd take days, not hours, to show up – which was hardly surprising really. So we spent a night with the guerrillas, slept in this schoolhouse; they put on dances for us – it was all rather surreal.

Yannoulis, their commander, was a friendly chap – kind of intellectual, barely out of his teens. There were lots of girls there too. Twenty percent of the Democratic Army is women. Can you imagine? So anyway, after a third bracing night in the mountains, the majority decided to head back. It was kind of ignominious. We sneaked out at the crack of dawn like chicken thieves. They were stunned. We'd let them down, we hadn't waited for their king. The communist representatives stayed – they were determined to wait for Markos. But of course it was hopeless. Their interviews alone wouldn't count as a report for the commission . . .'

'Why didn't you stay on with them?'

Michel gulped his third whisky and leaned back wearily.

'Because it wouldn't have made any difference. And because . . . I suppose I was representing the West. And because I had to send off my dispatch. A day later would have been too late – *Le Monde* wouldn't have run it.'

'So professionalism above all else, huh?'

'Something like that.'

'Did this American, George Polk, come along?'

'Oh no. There's talk that he has an ambition to go by himself, do the Markos interview solo.'

'That's an idea!'

'Don't even think about it! You'll get blown up by the first mine. Just forget about it. George is American, he thinks everything's possible. Hubris, that's what it's called – the Greek sin. It's every journalist's dream to interview Markos, but nobody will do it, not even Polk.'

Pascal noticed his heart was beating faster.

'And part three?'

'Part three . . .' Michel slumped. There were three empty glasses in front of him and he eyed them despondently. 'Part three is where the commission representatives trotted off to Geneva to compose their masterpiece on the failure of the mission. And where the big massacre takes place. To be continued.'

Michel smiled at Pascal inconclusively and his haggard green eyes confirmed Pascal's impression that it was time for Michel to take a break from Greece and war. He put an arm around his friend's shoulder.

For days, Pascal wandered around the streets of Athens, hungrily absorbing every tell-tale detail. Pale, whitewashed graffiti on a wall: *Democracy*. 'Like a drowned face floating up to the murky surface of a lake,' he wrote. The sphinx of the Parthenon squatted barrenly above the city, an unresolved enigma. The swastika had flown on top of it a few years ago and a young man had climbed up to tear it down, miraculously surviving both the climb and the Nazi bullets. Now the blue and white flag brightly signalled a free Greece. 'Now that the barbarians are gone, what is going to become of Greece?' Pascal wrote.

For the past two years, Michel Franchitti's dispatches in *Le Monde* had created in Pascal's mind an image of a country bloodily submerged in vendetta-like intrigues. But for weeks, the overwhelming mood in Athens was one of paranoia, of hushed conversations, of bending of heads before anticipated blows. Pascal's fascination with Greece was taking on a corporeal form – not a pretty one, but a rich one. Where is the war? he wanted to ask Polk, but he knew very well where the war was. He felt that his duty was to follow it, not to sit in the grim cosiness of the capital where all news from the front was second-hand and instead of action there was speculation. Why don't we go where the war is? he wanted to ask Polk but he knew the answer himself. He wasn't the only one who thought about it.

One afternoon, walking with Polk to the post office to send off his latest dispatch, he was being instructed on how to be cautious.

'Never sit in restaurants with your back to the door.'

'You mean so that *you* can sit with your back to the door?'

They laughed but not for long. The American nudged Pascal and pointed to a well-padded, impeccably turned-out middle-aged man emerging from the Ministry of War on the other side of the street.

'General Kalamatis, a favourite of the king and the American mission . . .'

Polk had no time to elaborate. An unshaven young man in a shabby overcoat crashed into the general who swore loudly and filthily. The young man continued on his way for a few seconds but then turned around and yelled in a hoarse voice: 'Death to the fascists! The people will triumph! Stick your Truman up your arse!'

Pascal had no time to congratulate himself on understanding the idiom because the general pulled a small gun from his coat and fired at the young man three times, although one shot from such a close range would have achieved the desired effect generously. Brains spluttered out, soiling the soft grey coat of the general. The young man without a face was thrown against the ministry wall by the second blast and instantly collapsed into a shapeless heap, leaving a large black stain on the wall above him. The general cast a quick glance around and sprang back into the ministry. A couple of passers-by slowed down hesitantly then walked on with some urgency. People on the wrong side of the street nervously crossed to where Pascal and George Polk were standing, frozen.

'Do you have a camera?' Polk enquired in a choked voice.

'No.' Pascal was remembering the contents of his stomach.

'Then let's get out of here.'

Pascal walked in a daze.

'Welcome to Greece, paragon of democracy, friend of the United States of America,' said Polk through gritted teeth.

'I'm going to put this in my story,' Pascal said.

'Go ahead, peg it on. After two more of these occurrences you won't even bother.'

'But I will,' said Pascal with grim determination. He cast one last glance behind at the bloodied heap and continued on unsteady legs.

He held the malodorous telephone receiver with a shaky hand, his shrunken throat finding nothing to say to an agitated Pauline except to reassure her that all was well and Athens was perfectly safe for foreign correspondents.

SEVEN

April 1998, Thessaloniki

Thessaloniki became a labyrinth in which he looked for the white-haired Amazon. If he were to extend the metaphor, he wouldn't be sure which one of them was the Minotaur. He sat in 'her' restaurant a couple of times, hoping she might return to read her book over a *horiatiki*. A slight hollow appeared at the base of his chest – what if she had left town?

One day, he was browsing through some unaffordable editions on Greek mythology on the second floor of the Tsimiski Street bookshop when, in a shock of recognition, he saw her. She was arranging some books on shelves, with her back to him. The short peroxide hair, the trim behind in pale jeans, the slow, somehow pensive movements. He stood watching her, hoping she would turn around, until he became aware that a bearded man behind a desk was looking at him severely over his glasses. He left while she continued to put stacks of books on the shelves.

He came the next day but found only the bearded man who peered at him even more disapprovingly without even saying, 'May I help you?' He decided to ask about her next time, but there was no need to, because next time she was sitting behind the desk, looking through a fat register-book, writing something down. He pretended to occupy himself with a row of albums, until he felt her eyes on him. Suddenly nailed down with emotion, he attempted a smile, but it was probably unsuccessful. At that point the entire row of large-format albums swooned to one side and he reached to straighten them, embarrassed in a schoolboy way.

'It's all right. Don't worry. It's only Alexander the Great.' Her English was accented.

'Okay,' he said and, not knowing what to do or say next, looked at his watch and pretended to be in a rush. He nodded goodbye to her dreamy, amused smile and went down the stairs in a daze. Normally, it would take him much less time and sweat to strike up a conversation with a woman.

The next day, he sat at 'her' restaurant for a quick coffee, planning what to say when he went into the bookshop. And suddenly, there she was, sitting at the other end of the row of white-clothed tables. His heart stopped, like a dreamy sentinel crashing into the wall of the enemy's abrupt apparition. She noticed him in her usual composed way, perhaps even smiled. He overheard her order in very reasonable Greek; the fat waiter chirped at her adoringly. He tried not to stare. He sipped the sweet coffee and wondered why she had spoken to him in English in the bookshop. She stabbed her salad and chewed, full-cheeked and oblivious to him. He could see her nipples poking through the soft fabric of her white top. It wasn't the warmest of spring days and she didn't have her suede jacket. The coffee gurgled in his empty stomach. She was served coffee too, which she drank while reading a paperback.

She left some money on the table and headed down Ayas Sophias Street. As soon as she got up, the wind lifted up two of her banknotes and blew them up the street. He got up, briefly considering chasing them, but instead found himself walking down Ayas Sophias behind her. Following her was not as ridiculous as it would have been to follow another woman. The vardari pushed him along the street, trying to bring him closer to her, as if he was running despite himself. People got in the way. If he'd remembered the universal rule of port towns, he could have guessed her itinerary. In port towns you always found yourself walking either along the waterfront, or parallel to it, or towards it; there was no other way. But it had been a long time since he last walked towards this waterfront. In Australian coastal towns different rules applied because the Pacific was more impersonal than the Aegean; you didn't have the same urge to get close to it.

The early afternoon sky cast its premature shadows over the waterfront. People strolled past Theo, but he felt that he was moving in another dimension – the one she was moving in, like swimming in a stream of white light emanating from her hair. Suddenly, in the narrow passage between a sprawling waterfront café and a kiosk, she stopped and turned around. He froze. Her gaze was neither friendly nor hostile.

'You've been following me,' she said, this time in a softly accented Greek. Her voice was so velvety that for the first few seconds he didn't register what she said. His faculties deserted him. He shrugged and grinned.

'It looks like it, I guess.'

'It's okay, I've been following you also.'

She smiled without showing her teeth. A devastating dimple appeared in her left cheek. He was miserably stripped of the words he had woven carefully and cunningly like a net in which he would catch her.

'Have you?'

'Yes.'

And they were walking again. Together. She was only slightly shorter than him.

'When?'

'Just now.'

'Oh.'

'I mean that you were following me, but I made you follow me. So in a way I was following you first. It doesn't matter that I was walking in front.'

He had to think about this.

'You speak English?' he asked in English.

'Sure.'

He craved to see her face close-up. Now that she was only a step away from him, the proximity was uncomfortable. He glanced towards her tentatively and caught a glimpse of her mouth – pale, large and exquisitely defined. She caught his glance and for a few seconds her liquid eyes ran over his face. The amused dimple reappeared.

'You don't mind if I walk with you?' Theo asked.

'No. I'm actually going to the White Tower. I haven't been up there for a while.'

'I haven't been up there at all,' Theo rushed to remember falsely.

'What do you know about the tower?'

'Well, once it was called the Bloody Tower, then it was sort of whitewashed of its reputation. From the Bloody Tower, it became the White Tower, as things often do in history. And now it's pinkish.'

'Like all Mediterranean forts.'

'Once, rebellious janissaries were executed here. Prisoners' screams could be heard in the streets,' he continued, inspired.

'You know local history, I can see.' She smiled.

I am a fool, he thought.

Once at the top, they faced the sea. To the far right, cranes had frozen in the harbour like giant, melancholic insects in a half-hearted attempt to take the city. Up above them, the blue and white flag flapped crisply in the wind. The clouds were letting through just enough light to induce a sense of fatefulness about the view and about being here. They walked around to the other side until they faced the handsome panorama of buildings. Her pale face was brushed by the wind to an unripe peach colour. The white of her top and the white of her hair framed the olive strangeness of her face. She shivered.

'The disquieting city,' she said.

'Sorry?'

'Something my father used to say about Salonika. Apparently, it was an Italian marine officer called Alberto Savinio who first said it.'

'Disquieting . . . And much coveted. Everybody wanted it. Everybody passed through it. The Turkish sultan Murad had a dream in which Salonika appeared to him as a rose.'

'And did he pluck the rose?'

'Yes.'

They had to out-shout the wind. He took off his jacket and put it over her shivering shoulders. At the foot of the tower, she looked at her watch.

'What were you reading at the café?' He was trying to prolong the moment.

'A novel by a Greek poet.'

'Is it interesting?'

'It's about sailors on a straying ship talking about past adventures.'

He listened to the uneven stressing of her words, the creamy thickness of her voice. He discovered her eyebrows – dark, even and straight, as if drawn by a naïve and gifted hand in an effort to represent melancholy with one perfect line. Unlike normal eyebrows, they didn't follow roughly the curve of the eye; they were uncompromising. They contrasted arrestingly with the dazzling peroxide of her hair.

'Would you like to grab a coffee somewhere? Or lunch perhaps. Sometime?'

'Sometime. I must go to the shop now.' She looked at her watch again. 'It was nice to meet you. I'm Véronique.' She put out her hand. He felt the bones in it. At the same time as he said, 'I'm Theo', he realised the watch she'd been looking at wasn't there. The wind messed her hair.

'You must be lonely here,' she said, out of the blue.

He shrugged in dismay and said, 'I have family here.'

She looked at him for a mute, piercing moment.

'So, lunch tomorrow?' She lifted those unbending eyebrows.

Traffic roared past him. People strolled. Shadows rose from the water and crept into the city.

With devastating precision, Theo was in love.

As if love was a mythical place he had studied and now, suddenly, without a warning, he was there. His eyes were in love, his chest was in love, and so were his knees, his hands, his ears and his memory, which consisted entirely of the last fifty minutes. His future was in love.

If he had been Paris – the shepherd who was given a golden apple and told to be the judge of the three great goddesses, Athena, Aphrodite and Hera – he wouldn't have had to think twice. Because all three of them would have been Véronique. On the way back to the Philipidis' sad apartment, he breathed in the aroma of the budding Aegean spring and exhaust fumes, feeling the brand-new immortality of his blood branch inside his veins.

A woman should be given the opportunity to be late. Theo arrived at Patsas Nikos just before noon. A strange choice of venue on her part, one of those faintly canteen-like places with traditional dishes like the smelly *patsas*, and not entirely white tablecloths. It wasn't even in a fashionable part of town. Before he finished his first cigarette, Véronique appeared, more striking than he thought possible, a bright shock of hair framing the olive paleness of her face, her large, pale aphrodisiac mouth smiling. After they ordered, Véronique took a slice of white bread from the wicker basket, kneading it in her slender, short-nailed fingers, and asked, 'What is it that you're doing here, Theo? Visiting relatives?'

'I'm here for research actually. I'm doing a PhD in classics. Alexander the Great and his relationship with the gods.' He felt as if he was at the airport again.

'And where do you live normally? Australia?'

He was startled. 'How did you know?'

'Your accent gives you away.'

'And yours doesn't. I mean, I'd hesitate to guess your nationality.'

'My nationality is French. But nationality doesn't mean anything.'

'It does here, in this part of the world.' He was tempted to tell her about Papadopoulos but thought better of it.

'So, are you Australian? Or Greek–Australian? Or something else?'

Their tripe soup arrived, steaming and smelly. She tilted her head to one side to see him better, out of the steam's way, and for a second it was not unlike the way Hrisoula had looked up at him: 'What's a eunuch?' He picked up his spoon but the thick soup retreated into the future as if sucked by a playful tentacular force.

'I'm half-Greek, half-Macedonian, and predominantly Australian.' She swallowed. He could see the tripe soup travel down and wished he was tripe soup. She dipped a piece of bread in her bowl and sucked the liquid from it. Theo swallowed his first spoonful which should have been delicious but, because of his nervousness, only scorched his tongue.

'So, like the different colours of your eyes, you are somehow a living paradigm of transnationalism. Greek and Macedonian, Australian and European. Although one is obviously stronger than the other, like the brown eye is darker than the blue.'

He felt himself blush. 'I don't think I'm a living paradigm of anything.'

She dabbed her mouth with the white napkin. Was she amused?

'My grandfather had an obsession with Greece. He wrote a book on it.'

'What kind of book?'

'About the Greek Civil War. It was translated in English as *Land of Midas: the Catastrophe of the Greek Civil War.*'

'I didn't realise you had such a connection . . . Our family has a connection to the civil war too.'

'Which side were they on?'

'The side of the dead.'

The straight eyebrows went up and she studied his face with a detached look as if she wasn't listening but observing. They were silent for a while.

'And what are you doing here? If you don't mind me asking,' he said.

'I lived here for a couple of years when my father was a cultural attaché. I'm just revisiting.'

'Has it changed much?'

'I'm not that old, you know!' She laughed discreetly. Her laughter was low, throaty, indulgent and arousing, like a strip of velvet just too small to wrap yourself in, so you pressed it against your skin and wanted more.

Theo rushed to exonerate himself. 'I'm asking because I was last here ten years ago and it's hard to tell sometimes if the place has changed or it's you that's changed.'

'Exactly.'

The greasy-haired, dreamy-eyed waiter was singing along to the music that filled the semi-empty restaurant, broodingly: '*Ayie Nikola filaye k' Ayia Thalassini* . . . Saint Nicholas save us and Santa Marina . . .'

Véronique smiled. 'They must be fans of Nikos Kavadias here.'

He realised he was leaning forward, elbows resting on the table, with only two tripe soup bowls between their faces.

'Where are you staying, Theo?'

'With the family. But I need to move out very soon.'

Her sharp shoulders were pointing up. Her sharp breasts were pointing towards him.

'I've got an apartment in the old town and I know there's a similar one available in the same area. They belong to the same landlady. Maybe that's what you need. They're new apartments built in the old style.'

'Sounds good.'

'I could ask her to show it to you, but she's in Athens until next week. You could come and see mine. And you can decide if you want the other one.'

He wanted the other one.

The small balcony had a postcard view of the old town and the sea beyond it. Theo tried to look at the place pragmatically but he felt as if he had walked into a fantasy.

'Bedroom. It's not huge but you don't need a big bedroom.'

Whatever that was supposed to mean! A double bed, hastily made, with a few books strewn around. A sterile lampshade, a built-in wardrobe, shoes, a standing rack for drying clothes. In a moment of untypical lucidity, Theo noted that she was good at creating disorder with a limited number of objects – because there wasn't much in the lounge apart from a few pieces of new modern furniture, stacks of books along the wall, and a beautiful turquoise rug carelessly and uselessly laid in a corner as if it had landed there in her absence.

She went to the mini-kitchen to make coffee. A microwave. A kitchen bar. A humming fridge. A flash of amber. Fingers of blind possibility stroking his back. He picked up a book from the coffee table. On the cover, a strikingly unpleasant painting of a mulatto girl, naked, with a shawl over her shoulders, cheap-looking jewellery, long black hair, red lips, hands shamelessly on her hips, breasts small and in the wrong place, clitoris drawn across the pubis in that crudely erotic way popular artists sometimes have of marking femininity. The poems inside were in Greek and English. She sat on the sofa opposite him.

In an atypical, surprising bout of vocality, Theo read an English stanza:

Where are you from? From Babylon.
Where are you going? To the eye of the cyclone.
Whom do you love? A gipsy woman.
What is her name? Fata Morgana.

Few things are as pretentious as opening a book and reading out a poem for no good reason, he thought. But she smiled.

'I've come across Fata Morgana before . . . What was it?'

'In the Messina Strait, there are dangerous currents. Sailors see distant landscapes as castles in the sky. They see a combination of an inferior mirage, where the false image appears below the true position, and a superior mirage, in which a double image appears, one below the other.'

'I see. I thought Fata Morgana was a woman.'

'That's right. Fata Morgana is also a mirage of a beautiful woman who appears to the sailors and brings catastrophe.'

She didn't pronounce the e at the end and it sounded like 'catastroph', with the stress on the o.

The dangerous dimple appeared in her left cheek. He knew that after making love to her, nothing would be as it was before. It already wasn't the same. He felt this with frightening certainty. At this point, the coffee in the small pot boiled over with an angry hiss. Véronique got up without panic, removed it from the hot plate and dumped it in the sink.

'So much for coffee,' she declared, her voice entirely lacking in disappointment.

She held the door open and leaned on it, but somehow tensely, as if the door were leaning on her.

'So, when will I see you again?' He clutched the book with the

obscene woman on the cover which he had asked to borrow in a fit
of sudden interest in the poetry of Nikos Kavadias.

'When do you want to see me again?'

'Tomorrow,' he said.

Her hand rested on her exquisite collar-bones, fingers stretched
out.

'Tomorrow I can't. Saturday? We can go to Halkidiki. It's getting
warm; we could have a swim.'

'Excellent idea. I'll pick you up on Saturday morning – I have a
car. I loved climbing rocks there when I was a kid.'

'Me too.'

'Maybe I saw you there, on the rocks, but didn't recognise you. I
mean, we would've been there around the same time.'

Her head cocked at the angle of perfection, she smiled with radiant
sadness. Four long, short-nailed fingers over the door's ridge – this
was the last flicker of Véronique imprinted on Theo's retina.

On Uncle Panayotis's balcony, Theo blew overexcited clouds of
smoke against the sprouting spring sun. Hrisoula, restless and
ingratiating, kept asking him to tell her a story, offering him with
sticky fingers sweets semi-wrapped in foil. Unable to think of a story,
Theo read to her, in Greek, some of Kavadias's story-poems: 'All night
you soaked him with Midas's wine and three light-house flashes lulled
him to sleep . . .'

'What's Midas's wine?' asked Hrisoula with a mouth full of fudge.

'It's . . . the wine that King Midas drank,' Theo said, not quite
sure.

Bored, Hrisoula planted herself in a wicker chair, turning her back
to him, spread her hair over the chair-back and commanded, 'Uncle
Theo, play with my hair.'

So Uncle Theo fingered her blonde hair awkwardly, glancing at
the page where an arrow pointed from 'Midas's wine' to a question
mark and sharp, barely readable handwriting: *The gardens of Midas?
Midas touch?*

EIGHT

March–April 1998, Thessaloniki

One clear evening, after work, she was sitting on a waterfront bench by the White Tower, with an ear of steaming, salty corn. She felt almost content. Traffic thundered behind her like a spring river. There was only one other pedestrian within sight on the promenade: a young man in a leather jacket some fifty metres away, walking in her direction, at the edge of the promenade, looking down at the murky water, hands in his pockets. As he approached, she could see his profile. It was vaguely familiar, beautiful but irregular. All memorable beauty must, of course, have some irregularity. His jaw was decisively outlined, but not vulgarly masculine. His nose was straight and perhaps a little too fleshy, it was hard to tell. His short dark hair had an unremarkable cut. It would perhaps tickle the hand. She had the sudden desire to run her hand over his nape. He was tallish and well built, but slightly stooped. He looked towards her and their eyes met for a couple of seconds. His face was even more interesting than she had thought, and his nose was not so much fleshy as wide-ridged. Many Greek men were big-nosed. But was he Greek? He walked on past her. The faint familiarity still lingered about him. She glanced at his taut butt. He was younger than her. She hadn't felt desire for a man since the boy in Istanbul, almost a year ago.

She started looking out for the leather jacket with the hands in its pockets, but there were too many young men in leather jackets with unremarkable haircuts. When finally she spotted him again, it was in the bookshop, only metres away from her desk. He was browsing through some books in the classics and history section, with his back half to her. She was surprised to feel her pulse accelerate slightly. This didn't happen often these days. She caught his eye. He smiled a tentative, almost timid smile and an entire row of luxury albums on Megalos Alexandros collapsed to his right. At that moment, they picked each other out as foreigners. They smelt the foreignness on each other. He tried to straighten the row but order had been irrevocably compromised. She didn't know why she spoke to him in English then. This brief exchange had on her the effect of sudden tender pressure of moist lips on a melancholy nipple that had been buried under layers of winter clothing.

When finally she saw him close-up, there was a look of vulnerability about him. His dark eyebrows were like a dismembered gull in flight, the two wings barely joined by the shadow of a suspended soaring. And his eyes of course, his eyes. Apart from hearing about her Grandfather Pascal who apparently had odd eyes too, she had never seen eyes like his – one golden brown, one dark blue. They gave him a slightly squinting look, as if each eye observed a world of its own. His nervousness was irresistible. His chain-smoking was desperately self-protective. His voice had the slight huskiness of the chronic smoker. It chafed her the way his hair would her hand. It made the hairs on her arm stand. Theo. He exuded his name like the musk of his skin, not that she saw him as a young stag at any point.

Then the phone-call came from her mother.

'Grandmother Pauline is deteriorating very fast. You'd better come home.'

She shuddered at the sound of 'home' but packed a few things and took a week's leave from the bookshop. She didn't know whether she wanted to come back to Thessaloniki, but she had nothing to go back to in France. Or anywhere else. She didn't explain all this to Theo, of course. He was beginning to grow on her. Hour after hour, desire fed her starved future, like a zoo-keeper feeding red meat on a rod to a depressed lion. She left him a note on her door, regretting the missed weekend at Halkidiki.

NINE

April 1998, Thessaloniki

On Saturday morning, clouds threatened to envelop the city in their moist mood. Theo forced Uncle Panayotis's battered Volkswagen through the traffic-unfriendly streets of the old town until he reached Véronique's building in Dionyssiou Street. He waited outside for ten minutes before he went up the sharp, concrete stairs, his heart pounding with the anticipation of her at the door, sleepy-faced and exquisitely bare-legged. Her alarm hadn't gone off, although it was past ten. She had had a late night reading. She couldn't sleep until the small hours from excitement. She would invite him in for coffee which would boil over aromatically.

On her door was taped a square white envelope which he ripped open. Inside was a folded piece of blue paper and a shiny key, warm as if she had dropped it there only seconds ago. He could smell the metal. The blue paper rustled matter-of-factly as he unfolded it with anxious hands.

> Theo
>
> I have to leave today, Friday, for Paris. My grandmother is dying. I don't have your number so I couldn't call you. I leave the key to the apartment. You are welcome to stay here for the time I'm

away (about ten days). I've left most of my things but they won't get in your way. There is a couple in the apartment next door who make love very noisily. Otherwise, keep the key until I return and put it under the rug in ten days' time please.

Véronique

The key felt cold, although he had been holding it tight in his fist. He realised he hadn't been breathing. His lungs flopped like fish on sand. He unlocked the door with a pleasant click and stepped in. He gazed dully at the marble kitchen bar, the sofa where they sat, the lamps, the Turkish rug, the glass door to the balcony, the strip of blue in the distance . . . Her world, terribly deserted but still hers.

I've been following you also. What if she was a spy? He scanned the note again, frantically searching for meaning between the lines. Her handwriting was elongated and crammed, the same as in the book, but was it genuinely hurried? She had been in the service of the intelligence service and they in turn had been alerted by Papadopoulos. But there was admittedly something odd about a French spy working for the Greek intelligence. Except that she didn't have to be French at all. She could be of pure Greek stock. It could all have been an act – her foreign accent, her diplomat father, her writer grandfather. And the impromptu trip to Paris, and the absurd grandmother.

There was a half-full packet of ground coffee on the bar, white sugar and sesame breadsticks in a packet. He looked in the bedroom. The bed was unmade. The cream blinds were closed. In the bathroom, a tube of shower-cream in the shower, a bar of translucent soap in a dried-up puddle. He caught himself looking for white hairs on the light blue tiles. He didn't touch anything, though – the place was so imbued with her that to touch anything would be to touch her.

'Anything could still happen in Greece,' his father would say. His mother disagreed: 'You still live in the late sixties. It's changed since then, you know.' 'Is that why they still won't let your mother in?' They took turns in assuaging each other's outbursts of despair. Theo was tired of them. So, should he now expect the secret police to round him up and send him back to Australia, because he wasn't trustworthy enough to do a PhD on Megalos Alexandros?

The room spun around him and for a moment he doubted that

he had ever really met Véronique, or rather that the woman he had met was really Véronique. For a moment he doubted that he had ever left the benign buzz of Melbourne where he was perhaps having a bizarre dream right now, a drawn out, unending dream. When he woke up, he would find himself in the university library or at his desk at home, in the drowsy Australian afternoon. And he would sit there for a while, dazed by the murky, compelling world from which he would have just emerged, heavy-limbed with longing for Véronique, the tall, elusive Amazon who didn't exist.

And, stronger than his suspicion and disappointment, longing flooded him at once with crippling intensity – for the velvet laughter, for the dreamy shimmer of those mineral eyes, for the one or two moments of intimacy that went through him time after time, like knives of pleasure through unexpecting flesh.

The family made a scene. 'You come once in ten years and you want to live in a rented room! Is that how you do it in Australia?'

The worm of remorse wriggled inside him, but not too much. 'I'll be back in ten days.'

On his first night in Véronique's apartment, he found some eggs in the fridge, fried them in olive oil and had them straight off the frying pan, between his laptop and the obscene cover of the Kavadias poems. Her food, her book. He studied her note, to reassure himself that he hadn't simply read what he wanted to read in it, that she had really invited him to stay. He picked up one of the white towels in the bedroom. The shower-cream, half-used, was heavily fragrant, musky, reminiscent of her smell, permeating his senses. The water pressure wasn't strong enough, so he stood under the frugal stream for a long time, washing off the Véronique-like slipperiness, not wanting to wash it off. Wrapped in the towel, he lay on top of the unmade bed, her crumpled sheets at his feet, not daring to slip under the covers yet. He craved a cigarette but she was a non-smoker and perhaps wouldn't like a lingering smell in her bedroom when she returned. When she returned . . .

A series of distant but dramatic moans came from next door. He lay motionless, his cheek against her pillow which had a faint citrus fragrance mixed with the even fainter smell of hair. He was grateful to the unrestrained lovers for bringing him closer to her – because, somewhere in time, Theo and Véronique were lying in the same bed, face against the same pillow, alone, listening to the same anonymous sounds of rapture.

On his first day in Véronique's apartment, he decided to do some work. He installed himself at the coffee table, which was highly uncomfortable, and tried to hypnotise himself into thinking about Alexander.

Remove yourself from this lounge. Remove all contemporary figures from your mind, like bedraggled, unshaven clandestine passengers from a private train. Skip the last two thousand three hundred years, flash through the short twentieth century of wars, the Napoleonic terror, the Enlightenment, the dark Middle Ages, quirky, opulent Byzantium, the cruel excesses of Rome, the decline of Greek city-states, and stop there.

Witness Alexander stretched out, powerful and young in his death. Alexander drinking into the night and to his death. Crowning himself as Ammon, with a horned helmet. Howling with grief for two days over the body of his friend Haphaestion. Drunkenly overlooking the carnage and sacking of Persepolis, and burning the seventy-two-column Persian palaces down to a mere thirteen columns. Handsome, stocky Alexander at twenty-four already a king of Macedon, hegemon of the Corinthian League, overlord in Anatolia and the Levant, pharaoh and the son of Ammon. He wanted to surpass not just his father, but Dyonysius and Heracles, the gods themselves. To travel further. To be more invincible. He did, he was. He was short. He had one dark brown and one grey-blue eye. He wasn't that keen on women. He had an ambitious and powerful father. He conquered the world, naming every second city after himself, but even his megalomania didn't conceive that two thousand three hundred years into the future two neighbouring countries happening to live within his kingdom would drown themselves and each other in a pool of unredeemed Alexander genes, that the war of his wild Macedonians with the disdainful Greeks would become a war of words all the way across the globe in a land that was even further beyond his reach than India . . .

And Theo? What had he done in his twenty-four years? He was of average height. He had one dark blue and one gold-specked brown eye. He had a supportive father, a loving mother, both hideously damaged by a war they hadn't even taken part in. He had no ambitions of greatness, except to conquer a landscape of knowledge, as it were. But something presently escaped him the way Carthage escaped Alexander – not that there was any comparison, of course. Alexander crossed the Indus, the only one after Dionysius. Theo had crossed Dionyssiou Street to come into momentary possession of a vacated apartment.

And again, the room was flooded with Véronique. Brushing hair away from her forehead, rolling the vowels of English off her tongue which spilled over her lap musically, her elaborate lap where so much could be found. Her hands slender like her feet. Although he hadn't seen her feet, he could imagine them narrow and tanned in his hand, toe-nails like pearls. Small white hairs on her graceful neck . . . What if she didn't intend to resurface at all? She hadn't left a number or address in Paris.

He looked through her books, stacked along the walls – there wasn't a single bookshelf in the apartment. He browsed through volumes of Greek poetry in Greek and English; dog-eared science-fiction novels in English and French; serious, brooding-looking novels by Greek authors without a single line of direct speech; a concise, heavy *Salonica Through the Ages*; a non-fiction book called *Salonica Station*, which seemed to be on the multicultural history of the city; and a curious *American Poets Writing About Their Fathers*.

TEN

Spring 1948, Athens / Thessaloniki

All along, Pascal wanted to go to Thessaloniki; the real action had shifted irreversibly to the north. In Athens, he covered events like the death of the dull King George and the succession of his equally dull brother Paul and his wife Princess Frederika of Brunswick, granddaughter of Kaiser Wilhelm II. Assassinations and subsequent executions of scapegoats, of which there was never a shortage. Mass arrests of suspected leftists and their internment on Aegean islands, which sucked the life out of the guerrilla army. At every turn, Michel's pronouncement about the fatal rift in the KKE was confirmed. Then came General Van Fleet, head of the US Military Advisory and Planning Group, who checked in at the Grande Bretagne with his wife and left immediately for the military training camps to help the national army, in the words of an American correspondent, 'to get off its fanny and fight'. Then the winter of the controversial *pedomasoma* or rounding up of children in the 'Free Greece' of the north to take them across the border into the Eastern Bloc. From distant Athens events in the north appeared fantastically distorted.

He listened to the radio of the Armed Forces: 'The National Army of Greece is ready to clean the north of the Slavo–communists. Greece for the Greeks. America is behind us.' Its programme ended triumphantly with the national anthem. He listened to Radio Free Greece from Belgrade: 'Any day now the USSR will drop food and clothes for the fighters of the Democratic Army because the Comintern is with us in our struggle for a new world, for a new, free Greece.' Its programme ended triumphantly with the national anthem.

Two events propelled Pascal to finally undertake the difficult trip to Thessaloniki. The first was witnessing the routine shipping of prisoners of war to the islands.

Minutes after a raw, cool dawn, Pascal sat at a wharf café called My Ikaria. It was the haunt of police officers who supervised the deportation of prisoners. Pascal watched a slow ship furrow the pale harbour waters on its way to Australia. These were the voluntary, economic exiles, the happy ones, if ever there was a happy exile. Next appeared the women and children with their bundles. They gathered at one end of the small square and anxiety flooded the morning. A police sergeant with a sharp moustache startled Pascal, asking to borrow his matches. Pascal obliged. The next moment, the sergeant shouted at the women, 'I don't want any trouble, understood? No hysterics!' There was silence. He turned to Pascal. 'They come to stir shit, I know it. It's the same tantrums every time. But we're humane, we let them come. We're too humane.' He sighed, shaking off the ash of his American cigarette near Pascal's foot. Pascal put his hand on top of his cigarette box so the sergeant wouldn't see the giveaway Gauloises.

The prisoner convoy appeared at the other end of the square, sudden and dark in the radiant morning like a flock of black crows blocking the sky.

'Where are they taking them?' Pascal enquired of the sergeant who sat down at the next table, joined by two others.

'Ikaria, Mykonos. The further the better.'

'Are they recent captives?'

'A mixed bag, actually. Some from up north, some from the Peloponnese . . .' the sergeant replied, misunderstanding the question.

Pascal put his cigarette box in his shirt pocket and got up. He nearly crashed into a tall young woman with sculpted cheeks and eyes swollen with tears. She knelt by the table where the three sergeants sat, placed a wad of drachmas on the table and let out a sob.

'I beg you,' she said. 'Tell the guards not to be harsh on my fiancé. Georgi, Georgi is his name. He's sick, he's got an ulcer and a shrapnel wound in . . .'

But whatever she said next was blocked by the coarse laughter of one of the sergeants. 'Ulcer? I've got an ulcer too, my beautiful! And is anyone pleading for me?'

But another sergeant said, 'I think we could arrange something. Get up, girl. Don't dirty your pretty knees.'

She got up, her face contorted with anguish. The compassionate sergeant leaned towards her and said tenderly, 'How about we go in the back and you show me what you have under that skirt.' He grabbed her leg. 'Then we could think of arranging something for your Georgi.'

Pascal could hear the spittle gather in the woman's mouth before she spat at the compassionate officer. The officer got up, knocking over his wicker chair which fell softly to the lino floor. 'You filthy communist whore!' He grabbed the woman's hair and twisted it, throwing her against the wall. Pascal rushed to him but the other two officers got up and pushed Pascal away.

'You stay out of it.'

The woman didn't make a sound.

'Let her go!' Pascal groaned.

'Bastards, let her go!' shouted a man from the prisoners' crowd and leapt towards the café. Three soldiers stopped him with their bayonets pointed at his stomach. At that point the thick, elephantine horn of the ship blocked out all other sounds. The three sergeants let go of the woman and walked out to do their job. She slumped slowly against the wall, dishevelled.

Pascal bent over her uselessly. 'Are you okay?'

She looked at him and in her once clear eyes he saw the cloud of this war's madness, a vortex of black silence. Sullenly, he walked out of the café to get a better view of the scene. Many of the men were boys, their faces sunk into a premature middle age, their angular frames hovering between awkward adolescence and haunted deprivation. The murmur of the women on one side and the men on the other rose to a roar as the ship docked and they still weren't allowed to make contact. 'Come on!' came a male voice. 'Let them through! Be human!' The sergeants exchanged looks.

Pascal stepped towards them, forgetting his vow of impartiality. 'Major!' he said to his mustachioed acquaintance, knowing he would be flattered, 'let them have it, there'll be less trouble.'

The sharp ends of the moustache went up inquisitively. Then, miraculously, one of the other sergeants yelled, 'Five minutes!'

A great rush ensued – weeping, hurried instructions, silent clasping of bodies, faces held in hands. A man stepped away from the rest and limped towards Pascal.

'Keep off!' shouted the guards, pointing their bayonets at him. The man lifted his arms.

'It's all right, I'm from the Red Cross,' Pascal lied and walked towards the man, expecting the prod of bayonets in his own back. They let him off though. Pascal came face to face with the man. He was tall and powerfully built, his age effaced by hardship.

'Are you a correspondent?' he whispered.

'Yes. For *Le Monde*, a newspaper in Paris.'

The man shook his hand feverishly. 'Égalité, liberté, fraternité!' Pascal couldn't tell if he was being ironic. He stank of unwashed flesh and stale blood. 'Tell the world, tell what you've seen here. We may not live to tell. We're going to hell. Do you know what Ikaria means? Hell in the Aegean.'

As inconspicuous as he could be, Pascal slipped his Gauloises inside the man's coat pocket. The man lowered his voice.

'You're a good man. Do something for me. My wife, she doesn't know I've been captured. If you go north, please find her, we're from Edessa, west of Thessaloniki. Her name is Hrisoula, Philipidis Hrisoula, we have three children but two of them are . . . never mind, you know about the *pedomasoma*. I managed to scribble something in the cell, they don't allow us pencils so I had to open a vein . . . Will you do this?'

Pascal nodded, speechless. The man shook his hand again and

Pascal found a grubby, folded piece of paper inside his palm which he pushed up his own sleeve.

'What's your name?' he asked.

'Philipidis Angelis.'

The situation made normal introductions somehow awkward so Pascal simply said, 'I will do my best.' He wondered if this wasn't a blatant lie.

'Tell the world what's happening in Greece, that it's a Midas complex in reverse, a Midas nightmare, that we wanted to touch Greece with good hands, with loving hands, to turn it to gold, and instead it's all turned to shit. They, the fascists, the torturers, see them ganged up there, the coyotes of Greece, they want to petrify every living thing. Listen to me, every honest man is either fighting in the mountains or on a prison island breaking rocks. Tell the world there are no gods here, no myths, just this: the land of Midas, a petrified land . . .'

The guards pushed Angelis away and a whistle announced the end of the farewells. The women shuffled away without a single wail. The prisoners trudged towards the ship, walking over the large and now faded writing someone had scratched in the soft cement when it was first poured: 'Cursed Land.' Angelis turned to look at Pascal one last time, his eyes still burning with the fever of his message. Someone behind Pascal said loudly, 'Mother of Jesus!' He turned around and froze.

Inside the My Ikaria café, from a red curtain cord tied to a ceiling beam, hung the handsome young woman who had pleaded for Georgi. The sergeant she had spat on was staring at her stiff body. 'Crazy bitch!' he swore and spat on the floor. The owner of the café had gone inside the kitchen to make breakfast for the officers. During these departure scenes, he tried to sink out of sight. Now he clutched the steaming plates before the dead body, his business flashing before him.

Numb, Pascal looked out to the prisoners, anxious that Georgi should not see his beloved like this. Then he helped to cut the rope and take the body down. The beautiful face was a bluish white. The wad of drachmas was still on the table. He took it and slipped it in the woman's belt – it was still hers, even if she no longer owned it. He was moving with the patience of a man in a nightmare, expecting to wake up at any moment. The ship glided on the smooth surface. The dark prisoners stood on board, immobile, and so did their dark women on the cement. Suddenly, there was a stir among the prisoners on board and a man frayed himself a passage through to the railings, climbed over and jumped – or rather fell – into the water. It was all so quick that the guards, surprised, didn't fire immediately. They waited for the man's head to bob to the surface and when it did, five or six of them fired. The horn of the ship sounded again, with a new despair, muffling the shots so that they seemed to come from under the water. There was a single shriek from the women's crowd, like a human extension of the ship's horn: 'Georgi!' and an elderly woman rushed towards the water. The guards stopped her. She fell to her knees and bent over as if she had been shot in the stomach, rocking without a sound. Total silence descended on the quay as if the sound had been turned off by someone who could bear it no longer.

'I told you.' The moustache nodded at Pascal. 'Nothing but trouble.'

Pascal walked away in his nightmare, past the carefree morning shops along the waterfront, past the boys selling *koulouri* and newspapers, past the closed kiosks where guerrillas used to enrol clandestinely for the Democratic Army. He reached instinctively for his cigarettes but instead he found Angelis's letter. He opened it. Angelis had used a wire dipped in his blood. Pascal folded the paper again and put it back in his pocket with a shaking hand.

That night, chain-smoking at the open window of his hotel room and staring blankly at the ghostly whitewashed wall across the street bathed in yellow light, he was tormented by a double remorse. First, he hadn't tried to do anything for the woman when he saw the cloud in her eyes; he had turned his back to her. Second, he hadn't told Angelis his name, as if they weren't equals by virtue of the man's prisoner status. As if Angelis was already a non-person.

Pascal opened the letter again. 'Hrisoula my beloved wife . . .' He folded it back and put it on the desk.

ELEVEN

April 1998, Paris

Grandmother Pauline was in a coma. 'She wanted to speak to you,' the family said to Véronique accusingly, 'but you are too late.' Didn't she leave a note? No, she left a will.

Overnight, Véronique came into possession of half the shares, the villa in Nice, along with the second house in Paris, plus the near-derelict house in Marseilles which had belonged to Pascal Loublier and, later, to Véronique's father. Pauline's second husband François had his share too but the Martinière estate was substantial.

At the funeral, there was the who's who of Paris, in hats and heels, sad little voices from the women and handshakes from the men who ogled Véronique and the other young women in the family looking superficially bereaved in their sombre clothes. There were scented kisses, cigar kisses, mint kisses, halitosis kisses, kisses to be endured. Véronique clenched her jaw and endured. The funeral was pompous but somehow weary, as if there were no more grieving energy left after her father's funeral six months before. Perhaps that was precisely why. The fact that Pauline had died of a broken heart was not mentioned, but the knowledge of it became the very stuff of the event's weariness. It was like burying Alex Loublier for the second time alongside his mother. Véronique was dazed by the sudden coffin, the sudden wealth she was in possession of, the sudden cold spring in Paris. Her transplantation from the shabby charm of Thessaloniki had been too quick and she regarded the family's muted drama with bafflement, as if she had been picked out of a dozing audience, pushed onto the bright stage and expected to perform alongside the professionals. As speeches resounded in the splendid chapel, Véronique composed her own.

Pauline de la Martinière: crème de la crème of Parisian society. A very fine lady with one big, rough chip on her shoulder: Pascal Loublier, the elusive and dysfunctional ex-husband, the obsessed writer, the wandering spirit, the bastard. He had eluded her for twenty years until the final elusion in 1967. Presumed dead. Presumed alive and well somewhere else. Presumed madman. Everyone had their version. Pascal Loublier had an enviable collection of personas. The shadow he cast over the family flickered like an everlasting flame. When her father died (though she never used that word in her mind – he crashed, had an accident), Véronique's mother's family just about lynched him posthumously. He had proven to be a Pascal Loublier number two – went to Greece, didn't tell anyone anything, and never made it back. And here was Pauline, a woman who had been born with a silver spoon and who lived and died with a bitter taste in her heart, having had everything except what she really wanted. She died, barren with her only son's death, stunned with poverty in the midst of her wealth.

Pauline did not see much of Véronique after she turned ten and the family left for Greece. Pauline called her 'l'enfant sauvage'. But, after all, everyone said with badly disguised envy and resentment, it was in the order of things that so much should go to Véronique; she was de la Martinière's only grandchild.

She tried to fall in love with Paris again, the way she had done when she returned from Colombia, three years ago. After the frank chaos of Cartagena, Istanbul and Thessaloniki, Paris was like a polluted sugar cake. When she closed her eyes, she saw mangled pictures of Byzantine Thessaloniki, the endless, unbending Egnatia drive, Theo looking at her with his odd eyes, with that irresistible mix of shyness and defiance.

At the wake, Véronique was pulled aside by Pauline's second husband François, a right-wing politician with a brilliant past. Pauline's marriage to him had a tinge of lunatic revenge against the leftist misdemeanours of Pascal – and she had no doubt regretted it ever since. François breathed a mixture of valium and cognac in Véronique's face.

'You should know something, dear. Pauline told me that she knew where Pascal had vanished, after all.'

He squeezed her elbow. Véronique wasn't sure how seriously to take this.

'He went to his other woman in Greece.'

'What other woman?'

'The woman that he met when he was roaming in the Greek mountains with the commies.'

'That's just a load of . . . dross.' Véronique pulled her elbow away. Spitting on her grandfather's memory was their favourite pastime. And however she had grown to resent Pascal, she took attacks against him personally, as they somehow reflected on her father. François leant back and swirled his glass between knotty fingers.

'She told me, in confidence, that Pascal was never the same after he came back from the Greek war. When he left for there that last time, he went to look for his partisan sweetheart. He must've found her since he never made it back. That's what Pauline believed. That's why she burnt all his stuff.'

'Look, François . . .' But he placed a hand on her shoulder.

'I know, I know. We've all been through this before. It's a finished affair, but I'm just telling you that Pauline believed it until the day she died. But she only told me in the last year or so. I don't know if she told anybody else. And frankly, I don't even have to bring it up. It's been a nightmare for me. And just when things settled down, Alex goes off and gets himself killed . . .'

His voice broke down. Véronique put a hand on his pale sleeve although she didn't know whether she felt any compassion for him, whether she felt anything at all. Reading too much into her gesture, he put his arm around her, leaned against the heavy curtains, and she felt something inside him cave in. He whispered in her hair.

'She blamed him for Alex's death . . . She didn't forgive him – a dead man. She died without forgiving him for Alex . . .'

Véronique patted his sleeve until the merciful apparition of drinks on a tray.

The 'other woman' had never been mentioned to her before. François was getting senile. Or Pauline's re-evaluation of the past had been clouded over. Even so, Véronique took out the file of the Daphne Grigoriadis woman and looked at the photograph. Did Michel tell her everything he had to tell?

Her mother handed her a bunch of heavy keys – to the houses that Véronique now owned. Véronique didn't feel like an owner; she just felt like someone holding a bunch of keys.

Her mother sat across from her and lit a cigarette. Véronique saw a kind of ersatz ruin that she had no tools to restore. She could only identify the chronology and nature of the damage. Véronique had pity for her mother but no compassion, just as her mother had love for her but no understanding.

'What is this?' Her mother pointed to the sheet.

'A file from the Greek police archives.' She didn't have the energy to lie, but the effect was the same since her mother took no notice.

'Véronique,' smoke curled from the impeccably rouged mouth, 'you've been withdrawn ever since you came back. You aren't making any efforts to contact family and friends.'

'What friends?' Véronique said. 'You know I have no real friends here. And I saw the family at the wake.'

'You know, it's because you're so withdrawn that you have no friends any more, because you never settle in one place . . .'

'Please don't start.'

'I know, I won't start.'

Her mother feared what she didn't understand.

'And you still haven't dyed your hair.'

'It is dyed. It's peroxide.'

'You call that dyed? I call it killed. It's white, for Christ's sake. You're only thirty, you don't have to look like an old woman. Every woman tries to look younger.'

'But I *feel* like an old woman, Mother,' Véronique said, instantly regretting it. Her mother didn't need this. They looked at each other for a short uncomfortable moment.

'I know it's very hard for you, darling.'

This was all she could come up with, all the help she could offer. Véronique guessed she was expected to cry, or do something emotional, so that they could bond. Véronique felt sorry for her mother. Her movements had become jerkier. She constantly tossed her black (dyed) fringe in a nervous tic. But instead of reaching out, Véronique swirled the cold café-au-lait in her bowl and said impassively, 'I'm going back to Greece on Tuesday.'

Her mother's face fell. 'But . . . I thought you were staying!'

'No, I left my things in the apartment there and I'm going back, I don't know for how long.'

'Véronique, I swear, this family is cursed. All of you, all the Loubliers, there's a curse on this family! Always going somewhere, no peace, nothing but trouble. You go away and you don't come back! Or you come back and then you go away, until you don't come back one day. I thought you'd be different, you're a girl after all, but no! Damn suicidal, that's what you are! Suicidal!' Her breathless staccato collapsed into weeping.

She wept on the heavy mahogany table, face in one hand, unconsoled, holding in her inert fingers a still burning cigarette. Her padded, well-meaning boyfriend Jean-Loup pottered around, stroked the dog, glanced at Véronique imploringly. Véronique sat without moving, not sure whether she was numb with a dull pain or just numb.

'Why, why do you have to be like them? What's wrong with staying here, where you have every opportunity to live like you should. Now you're an heiress too! You have an entire estate. Why another senseless trip, why these obscure destinations? What do you find in those places? Haven't you had enough uprooting, enough of the moving house, enough foul cities, enough Arabs?'

'Mum, there are no Arabs in Greece.'

'I know, I've been there! And what will you find there? What will you achieve? Your father is dead and you must understand there is no solution to this.'

Véronique got up. Her knees felt weak. Her voice whimpered at the bottom of a pit somewhere in her chest. 'I understand, Mother,' she whispered, 'but sometimes it's not enough to understand.'

And she made a dramatic exit.

At the airport, Véronique was seen off by her mother, Jean-Loup, the dog and her elegant and neurotic aunt who said, 'Véronique dear, you're a bit pale these days. You should at least do something about your hair – it adds years to your looks. Even your grandmother made an effort to dye her hair to its original colour.'

'You call orange her original colour?'

Her aunt shook her head.

'You don't look after yourself when you're young and pretty. And not even that young any more! When you're old, you'll have no choice! You just wait and see.'

Ugly women must take special pleasure in the idea of age, Véronique thought – there is some measure of equality in the damage it inflicts.

'Leave her alone.' Her mother was conciliatory. Trying to smile, she put out a hand to stroke her daughter's white hair. Véronique felt something inside her mother cave in, as she had felt it in François. Or was it inside herself?

The continuity of the family had crumbled – her father gone, her mother floating helplessly into menopause, her never-ending childhood of Greek beaches and Rivieras swelling into the turbulent time of her parents' divorce, then taming the world alone and full of vigour . . . The family had shrunk, and so had the world. It was over, for her and for everyone else. Her mother knew it too. Véronique fled, waving to the sorry bunch. Her mother stood, frail and blowing a kiss with her already age-spotted hand. Under her immaculate black fringe, two thin streaks of mascara leaked down her cheeks.

TWELVE

April 1998, Thessaloniki

The days started to roll – a torrent of stones kicked into motion by a wandering foot on a hill-slide. Theo ticked off every passing day approvingly. Borrowing Uncle Panayotis's car, he went on a confused search for Dionysius. He intended to fill his mind with the fat, contented Dionysius, to push the slippery Véronique out. At Pella, royal seat of the Macedons, Dionysius, young and effeminate, was riding a panther with bloody flesh hanging from its mouth, holding a cantharus – the God of Alcohol's sceptre. At Dion, a Dionysius statue from the baths. Dionysius's triumphal epiphany. Dionysius on a chariot, post-Alexander. At Mount Olympus, a modern, sumptuous Monastery of Dionysius in progress. The ever-changing, sly Dionysius. Alexander's Dionysius. Or Dionysius's Alexander?

When he first saw photographs of these mosaics, Theo was captivated. Now he tried to merge them with the photographs, to create a continuum of intention and action. He couldn't. Those pictures were a small part of his physical reality in Australia. Now, he was a small part of their reality in Greece. He had been visited by these places but now he was visiting them. There was no continuation. Something was always contained by something else, something was always bigger than something else, and there was no exact correspondence, only the incessant, distorted fluidity between an image and its reality. He screwed up his eyes and the graceful Dionysius on the panther rearranged himself into an Amazon. She had short white hair, a tanned, lean body, and a panther's skin draped across one shoulder. Her eyes, amber hardened by the ages, gazed at him inscrutably. She held a bow and arrows.

He got up and the blood rushed from his head. The country stretched dully on all sides, bare and still impoverished by a harsh winter. He shivered in the windy emptiness. He was disconnected from the original purpose of his coming here. Greece appeared closed for the day, and for the day after. He could have done the research back in Melbourne. Two years of feverish planning and daydreaming of this trip to freedom, and now he didn't know why he was here. Being here hadn't brought him closer to the past. It had only brought him close to the crude retailoring of the past in order to dress the shivering skeleton of the present. He felt an unpreparedness in himself, in spite of all preparations. He didn't know where to start. He didn't know how to continue. He was suddenly angry at himself for being too easily impressed – by Papadopoulos, by Véronique, by simply being here. The seven remaining days before Véronique's return stretched to fill an entire calendar of uncertainty.

Two days later, the telephone rang piercingly.

'Theo?'

'Véronique!' His heart stopped but that was fine. He didn't need his heart any more.

'You settled in okay?'

'Yes, thanks. I mean, not really, just camping here, as it were.'

She laughed for a fraction of a second and velvet brushed his ear.

'How's your grandmother?'

'She's . . . dead.'

'I'm so sorry.'

'Thank you. Look, I'm coming back on Tuesday.'

'Great. I'll come and pick you up at the airport.'

'I'm getting a déjà-vu feeling.'

'As long as you don't leave a note at the airport for me.'

When he put the phone down, Tuesday was a door that opened with a slow creak, letting the sunshine stream inside, revealing the dingy cell in which he had been crouching, occupying himself with the rats in the corners, ignoring the fact that he was a prisoner. A prisoner of the suspicion of her. A prisoner of a relentless desire for her.

On Monday night, unable to face the Philipidis family's questions again, Theo moved into a cheap hotel room as close to the old town as possible and in the humming, unhurried Aegean spring he waited for Tuesday as if it was a person.

THIRTEEN

April 1998, Thessaloniki

On the plane, Véronique thought of Michel Franchitti. And, of course, she thought of Theo. There was something else too, which she didn't want to dwell on. For some time now, she had felt that she had lost the ability to be surprised, to feel much at all. The world – this once unfailing panacea, narcotic and aphrodisiac – was loosening its grip over her. It was not just the shock of her father's death, if she was honest with herself. Even before that, she was listless. She went from Cartagena to Paris, then to Istanbul, pretended to teach French, tried to be interested. But some part of her failed to be convinced. Somewhere, a corner of her was swept and empty. Something giant, perhaps a giant doubt, had cast its shadow over her. When had it started? Perhaps in the space of the last two years, perhaps earlier. Perhaps it started in Cartagena, or way back in Canada. Whatever movements she made, the shadow mimed them. It was bigger than her. She was a globe-trotter, yes, but something in her step was haltered. She consumed the world but there was no flavour left in it. She had always had a silver spoon, but it was beginning to gag her. What was left there to experience or to desire?

She landed in Thessaloniki with the sense of being given a last chance – for what, she didn't want to know. Theo stood out from the welcoming crowd, odd-eyed and intense in his leather jacket. The sight of him jolted her in the familiar way. It was a relief to be jolted in that way, like a loose spring that was being wound up again. She smiled and let him take her bag.

FOURTEEN

April 1998, Thessaloniki

They had to shout over the engine's roar. The butterflies in Theo's stomach were breeding fast.

'How was Paris?'

'The same as last time. Minus one person.'

'I'm sorry about your grandmother.'

'How did you enjoy the apartment?'

'It was great, thanks. And you were right about the couple next door.'

'Yes. They are tireless.'

'Actually, it doesn't have to be the same couple.'

'You mean that I've lived in a brothel for six months without noticing?'

They smiled. He had made some decisions about how to act, what to say, but having her next to him like this numbed his brain. He felt like a hapless Theseus who had lost track of the Minotaur. And he was sick of these stupid mythological comparisons . . . He drove to the now familiar house in Dionyssiou Street and took her bag upstairs. She opened the glass door to the balcony and stepped outside. The sea was a dark grey under a pink sky. Theo sat on the couch, unsure whether to be a guest or an ex-resident. The shock of a car crash reached them from the city. She went back inside.

'That sounded nasty,' he said.

There was something new in her face. But she simply said, 'Let's go and have dinner.'

At Taverna Dedalou, surrounded by plants and decorative plates on the walls, she looked more honey-hued and amber-eyed than ever. And her arms in the thin white polo-neck were swan-like. An entire country shrank into a remote backdrop as she filled out the picture. She ordered cuttlefish and spinach in wine. They drank too much of the acrid retsina, he filled an ashtray with impatient butts, she smiled closer to his face than ever, making the hairs on his neck stand. The café swarmed with people.

'Theo.'

She leant back in her chair.

'I've spent nearly six months here. I'm thinking of taking a trip around the Mediterranean.'

The world fell back into its original chaos. Thessaloniki loomed huge and ugly without her. He waited intently.

'I'd like to go up the Adriatic coast, then across to Italy, then to the French Riviera. We, I . . . we have houses there. Then down the Spanish coast and maybe across to Morocco. Have you been that way?'

'No.'

A moment of silence slipped between them, as if to clear enough space for the enormity of what followed.

'Would you like to come?'

The world fell into an even greater original chaos.

'On this . . . trip? With you?'

'Yes.'

He searched feverishly for the right attitude to this. But what is the right attitude to being told that you've just won a million dollars? It was one of those pieces of news that instantly disfigured your world with fierce possibility. Travel with her? But being with her was already travel. Sitting there, in the smoky, cluttered taverna, was already travel. And they hadn't even touched.

'What's the purpose of your trip? Do you have a mission?'

The straight eyebrows went up. 'Perhaps I'll find one on the way.'

He meant to say 'I need to think about it' but by some strange misunderstanding between tongue and intent, he said, 'I don't need to think about it.'

'Oh,' she said.

A strand of white hair fell over her right eye. He felt a blush spread up from the base of his stomach. But it wasn't a blush. It was something else. Something like a multiple emotional orgasm caused by the following realisations:

She wanted him.

He would go to the end of the Mediterranean world with her – and she had just invited him.

The world for once was beginning to make sense.

Only a table was between them.

He leant forward, and so did she. He reached over to her face – the only face in the world – and touched it with the unsteady fingertips of his right hand. Her skin was softer than he could have imagined, and cooler. He felt the tender, silk hollow under the cheekbone, the exquisitely defined jaw, the large pale mouth, warm like a sleeping creature. The event of his hand's contact with her face was unendurable. She was still, careful. This moment would never pass. The moment when he leant his face towards her face, when he lost her from sight and felt her instead, when the moment was drowned in the eternity of the Kiss.

He couldn't say how long the Kiss lasted. Their tongues were unsure, blind, only getting acquainted. The table between them grew until it pushed them apart. He looked at her with more than his eyes. Her face was more than a face. His body was clenched and pulsing. Time passed. They sat in silence. Theo felt changed forever. Then her husky voice populated his mind.

'So you are coming.'

He nodded, his voice anaesthetised. The cigarette in the ashtray had burnt down to its root. He raised his glass. She raised hers. They clinked without a word and perhaps managed to take a sip.

When he finally retrieved his voice, he said, he didn't know why, 'All night they soaked him in Midas's wine.'

She smiled with new complicity. 'Do you know what it means?'

He felt newly invincible with sudden knowledge.

'Do you know that we are very close to the Gardens of Midas? We're about ninety kilometres from the Precinct of the Nymphs, a wine-growing district also known as the Gardens of Midas, where King Midas . . . drank wine and waited.'

'For what?'

'For the secret of life, of course.'

'Of course,' she echoed ironically.

'Midas drank wine with sacred water, and waited for Silenius, the teacher of Dionysius. Silenius was half-man, half-goat, a satyr. He roamed the world, constantly drunk, accompanied by nymphs, bacchanalians, satyrs and other sinister creatures.'

'Wasn't that Dionysius?'

'Well, he did too – like teacher like student, you know. Dionysius's son Priapus was more of a freak, of course – he needed a wheelbarrow to carry his genitals.'

Véronique laughed. 'We can go to the Gardens of Midas if you want.'

'Do you know how to get there?'

'Just follow the Via Egnatia, and – you know, all roads lead to Rome.'

The night was chilly, the road deserted. The drive lasted perhaps half an hour, perhaps two. Theo drove fast, the wheel feeling thick and obedient in his hands. He glanced at her every now and then. She was withdrawing into herself. It was so dark he could make out only the shadows of trees and hills. He had missed the turn-off for Naoussa. He pulled over and turned to her. Maybe it had been a bad idea.

'Let's get out,' she said.

The late-night chill entered them at sharp angles. She buttoned her jacket up. The dry vines stretched indefinitely in a multiplying dream, the hills slept a menacing sleep, the moon crescent was bleak and fabulous. They trod on damp earth and smelt the low cloud. She walked, hands in her jacket pockets.

'So, Midas drank wine and waited.' Theo broke the silence.

'Eventually, Silenius came. Midas ensnared him and tried to obtain from him the secret of life. But, in the meantime, Dionysius appeared and released his teacher, promising Midas to grant him any wish in return. Midas asked to be given the gift of turning everything his body touched to gold. And so it was. But soon Midas realised his folly. He was surrounded by gold but unable to feed himself or to quench his thirst, because everything he touched turned to gold. Even wine turned to gold-powder and crumbled down his beard. He was starving. He was the richest and most wretched of kings and men. And he begged Dionysius to lift this curse.'

In the moonlight, her eyes were burning whisky. 'And he did?'

'Yes.'

They stood on the desolate road, alone against the moon. Their voices were crisp.

'Something else happened around here,' she said, 'but I can't remember what.'

'Alexander the Great was taught here by Aristotle?'

She nodded vaguely.

'And Aristotle's version of the myth is that Silenius spoke in fact, and revealed the secret of life.'

'And the secret was: life is full of grief,' she said.

'How do you know this?'

'What? That life is full of grief?' One corner of her lips stretched into a dry semi-smile.

'Aristotle's version.'

'It's my version of the myth, not Aristotle's. Or maybe it's a case of great minds thinking alike.'

He put his hand on her cold cheek. Her eyes were in shadow. She gripped his hand with her cold palm, gently removed it and walked back to the car. Theo followed in feverish sobriety.

They didn't speak on the way back. The jealous night had sneaked between them and pushed them apart. When he stopped under the street light in Dionyssos Odos, she put a hand on his arm to stop him from opening his mouth.

'I'll call you tomorrow,' he said.

No kiss. Just her hand on his sleeve. And her foot on the pavement.

And a last look, not friendly, not hostile, but a hooded, sepia look.

'Kalinichta, Midas.'

Lying on his austere hotel bed, the Kiss stung his lips. The tale of Midas was fundamentally flawed: Silenius the hoodwinked wasn't the one ensnared, Midas was the captive. Perhaps they were one and the same . . .

Theo had an erotic dream with a worrying woman who had Véronique's face and upper body, straw hair and the lower body of a faun. They chased each other around an ochre wood and copulated clumsily against sinuous trees. His pleasure was intensified by his fear of her. They merged into one confused but rapturous being.

FIFTEEN

May–June 1948, Thessaloniki

The second reason why Pascal decided to go to Thessaloniki was the fact that George Polk had finally made it to the city and possibly even into rebel territory.

Pascal's trip took three days and two modes of transport. The recently restored railway from Athens took his train proudly all the way over Mount Parnassus and into Thessaly, and just as the passengers were relaxing into a sweet sense of safety, something happened which instantly convinced Pascal – who was in the second passenger wagon – of the profound wisdom of placing a string of empty carriages in front of the passenger wagons. As the mines ripped the tracks, sending the empty wagons up in a deafening storm of metal and dust, and angrily shaking the full wagons from which screams rose in a similarly deafening crescendo, Pascal thought how propitious this was for his journey into the dark north. So much for normality.

There was a division of the national army on the train. They rushed about, waving their guns, threatening to blow up any bandit who dared show his ugly communist face, but they didn't venture far beyond the railway tracks since the woods were veiled by a devious fog in which any number of bandits could be lurking. The civilian passengers were forced to spend a hysterical night on the train, unprotected by the national army which had more urgent designs up north. Jeeps and vans were sent from the capital to transport the army. Some soldiers asked to stay on and protect the ladies from bandits, but the officers were not in the mood for romance. Pascal, as an honorary Westerner, was offered a ride, which he accepted. He travelled through the bumpy, starless night in the back of a van, among a crowd of fresh-faced soldiers just out of American training camps, yet unmangled by war. After carefully dodging questions about his mission, he was left alone. The soldiers sang Klephtic songs from the war of independence, laments such as 'The Black Crows', deploring the 'nation wounded by the guerrillas', and told jokes.

'This mule from Albania goes wandering around the border and crosses it. The Albanian border guard asks the Greek guard to pass it back over – it's their mule after all. The Greek guard says it's out of the question since the mule has violated the territorial integrity of Greece and is currently being interrogated by the UN Special Commission for Observation on the Balkans . . .'

Pascal laughed with the rest of them and thought of Michel and the commission's inglorious search for Markos the previous year. But Michel would be proven wrong in his assertions that George Polk wouldn't dare cross into rebel territory. Pascal was following in his steps. First get to Salonika, then find a reliable guide to take him to the mountains. He might run into George who wouldn't be pleased – after all, he wouldn't want his laurels stolen – but then they might end up in different parts of the Grammos Ranges. Of course it was going to be a chase for the first interview with Markos. He wouldn't give two interviews to two journalists; he had too much else to worry about, such as his head, for which there was an official reward of twenty million drachmas and for which there were many candidates exquisitely trained in decapitation. Polk had not publicised his pending journey. He had not even confided in Pascal. Polk was not going to be intimidated by recent threats from anonymous sources that 'someone was going to be hurt', following the publication of his indignant article in *Harper's Magazine* exposing the excesses of the government. Pascal told himself that he would have made this trip regardless of George's movements. It was the natural, and only, progression of his work here. It would be easy for him to get the sympathy of the guerrillas; he was not American or even British, and he had socialist, if not communist, leanings.

There was less light in Thessaloniki than in Athens, or perhaps the tissue of light itself was different, unevenly distributed, trapped between buildings. There were more shadows, more paranoia, more unchecked graffiti: 'Death to the fascists', 'Death to the bourgeoisie', 'KKE', 'ELAS'. Thessaloniki was a besieged city. The guerrillas, invisible and terrifying, lurked at its very edges. The curfew was strict and people scurried past each other, quick steps fading inconclusively into small side-streets.

Pascal looked in vain for the scars of the recent deportation of the entire Salonician Jewery to the gas chambers. The city had closed over the wound left by its fifty thousand Jews, just as the water of Piraeus Harbour had closed over the body of Georgi. There weren't even mothers left to cry here.

A couple of months before, the rebels had attempted to seize Thessaloniki by shelling the centre. Every window of Hotel Cosmopolite, where the UN Special Commission was staying while investigating allegations of child abductions to northern countries by the guerrillas, was broken. This was possibly a third reason why Pascal decided he could no longer stay in uneventful Athens.

Polk had apparently left town the day before to cross the front line. Pascal was very keen to find out exactly how Polk had managed this. He knew the standard practice for new rebel recruits in Athens and other towns in the south was to hire a guide who would take the novice up north, across the front line and to the nearest post of the Democratic Army. This was fraught with danger, of course, not only because of possible capture by government forces, but also because the prospective guide could be better paid by the police to hand over potential enthusiasts of the mountains. But there was no standard practice for foreign correspondents, simply because there was no precedent of a single Westerner crossing into 'Free Greece'.

While Pascal was making careful and fruitless attempts at enquiring about Polk's guides, the American's ID was sent by mail to

Thessaloniki's third precinct police station by unidentified persons. Polk had gone missing. Pascal felt less keen to meet his presumed guides and more anxious to find out what had happened. Rumours began to circulate about Polk being murdered in the mountains. Pascal dithered for a day or two but was soon put out of his indecision. Polk's bloated body, his neck broken by a bullet, was spotted by fishermen in the harbour.

If he left immediately, Pascal would avoid being dragged into a potentially torturous inquiry as a witness. But then he wouldn't make himself available as a potentially useful source of information – after all, he had known Polk and his Greek wife in Athens. There was no doubt that now was the safest time for him to sneak out of Thessaloniki – whoever the assassins of George Polk were, they were not likely to strike twice at a similar target within a matter of days. But what if he was subsequently suspected of being involved in the murder? His motives would be either professional competitiveness, or his well-known leftist sympathies; he could be accused of being an agent of international communism and part of a conspiracy to murder Polk in order to frame the right-wing organs of power and discredit them in the eyes of the West.

After only a week, Pascal concluded that anything was possible in Thessaloniki. He could smell it in the air, fragrant with the coming spring and the sewage stench rising from the harbour when the vardari struck from the north. Polk had taken a chance; Pascal was about to do the same. Pauline sounded hysterical on the phone. 'Go back to Athens, if you won't come back here – for the love of your son! They'll kill you too!'

He was pierced by the strange feeling that his time with Pauline was over, that whenever he returned, they would not go back to their previous life, that a vital thread had been severed and she was to him little more than an anxious, uncomprehending voice down a telephone line and his son Alex little more than a bundle of augmenting consciousness which did not include his father. He felt suddenly emptied. Things back in France shed their nagging importance. He had been blind not to understand that this war had acquired for him the intensity, if not the features, of that other war in which he was so ashamed not to have taken part directly. He had buzzed on the periphery of the Résistance, held back by his wretched health history, armed only with his pen and his nom-de-guerre for which, strictly speaking, there was no need. Was he repeating that experience here, in this war that was not his, in which he could take no sides?

Tito was definitively denounced by Stalin and all communist satellites, placing the Greek guerrillas in a most delicate position. 'Their main source of aid was Tito's Yugoslavia,' said Pascal's cable. 'The KKE's ideological allegiance is with Stalin, though Stalin certainly isn't with the KKE and indeed relies on the elephant of the West to crush the annoying rebel bug.'

For the next couple of weeks, as the inquiry gathered speed, Pascal had to keep a low profile. The American officials ignored him. The police groped for the main suspects in a darkness created by themselves, in order to obscure other, more embarrassing possibilities. Pascal could have easily become a suspect had the police not decided to focus on Polk's wife and his closest journalist friend in Athens, then a local, a Reuters stringer from Thessaloniki. One day, Pascal received an unsigned note, in French, in his hotel room: 'Monsieur Loublier, please tell the world about this injustice. A conspiracy has been engineered by the security police and the American embassy. Someone will have to tell the truth. I may not be able to.' He assumed it was from the Greek scapegoat. In his helplessness Pascal made a mental note to uncover the fallacy in his future book, once he was safely out of there. But it would be too late to help anyone. And, to describe it all, he would have to be present at the trial, which involved putting off his trip indefinitely. At that point, talk of a major government offensive against the rebels, scheduled for mid-June, began to circulate under the slogan 'May the Grammos Range become Slavo-Communism's gravestone!' Speculations leaked into journalistic circles that an early summer attack would be premature and inconclusive because of the current strength of the rebels. In any case, Pascal had to make sure he would be back before mid-June, so as not to be buried himself under that gravestone.

On a night without moon, Pascal sat in a caique with two fresh-faced boys. They steered across the Thermaic Gulf in the direction of Mount Olympus, grinning whitely at the nervous Pascal like some unorthodox, underage Charons taking a reluctantly dead man across the Styx to the underworld.

SIXTEEN

April 1998, Thessaloniki

She watched Theo with bemused infatuation as he spoke of Alexander the Great and political subtexts, of the 'archaeological Mafia', blowing apologetic clouds of smoke away from her face, though the smoke always came back, stinging her eyes. His impetuosity was contagious. His conversation was nervously diligent, like a top-grade essay written in a hurry, especially when he regaled her with Greek mythology. But she decided to resist the pull of his body until they left Thessaloniki. She had the feeling that if they consummated their lust before leaving, there would be no impetus to go anywhere. She also felt that, had she not met Theo, she wouldn't have been able to leave at all. She would have never gone on a trip without him, even though staying in the same place, whether it was Thessaloniki or Paris, would have been unbearable. Looking at his animated, candle-lit face at the Taverna Dedalou, listening to him talk about his family in Melbourne, she was roused as though after a long and numbing slumber. When they kissed for the first time, his tongue was firm, his face eager. His long curled eyelashes tickled her cheek. For the first time since that phone-call in Istanbul, excluding tripping, she forgot about her father, drowned in the moment. Of all the kisses she had tasted, none had tasted so much like water to a parched palate.

When, at night, they drove along the ghostly Via Egnatia, she had a moment of claustrophobic panic – the dark silhouettes of hills nudging in, the fields brown and reeking of freshly turned earth, the hopelessness of this never-ending road like a cut through time that wouldn't heal. She was running along this gaping crack, too close to the edge, and Theo's presence was the only thing that proved to her she hadn't fallen. She stared at him in the harsh beam of the car's headlights, as he went on drunkenly about Midas's misadventures. Her father could be around, listening. Her father would have wanted to add something to the story; he knew the myths. Which version of the tale would he have preferred? The one where Silenius reveals that life is full of sorrow, or the one where Silenius is released by Dionysius, and Midas is granted his wretched wish? Or both of them at once? So that Midas knows there is nothing to know beyond sorrow, and at the same time ends up killing everything with his touch.

Véronique never asked her father what he thought about Midas. Standing next to Theo, she wished she had, as if that would have been a solution. Perhaps being here with Theo, in the middle of the damp Precinct of Nymphs, caught between winter and spring, was not the result of a mere encounter. She hoped it was love at last, at last. She hoped it wasn't, for surely she wasn't capable of ever loving again.

Aware of Theo's subdued presence in the car, Véronique felt as if they couldn't touch before they crossed the border. Any border, as long as she could wake up and taste in the sour breath of morning the sweet promise of things being unknown, worthwhile. With Theo odd-eyed and curious by her side.

But there was one more thing to do before that. On the phone, Michel Franchitti went quiet at the news of Pauline's death. 'Come over, Véronique.' His voice was diminished and chillingly intimate. 'I haven't told you everything.'

SEVENTEEN

April 1998, Thessaloniki

He followed her casual finger across the map, which was so diminutive that her finger currently blotted out a third of Italy. Going to all those places together was clearly a fantasy. Theo knew that something in this map and this exquisite, short-nailed finger didn't correspond to reality as he knew it. That this voice was precisely the kind of voice that one remembers from a dream. His or her dream, he couldn't tell yet and he didn't care, as long as the dream didn't end. He slid his hand under hers and his fingers felt the tender skin of her wrist.

'. . . Then we'll stay in Nice and Marseilles, in our family houses, and continue down to Barcelona, down the Spanish coast . . .'

Her finger travelled down vast coastal zigzags. This journey was more insane than Alexander's campaigns across Asia.

'. . . We can cross over to Morocco and continue towards Algiers, Tunis, Tripoli and Alexandria. Then from Alexandria we can cross to Turkey. And from Turkey, guess where?'

He couldn't, he was too preoccupied with her elbow cupped in his hand. 'Back here. The circle will be closed.'

'I like your itinerary,' he said.

'Oh, and something else,' she said casually. 'Because I'm inviting you, I expect to take your expenses on myself.'

He hadn't choked on smoke since he was fourteen.

'Well' – she didn't abandon her casualness – 'you don't realise this, but my family is wealthy. Money is not a problem.'

He smoked in shocked silence.

'That's very . . . kind of you, but I . . . It's just not in my . . . culture.'

'I know, but to me it doesn't make any difference. I just inherited a large estate from my grandmother.'

'But . . . how do you know that you can trust me? You don't know me.'

Her pupils dilated like bugs flying into the liquid amber of her irises.

'So *can* I trust you?'

A gull passed over them, dropping a white splatter in the middle of the table. She smiled with her large mouth. An incontinence of wellbeing flooded Theo. He said, flippantly, 'And can I trust you?'

Her smile merged into a thought. Without any playfulness, she said simply, as if announcing the end of the joke, 'I don't know, Theo. You have to decide for yourself.'

And she got up, took off her jacket and let it hang in her cradled hands. Her elusive scent hung over the table. Theo felt drugged, his tongue numb.

'Have you noticed how we keep coming back to Thessaloniki?' she said, all laughter suddenly gone from her.

'What do you mean?'

'Why did you come here, for example? You didn't really have to come here to do your research. I didn't have to come back either.'

She was somehow putting her finger on a sore spot. But what was the spot? He stood up. They walked in no particular direction. His black Reeboks and her moccasins. Just how rich was her family?

Thunder startled them.

'Perhaps we'll never leave here then,' he suggested. They stopped, in the middle of the midday market bustle.

'And it will always be today,' she said. 'We'll keep replaying the same day over and over.'

A warm rain without an edge enveloped them. She looked up, closing her eyes. The raindrops teased her eyelashes and for a moment she looked as if she was crying, despite her breezy expression. Her long neck was exposed. He could smell her hair, her damp skin, the dusty smell of new rain on the pavement, the fruit on the stalls. He brushed his face against her cheek and ear. A group of young men with motorbikes whistled from the other side of the little square. A short, square woman yelled at them to move aside because they were blocking the access to her vegetable stall. They stepped aside.

Véronique looked at her watchless wrist, breaking the spell. 'My bus is leaving soon.'

'What bus?'

'I'm going to Edessa.'

'You're going to Edessa? What for?'

'To see an old friend of the family.'

'I'll drive you.'

'No, it's okay, thanks. I'll be back in the afternoon. I heard it's a beautiful town.'

Véronique placed a sudden, enigmatic kiss on the corner of his mouth. And she was gone.

He stood entranced in the middle of the market, ready to wait however long it took, the kiss flowering in a corner of his lips like a fresh sore. The spring rain drummed sonorously on the plastic awnings. Two of the young men straddled their motorbikes and revved them, then continued talking.

'Uncle Panayoti, I need to borrow your car again.'

'Sure. Where are you going now?'

'To Edessa.'

Shocked silence.

'Edessa! What for, my boy?'

'I want to . . . look at your old house. I've never seen it.'

A sigh.

He drove like a madman until he caught up. For the next hour, he was stuck behind the retarded bus, which rewarded him with puffs of black smoke. She was inside, so close that he couldn't think about

her. His head spun from sleeplessness. He had no idea what he was
going to do.

When they arrived, Véronique got off the bus and talked to the
driver briefly, then headed for the town centre. Theo parked nearby
and followed her, walking a safe distance behind. She crossed a plateia.
Eventually, she turned into a steep, deserted street. Theo stopped at
the corner and watched the movement of her legs until she stopped
at the gate of what must have been a whitewashed house (they were
all whitewashed in that alley) and disappeared from his view. He
waited for a few minutes, smoking and unsure, until his dignity
prevailed and he retraced his steps back into town. Across from the
Edessa Museum of Folklore he found the Philipidis' house. There
was nothing to see, of course – it was an ordinary house in dire need
of a paint job. A family was living in it. Mother, father, two kids,
maybe a grandmother, maybe a dog. The Philipidis lost the house
after the civil war and when it was restored to them, in '85, they sold
it because they had moved to Thessaloniki. The icon-faced Hrisoula
had lived here with Angelis and their three children, two of whom
had been taken in the 1948 *pedomasoma*. They had ended up in
Tashkent, two kids of five and eight, Theo's father and aunt. They
had come back to the border twenty years later to see their father
Angelis in a coffin and wave to their mother on the other side. They
had married and gone to Australia. Life went on. They had children.
And so here he was, living it up, trying to ignore the nightmare that
rippled through the family like a radioactive breeze. Angelis's black
feet the size of watermelons after *fangala* torture, the castor oil which
damaged his intestines forever, his sixteen years on the prison islands,
and finally, his death in jail in '67. Panayotis's three years in jail under
the colonels. Theo's father's ulcer. Theo's childhood resonated with
his father's insomniac pacing around the house, his knuckles
permanently grazed from punching the walls at night. The
Grigoriadis, his mother's family, also came from Edessa, except their
house was never restored to them.

He sat at a café near the thundering waterfalls and had a frappé.
He had neither the nerve nor the need to wade through the queasy
quagmire of the past. It wasn't his quagmire. But every day spent in

these places sucked him in deeper. He needed to get out and he needed to get out with Véronique, whoever she was, wherever she was headed. The thesis would somehow write itself later. Somehow, he could afford to do this. Somehow, Véronique would help make things simpler. There was none of this vestigial squalor in her cosmopolitan, slightly melancholy world and he would be a denizen of that world for a while, whatever risks the visit involved.

He drove back, punishing Panayotis's old Volkswagen, swerving dangerously at turns, speeding like any young Mediterranean male – only he was speeding into the shallow future in order to leave the fathomless past behind.

EIGHTEEN

May 1948, Pieria HQ

Standing before the indoctrination officer, Daphne Grigoriadis shook from head to foot. Every breath he let out from under his moustache moved her closer to the dawn, as if she was made of paper.

'Please, comrade,' she said, 'he made a mistake. You know he's a good fighter.'

'As I said, it isn't up to me. You ought to plead with Commander Achilles.'

'He has gone away for the week.'

'I know!' He pursed his mouth in irritation. 'Look, the execution order has already been issued.'

'But there's been no court-martial!'

'But the order has been issued and approved by HQ. Or do you expect comrade Zachariadis himself to be overseeing every petty execution?'

'Our family has already given a heavy toll. My mother and my father . . .'

'Comrade Daphne, we aren't interested in your parents. Every family has sacrificed members. And I'd advise you to be more careful about what you say.'

The indoctrination officer placed a hand on the small of Daphne's back and pushed her gently towards the door. Her shaking legs took her out into the bloody incontinence of a sunset spilling over the scorched peaks of Vurinos.

'Comrade Daphne!'

'Yes?' She turned, hope lacerating her heart.

'You are allowed one last visit to the condemned.'

For a second, dazed with disbelief at what was going to happen, she didn't know in which direction to walk. The cliffs, perhaps, to end it once and for all? And yet she had seen many executions of comrades. This one was no different. She must try to overcome her emotional involvement and look at it objectively, from the Democratic Army's point of view. Her brother was a 'demoraliser', a 'winger'. She couldn't.

Alexis was sitting dejectedly on the clay floor of the cell, together with the other two condemned: one who had been caught making love and another one, even younger – perhaps fifteen – who had been caught asleep on his night-watch. Daphne knocked on the window.

'Alexi,' she whispered.

He looked up, and something approximating a smile lit his yellowish face.

The guard opened the door and she went in. Alexis got up with visible effort. She could see that prostration was his way of preparing to let go of life. They embraced. The cell was unbearably stuffy.

'Alexaki,' she whispered, holding onto his arms. 'I tried. I tried but . . .' – she wanted to say they were monsters, they had no humanity, they were losing the plot – '. . . but Commander Achilles has gone away for the week and the indoctrination officer . . .'

'Daphne,' Alexis's black eyes burnt with the dull intensity of doom, 'nothing could've saved me. You can see they have stepped up executions since the break with Tito. These are the forces of history and I'm just a small pebble tumbling down the hill before the great avalanche.'

'My philosopher.' Daphne stroked his hair, still whispering so he wouldn't hear the panic in her voice. 'Perhaps someone will intervene, something will happen before dawn comes, an earthquake to swallow us all, or a surprise attack from the army . . .'

Alexis smiled. His smile had aged in the last twelve hours. 'No. You and the others must carry on until the end. I'm not such a great shot anyway.'

'Me neither,' giggled the boy who had been caught asleep, and a sudden sob escaped his throat. Grimacing, tearless spasms shook his beautiful glabrous face. 'At least you've got your sister to kiss you. I've got nobody.' He turned to the fornicator: 'And you, at least you've had a woman. I have to die a virgin.'

The sinner lay in a heap in the corner, facing the wall, inert.

Daphne went over to the boy, who by far wasn't the only virgin in the room, and crouched beside him.

'I will kiss you if you want,' she said confidently.

'On the lips?' The boy was incredulous.

She leant forward and placed her cold lips on his. He shivered, his limpid blue eyes enlarged with wonder.

'Die like a hero,' Daphne said to him solemnly, sensing that was the only way to instil some strength in him. 'Die as if you are dying for your fatherland. Or for the girl you would've loved.'

'As if,' Alexis sneered bitterly. 'If only I knew I'd end up being shot by my own . . . I would've . . .'

'What? Never joined?' Daphne's voice was restored to its normal volume but they had to speak quietly because of the guard who was smoking just outside the door.

'No, I didn't mean that. I don't know what I meant. Daphne!' He gripped his sister's arms with sudden urgency. 'Promise me something.'

'Anything.'

'Tell Illias that I died like a hero. That I didn't shed a tear. That I was proud to give my life, whatever . . . You know what to tell him. I want him to be proud of me, for once.'

'Come on, Alexaki, he is proud of you!'

'Please promise me. And if one day . . .' His voice broke but he cleared his throat, frowning at his weakness. 'If one day you see Dad, if he gets out of the islands alive, tell him the same. That I was a proud son of my father.' He looked at Daphne, inspired by his own words. His sharp-featured face pierced her. She would carry his face lodged inside her to the last day.

'And Daphne, promise me . . .' He combed her cropped black hair with his fingers, 'Promise me you'll grow your hair back when the war is over.'

She tried to smile but her face was struggling with too many other things.

'Remember,' she whispered, 'when you were little, how I would sit you on my knees and teach you to read from that square book with the nice illustrations?'

'Yes, and I was hopeless.' Alexis smiled.

The guard coughed. 'Time's up, comrades.'

Daphne gripped Alexis's sleeve and, like a blind woman, her shaking hands groped for his face, ears, neck, hair, desperately trying to capture these bits of him, to take them with her, to salvage them. She pressed her dry lips against his warm eyes, his damp temples, his small ears, his unshaven cheeks, his sharp nose, his chapped, bleeding lips. She wanted to say, 'I'll fight with a doubled strength, I'll fight for you too, we will win this war', but no voice came out, not even a whisper or a whimper. Alexis returned her kiss and put his hands on her cheeks, his eyes suddenly drowned in the same wave of terror that was choking her. She walked out without looking back. Outside, the guard apologised – he had orders. Daphne nodded indefinitely, her vocal chords unwound and hanging loose somewhere inside her hollow body. She couldn't help taking one last look at Alexis through the window. He looked back, and they stood like this, she with her face against the window-bars, he with his elbow propped up on his bent knee, his head leaning on the dirty whitewashed wall. She stroked the glass with the tips of her fingers and moved away.

She walked like those she had seen walking after shell-shock – in no particular direction, suicidally carefree.

Her comrades teemed around, some with unsure words of comfort, some without, convinced that her brother was indeed a 'winger', bringing the morale down, encouraging deserters, and therefore deserving the firing squad. Irini, the young woman who had been caught fornicating with the prostrate man in the corner, looked at Daphne from a distance of terror, not daring approach her for fear of being seen as conspiring.

She lay all night with open eyes, listening to the macabre orchestra of the mountains: crickets, then a typewriter, then crackling of fire, then simply stars – but no moon. They had lain like this, she and her little brother, years back, before the war, and the one before; they had listened to the cascading waters of their town Edessa, and their lives had stretched before them like Turkish carpets, and they had giggled, then argued when Alexis had suggested that he would become a resistance fighter if the Germans invaded, Daphne protesting that she wanted to fight the Germans too, and he condescendingly explaining that women couldn't fight. All night she fed good memories to the beast of terror to pacify it, to stretch its night of repose, because dawn was its awakening. She knew that even if she went to the indoctrination officer and took off her clothes, she couldn't save Alexis. Such was the system that once an order was issued, the original reason did not matter. The responsible vanished; only the executors remained.

The shots of the firing squad came just as the sun's plucked rooster-head began to emerge between the mountains. In the cool morning breeze, she felt the fresh tatters of her life stir like rags on a maimed body. She got up and stumbled around the church, the barn and the school to where the three bodies lay on the earth still damp with the chills of the night. They were all barefoot and naked from the waist up, having 'volunteered', in the guerrilla fashion, hard-to-come-by articles for the survivors. Captain Telemachus, who was in charge of the firing squad and who, like many others, had a soft spot for Daphne, took a brief, shifty look at her and whispered confidentially, 'You can have his things.' 'Can I dress him in his shirt?' 'No.' She made a small bundle of Alexis's boots and shirt and obtained permission to dig his grave. Around his neck was a gilded medallion with a photograph of their parents – young, humourless and felicitously retouched by the photographer. She left it there, on his slender, hairy, still warm chest, next to the red hole where his heart had been only five minutes before. She closed his lids over his obsidian eyes.

Later, she didn't know how much later, when sweat and tears ran down her face and the spade dug into her blistered hands, the reptilian voice of Telemachus hissed behind her, 'Antigone, Antigone, if you bury your Polyneuces, sooner or later you must incur the wrath of Creon.' She turned to give him a look which she hoped sent him straight to hell and continued her labour next to the quietly weeping Irini and two others. She threw spadefuls of soil on her brother's perforated naked chest and his sleeping face, and prayed with gritted teeth for the decisive battle to come soon, and for the Grim Reaper to tap on the shoulder of Commander Achilles, and Telemachus, and the indoctrination officer, whose name she didn't care to remember. And to cut off her own life at the rotten roots, so that she could share the arid soil of this land with her little brother.

She was given the rare grace of marking her brother's side of the common grave with a crude metal plate she made from the lid of a Hungarian meat-tin. On it she scratched thinly with a nail: 'Grigoriadis Alexis, 1928–1948'. There was no space on the lid for 'Died like a hero, as if dying for his fatherland'.

NINETEEN

April 1998, Edessa

'I haven't seen Pauline for seventeen years, with the exception of one brief visit ten years ago. We became estranged while Alex was in Greece. Then of course I left France to come here. That time at the Villa des Marées was the time before I last saw her.'

He looked at Véronique imploringly.

'You see, Véronique, Pauline and I . . .' He started shakily, then gave a dismissive wave of the hand. 'No, nonsense. There was no Pauline and I. It was just me. I was in love with her for many years.'

He gave her such a helpless look that she forgot to be shocked.

'You didn't know, did you? Everybody knew. Alex knew.' He sighed and rubbed his forehead. 'I was mad about her. It's always that way, isn't it? Always, we love the wrong person. Or we are the wrong person to love. Like Pascal was for Pauline. I'm talking about real love. The rest of the time we just pretend, and at the price of pretence we reach some approximation of happy convenience. Right?'

Véronique wanted to reach out and touch his hand, thank him for his frankness. But she only took a sip of coffee.

'Are you in love?' he enquired gravely but tenderly.

She choked on the thick coffee. 'Why do you ask?'

'Because you look different from last time.'

'Do I?' she said flatly.

'When you are, when you truly are, one day, you will know. You'll have no choice but to know. Like I knew with Pauline.'

Véronique bit her lip. Did she know already? No, she didn't know anything. Thessaloniki and Theo seemed far away.

'Have some baklava, please.' Michel pushed the plate towards her. Véronique hadn't tasted the sweet pastry since her father had said, 'Keep some for me.'

'Pascal and I were friends, of course. We knew each other well, although I can't be sure of that any more, after all that's happened. Pascal and Pauline had a strange relationship. By the time Pascal went to Greece, that last time in 1967, you could hardly say they had a relationship . . . He spent most of his time in Marseilles.'

He stopped, as if scared by what he was about to say. A fat black fly buzzed over their heads, aiming for the syrupy plates. Michel took a newspaper and folded it, his eyes on the fly.

'I don't know if you need to know all this.'

'She was a complex woman, wasn't she?'

'A formidably complex woman. Afflicted all her life by her love for the wrong men.'

'What do you mean?'

'Well, what do I mean?' He was comically irritated. 'Pascal was a fiendishly difficult man to be around, and François, well, just look at him, with all due respect . . .' He lit a cigarette. 'Don't get me wrong.' He blew out a reconciling cloud. 'All men are simple when it comes to emotions. Let's take Pascal. Pascal had an intellectual's mind, and a humanist's heart. He was destined for big things. But he was also headed for disaster. For twenty years, disaster eluded him, so to speak. When he came to Greece the first time, during the civil war, I was in Athens, a correspondent for *Le Monde*. He took over from me, I'd had enough. Alex was only two. In Paris, I found Pauline beside herself with anguish. I did my best to support her. I loved Alex and we got on better than he ever did with Pascal.' He sighed. 'But I guess . . . I admired him. He was fearless and he cared. He cared about what happened to Greece. He cared even about the

Macedonians in the civil war, for Christ's sake. He cared for the underdog, always. That's more than most people can manage, including myself. But in the end, he didn't care about Pauline. And I never forgave him this.'

With one devastating blow of the lethally folded newspaper he swatted the fly, which was feeding in the baklava plate, inspected it to his satisfaction, then pushed his sacrificed pastry away.

'When it came to emotions, you know, he was hopeless. He didn't deserve Pauline. He punished her continuously for not being interested in the things he cared about. He despised tyranny and injustice – he was the walking paradigm of the Western socialist, this strange, misunderstood beast. And Pauline wasn't interested in politics. She preferred her art uncontaminated, as she used to say. But deep down, I suspect he simply stopped loving her.'

'Did Pauline know this?'

'Of course. She was a very intelligent woman, nothing escaped her. But she believed for a while, after '67, that he had deserted her. Poor Pauline. She was prepared to believe that he'd left her for another rather than believe that he was dead.'

His partisan sweetheart, François had said. *His other woman, in Greece.*

'Another woman?'

'Well . . .'

'Who?'

Michel opened his arms, encompassing the entire female sex. 'God knows.'

'My father, I wonder if he knew any of this.'

Michel shook his leonine head.

'You were close to Pascal.'

'Pascal was a private man. After he came back from Greece, he shut himself in his Marseilles house. For months we wouldn't see him. He was traumatised, I think. I tried talking to him but he was elusive. Then he went back to Greece, this time only for a week. When he came back, his hair was grey. He was only twenty-eight then. He didn't speak to anyone about what had happened. He moved to Marseilles where he wrote his book in the next two, three years.'

Véronique saw a sudden shift in Michel's mind, as obvious as if his eyes had changed colour.

'I must say, however, that on at least one occasion he showed me a photograph, a group photograph of partisans in which there was a woman . . .'

'What was her name?'

'I don't know. But I think she made a deep impression on Pascal. His relationship with Pauline was mortally wounded, so to speak, by what'd happened in Greece, whatever that was. He became an exile in Paris, as if he was a refugee. I don't think anyone knows, or knew, the whole truth of what Pascal had been through, psychologically. I know about war. I was a correspondent too, don't forget that. In a sense, you never recover. And of course he had concussion from the first time around in Greece . . .'

Michel's voice had gone hoarse.

'What about that woman Daphne from the archives I showed you last time? Does she look anything like the woman he showed you in that photo?' asked Véronique.

'It's hard to say. I wouldn't say so.'

'There's got to be an explanation of these photocopies. Dad thought he was on to something.'

Michel looked at her for an unguarded moment and quickly shifted his gaze but it was too late – she had seen him say, 'Please don't insist.' She didn't insist.

'I didn't want to tell you,' he said, 'but I'm going to anyway. These so-called records . . . They're incomplete. The real files are huge. They've only given you the headings, as it were. But in any case, even the complete files wouldn't be of any use any more. I'm not even sure if they haven't given you fakes.'

At the door, Michel took her hand between his large, soft palms and held it.

'You know, about Pauline . . . It's all so long ago, of course, but I feel I ought to say it . . . I did love her deeply. For many years. It wrecked my life. It was desperation that made me do what I did.'

He leant against the open door, still holding her hand, not unlike the way François had leant against the velvet curtains a couple of weeks ago, something inside him caving in.

'When Pascal first mentioned his idea about writing a second book, going off on a long research trip, it was still very much an idea. He wasn't sure. I . . . encouraged him. He had been depressed for many years. I convinced him I would find a publisher for him; it would be a terrific book, revealing, sensational, better even than the first one. We even had a title for it. *Night Without Moon*. It's the opening line of a popular rebetiko song which was made illegal during the civil war.'

He let go of Véronique's hand and crossed his arms.

'Pascal needed something to live for, a mission, a sense of worth as a writer and a human being. That's the kind of man he was. That's why I encouraged him to go. But the truth is, he'd already had a crack at the civil war theme, and it wasn't that smart to write another book on the same subject.'

Véronique waited without a word.

'You see, Pauline was unhappy with him, but she was enslaved by her emotional dependency on him. She suffered atrociously. I wanted to have a chance to make her see her mistake. I was divorced by then. I'm not saying that I feel responsible for what happened to Pascal. But I . . . made a mistake. I killed off any chance of getting closer to Pauline. Especially after the passport was recovered. I lost her completely then. And I lost Pascal, who was a dear friend after all. A dear friend.'

Michel swallowed and smoothed his left eyebrow with the tips of his upset fingers. Véronique realised that her silence was becoming accusatory but still said nothing.

'When I heard about Alex's accident last year I . . . I called her, though I didn't know what I'd say. She never came to the phone. I left many messages with various people, including your mother. Pauline didn't want to speak to me. Alex's death was like reliving '67 all over again for me. And much more so for her, of course.'

Véronique needed to flee. The last bus was leaving soon. 'Thank you for being so sincere.'

But his hand gripped her arm. 'If you look in Pascal's book, you'll find a passage where a village elder told him: "They are trying to liberate Greece from the Greeks." When Pascal set off in '67, he said to me, "Michel, I'm going back there because only one thing can liberate Pascal from Pascal."'

'And what was that?'

'I don't know.'

She could not read him.

'And, Véronique, I'd give five years of my life to find the man who killed Pascal. But, as I said to you last time, things just sink here, get lost in the labyrinth. Such is the nature of this country that its fate becomes the fate of those who get too close.'

'What about you?'

'Me, too.'

The green eyes farewelled her ambiguously.

When she reached the corner, she looked back. Michel stood in the doorway, twisted like a tree after a thunderstorm. He waved and she waved back.

The town clock tolled. Where was she? Greece. France. Italy. Colombia. Turkey. A languorous clock calling for siesta. Or the end of siesta. Or the end of something. She rushed through town, retracing her steps from a few hours ago as if erasing them, as if cancelling her visit, Michel Franchitti's guilt, Pauline's despair, Pascal's torment, whatever it had been, her father's pointless sacrifice in the attempt to make sense of it all. It was too much to fathom. If her father had failed, she stood no chance. She must forget what she never knew.

Waterfalls pounded the earth with the youthful violence of spring.

TWENTY

April 1998, Thessaloniki

In the morning, Véronique turned up at his door. His loins wrapped in a towel, naked from the waist up, he was shaving. The shaving cream was a convenient shield against the blush that invaded his neck at the sight of the unexpected visitor. They stood at the door for a moment, closely facing each other.

'Good morning, Midas,' she said.

He stepped aside to let her in.

'Please, finish your toilette.'

Her moccasined feet softly crossed the room. She went out on the diminutive balcony and surveyed the bustle below. The noises coming from the balcony and from adjacent rooms – a radio, the buzzing of a vacuum cleaner, a confident male voice singing 'Amore Mio' – made the world distant and fascinating, like a freak exhibit behind museum glass. He wanted that sudden world, because she was in it.

'How was Edessa?' He shaved briskly.

'Nice. Especially the waterfalls.'

Theo pushed the door. Papadopoulos was at his desk, biting into a greasy cheese pastry and sipping aromatic coffee. He jumped up in a flurry of crumbs. Then he saw the second visitor and dabbed his mouth with the serviette he was holding. Véronique nodded.

'This is my colleague from France, Véronique Loublier. Véronique, this is Mr Papadopoulos, assistant director of the museum.' Theo spoke in Greek.

Papadopoulos looked from one visitor to the other, sat back in his chair and lit a cigarette.

'What do you want now?' he said.

'I'd like to have admission to the museum facilities,' Theo said brazenly.

'Oh. But we discussed this already. I told you not to come here again.'

Theo stepped forward, walked around the desk and stood next to the seated Papadopoulos, who sprang up. His planned offensive crumbled in a heap of pity for the little man caught mid-breakfast, and in the sheer physical incapability of violence. He looked at the desk as if for help, reached for the coffee cup and emptied it on top of the pastry, which turned a soggy brown. Papadopoulos watched this with concentration.

Véronique stared, her lips semi-open in the abandon of shock. She shook her head at Theo in a mute request for explanation.

'Let's go,' Theo said in English, with the regret of a real gentleman forced to resort to ungentle measures. He hailed a taxi. 'I'll explain to you in a minute. But I have to say goodbye to the family. Would you like to meet them?'

Véronique shook her head. 'If it's going to be as entertaining as this! Why did you punish him like that? Now he'll have to get another pitta for breakfast.'

'Believe me, he deserved it.'

'Where are you from?' shouted the driver over the loud bouzouki.

Theo and Véronique exchanged unsure looks.

'Australia,' Theo shouted back.

'Ah, Australia!' The man's face lit up like a plundered Christmas tree. 'My son and daughter are in America. New York, Sydney. Ah, my dear boy. It's good that you're in Australia, you're living the good life . . .' He lit a cigarette and turned up the music.

Panayotis kissed Véronique's hand with ebullient delight and Paraskevas served freshly baked buns, sweet quince preserve and coffee. Véronique sat in their lounge, looking conspicuously foreign with her light cotton trousers, bleached hair and subtle gestures. Panayotis engaged in a conversation with her immediately, she speaking Greek, he experimenting with his school French.

'Where did you learn to speak Greek so well?'

'Oh, I don't think I speak it well, but thank you. I lived here when I was young.'

'Is that right! How extraordinary, a French girl in Greece! You were here with your family?'

'Yes, a long time ago. I decided to revisit.'

'Extraordinaire!'

Theo's bun got stuck in his throat. The old fool. He wanted to leave quickly but Panayotis was only warming up, basking in the presence of the visitor. Véronique sipped her coffee. Theo took out a cigarette.

'Not inside.' Paraskevas wagged an affectionate finger at him.

'I know.'

'Eh! Let the boy smoke where he wants!' Panayotis said, hoping Véronique would appreciate his democratic personality. But Theo only fingered his lighter.

'And what is your . . . field of expertise?' Paraskevas enquired softly.

Véronique looked at Theo with alarm. They hadn't expected such detailed questions.

'She is doing research on Apollo.' Theo saved the day. Véronique smiled competently.

'Aha.' Everybody nodded, finding the answer fairly exhaustive.

'Well, we must make a move.' Theo glanced at his watch.

'Right.' Uncle Panayotis snapped into action. 'I'll drive you to the bus.'

'Oh no, no, don't,' Theo almost shouted. 'We'll take a taxi.'

Panayotis looked at him as if the boy had lost his mind.

'Taxi? Will I let you spend money on a taxi? Get your stuff and let's go.'

'Uncle,' Theo began.

'No uncle.' Panayotis winked at Véronique. 'Please don't deprive me of the pleasure.'

At the station, Theo and Véronique insisted they didn't need to be seen off on the bus and Panayotis had the grace not to insist. He winked at Theo. 'You have a good time, eh? And do lots of work on Apollo!' He hugged his nephew and whispered in his ear: 'Why is her hair white?'

Theo gave a shocked shrug. 'I don't know.'

Then Panayotis turned to Véronique and kissed her hand. 'Bon voyage, Mademoiselle! Vous êtes très belle!'

They took a taxi to the airport.

'Look,' Theo said, 'we're leaving Thessaloniki after all.'

Véronique laid her cool hand on top of his. He pushed his fingers up through hers. She wore a flat-headed gold ring on her small finger, with a miniature coat of arms engraved on it. Her complex face turned to his for a moment. Platoons of adrenalin raided his body. He was committing the biggest single act of madness in his life and it felt just right.

TWENTY-ONE

June 1948, Pieria HQ

Commander Achilles kept his dark glasses on as usual, despite the haemophilic bulb in his office. Daphne could never be sure where he was looking – which was no doubt the intended effect. But it was better this way, for she had seen his eyes once and they were repulsive.

'Comrade Daphne, as one of the brightest fellow strugglers in your regiment, and also in order to purge the name of your family from the disgrace of your brother who, if I remember correctly, was executed a week ago, I am entrusting you with a mission of high responsibility and honour.'

Daphne looked at the black glasses and said, 'Comrade Achilles, the Democratic Army of Greece is generous to its fighters. I will be proud to serve the Democratic Army in whatever way I can.'

She knew this was a trial for her, following the execution of Alexis – the less enthusiasm she showed, the closer she got to her own bootless dawn. The commander nodded and, for a moment, it looked as if he actually had a neck. He rolled a coarse cigarette in his thick fingers.

'You have been assigned the task of taking a Western journalist across to General Markos.'

Daphne froze.

'Comrade, how will I know the whereabouts of the general?'

'General Markos is expected to be in his Aetomilitsa HQ in approximately fifteen days. This gives you plenty of time to get there. Our journalist who has arrived from Thessaloniki will rest here for two days before setting off.'

'Comrade, I am honoured but I have not done this itinerary before. I come from Edessa and . . .'

'Worry not, you'll go with Kallistos who knows the area. You'll be given two mules and provisions for a couple of days until you reach the first village under our control. You will get provisions at each village. You will take a letter of introduction from our HQ which you will present at checkpoints. Here is a list of the villages we control. You will circumnavigate the rest. If you get ambushed or caught by the national army, hand him over, don't resist. They won't touch him. Then ask him to intercede for you. Kallistos knows the itinerary. When you reach your destination, the foreigner will no longer be in your charge. Someone else will take him back via Kastoria or Ioannina. You may then continue with other comrades on to Smolikas, just in time for the offensive, where you'll join our battalion. And you must realise the importance of this assignment. This is the first correspondent to make it alone to Free Greece and, following the murder of the American Polk, it is very important that he be treated well and given an excellent impression of life in Free Greece. Is that understood?'

'Yes, Comrade Achilles. When may I meet the foreigner?'

'Tonight, if you like.' His voice softened. 'You may in fact join us all for supper in my HQ in half an hour. You are now dismissed.'

She turned towards the door.

'Comrade Daphne!'

'Yes?' She looked back.

'There is one more reason why I chose you for this mission, apart from your intelligence and fearlessness. I believe that it will take your mind off your brother. I know how close you were.'

Daphne was astounded. He took off his glasses. His eyes were pulsing and naked on his pasty face, frogs on a pond-lily.

'You think that I'm a monster. I was only doing my duty. We cannot tolerate, in these critical times, our fighters encouraging deserters and bringing the morale down. It was unfortunate Alexis didn't keep his views to himself.' He put his glasses back on. 'You are dismissed.'

Daphne knew she should thank him but her voice had gone again and she just nodded before turning on her heels and walking out, dazed by another spectacular sunset.

The foreigner was sitting between the glassless Commander Achilles and the indoctrination officer, smiling confusedly at something they were telling him. There were also three kapetanios, among them Telemachus.

'Ah, Comrade Daphne! Pascal, meet your beautiful guide Daphne Grigoriadis, also known as Dawn. She will keep you company on your trip to General Markos.'

The foreigner got up and stretched across the table to shake her hand, his face suddenly serious. His hand was warm and surprisingly soft; she couldn't recall touching such a soft male hand. Her own hand was calloused. She felt herself hard and graceless from head to toe. She remembered that she was a woman – or rather that once she had been a woman – and wished it showed more on this occasion. She blushed. Ribald laughter rattled in throats like machine-gun fire across gullies. The foreigner offered her his chair since there were no other chairs available at the table.

Commander Achilles slapped him back down. 'Where are you going? She'll be all right. Women and men are equal in the Democratic Army. It's not like Paris, eh?'

The foreigner smiled uncertainly, his unsettling odd eyes on her. Telemachus produced a chair as if out of thin air and slammed it on the floor for her, next to himself. She sat down shyly.

'So, as I was saying, we have a lot of national army deserters, really good fighters, trained by the Americans. They run from the monarcho-fascists and come to us. But they're lousy fighters because the Americans and their butcher general Fleet don't know how to fight. They're nothing next to our lions!' Achilles had had too much to drink but the foreigner was polite and listened. Someone poured retsina for Daphne and she threw it down. There were olives, bread, goat's cheese, ouzo, hard-boiled eggs, even some smoked meat – a feast.

'Eat up, Comrade Pascal!' the indoctrination officer urged him. Everyone else was picking at the food, as if they weren't hungry, but she knew these were precious reserves specially produced so the foreigner would see that they were well fed.

'They think they can scare us with their Spitfires but we have lions' hearts!' Achilles thumped his massive chest with a fist. 'They are puppets of the Americans but we are free. We'll create a new, free Greece, a Greece that won't be a lackey to any fascist kings and queens!'

'And this' – Telemachus pointed to Daphne – 'this is the face of the revolution. Take a photo of her face and send it to your newspaper. A face like a statue! Proud, free. They call us bandits. Is this a bandit, tell me?' He leant towards Daphne's face, gesturing. She felt like fresh produce praised by a peasant at a village market.

'You speak Greek?' She turned to the foreigner. His eyes were very odd – one dark blue, the other a speckled brown. He was unshaven and tired.

'Yes, but not very well.' He smiled in his unsettling way.

'Which way did you come?'

'Across the Thermaic Gulf, in a boat, and then on foot and mule . . .'

'Daphne, don't tire our guest with questions.' Achilles intervened with almost genuine bonhomie. 'He's been travelling for days. He needs to be entertained. And he will be! Tomorrow, Comrade Pascal, we'll put on dances for you. We have dances anyway – our fighters like to dance and sing, their morale is very high. But at present we're also busy with drills because the monarcho-fascists are planning an offensive against us. We'll show them.'

The foreigner seemed dazed by what must, for him, be an adventure. He reached his drinking limit fairly soon and, after exchanging his own cigarettes for a home-made rolled-up tobacco leaf which he smoked chokingly, he began to look quite sick. She was suddenly flooded with contempt for him. How pathetic they were, these foreigners, coming from their smug West, with their soft handshakes and perversely avuncular governments, with their bloodthirsty nostrils stuck in other people's business, with their well-disguised opinions feeding on the fertile turf of ignorance and preconceptions . . . Yet, the American Polk was murdered for wanting to cross into this territory and here was a second, luckier Polk. Perhaps he really wanted to know the truth.

'Tell me,' the foreigner turned to Achilles, who by now didn't look like someone whose opinion could possibly count, 'who killed George Polk?'

The table burst out in merriment.

'My dear Pascal' – Telemachus was showing off in front of his captives – 'I don't believe you are serious in asking this question.'

'When I left, they were trying to pass off two guerrilla commanders as the murderers . . .'

This foreigner was almost brave, in his own ignorant way. A heavy hand was placed heavily on his shoulder.

'You mean Mouzenidis and Vasvanas? Do you know that they're both dead?'

'See how incompetent those thugs in the secret police are!' Another kapetanio turned to Pascal. 'They can't even frame us properly – they go for dead men!'

More chuckles went around.

'Were you friends with him?' Daphne asked, her voice sounding strangely naked amid the male cacophony.

'Yes.' The foreigner smiled and the thin, tired melancholy veiling his features made her want to ask him many things, but she had asked enough questions tonight. It made her want to tell him many things, but the things she most needed to tell someone, she knew she never could.

For the next two days, she saw little of the foreigner but much of the effervescence whipped up for his benefit. She hadn't asked about his nationality but everybody knew, even the sweet village idiot – by some tragic mistake named Adonis – who went around singing his idiot version of the 'International', conducting his invisible joyful chorus as he went along. Then someone started singing 'La Marseillaise' in what she presumed was bad French. Spontaneous dances were organised in the square and the brown-uniformed partisans were joined by the villagers in their homespun clothes. Rapid-fire demonstrations of lethal military skill were performed for the foreigner – the girl guerrillas emptied magazines of precious bullets into targets. The whole village came out voluntarily – a rare occurrence – and the spirit of festivity spread, like a wool rug catching fire. The mountains rang with the echo of song which to Daphne sounded strangely hollow: *Osa sithera o Truman na rixi nikitis tha ine panda o laos.* 'No matter how much iron Truman throws in, the people will always be victorious.'

PART TWO

*In
the
Land
of Midas*

TWENTY-TWO

April 1998

'Look, we're leaving Thessaloniki.'

It didn't feel as if they were leaving. Thessaloniki was a difficult place to leave gradually. You had to jump on a plane and instantly fall asleep. Her cool hand answered his warm hand and their fingers locked. Theo was clearly terrified of their destination, and right to be so. She was the one without a self-preservation instinct.

On the bus to Durrës, among the locals with battered bags and rifles who stared at the two foreigners in murderous intent, Theo's tense face told her that this was an act of unaccountable insanity for which they might have to pay the ultimate price. She was amused, and observed him at an oblique angle from her seat in the other isle. The driver had a gun next to the gearbox. Theo sullenly watched the paranoid bunkers scattered alongside the bumpy road, the abandoned tractors in ravaged fields. The only vehicle the battered bus overtook was a donkey-driven cart with peasants transporting Kalashnikovs among severed tree-trunks. Dusk fell lazily over the bare hills and the Adriatic flashed its scaly tail in the distance. She had arrived somewhere new – with him – and that was all that mattered.

Theo sat on the edge of the bed in their Romeo hotel room,

smoking and watching the soundless TV screen which was showing CNN news about how many people had been shot in the Albanian countryside in the last week. Many. He pulled the curtains, closing off the view to the vast, deserted sand strip. Véronique stood in the doorway behind and watched him for a while. They had checked into the same room with two Spartan single beds because it was too unsafe to have separate rooms – they would be too vulnerable to break-ins. When they checked in, Theo asked the bright-faced receptionist in Greek if he could borrow a spare gun. He could. Now he fingered it with horrified bemusement.

'I have no idea how to use this thing. I don't even know if it's loaded,' he said.

'But the main thing is, it makes you feel better.'

'Nothing can make me feel better except getting out of this hole as soon as possible.'

'Okay,' she said blithely. 'Let's see if we survive the night and tomorrow we'll take the ferry.'

'Together with all the bandits trying to cross illegally.'

'Oh, come on.'

He looked for an ashtray as a temporary solution. This place wasn't even safe enough to make love.

'Tell me about Alexander. Did he fight the Albanians?' She was talking to a child, asking him what they did at school today.

'His father Philip fought the Illyrians who are supposed to be the ancestors of the Albanians. Philip's mother was in fact half-Illyrian. When Philip married Cleopatra, his nth wife and thirty years his junior, at the wedding the new bride's uncle insulted Alexander, asking the gods for a legitimate heir to the Macedonian throne – which implied that Alexander wasn't good enough, his mother being from the Epirus . . .'

'Cleopatra? The Egyptian one?'

Theo looked at her with shock.

'No, this is another Cleopatra. It was a common name, you know. But of course the other Cleopatra was also Macedonian. Anyway, when Alexander was insulted, he threw his skyphos, which is a drinking cup, at Attalus, and at that, his drunken father drew his sword, stumbling and falling over in the process. Alexander looked down at him and said, "So this is the man who intends to conquer Asia and who can't even get from one table to the other without falling over." He had a point. After this, he and his mother left the court and Alexander found haven with the Illyrians. It was a dangerous moment for the Macedonian kingdom, because Alexander could have consorted with the Illyrians, who were sworn enemies of Philip, and invaded Macedonia. Philip realised his mistake and sent for his son.'

'Why did he marry Cleopatra anyway?'

'Well, he . . . fell in love with her, I guess. He lost his wits over her, which is why he put his family and his state at risk.'

'Foolish man,' Véronique said dreamily.

Theo shrugged, wizened and fatalistic.

They decided not to venture out of the hotel and had a dinner of fries and kebabs in the hotel's restaurant, speaking in Greek all the while.

'You seem to prefer third world countries,' he said accusingly. 'Why is that?'

'I want to be surprised. To learn something I don't know, or that I know but need to be reminded of. And what you call third world countries can perhaps do that.'

'If you mean poverty, you can see that in any big city, you can see it in Sydney or Paris, you don't need to go to those places.'

'No, it doesn't come down to poverty. In fact, I don't know what it comes down to. A kind of honesty . . .'

Theo raised an eyebrow.

'A kind of frankness about the human condition. It sounds pretentious now but . . . that's how I feel. It must all be rather selfish. I'm looking for something both to surprise me and to . . . bring me closer to the world, to make me feel.'

'Feel what?'

'Just feel.'

He looked at her, dimple in his chin, tension in his shoulders, and didn't understand. Back at the hotel, Véronique knew he thought the same as her: was this the night? Neither of them was drunk. One of them would rather be elsewhere. One of them didn't care where they were, as long as it was not somewhere familiar. They sat on a settee by the window in their room. She was unsure how to move inside this new, unlimited closeness. They heard the sea splashing anxiously on the other side of the darkness.

'You know, it occurs to me that if you want to feel, maybe you should be looking inside yourself, not inside Albania.' Theo smiled, pleased with his insight.

'Thank you, Mister Analyst. I've looked inside myself and frankly, it looks very much like Albania in 1998.'

He laughed. 'What did you find?'

'Oh, this and that.' Her father's evasiveness. 'Mainly useless concrete bunkers scattered in a ravaged countryside.'

'Maybe I should have a look. You never know, I might be able to recognise these things. Or just . . . like them.'

Again, each eye had its own agenda: the blue one thin on substance and prone to weakness – almost a latent alcoholic's eye – the brown one passionately committed. His body shivering with desire. Her body stunned by desire.

He moved over. His hand on her cheek, brushing away hair that didn't need brushing away. Her hand on his neck, feeling the unshorn growth at the back.

'Your neck needs to be shaved by an expert hand.'

His electric shaver buzzing in her hand, Véronique had a flashback to that lonely and grotesque night in Jamaica when she held a vibrator – her bewilderment at the idea of inserting this mechanical object inside herself, her horror at the sight she must have been, her warm, desolate body open to the noises of the Caribbean night, so full of other people's laughter outside her window, and only a nasty vibrator for company. She had just left her Colombian lover, a captivating fifty-year-old psychologist who turned out to be simultaneously having another affair in Bogota. She went to Jamaica to get away from their old haunts in Cartagena. She held the vibrator like an exorcist's instrument of torture. Not that she had imagined a life with him – she had just been in love with him. She threw the ugly object on the floor where it continued to buzz and vibrate until she smashed it with a chair. Then she snorted some exorcising substance and went out dancing until she dropped. But she didn't want to remember that now.

She pressed the delicate blades against Theo's skin. With drawn-out sweeps, she cleaned long ribbons of flesh of the dark growth. He sat still. She stroked his neck with her free hand before applying the metal head.

'Something about having your hair touched . . .' His voice was muffled. 'My niece Hrisoula wanted me to play with her hair.'

'I don't like my hair being touched.'

'Which part of you do you like touched?'

She turned the buzz off. Silence flooded the room like a lavish flush over pale skin.

'Whichever part you can reach.'

Theo turned around and the face she saw was made to be looked at, touched and inevitably, imperatively, loved. Each eye separately, each half of the slightly cleft chin, each set of curled dark eyelashes. Then the kiss. Then the hot, hungry hands, the knot inside, the many knots inside. Véronique extracted herself from the glue of lust and put her feet up between them, leaning backwards on her hands, feeling the bolt of desire split her head and race down her body. His pupils were dilated, and he reached for a part of her to bridge the sudden distance. His hand cupped her knee. He took a deep breath.

'It's so strange.'

'What?'

'Everything. This hotel in the middle of nowhere. Being here, like this, in bandit country. What happened in Thessaloniki . . . The way we left.'

'Does it worry you?'

'No. It's just that I think we shouldn't have rushed. We should've waited. We could've been somewhere else now, Italy for example.'

'We can go to Italy tomorrow, if you want. It's just across.'

He smiled somehow ruefully.

'You know we can't. The ferry service has been suspended because of the hijacking. Do you like Italy?'

'This is like asking if I like culture, history, and the constant renewal of the human spirit.'

'Okay, do you love Italy?' He stroked her knee.

'Italy is vital. It's an essence. I don't know if I love it.'

'An essence of what?'

'Just an essence. Do you know Italy well?'

'I've never been there.'

'You'll love it. It's full of ruins.'

'I enjoy ruins only when there's nothing else to enjoy that's alive.'
He crouched in front of her, his legs long and his crotch tight under
his pants, and took her hand.

'A bit like an inverse Midas,' she said.

'More like a happy Midas.'

'That's what I mean. An inverse Midas is a happy Midas, delighting
in the ruins of things that should've been alive.'

'He creates those ruins, though. I wouldn't want to create ruins.'

'He didn't either.'

'But he wanted to touch things too much.'

His age was against him, but then age is always against us, first
when we are too young, then, suddenly, when we are too old; there
is no transition, no time of grace. She too seemed to have missed it.
Youth had its advantages.

'So how much touching is too much?'

'Maybe we should find out . . . um, what's the word . . .
empirically!'

Absurdly, Véronique thought Too late. It's been done already and
Midas is cursed for all eternity.

'And if you turn to gold, I'll be a very unhappy Midas,' he added,
gazing at her both longingly and aggressively with his unnatural eyes.

He displayed astonishing self-control – for another three minutes,
after which they were both kneeling on the floor, erratically
unclothed, then standing chest to chest, she leaning on the impure
wall, he leaning on her, and finally, having achieved a more definitive
state of nudity, on a quickly and ineptly stripped bed. Theo, in his
consistent eagerness to please and impress her, was taking his time,
accustoming his eyes, hands and lips to her body in the thickening
darkness. Véronique was nervously impatient, which made her
indecorous. Where previously a new sexual experience had been a

sumptuous island bay, in which she immersed herself with open eyes, studying and marvelling at the exotic flora and fauna, now she found herself plunging head first, ripping the water, struggling to sink as deep as she could, wanting her pleasure to be a raw trail in the unexplored current that pressed her from all sides and eventually carried her towards a violent whirlpool. Only then did she drift, with the promise of what she would find there. Their first and only Albanian night was short and varied. They made love six times, in a crescendo of pleasure and urgency, as if chasing a quota.

'I feel like I've died and I'm in Paradise,' Theo whispered in a fallen angel's voice.

'Perhaps you're visiting me then. I feel like I've been dead for a while anyway. But having you there really makes a difference.'

'Thanks,' he snorted and gazed at her wonderingly. 'It's nice to feel wanted.'

Yes, she was alive after all. There were questions he didn't ask that first night which she saw form like beads of sweat on his upper lip.

When Véronique awoke in the early morning, after an hour of slumber, Theo was asleep. With a phantom finger she outlined his harmonious profile, admired the Spartan purity of his slender and almost hairless torso that would expand and become heavy and sagging in twenty years' time, his dark nipples, the retreating spiral of his ear – and a vast sadness flooded her. She almost choked on it.

She wanted to be able to take that first plunge with him again, and now she never would. A city where she had lived before was always a diminished version of itself the second time around, and it only kept diminishing with each subsequent visit, like Thessaloniki, like Paris. Never again the bitter-sweet tang of the Aegean wind, the thrill of reckless traffic, the alluring dissonance of a foreign language, the inherently cruel enigma of medieval fortresses, the lives of people that were out of reach and yet moving around kaleidoscopically in magnificent bursts of beauty and squalor.

Theo had stopped moving in magnificent bursts of exotic novelty. He had frozen into possession already. Véronique lay, stunned by the suspicion that from now on she might have to rely on his ability to see the crepuscular world for her – with the wonder and passion that no longer came to her easily. That his unjaded, unmatched eyes might be the only living sense between them and, more terrifyingly, that his eyes might be the only life-sustaining organ she could rely on, like a heart shared by Siamese twins.

In the glorious morning they climbed the quietly ruined street leading up to the former palace of King Zog. Theo's jubilance was slightly overshadowed by the fact that they were not in Italy.

Two boys sat on the pavement, smoking in adult silence and cleaning a Kalashnikov. They said something in Albanian to which Theo replied in Greek, 'We don't speak Albanian.' The boys gazed at them dully.

'I hope they don't have ammunition so they don't blow themselves up,' Véronique said.

'So they don't blow us up, you mean.'

They climbed another, more arduous hill, to reach the lighthouse. Young, chain-smoking guards stood around like monuments to boredom. Delighted to have some diversion, they attempted to start up a conversation in English with the new visitors, asking where they were from. 'Ellada,' said Véronique. 'Ellada,' said Theo. Theo was offered Marlboro cigarettes. He took one and offered the guards his own Marlboros. They clicked their tongues in deference and helped themselves timidly.

From the top, they contemplated the sprawling spectacle of the coast, a surprise amphitheatre nesting at the bottom of a hill, and each other.

She reached for his rough cheek. He drew her to him but then, remembering where they were, his grip slackened.

'Let's leave today. Let's go anywhere. I want to live.' He took out the Marlboro cigarette and lit it but then made a face and stubbed it out. 'A fake.'

'If you really can't stand it here, we'll leave today. What worries you the most? '

'Well, nothing in particular. It's just that the economic pyramids have collapsed, there are two Kalashnikovs per man, woman and child, and chaos is an understatement when describing Albania. And you are here with me. We could have thugs break into our room any moment and rape you and murder us. That's all really.'

Véronique put a hand on his waist. Perhaps she was slightly taller than him after all.

'This trip was my idea. I'm the one responsible. And we'll leave as soon as possible.'

Downstairs, the soldiers were speaking excitedly among clouds of Marlboro smoke.

'What is it that you are guarding?' Véronique enquired.

For a moment, there was a puzzled silence. Then an answer came in English: 'Secrets of state!'

Laughter.

'We are guarding view because Albania haven't nothing else.' A soldier with azure eyes flashed his tooth-gap like a tender and naughty secret. No laughter this time – the other soldiers didn't understand the Greek. Véronique shook his hand, she didn't know why. His hand was soft and vague like a mollusc. He blushed as the others cheered. Véronique followed Theo who was already heading down the hill. A gunshot was fired, startling them like rabbits dashing across a field. But it was only a salvo in their honour.

They chased each other down the hill and ended in a breathless scuffle of stretched clothes and bitten lips. The two boys had finished cleaning the rifle and contemplated the two silly foreigners through clouds of contemptuous smoke.

TWENTY-THREE

June 1948

'Why are we travelling by night?'

The foreigner was just hopeless.

'Guerrilla rule number one: never do by day what you can do by night.' Kallistos indulged him with an answer.

Spiridon the mule went first, followed by the inhumanly tireless and cheerful Kallistos, then the second mule, to which someone had omitted to give a name and a brain, but not the muscles to carry the luggage, and finally Pascal and Daphne. After a couple of hours of silence which the foreigner tried awkwardly to disturb, turning foolishly to make eye contact with Daphne in the darkness, Kallistos said, 'Save your breath, Mister. We have a lot of walking ahead of us.'

This resulted in another hour or so of silent ascent along the ridge of the mountain, followed by descent. The sharpened crescent moon hung menacingly ahead of them, like a Damocles' sword. Daphne could almost hear the mountain hum to itself.

'Isn't there a shorter way?'

Daphne didn't even deign to respond.

Kallistos said, 'This is the shortest way for guerrillas. We have to stay out of the observation range of the national army because they're camping in the south, not too far from here. We don't actually know how far. Things change every day.'

It was a night that to the foreigner must look beautiful and mysterious. But he was already tired; his stride became less tidy and Daphne had to slow down not to stumble upon him.

'Are you tired?' she asked threateningly.

'No, not at all.'

'Good.'

'Tell me,' the foreigner persevered, this time without turning, 'where are you from?'

'Edessa.'

'Edessa? I have a letter to deliver to a woman in Edessa. Philipidis, Hrisoula. Her husband gave me a letter for her before he was shipped off to the islands.'

'We won't be going to Edessa,' Daphne said curtly.

'I know, but I just wondered if you knew them.'

'Yes.'

'You know the Philipidis?'

'Of course I know them.'

'They have three kids.'

'Panayotis, Kostas and Sophia.'

'Two of them were taken in the abductions.'

'It wasn't an abduction.'

'What was it?'

'It was an organised humanitarian effort to save the children from the war.'

'That's not what I've been hearing.'

'Comrade Pascal.' His name tasted unnatural on her tongue. 'You're a journalist. You can't tell me that you take everything you hear as the gospel truth, especially in a place like Greece, ruled by the monarcho-fascist stooges of an imperial power.'

He turned and stopped. She had to stop too.

'I get the feeling that you'd rather not be on this journey,' he said softly.

'I am acting under orders from Supreme Headquarters. I have no preferences.'

He found nothing to say and they walked on.

Kallistos was whistling. The rest of the walk was silent and laborious. She could see the foreigner had never walked for so long in his life but was too proud to admit to tiredness and just stumbled on. She could have suggested he got on the second mule but didn't. He had come to them and so he must endure at least the best part of what they had to endure. Besides, observing the way he walked, she began to suspect that he had fallen prey to saddle-burn from his previous trek. She whistled along with Kallistos.

The moon shed its rust over their heads.

At dawn, as they came upon the first village, she and Kallistos asked to see the commander. There was no commander. There were no rebels, in fact – they had left a few days ago, and the government army hadn't taken over yet. Despite Daphne's wariness that they were easy prey to village informers, the three travellers collapsed inside a room they were given in a local house by a woman. There was one bed in the room and mattresses on the floor.

'You take the bed,' Daphne said to Pascal and took off her boots.

'No, I couldn't possibly. You will take it.'

'Look, don't be a gentleman. I'm a guerrilla, you're the opposite. You take the bed.'

'Only if we take turns and tomorrow you take the bed.'

Kallistos was already sleeping, his cap over his face, curled up like the child that he was. Daphne prepared for sleep: she took out Alexis's shirt, folded it and put it under her head. She hugged her rucksack with his boots inside.

'What is the opposite of a guerrilla?' asked Pascal just as she was on the point of drifting off. She grumbled.

'A journalist from Paris.'

There were no more questions.

When they reached some railway tracks, Pascal said with an air of competence, 'We must be extra careful here, I suppose, because they lay mines along the railway. When I was on the train from Athens . . .'

Kallistos and Daphne pointed to the monstrous silhouette of an overturned wagon further down, with its wheels in the air.

'The railway hasn't been used for ages.' Kallistos kicked the ripped-up tracks. The foreigner was embarrassed.

'Is this the guerrillas' work?'

'It's everybody's work. The Germans, the guerrillas, the national army, armed bands from a few years back, you name it. We're very international here.'

'When it comes to destruction.' Daphne's tongue slipped and she bit her lip, but the foreigner naturally seized the chance.

'Surely you also have international aid?'

'Surely,' Daphne said and busied herself helping the mules across.

On the outskirts of a village, all five of them froze when a voice came from the shrubs. 'This is Free Greece. Freeze or I shoot.'

'Fellow struggler,' Daphne yelled. 'We are coming from Pieria, on a headquarters dispatch. We're taking a foreign journalist across to General Markos.'

'Step into the light.'

A torch was shone at them and Daphne stepped into the dazzling circle of burnt grass.

'We have a letter from Major Achilles.'

'Is the foreigner English?'

'No.'

'American?'

'French.' Daphne wasn't sure if this would warm the guard's heart.

'Good. Bring the letter.'

Daphne stepped into the shrubs. A young, twig-thin man with a Russian cap too big for him pointed his rifle at her, grabbed the paper from her hand and told her to step back. There was shuffling behind him. Another silhouette emerged, also pointing his rifle at her. The weedy one got up and his face cracked into a grin so childish her heart sank — it reminded her of Alexis.

'Welcome to Free Democratic Greece.' He handed her the letter back. 'Where is the foreigner?'

Daphne pointed at Pascal who waved tentatively.

'We're staying for a few hours.'

'Just for a few hours?' The guards looked pathetically disappointed.

The second one stepped into the light to shake Pascal's hand. His left arm was missing.

The roosters of the village announced their arrival, and so did the dogs. Soon the village school poured forth half a dozen armed men.

'Bloody guard, I'll have him shot!' one of them shouted.

Daphne was greeted by half a dozen rifles. 'Comrades, we're from Pieria, travelling with a foreigner under headquarters' orders.'

She received the gruff looks calmly and produced the life-saving letter.

'This is the rest of your brigade?' The gruffest of them all scratched his untrimmed beard as he screwed up his eyes at the sorry bunch.

'They send a woman, a village boy and two donkeys to look after a foreign visitor?' He shook his head, then noticed that some rifles were still pointed at the visitors. 'Lower your guard, you're not going to shoot at French journalists and mules now, are you?' And a hollow, unpleasant 'Ha ha ha ha' rattled in his big throat as if someone was shouting down a pipe.

'Welcome, Comrade Pascal. I'm Kapetanio Ares.' Of course, Daphne thought, one wouldn't expect a lesser name from him. He clenched Pascal's hand and slapped his back, which visibly caused Pascal some discomfort. The other men were more interested in Daphne.

'Captain,' she said, 'we've been walking all night. We need a bed.'

'A bed? You're all going to sleep in one bed?' A ripple of snorts went through the rank of his men. But the kapetanio became serious: 'Of course. We'll give you beds. And we'll feed you, and whatever else you need. We welcome foreigners, as long as they report the truth when they return.' He gave Pascal a look full of menace.

'Captain, if I wasn't interested in the truth, I wouldn't be here,' Pascal said firmly. Daphne was proud of him, if that was the word.

'And you speak excellent Greek too!' The kapetanio nodded respectfully.

An abundant breakfast was put out on two tables in front of the school. The three of them ate ravenously, watched by the village people, who were beginning to emerge tentatively as if a natural disaster had struck during the night and they were now coming out to assess the damage. The *andartes* surrounded the table and cheered the three arrivals. The kapetanio pulled one ruddy, anguished-looking village woman aside and had a brief one-way exchange with her after which she scuttled away. This was going to be their hostess.

'A toast!' Ares lifted his tiny ouzo glass. 'To our victory over the monarcho-fascists!'

Everybody who had a glass raised it. The guerrillas shouted 'Long live Democratic Greece!', 'Stalin is with us!', an adventurous 'The French Communist Party is with us!' and an unfortunate 'Tito is with us!', which was shushed and greeted by the kapetanio with 'Who said that?' A frail girl with red hair stepped forward.

'Magdalena, if you weren't the daughter of the brave commander Christos, I'd have you shot.'

The girl blushed deeply but didn't budge. Another woman who had the dry, unblinking look of an indoctrination officer, said 'Comrade, she didn't come to her indoctrination class yesterday. She was indisposed.' Stifled giggles.

Daphne glanced at Pascal, whose mouthful had frozen in his mouth. The kapetanio started quizzing him on French opinion on the war and Pascal said things like 'The French Communist Party is with the partisans. The French people support your cause.' Kallistos had fallen asleep in his wicker chair, still holding a piece of bread with cheese on it, which crumbled down in his lap.

The anxious-looking woman gave them a bedroom with a luxurious double bed, probably her wedding bed, and another room with two beds.

'Where is your husband?' Pascal asked.

The woman glanced at Daphne unsurely and said apologetically, 'With the government army, Kyrie. But he only joined because our elder son was killed by the communists. My other son is with the Democratic Army, though.' She straightened up at this.

'What would happen if they found themselves in opposing camps in battle?' Pascal's questions were too direct.

The woman thought so too. She covered her face with her cracked hands. 'God be with them to keep them from the worst sin.'

Pascal had acquired some of the mules' personality traits and wouldn't budge from his position on the beds. So Daphne lay in the double bed, behind closed shutters, in snow-white embroidered cotton sheets, so unused to this luxury that she couldn't sleep. The noise from the guerrillas' morning drills helped to keep her awake. How different life had made her from what she would have been. She who had slept in a bed like this between her parents, who had smugly patted her dowry in a coffer by her mother's sewing table, who had sat with her girlfriends by the rushing waters of Edessa, giggling about boys. She who had wanted to go to Thessaloniki University when the Germans left, who was her father's 'doll' and her mother's 'hope', who had talked so confidently, like everyone else, about the new life they would have when the Germans left, when Father came back, when the spring came, when . . . She whose youth withdrew from her in terror as if from the touch of a disfigured stranger. She who had to order herself harshly to sleep, thinking of her elder brother Illias who was still alive, so that she wouldn't start crying for everyone and everything that she had lost. Because she knew that if she started crying, she would never be able to stop and would have to be shot.

At dusk, their hostess fried eggs for them, apologising that she had nothing else.

'How come,' asked Pascal, who really could be a pain sometimes, 'the guerrillas have plenty and the peasants don't?'

The woman busied herself.

'Because whatever the peasants have goes to the Democratic Army,' Daphne said. 'Or the Government Army, whoever happens to take the village. It's called war.' Kallistos grinned at her with a full mouth.

'It's called terror over the civilian population.' Pascal's odd eyes bored into her. The woman, terrified, rushed in to save the day.

'I'm happy to help the DAG. My son is with them and they are fighting for a free Greece. We all ought to help . . .' The woman slumped on a chair and sudden tears flowed down her wasted cheeks with their broken capillaries. If Daphne had been a dedicated communist, she would have handed the woman over to the kapetanio as a traitor, but she reached out and put her hand on the woman's shoulder.

The woman wiped her tears and turned to her. 'Child, your mother must be worried about you. Where are you from?'

'Edessa.' Daphne's throat shrank around the word. 'My mother doesn't worry about me any more.' She got up abruptly. Pascal and Kallistos were still eating. 'Come on, guys, let's go. You can't eat all night.'

'I'll make you a little bundle to take along.' The woman fretted about, looking for food that she didn't have.

'Please,' Pascal stopped her. 'Kyria, we have plenty.' It was a lie and Daphne gave him a red star for it. 'I will never forget your hospitality. May your husband and your son return safely when this is over.' He kissed her hand and her tears started flowing again. Kallistos had the mules ready. The woman gave Daphne a small bunch of wild geranium and placed her chapped lips on Daphne's cheek, scraping her skin.

TWENTY-FOUR

April/May 1998

Adriatic white-scapes in the day, body-scapes in the night, merging into one another with the jubilant repetition of novelty. Summer approached absent-mindedly, fragrant with good intentions, a messenger of favourite news. Véronique blossomed after a long drought.

They wandered for days, sometimes hand in hand. Ascending and descending the cobbled labyrinth of unpredictable streets. Sheltering against fortress walls when the wind blew with a sudden cleansing ferocity. Discovering a blue glass bead in the bullet hole of a pock-marked stone wall, then incorrectly identifying the different types of bombardment scarring other walls. Véronique speculated about the bead, which preoccupied her all day. A young refugee girl from Bosnia who was temporarily sheltered in this building and, when leaving, placed this bead in the bullet-hole to mark her presence? A tidy old man who trudged along this street, saw the bead on the ground, picked it up and, not knowing what to do with it, put it in the nearest bullet-hole? A teenager living on the ground floor of the building who had an arrangement with her teenage lover to leave this bead here to signal it was safe/unsafe for him to climb over the balcony?

'Oh, come on,' Theo said, 'families here aren't that traditional.'

'That's true. They can be more traditional in Italy.'

'Sometimes, though, tradition produces amazing things, like *Romeo and Juliet*.'

'Vendetta. The best examples of which are in Albania, I hate to disappoint you.'

'Yeah, the Mafia influence.'

'No, there's a pure Albanian brand of vendetta. I wonder about you specialising in ancient history, you know!'

'Why, do you think I should specialise in modern history, so that I can come up with a credible theory on this bead and these bullet-holes.' He held the bead like an expert, between index finger and thumb, against the light. 'A fine example of blue glass, dating from . . . let's see, as far back as 1994.'

Invariably, they ended up mock-fighting and mock-pacifying each other in their favourite way. What had started as an outline of intimacy quickly filled out with the flesh and blood of their growing assurance of each other's pleasure. She taught him the word 'jouissance', which meant 'joy' and 'pleasure' as well as 'orgasm', and the enjoyment of things we do not own.

'English is such an impoverished, withdrawing language some-times,' she complained. Theo, taking this personally, charged himself with the physical enrichment of the situation. His diligence and passion were so great that Véronique sometimes smiled at him in the middle of lovemaking. She was already sensing in him the unmistak-able limitations of decency, which she tasted in his kisses with a kind of confused nostalgia. He had never had and would never have the malignant intensity of a pornographic imagination.

Only after two weeks did he ask the obvious question. Stroking her flat belly, he said, 'Why do you dye your hair?'

'Because I'm grey.'

'But you're too young to go grey.'

'That doesn't mean anything,' she snapped, without meaning to.

'When did it start?'

For some reason, she was irked by his inquisitive face, although she had expected this. 'It didn't start. It happened over a few days.'

'When?'

'Last year.'

'Was it . . . triggered by something or just . . .'

'It happened after my father had an accident.'

'Did he . . .'

'Yes.'

The simplicity and flatness of this one word wounded her. She wanted to get up and walk out, slam the door in his shocked and uncomprehending face, be alone for a long time, for the rest of the time. But which time and when would it end? She couldn't talk about her father to a virtual stranger, even if he was her lover and travelling companion, even if he was exceedingly decent. Even if he was Theo. One word, unchangeable, and so brutally, callously casual. Yes. He could've asked her if she'd had breakfast. If she'd come. If she'd ever sky-dived.

Theo had no immediate reaction. He lay smoking for a moment, then turned to her and, without scrutinising her face – for which she was grateful – he took her inert hand from her inert thigh and not so much kissed it as pressed it to his face, as if sheltering it from a vicious storm.

'Véronique, I didn't realise. You never told me,' he said with what sounded like emotion.

'Never,' Véronique said dryly, 'is only a few weeks. Besides, you hadn't asked.'

'What kind of an accident was it?'

'A car accident.'

'In France?'

'In Greece.'

He stubbed out his cigarette. There was, predictably, an effort in him to reconcile this new information with what he already knew of her. He put his hand through her hair, kissed it, then laid his head on her stomach, all with such grace and feeling that her eyes suddenly filled with tears, which quickly overflowed into streams that formed small pools in her ears. She hadn't cried for months.

'You've told me so little about yourself. And I don't want to ask because I have the feeling that you'll somehow avoid the subject basically, like you often do.'

'Do I?' said Véronique calmly, despite the pools in her ears and the hot spring in her throat.

'I've told you everything about my family, probably bored you to tears. And about myself. And what do I know about you? Where you've lived, that your grandmother was an aristocrat, that your grandfather wrote a book about the Greek Civil War. That you're not exactly a French patriot. That you have a thing about Greece and Greek poetry and speak several languages. '

'You mean you have information, but no knowledge of me.'

'Something like that.'

'There's nothing much to know. My life has no dark secrets.'

'Your life . . . maybe. But I think that *you* have them.'

Theo was looking at her intently and she knew it was time to end the conversation.

'I have hardly anything, in fact,' she said.

'That's absurd. You have everything, as far as I can see.'

'Yes. As far as you can see.'

He gave up and she was glad. He kissed the pools away. For the first time in years, she felt she was being taken care of – and by a man six years younger than her.

When he regained his speech a few moments after the act, he sometimes surprised her with his observations.

'Do you know that you have Amazon breasts?'

Véronique looked down at her breasts, amused.

'I never realised.'

'Of course real Amazons only had one breast. They basically cut off their right breast so that they could have a better grip of their bow.'

'So I'm not a real Amazon. Maybe I should look into it. Would you still want me if I had only one breast?'

He spoke to the hair just above her ear. 'Why, do you intend to get a bow and arrows and shoot me?'

'No, just experiment with your aesthetics.'

'Well, don't bother, because I would love you no matter how many breasts you have.'

The word flashed its shocking, frail nakedness at them and they stared at it for a still moment. But there was nothing to be done about it. Except to make love again, to smother the word in carnality, like a suicidal sleeper who presses a pillow over his face.

Her father had unforgettably quoted Pascal on love: 'Marriage is to love what the church is to spirituality, legalising institutions which end up spawning rebellion, persecution and inquisition – self-inflicted or otherwise.' Despite this manifesto, however, Pascal the proud atheist in religion and in love, never left Pauline unless one counted his disappearance.

Her father would have approved of Theo. But she wasn't sure that her father would have approved of her. There had been a sadness about him these last couple of years, a helplessness to give his daughter what he instinctively sensed she missed – a focus, a meaning, perhaps love. Or was it his own sadness, his own lack of meaning that he extended to her? Except that last time they spoke, when he sounded lively and even playful as he used to be years ago.

'Sometimes I wonder where you are.' She had thought Theo asleep in the dark next to her.

He groped for her and when he identified her face, he bent over and kissed her with such inspiration that her chest tightened. This tightness was not simply the angst of new love; it was a Gordian knot (as he would say) of insoluble fear. Fear for him, who was so deserving of being loved. Who had stepped into her world like a brave Theseus entering the labyrinth without a ball of twine. Fear for herself, who dwelt in the labyrinth alone and sick.

If there was an innocent kind of sleeper, it was Theo. He slept purely, drained of all the knowledge he possessed in waking life. It was as though he were perched on a branch and about to tip off, but unaware of the danger. He was malleable in his sleep, impressionable. If she were to whisper obscenities to him, he would smile coyly. If she were to say I love you, he would believe it but not remember it later upon waking. It felt almost indecent to watch him sleep.

Twenty-five years ago, in the zoo, by the deer cage, her father had held her up to stroke the velvet horns of a large, solemn deer. When she withdrew her hand, there was blood on it. She thought it was hers, but in fact it was the deer's. Her father explained that the deer's horns were so sensitive that even her small hand had wounded them. She had cried for the deer who kept trembling. Her mother had chided her father: 'Stop telling her horror stories'. Some time later she had gone to the zoo with her Grandmother Pauline. That deer was no longer there. She knew he had died from being touched too much by careless strangers. Grandmother Pauline had sighed: 'Yes, my treasure. That's how it goes. Some animals die from being touched too much, others from not being touched enough.' Véronique was puzzled but refrained from asking questions, fearing Grandmother Pauline might suffer another of her terrible attacks of sadness.

Watching Theo sleep was like stroking the deer's horns – she couldn't do it for too long.

These were days of shallow and expansive promise, like the coastal water, still too cold to swim in, but gaining summer langour by the day. They were getting closer to Italy, much to Theo's visible ecstasy. And to Véronique's relief, they were far enough from familiar places, even if the Dalmatian coast offered typical Mediterranean sights.

Véronique had noticed an imposing, slightly battered-looking white building which announced promisingly 'Art Gallery'. They went in one day. There was no one in the lobby to collect the door-charge. There was no one inside at all. The high ceilings were missing in places and the sky peered down at them indifferently. There were light patches on the walls where the exhibits had been. Elegant baroque arches lead them to a courtyard full of sun and twisted, charred trees. Véronique sat on a stone bench overgrown with weeds.

'So much for culture,' Theo said. 'Culture is a graveyard.'

'When you think of it, all of Europe is a graveyard. Sometimes I really hate Europe.'

'It's not Europe you should hate.'

'What then?'

But Theo didn't know.

'It's the spell that I hate.'

'The spell?'

'The spell that Europe is under. She has been under a spell most of this century.'

'What kind of spell?'

'I don't know. Like the spell of Midas. A blind grasp that . . . that petrifies everything in its longing to improve. And then a long wait for the horrible Silenius, when everything has finally turned to . . .'

'To shit,' Theo guessed correctly.

They sat in silence for a while. There were invisible birds in the blackened trees.

'What happened with your grandfather? Did you say he went missing?'

'Yes, in '67. The year I was born.'

'That's the year my grandfather in Thessaloniki died too.'

'How did he die?'

'He was tortured to death, basically.'

Véronique was startled. 'I'm sorry.'

'I didn't know him.'

'You make it sound as though it's okay that he was tortured to death since you didn't know him.'

Theo thought about this for a moment.

'My other grandfather was killed before my mother was born. He too died from torture, on an Aegean island.'

'What a history.' Véronique looked at him; he was smoking, unperturbed. 'And to think that those islands are swarming with tourists these days, as if nothing happened. And we talk as if nothing happened.'

'It's basically self-preservation, I guess.' He stroked her bare arm.

She was unpleasantly reminded of her own avoidances. The parasite of irritation settled inside her mood.

'But you didn't tell me about your grandfather,' he continued.

'There's not much to tell. He was never found. My father tried several times to set up an investigation, but each time it came to nothing. Basically.'

'Are you making fun of me?' He bent over her pseudo-menacingly.

'Of course not.' She couldn't suppress her smirk. He was such easy prey.

They were on an offshore island, sitting among the ruins of a Benedictine monastery. On the nudist beach in the distance a pair of naked stick-figures walked to the sea and back, bending and unbending in slow motion.

Before Theo could think of a suitable punishment, Véronique asked, 'What's the most difficult search you could undertake?'

He thought.

'Doing a search of all the strangers' photos in which you appear in the background, just by coincidence. Or by mistake.'

'Mmm . . .'

'You know, dishevelled, or sad, or eating an ice-cream, out of focus, you are the décor, the extra in somebody's photographic moment, and the person doesn't know who you are, and isn't interested either. How often have you have been snapped like that? You'll never know. Isn't that weird?'

'Yes.'

'What about remembering a dream that you've forgotten? Don't you hate that? You strain your memory, you know it's somewhere in there, lurking, the bastard, but it won't come out. Do you know what I mean?'

'It's the story of my life,' she said. 'Days spent uselessly trying to remember dreams I had the night before. Nights spent dreaming dreams I can't remember the next day.'

'You're a bit mellow today, I see. Basically, you're right, I suppose. Life is a dream.'

Véronique picked up a square stone and aimed into a small arch to the left. She missed and the stone hit the arch and bounced back, missing Theo's ear by a few centimetres. He ducked belatedly.

'Sorry,' she mumbled. 'Can you please stop saying basically? It's giving me an auditory rash.'

Theo picked up a bigger stone himself and aimed with greater precision at the same arch. The stone swished in the air and fell on a heap of medieval rubble. Theo got up and brushed the back of his jeans.

'I'm going for a walk in the botanical garden.'

When he had stepped over a few fallen walls and ducked despond-ently under a few arches, Véronique called out to him. He turned.

'Nothing,' she said. 'Nothing, go on.'

He shrugged with difficulty, like an angel with dislocated wings, and resumed his walk. Véronique took out the book of Seferis's poems she often carried with her.

We knew that the islands were beautiful
somewhere round about here where we grope,
slightly lower down or slightly higher up,
a tiny space.

She looked out to the mainland. The lovely coast of Dubrovnik was suddenly Greece's lovely coast, Turkey's lovely coast, the lovely Riviera – the Italian and French versions. The novelty was gone like a mirage popping in the haze, leaving her with the old arid infinity of the familiar. From now on, she would recognise beauty instead of perceiving it. She would remember it by groping for it. It was time to move on. To places where Theo hadn't been and where his eyes would caress objects and sights for her with a mesmeric, virginal spontaneity.

TWENTY-FIVE

June 1948

There was no moon and the crickets were crazed. A gentle mood without edges descended on the company. Kallistos at the front was trying to play a tune on a reed.

Pascal levelled his step with hers. 'Daphne, where is your family? Your mother, father? Do you have brothers and sisters? A fiancé?'

Daphne hesitated, then recited ironically: 'My tommy-gun is my mother, DAG is my fiancé. Stalin is my grandfather. Tito used to be my uncle, but not since last week. Hurray!' Pascal looked at her in confusion.

'You are full of mysteries,' he said, 'but I'd like to know the truth.'

'The truth? I'd like to know the truth too. Do you think we could ambush it somewhere? Booby-trap it perhaps?'

They walked in silence.

'You don't have to tell me if you don't want to.'

'Fine, I don't want to. What about you? Who do you have in France?'

'I have a . . . a sister but she lives in Italy. A mother in Marseilles. A little son, Alex.'

Daphne swallowed. 'How sweet. And a wife, no doubt?'

'Yes.'

Daphne stiffened, she didn't know why – it wasn't a sin to have a wife and a son after all, especially one called Alex.

'Your wife must be worried. Here you are, with dangerous bandits, roaming the mine-laden mountain roads of Greece.'

'I think my wife would be even more worried if she could see my guide.'

Daphne blushed. Thank God they were travelling by night.

'You mean him.' She pointed at Kallistos who was jumping over rocks, pushing the mules ahead.

'He's a little goat.'

'Yes, his ancestors were goats. Here in the mountains, it's hard to tell between goats and gods.'

Pascal laughed, which pleased her inexplicably.

'Except that goats exist and gods don't,' he said.

Walking beside him felt intimate.

'You don't believe in God?'

'No, I'm an existentialist.'

'I should've guessed. I once read something about Albert Camus. Do you know him?'

'Yes, I do. We used to work at the same newspaper during the German occupation, before I began working for *Le Monde*.'

Daphne was impressed.

'The slogan of our paper was "From Resistance to Revolution". But the fourth French Republic didn't quite make it to the revolution. Otherwise we would have had a civil war like you here.'

'My elder brother Illias used to tell me about Camus. He reads a lot. You might even meet him.'

'Where is he?'

'He's kapetanio of a division somewhere on Grammos.'

'Tell me, Daphne, you are Macedonian, right? Why are you in this war?'

Their steps crunched together musically. Kallistos gave up on his impotent reed and started to whistle.

'My whole family is in it. What could I do? Join the queen's army and kill my brothers?'

'I've heard that the Macedonians want autonomy, and that's why you had Tito's backing. Now that you've lost it because the KKE chose to stick with Stalin, what will happen?'

Kallistos had become interested in the conversation and slowed his step.

'Hey, goat-boy, are you eavesdropping?'

'Me? I can't hear a thing, the silence is so thick.'

They all laughed.

'Kallisto, tell Pascal about your family.'

'What family?' Kallistos said.

'The family you had, most beautiful one.' She turned to Pascal. 'Kallistos means best or most beautiful.'

Pascal rolled his eyes. 'Thanks for the Greek lesson.'

'I'm from Kozani.' Kallistos walked in front of them, speaking into the rocky void. 'My father was with ELAS in the Resistance. After the Varkiza agreement, he stayed in the mountains. One day, we kids saw some heads on display in the square. They were labelled. And just as well because otherwise I wouldn't have recognised Dad. Mum cracked after that because her two brothers had been killed too, and they took her to hospital. Me and my brother and sister went to live with my uncle. But then my uncle was suspected of sympathising with the communists and they executed him. They executed my aunt too because she called a government officer "fascist". We kids were told that we'd be taken to one of the queen's education camps for orphans and for communists' children. We didn't want to go because everybody called the queen Hitlerite Frederika and after all, my dad had fought the Germans, hadn't he. I was the oldest and I decided to take the other kids, six of us altogether, across the border with Yugoslavia. Or Albania, didn't really matter. We met all sorts of crazy people but it was hard on the little ones – we had to eat birds' eggs and roots. We were joined by some more kids on the way who like us didn't have parents. But then, when we got *this* close to the border, we ran into DAG and they took my brother and sister, together with my three cousins, and said they'd take them across to Yugoslavia where they would be fed and looked after. They didn't let me go with them. They said I was too old and should be in DAG.'

'How old are you?'

'Fourteen. I think.'

'He's also very good with mines. Kallistos is a hero.' Daphne caught up with him and put her arm around him. He glanced at her shyly. 'And he will find his brother and sister, and his cousins, when we win the war.'

Pascal was silent behind them. 'He is a greater hero than all the generals of Greece put together,' he slapped Kallistos on the back. 'There is a legendary character from the French Commune called Gavroche. He was a child-hero from the Paris barricades, an orphan, and the bravest of them all. You are the Greek Gavroche, Kallisto.'

They walked like this for a while – Daphne's hand on Gavroche's shoulder, Pascal behind them, the two mules in front. Pascal started singing a song that went like this:

Je suis tombé par terre,
C'est la faute de Voltaire.
Le nez dans le ruisseau,
C'est la faute de Rousseau.

'What does it mean?' she was jealous of the language she did not understand.

'It's the song of Gavroche. He says he has fallen on the ground and it's Voltaire's fault, he's in the ditch and it's Rousseau's fault. It's like this war really.'

Daphne had no idea what he meant but was too proud to ask for help in matters of French philosophy.

'See, I'm lucky,' she said instead. 'I might even have a father, still. And I have one brother alive. And all my limbs.'

'The night is young,' said Kallistos, and the two of them chuckled, but not Pascal.

'What about your mother?'

'My mother . . . After my father was shipped off to the islands as a dangerous Slavo-communist in 1945, my mother was taken to a government tribunal for communist sympathisers in Thessaloniki. They asked her various questions and she gave the right answers, but when they asked her if Edessa was a Greek, Bulgarian or Yugoslav town, she said, "I don't know." It was the wrong answer.'

'What happened?'

'What do you think happened, they gave her a medal for bravery? Executed.'

'Putain!'

'My two brothers and my fiancé were with the partisans. What were my choices, in your opinion? How much do you think I care about Tito's autonomous Macedonia?'

'What happened to them?'

'My fiancé Dimitri was deported to the island of Ikaria. He died there in February last year. I got a note . . . My younger brother Alexis was . . . He died last month.'

'No! How?'

'Like a hero,' Daphne said and started to hum. Kallistos was testing another, more promising reed.

'Quelle saloperie de guerre,' Pascal mumbled behind her.

From that night on, they talked much more during their treks. They heard consistent stories of mine accidents and had to circumnavigate the road from the north where the hills were brutal but at least they could move in the daytime. It was hot and it would get hotter. One afternoon, they ran into a crowd of villagers on the move.

When asked where they were going, an old man with shrivelled leather skin said, 'We don't know, daughter. We're from Mavropigio. The government army took over and we fled, fearing they would kill us for collaborating with the *andartes*. We left our animals behind. But when we arrived in the first village held by *andartes*, they didn't want us. So we're just wandering around.'

The women looked haggard, their feet bleeding, their children crying, their only men over seventy.

'Take us with you, daughter,' the old man pleaded.

'Let's take them along to the next village and negotiate with the *andartes* there,' Pascal suggested. Daphne was reluctantly for. Kallistos was reluctantly against.

'There are lots of them,' he said. 'They'll slow us down. We'll lose at least a day and I'm not familiar with this terrain.'

'They'll run into mines,' Pascal protested.

'We can't,' Daphne made up her mind. 'If we do, you'll miss Markos. You may even be late for returning before the national army strikes at Grammos. You may get trapped.'

'I don't care. It's important to help these people.' A lock of fair hair fell over his speckled eye which, in this light, was touched with gold. His stubble had grown again. She wanted to embrace him.

'Well, I care,' she said quietly. 'I have a mission. I have to look after you. These people will look after themselves. But I promise that when we arrive in the next village, we'll negotiate so by the time they get there, they'll be expected.'

Pascal opened his arms and raised his brows as if to say, 'You're the boss and I don't want to argue, but I'm not happy!'

Daphne explained to the village elder.

'God bless you, daughter. But I don't understand this war. During the occupation, they liberated Greece from the Germans. What are they all trying to do now? Liberate Greece from the Greeks? We don't want to be liberated any more.' Villagers tried to stop him – Daphne wore a uniform, after all, she was one of 'them'.

'Father,' she said, 'the Democratic Army is with the people. But we are all in the hands of greater powers.'

'We just want our houses and livestock back. And our men.' A woman holding an inert-looking baby sniffed.

There was nothing Daphne could say, nor Pascal, so they waved goodbye and walked down the hill, sullen.

They came across the ruins of a small temple in a wood clearing. An unshaven, haggard man emerged from inside and pointed his rifle at the startled group.

'Who are you?' Daphne said in her sternest voice, for he wore a government uniform.

'We are guardians of the temple of Demetra,' said the man.

'And who are you?' The voice came from far above them. They all looked up, including the mules. A man naked from the waist up was sitting on top of a tall column, grinning like a lunatic.

'Jesus, how did you get there?' Pascal hadn't registered that the uniforms weren't the Democratic Army's.

'We are Bedouins from the plains of Algiers,' she said.

'Is this some coded language?' Pascal enquired.

The rifle was lowered and a smile budded on the unshaven face.

'Deserters, huh?' Daphne smiled.

'Haven't eaten in three days. Do you happen to have anything edible, oh noble strangers?'

They had some bread and olives. The observer scaled down the column, using a rope that had been tied to the top by means of an extremely skilled manoeuvre. While wolfing down the food, they told their story of escape and Pascal took notes, as usual. This no longer irritated Daphne. It had become a ritual that she shared. She sometimes peeked over his shoulder to see him scribble incomprehensibly, which also had the advantage of legitimising a facial closeness that would otherwise be difficult to achieve. She liked the smell of his French cigarettes, which he shared with her and Kallistos.

'Why did you enlist in the army in the first place?'

'I was forced to enlist. My brothers and sister are in DAG. I don't want to have to kill them tomorrow.'

'Why were you hiding in the temple?'

'We don't know which way it's safe to go. But I couldn't see any major movement in the vicinity.'

Daphne hadn't ruled out the possibility that they could be spies. The safest thing was to take them under close supervision to the closest village where they would join the guerrillas.

'The safest way is to come with us,' she said. 'Only you'll have to hand me your guns.'

The soldiers exchanged looks and shrugged. 'You don't trust us?'

'As you can see, I have a foreigner here to look after. I have to make sure he's safe.' She blushed with pride under Pascal's gaze.

On the way to the village, the deserters told of their previous visit to the temple, some months ago, with the national army. There had been a guard there, from the village, who had let the guerrillas use the column as an observation post. The rope gave him away. He was executed. The rope had remained.

As they approached their destination, more movement appeared in the villages and on the hills. Bands of guerrillas were moving westwards towards Grammos, often accompanied by villagers.

'Why are old men sitting on donkeys while their womenfolk walk ahead holding the rope?' Pascal's innocence was staggering.

'It's the mine-detecting device of the Greek peasant. The woman gets blown up, the man and the mule survive.' Pascal laughed, not believing her. Kallistos laughed too.

Pascal was like a child, constantly curious, distracted by the slightest event, the most nondescript peasant, the most fetid goat. He would have gladly interviewed the mules if no one was watching. His curiosity slowed them down.

'Look, do you want to meet Markos or not?'

'I'm not only after Markos. Everything we see is important.'

She rolled her eyes and smiled.

One day, descending towards a village that spilled down a merciless rocky slope, they saw a frightful apparition on the rocks above. A tall woman naked from the waist down, wearing some rags on her upper body, her limbs badly scratched and covered in old blood, as if she had walked through a forest of thorns without noticing. Although her emaciated body was young, her long hair was grey and knotted, almost covering her face. Even the mules stopped, puzzled.

Daphne blushed, mortified.

'My God, what's happened to her?' Pascal gagged.

'I can think of a few things,' said Kallistos. The woman suddenly became aware of them and, startled, brushed the hair away from her face but didn't cover herself. She was perhaps only a year or two older than Daphne and, if she hadn't been a walking skeleton, her face would have been exquisitely beautiful. Her skin was weathered. She swayed like a reed in an imaginary breeze.

'Kyria,' Pascal yelled, 'we have some clothes for you, and some food. Please come down.'

'Yes, but do you have news of them?' the woman's voice came to them like the wind of a strange, distant season.

'Who?'

'The little one, Katerina, is four, with blue eyes and curly hair, it must've grown by now, and the other one, Christos, is six and a half, with a patch in his trousers. I should have cut them to shorts, it's hot now. A small characteristic scar on his forehead, his birthday is on All Saints' Day.'

The woman looked at them tensely, expecting the verdict. Kallistos cleared his throat and walked on with the mules, whistling. Pascal took a step up towards the woman, then stopped and looked at Daphne. There were tears in his eyes. She felt as if she really knew him now, as if they had been travelling together in these wretched mountains their entire lives.

'Kyria.' Her voice was so small she had to clear her throat and try again. 'Kyria, we have in fact seen them and they are very well. They have fresh bread and even chocolate. They live in a clean house with many other children. They will come back to you, but not yet. They send you their love.'

'Let's go,' she said to Pascal, avoiding his face.

'Kyria,' he said and wiped his nose with a sleeve, 'you must go home now and everything will be fine. Please go home.'

'Chocolate,' said the woman and scurried back up the hill with the agility of a goat, her vulnerable naked backside merging with the rocks.

Daphne and Pascal walked down to the village in silence.

They were offered either the church to share with others, or a barn to themselves. The village was full of guerrillas headed for Grammos.

Daphne found some fragrant dry herbs in a corner, wrapped them in a cloth and gave them to Pascal, for a pillow.

'This is very kind of you. But what about you?'

'Oh, I'm fine, I always sleep on Alexis's shirt.' She bit her lip.

'Your brother?'

'Yes.' She spread her blanket over the hay and lay down, uncomfortable under Pascal's gaze. He covered himself with a Russian jacket lent to him by a guerrilla who had studied in France and insisted on doing something for him. She noticed his shoes were in bad shape, his socks torn.

'Are your feet okay?'

'Fine, thank you,' he lied. 'You never told me about your brother Alexis.'

'He died.'

'In battle?'

'He was executed by our own.'

'What for?'

'He said that for every mule of foreign aid we received, the national army received a shipload of American aid.'

'Daphne, it is true. Your brother was right. And what kind of a Democratic Army is this anyway, killing its own.'

She blew out the decrepit candle flickering in a wooden box.

'That isn't the point,' she snapped.

'I know. I'm sorry.'

Kallistos whimpered in his sleep like a puppy somebody had stepped on. In the darkness, Daphne could see Pascal's gold-speckled eye only a metre away, but not the other one. He shuffled and his hand touched hers on the hay. She didn't withdraw it.

'You have lost a lot already and you are so young.'

'Nobody is young here any more. Look at Kallistos.'

'I know. But I am talking about you. Daphne, I feel very privileged to have met you. I will never be the same.'

She withdrew her hand. 'Don't say things like that. You'll forget everything when you go back to France. You'll forget my name.'

'No!'

'Shhh.' Something in her was uncoiling. 'I want to forget many things.'

'Forgetting doesn't help.'

'You mean that I should forgive too?'

'No. I don't know what I mean. But I don't want you to die or get wounded.'

'What happens to me doesn't matter the slightest. I'm just one of the many. In any case, I have no mother to weep for me.' Daphne put steel in her voice.

'You have a life in front of you.'

She sneered. He was propped on his elbow, his golden eye sparkling. He groped for her hand.

'I want you to have a life. You are brilliant, beautiful, brave.'

'Oh, please save your compliments for Paris.' She wanted him to continue.

'Daphne, if I tell you that I can find a haven for you in Thessaloniki, or better still, in Athens, will you come back with me in two weeks?'

She sneered again. 'I'm not a prisoner. I'm a guerrilla.'

'Markos is losing the war, Daphne.'

'Hush your voice or you'll have us shot. Are you a prophet anyway?'

'You were right about the greater powers. Greece is their plaything. Your army can't resist American aircraft forever, no matter how brave the guerrillas are. Tito has abandoned you. Stalin has never been behind you. Nobody supports you. They will crush you eventually. It's only a matter of time.'

Daphne turned her back to him and closed her eyes, her temples pulsing with shock and anger.

'Don't be a child,' he said. 'Listen to me.'

She flipped herself over. 'So you suggest that I abandon my brother, my comrades, everything we've been suffering for, and go to Athens where I'd hide like an animal or go on trial and spend my life breaking rocks on the islands?'

'I told you, I'll find you a —'

'Don't tell me anything. I'm not a deserter. Don't waste your words.'

Pascal fell back on his hay and puffed with frustration. 'It's suicide,' he said.

'I live in suicide country. It's what we do best.'

They listened to the pounding of each other's hearts.

'You know, Angelis Philipidis, the man who gave me a letter for his wife, said to me something strange. He said, this is the land of Midas, a petrified land. We have touched it with Midas hands, he said.'

Daphne floated pleasantly, carried by his soft accented baritone.

'Like the mad woman today,' she whispered. 'She is a rock in a land of madness. That land is Greece.'

Pascal squeezed her hand.

'You know what really got to me?' he whispered, 'The characteristic scar on the boy's forehead. As if anyone would notice.'

They were quiet for a moment, then she said: 'I don't know . . . The *pedomasoma* was meant to be a noble mission. Not a disaster.'

He did something strange then. He shifted his head towards her and put his lips on her fingers, then unfolded them and kissed her palm, the inside of her wrist, her bare forearm, finally putting his forehead in the fold of her elbow and staying there for a moment. She was so surprised she didn't react. She had never been touched by a man on any part of her body. Dimitri had kissed her a few times, true, years ago, but it hadn't been anything elaborate.

'Daphne.' He lifted his head. She could feel his breath, the warmth of his neck. 'Come with me to France.'

She was so astounded she couldn't form words for a moment.

'But . . . you're . . . you have a wife.' As if that was the only problem.

'Yes.'

'Pascal,' how she liked to have his name in her mouth, 'this is my country. I'd rather die here than live in your France.'

He squeezed her arm. 'I don't know. I don't know. I just want you to . . . I just can't bear to . . .' His face found hers and his lips stopped only centimetres away from hers. His hand stroked her cheek. His words were like a prolonged kiss.

'It doesn't matter that I have a wife. I will leave her if you come with me. I can't bear to leave you here.'

A terrible, unfamiliar weakness spread downwards from her stomach, and her loins and legs were paralysed with longing. She knew she must shake him off, but she couldn't. His lips were hard, chapped from the sun, delicious. His hand on her cheek, he kissed her eyes, her nose, her ear, her chin, her neck. She realised she was clutching the front of his shirt. She inhaled the scent of his neck – tobacco, sweat and another, subtler smell, a Pascal-smell.

Daphne was a sleepwalker on a narrow bridge over a deep gully. If she woke up now, she would fall.

They slept, their heads together on the hay, her hand in his.

'Daphne, Daphne, have you found your Apollo?'

'Oh shut up, best one.' Daphne jumped up, disoriented. Kallistos was binding pieces of tyre-rubber to the soles of his shoes with string. 'He must have shifted in his sleep.' She glanced at the sleeping Pascal.

'Yes, during the earthquake.'

'What earthquake?'

'Didn't you feel it? Have a look outside, there's nothing left of the village, everybody's dead, it's the end of the war, the end of the world. We can go home! Hurray!'

She smacked him tenderly on the back of the head but couldn't help smiling, as if something wonderful had happened.

'He's all right, your Apollo, not too much of a wimp.' Kallistos put on his fortified shoes. 'Like new.'

Daphne looked at Pascal's shoes. 'Could you do the same with his? They're falling apart.'

'Yeah, we can't let Apollo mess up his feet, can we.'

'Your hands won't fall off, you know.'

'No, but they'll get tired.'

She gave him another smack. He grinned and started cutting up more tyre. Then she remembered Alexis's boots in her rucksack. With her back to Kallistos, she took them out. They were half-worn, a recent gift to Alexis from a peasant girl who had seen him with his shabby bound feet and given him the boots of her brother – he had had his legs blown off. She put them in the place of his old shoes.

'Don't worry, best one,' she said, 'I've thought of something else.'

The guerrillas camped in the village were moving westwards that day. Daphne and Pascal tried to discuss with the kapetanio the disowned people of Mavropigio. His pock-marked face stretched into a sad grimace.

'Look at the people here. They barely have enough to eat. When the nationalists occupied this area, they requisitioned their livestock. Look at this woman.' He pointed at a middle-aged woman in black sitting outside her house. 'The nationalists took her sons by force, shot her husband, and then took her door to make a stretcher for their wounded. She's been sitting out there for weeks. She doesn't speak, she doesn't eat, she just sits, waiting. We put in a new door for her but I guess it's too late. What can you do?'

'We saw a woman . . .' Pascal said, 'on the outskirts of the village . . .'

'The mad one?'

'Yes.'

The kapetanio shook his head again.

'She's from another village, up north. Her husband was a partisan, killed in battle. DAG took her children across the border and the poor woman lost her marbles. She put fire to her house.'

'Why don't you enlist her in the Democratic Army?' Kallistos suggested. The kapetanio was called away.

'Kallisto!' Pascal protested. 'She needs to be taken to a psychiatric hospital.'

'This is not France, you know,' Daphne snapped at him, not knowing why. 'We have all lost our marbles. This is war.'

Pascal opened his mouth to say something and closed it. He stepped towards her.

'And don't play your romantic tricks on me.' She turned on her heels and went to help Kallistos saddle the mules.

From then on, they were rarely alone. The guerrillas, led by the sad, pock-marked kapetanio, were moving towards the same destination, accompanied by peasants and a 75-millimetre gun which had to be carried by several mules. One morning, they were walking along a narrow mountain path with a gorge to the left and a vertical cliff-face to the right. It was hard even for the heavy-laden mules. A sudden cry and a land-sliding noise made her stop and turn. Pascal had slipped perilously down the ravine and was holding onto a small, stunted shrub off the path. A couple of guerrillas rushed to pull him up. He was embarrassed, so Daphne pretended not to have seen him clinging to that bush. 'What happened?' she asked, levelling her step with his.

'You nearly got me off your back there,' he said, shaken but spirited. 'And wasted these boots.'

Daphne gave him a light push in the chest and strode on, swinging her rifle at him. She no longer had to walk behind him because there were others around. Now, when she walked in front of him, she felt his gaze on her back.

The days were becoming very hot, and progressing from goat-land to eagle-land in the scorching sun was impossible. They reverted to their night-shift.

'I need a post office to send a cable,' Pascal said one afternoon as they sat in the shade of a tree, sipping guerrilla tea made from a bag of herbs on a string which was dipped in the water for a second and kept for re-use. 'Back there, they must think I've been abducted or killed, like Polk.'

'You'll use the post office in Aetomilitsa. I guess you're worried about your wife worrying,' she added dryly.

'I'm worried about giving the wrong impression. But it's too late now anyway.'

'What does it mean, too late? You'll be back in Athens in less than two weeks.' Somehow, the thought was like a slip off a mountain path and Daphne's mood was plummeting to dangerous lows.

'If there were flowers here, I would put some in your hair,' he said. She blushed. 'But all of Greece is rock. You are the only flower.'

She kicked some stones and let her cropped hair fall on the sides of her face to hide her blush.

'Are all Frenchmen so hopelessly sentimental?'

'Would you rather talk about ammunition?' She loved the way his straight eyebrows went up when he was surprised, and his entire forehead seemed to shift backwards, making his hair recede further and conjuring an image of how he might look older.

A hawk circled over the peaks in the distance. The sunset was its nest.

'See that hawk?' she said. 'That's what we have against their Spitfires. Mules against ships, eagles against aircraft, that's right. And still we're going to win, because we have passion. A month from now, you'll be reporting from Athens that the Democratic Army is victorious. That the children can return from the north and, and . . . whoever needs to go to a psychiatric hospital, will go, and . . . and . . . a new Greece will be born.'

He turned her chin to him. His eyes were full of something intense she couldn't name. Pain.

'Daphne, my flower, do you believe this?'

'Yes.' She tried to steel her gaze but she suspected it didn't work because he drew her head to his shoulder and pressed it against his collar-bone, kissing her hairline and forehead as if she were a child with fever. She had received no such gesture of tenderness in her whole guerrilla lifetime, and perhaps beyond. She wanted to hold onto Pascal and not let him go.

Further down the hill, someone started singing 'Night Without Moon' – a famous rebetiko song, Daphne explained – and soon the whole band was singing the mournful tune. Daphne joined them. Pascal followed. A small fire crackled in the middle of the circle and a soft light carved the youthful faces. Pascal's golden eye sparkled at her.

Night without moon, the darkness is deep,
But a brave lad cannot sleep . . .

TWENTY-SIX

May/June 1998

On the long ferry ride, Véronique wanted to sit on the deck by herself for a while. There was a buzz of multilingual conversations around her. She tuned into one, in crisp English.

'. . . from the Greek nostos, "to return". And pathos, "suffering".'

'So there you go. You wanted an unusual malaise and here you are. Nostopathy, fear of returning to familiar places. Happy?'

'Yes, as long as we never go to the places where we've been happy before.'

Véronique turned to locate the source of this enigmatic exchange but a corpulent German group wielding Cokes blocked her view. The nostopathic couple had fled to a less familiar place.

Perhaps nostopathy ran in the Loublier family. Pascal's need to be liberated from Pascal was the ultimate nostopathy. And, essentially, the fear of familiar places was a fear of one's familiar self in those places, like a fear of meeting oneself in time – the ultimate nightmare of identity. Travel, love, adventure, drugs – these were only the different violences we did to ourselves in order to meet ourselves anew. Theo was right: she was looking for a new self in Albania. And now on this ferry. And in the next moment – in Theo's eyes, in his arms, in his voice.

There was only Theo left now: her drug, her trip, her love, her adventure, her trouble. She was investing in him more than a human could possibly accommodate.

She found him retching over the railing. She put a hand on his back while he finished and sat him down on a bench next to a placid couple who sat, thigh by fat thigh, limp but purposefully so, as if saving energy, only their eyes moving.

'At least now I know you're not insane.'

'What?'

'Only the deaf, those with no sense of smell, and the insane don't get seasick. I read it in a Greek novel.'

'Don't trust Greek novels.'

'What are you saying, that you *are* insane?'

'Actually, I wouldn't mind a temporary insanity, just while this trip lasts . . .'

'It might be safer to just go deaf or lose your sense of smell.'

'No.' He shook his head. 'If I went deaf, I wouldn't hear your voice. If I lost my sense of smell, I wouldn't smell you. I'd rather be sick.'

He leant on the wall and closed his eyes. He smelt faintly of sweat and cigarettes. Véronique put her arm across his chest as if to hold him upright, and laid her head on his shoulder. The couple next to them had been listening or at least looking – she could tell from the vague awakening that troubled their faces, like a distant memory of the original, long-lost purpose of this exercise of being together, thigh by fat thigh.

The more they approached Italy, the more Véronique advanced into the padded corridor of inalienable familiarity, like walking down a hospital ward.

They strolled across magnificent Roman ruins where their voices echoed. They stepped through the west gate of Diocletian's palace and saw camera-crazed tourists unmoved by beauty, snapping square deaths of the Venetian town hall, which stood unperturbed in its severity. Theo had to slip out of Véronique's sight to take photographs, she was so contemptuous of that 'barbaric practice'.

'It's barbaric *not* to remember this,' he countered.

'Photographs are the opposite of remembering. They violate your memory and your imagination.'

Theo sighed. 'I'm a scholar of ruins. Without visual records, classics wouldn't exist.'

'What a loss that would've been!'

Theo turned on his heels and marched off to indulge in his barbaric practice. Véronique watched unseeingly the dazzling ruins crawling with tourists. She was gripped by the apprehension of things slipping out of her control, a sense of slow and irreversible dilapidation.

That night, in their Beach Hotel, they lay side by side on the bed.

'I'd like you to stop paying for me,' Theo said suddenly.

Véronique waited, but he didn't elaborate.

'I thought you were okay about it.'

'I thought so too, but I'm not.'

She turned onto one side, propped her head on one hand and placed her other hand on his stomach.

'Just imagine you're my brother. That we share everything.'

'Yes, but we don't.'

'We share what we can,' she said quietly. 'And this, we can share.'

Their lips merged, followed by a merging of hips and loins, flat stomachs and sharp breasts, a swan-like neck, an arched back, pointed hips, hands which gripped not only shapes but surfaces, so avid were they. Véronique was released from herself at least for a moment that was an eternity of gratitude.

Véronique had been a toddler when she first went to Italy with her parents, and a teenager the second time, after the family had returned from Greece – their last holiday together.

On the ferry to Ancona, she and Theo had a benign argument about where to go. Véronique wanted to avoid being crushed by the tidal wave of tourists in the major towns. But those were the most interesting! Theo protested. He'd be surprised, though. Véronique wanted to go straight to Naples, her favourite place. Theo was too proud to plead for Rome but he insisted on Venice and Tuscany. Véronique felt too tired to argue.

'It can't be much worse than the Adriatic,' Theo said doubtfully.

She looked at him and much was said in that moment about his ignorant vitality and her knowing world-weariness, his optimism and her depression. She had to agree, though, that if she had wanted to avoid tourists at all cost, coming at this time of the year was not a smart move. 'But I warn you,' she said, 'I'm not queuing up for any museums and galleries. You'll be seeing David and the Uffizzi by yourself.'

In Florence, only the five-star hotels had rooms. Theo was uneasy. 'My grandmother loved five-star hotels, so this is a tribute to her,' Véronique explained helplessly. Theo gave her a look not dissimilar to the one she had given him on the ferry: her habitual wealth and his middle-class student poverty, her squandering generosity and his reticence to become its object. And they didn't smile this time.

A week went by and they saw each other intermittently during the day. Theo was determined to see everything there was to see. Véronique took strolls around the town. When they met, he would be cool from spending hours indoors, looking at art, and she would be sweaty and sun-struck from hours of covering every square metre in the town where her father had been with her.

'Sometimes Italy appears like the carcass of a once powerful animal picked by birds of prey.'

He laughed. 'Yes, but Italy lives from this.'

'If you call that living. Have you seen any Italians here yet? Except shop and hotel owners?'

'Well . . . the artists.'

When they walked past the artists in the Piazza del Duomo, some called out to her, 'Signorina, I paint your face. Beautiful face!' Some rushed to stop her and employed their powers of artistic and male persuasion to court her into sitting for them. One of them went as far as to offer, 'I paint your boyfriend too, if you want, eh?' Theo wanted her to have her portrait done, but not his. Finally, among the bustle of models, artists and voyeurs, she chose a small, dark, exquisite-faced artist in his twenties with dirty nails and feverish eyes.

'No English,' he apologised and brushed a chair for her to sit down on, although it was clean. As a crowd gathered to watch, and Theo looked on excitedly, Véronique thought how this was exactly the kind of situation she had wanted to avoid. The kitsch of wonder, the buzz of vulgarity, the cliché of Italy. She was only sitting here, in the scorching sun, surrounded by a sweaty, smelly, banal throng of tourists, because fifteen years or so ago she had done the same, at roughly the same spot, with her parents lovingly watching the pencil strokes on the sheet assume her facial shape and expression, though without great precision. Her father had commented, 'Como Venus de Botticelli!' and the artist had agreed. Then she had left the scroll in the Basilica di San Lorenzo and the next day it was gone. 'Oh well, someone got lucky,' was her father's response. 'It wasn't very successful anyway', was her mother's. Now she was getting her portrait back, updated.

'Americana?' hazarded the feverish artist.

'No. Francesca.'

'Française! Moi, je suis Albanais. Pour vous, 30,000 lire seulement.' They chatted Italy, France and Albania, somewhat to Theo's annoyance. Véronique told the artist of their trip through Albania, and he shook his head sadly. He was from Durrës. He had escaped four years ago on a ferry.

The audience clapped unanimously when he displayed the finished drawing. He insisted on shaking hands with both his model and her boyfriend, and only charged her the promised discounted fee. But she gave him three times the amount. His eyes were moist as he put the thick wad of lire in a pocket of his battered jeans, and his shy smile revealed a mouthful of broken teeth.

Later, they made an unlikely find: a scroll lying on the coloured marble floor of the Cappella dei Principi. When Theo unrolled it, they saw a pencil portrait of a young woman – a portrait in which it was obvious that the unfortunate artist had applied all his skill to flatter the subject but had possibly ended up reproducing a woman who didn't exist.

'I wonder if it's worth trying to find the woman,' mused Theo.

'I don't like her face.'

He gave her a baffled look.

'She paid money for this, you know – it's not any cheaper when you're ugly. Though it should be, as consolation.'

'Now who sounds arrogant!'

'How do you suggest we go about finding her?'

'I don't know. We'll give it to the reception. Oh, hold on, there's no reception here.'

'We can add this to our list of hard-to-find things. And all will be well.'

'All will be well,' repeated Theo, trying to make sense of the phrase.

TWENTY-SEVEN

June 1948

The roads became increasingly perilous due to mines laid by the guerrillas in preparation for the arrival of the government army. Vultures dined on the blown-up carcass of a mule on the side of the road.

'From now on, anyone waking up with limbs numbering less than four will be reported to the high command! Anybody found concealing a lack of limbs will be reported too,' Kallistos announced, causing sporadic laughter among the guerrillas. He fearlessly went ahead of everyone with the two mules.

'I feel like we're climbing towards the gods and I'll never see the sea again,' Pascal said.

'You mean you feel like you're going to die?'

He laughed. 'You're so extreme. You live in a black and white world.'

Daphne flashed him a black look. 'I live in the only world I've got.'

'I'm sorry. I'm an arsehole.'

'You are.' Then she added softly, 'Sometimes.'

They exchanged reprehensible looks.

'Noticed how the rations have shrunk?' she said with perverse relish.

'Yes.'

'They'll keep shrinking. The higher you get, the less you eat. The more you fight, the less you eat. The less you sleep, the less you eat.'

'You must have done a lot of climbing and fighting. You're like a reed.'

'The less space you take, the more chances of survival you've got.'

He seemed impressed. 'What would you be doing if there was no war?'

'Living, I suppose.' Daphne tucked her bouncy fringe under her brown cap.

'And in your spare time?'

'I'd be at Thessaloniki University studying philosophy. Or medicine. Or something like that.'

'Oh!'

'What does your wife do?'

He hesitated. 'Nothing. I mean she looks after Alex.'

Someone started singing 'With my gun on my shoulder I open the road to freedom', and soon the mountain silence was rippled by voices, pebbles cast into a limpid lake.

'It's an ELAS song from the Resistance,' Daphne explained. She was too embarrassed to sing in front of him but, to her amazement, he started singing along. His musical talent was zero.

'I didn't know you were so musical,' she chuckled, and deftly dodged his grab, hopping ahead.

'I'll show you musical.' He chased her among cheers and whistles.

'Apollo, Apollo,' Kallistos shouted. He had moved into the middle ranks. 'Don't chase Daphne for she will turn into a tree and you will mourn her forever.'

'This boy is too precocious for his own good,' said the pock-marked kapetanio to Daphne and Pascal when they stopped the mock-chase.

'I know,' Pascal said. 'I'll never look at fourteen-year-olds the same way again.'

'Greek youths are special, though.'

'Like Greek donkeys!' another guerrilla joined in.

'Paradise must be full of Greek donkeys.'

'What about hell?' Pascal asked with his pretended innocence.

'You stick with us and you'll see hell,' the kapetanio answered. He had the stoop and the lustreless eyes of the fatalist.

'Tell me, what did you do before the war?'

'I was a scholar of classics.' The kapetanio laughed, seeing Pascal's expression. 'You think we're brutes here? My father is a surgeon. I'm from a bourgeois family.'

'What are you doing up here then?'

'I'm fighting for a democratic Greece. For justice. For the oppressed.'

'Pascal, my father was a merchant and my mother taught at a sewing school,' Daphne said. 'What do you think, that we're all shepherds brandishing guns, a kind of monosyllabic cave-people with no concept of the world?'

She knew she'd gone too far. He stopped. She lowered her eyes.

'I think', he said seriously, 'that you're a bunch of extremely brave people with your hearts in the right place. And I wish you all the luck in the world.'

'Make sure the world knows this, my friend,' the kapetanio said, giving him a slap on the back.

They crunched on. Pascal's hand touched Daphne's.

On the outskirts of Aetomilitsa, loudspeakers thundered, 'Fight the mercenaries of America! Fight for a free Greece! The people will triumph over American imperialism!' There was much animation – guerrillas training, convoys heading up north, peasant women carrying firewood in their skirts. Pascal was somewhere behind talking to guerrillas, but Daphne made sure he was always within her sight. She was excited about their imminent meeting with the legendary king of the mountains. Illias couldn't be too far away either. Her mission was over and it had been successful. She congratulated herself and looked for Kallistos to say some nice words to him. Just then the sound of an explosion somewhere ahead sent a chill through her. She prayed it was the mules. She rushed forward. A few hundred metres down the road, she saw a small group gathered around something.

'It's the boy with the mules,' someone said to her. She ran on air. The indoctrination officer was right: there was no God.

Both Kallistos's legs had been blown off above the knees, and one lay a few metres away, its rubber-fortified boot still on; the other was lost in the gully below the road. He was conscious as the pock-marked kapetanio lifted him up onto an improvised stretcher. The boy's eyes were enormous with shock. His front was splattered with blood. 'Spiro, where is he?' he mumbled. 'He's fine,' Daphne wanted to say, although Spiro was blown to pieces, but her voice had deserted her. She smoothed the wet hair from his forehead.

'Who let him run ahead of the mules?' the kapetanio bellowed. 'Didn't I say let all the mules go first?' A silence descended on the small group attending to the stretcher and its contents. Guerrillas kept filing past. When Pascal appeared, she saw the realisation punch him. 'C'est pas vrai, c'est pas vrai,' he whispered, and Daphne looked away. He bent to the side of the road and retched continuously. Daphne held Kallistos's hand as they carried him quickly to the village. He was starting to fade. They had put rags to his stumps to staunch the blood but his face was as white as the rock that surrounded them and his shivering lips were turning blue. Pascal, just as white and shivering himself, walked beside Daphne, tears streaming down his face.

'Will he live?' he whispered.

'I don't know.' She squeezed Kallistos's cold childish hand. She didn't know whether she wanted him to live.

'I have a brother his age,' someone sniffed. It was the French-speaking guerrilla who had given Pascal his jacket and now covered Kallistos with it. 'Somewhere up north with DAG.'

Fight the mercenaries of America! Fight for a free Greece! The people will triumph over American imperialism!

The medics at the makeshift hospital shook their heads. 'We'll have to amputate without anaesthetic.'

'Are you out of your minds?' Pascal shouted.

'What is this foreigner doing here?'

The kapetanio raised his hand reconcilingly. 'He's with us, he's a journalist.'

'We have no anaesthetics!' The doctor, or whatever he was, shrugged helplessly.

Kallistos was delirious. 'Mama,' he whimpered, then 'Spiro.'

'Give the boy ouzo, quick.' A bottle was passed over and forced between Kallistos's teeth. Two doctors rolled up their sleeves. Kallistos's pants were torn up. A knife flashed.

'I can't watch this.' Pascal looked at Daphne beseechingly, as if saying 'Tell me this isn't happening.' She nodded, dismissing him. He fumbled for a moment then stepped outside, followed by the kapetanio. Daphne held Kallistos's hand and pressed an ouzo-soaked cloth on his forehead. A piece of wood was put in his mouth. While they separated his tattered flesh from his body, all her blood surged to her ears, blocking out his muffled screams. A red veil fell over her mind. She squeezed his hand to keep herself conscious. She had held a girl guerrilla's hand like this when the girl went into labour in the winter. She died anyway and her baby froze to death. Daphne was really squeezing her own hand, humming inside her head 'Night without moon, the darkness is deep . . .'

The next blow was being told that Markos had been here and was now gone. He was most likely to be in Pyrgos, Daphne was told, but again, no one could be certain. Her brother's division had left Aetomilitsa just two days before. Daphne kicked the wall of the makehsift hospital until the whitewash started to crumble. Angry tears welled up in her eyes but she was too proud to let them spill.

She explained to Pascal why she couldn't take him any further. She would be held responsible if anything happened to him. He could see for himself how unpredictable the roads were. Besides, he wouldn't be sure of making it back before the government army blocked the escape routes to the north. They were already fighting in Smolikas.

'I don't want you to be held responsible for me,' he said, after frowning in and out of a thought. 'If you don't want me on your hands, that's fine. I'll go to Pyrgos anyway, with the others. You are free to join your division and you don't have to see me ever again.'

Ever again. They looked at each other across sleeping Kallistos's bed. Pascal offered her a cigarette and she took it over the space where the boy's legs would have been.

'Why him?' Pascal leant his elbows on his knees. 'Why exactly him.'

'It's always someone.'

'It's always the best. The bravest.'

'I can't guarantee your safe return any more.' Someone irresponsible in her was rejoicing. Pascal got up, took his chair and put it next to hers.

'What are you saying?'

She shrugged. The smoke suddenly made her eyes water. He took her hand and put it on his knee, looking at it as if it was a creature. 'Look, I just want to be around you. Make sure you don't walk in front of any mules.'

She blew out smoke.

'Have you had a reply to your cable yet?'

'Yes.' He tried to conceal a smile. 'And have you seen the newspapers?'

'We're not allowed to read the monarcho-fascist papers without the kapetanio's permission.' She tried to conceal a smile too.

'Well, I've been abducted by the bandits, presumed murdered. Polk number two. I've cabled the embassy. They'll pass on the message to *Le Monde*.'

'And to your wife.'

He didn't like her mentioning his wife. Perhaps it was the way she did it. He glanced at her reproachfully and she pouted in mock-apology, lifting her eyebrows the way he would do. His speckled eye thought she was overwhelmingly sweet; his blue one was trying to be stern.

Kallistos let out a moan. 'Can I go home?' he whispered, without stirring or opening his eyes.

Daphne and Pascal froze.

'No, mikraki mou. They'll look after you here.'

'Will you stay with me?'

'Yes,' she lied.

'We'll stay with you,' Pascal confirmed the lie and stroked the boy's sweaty hair.

After a hideous moment of silence, Pascal began to sing quietly:

Je suis tombé par terre,
C'est la faute de Voltaire.
Le nez dans le ruisseau,
C'est la faute de Rousseau.

Kallistos drifted off again. Face in his hands, Pascal wept.

Daphne stroked his hair, which was the colour of golden acorns burnt to ashes.

Just before they were due to leave, and after Daphne had cabled a report of their journey to supreme HQ, Pascal showed her a statement he had typed in the gymnasium. 'I continue towards Pyrgos on my own initiative. Grigoriadis Daphne is no longer my guide and may not be held responsible for my fate henceforth. Signed: Pascal Loublier. Stamped: Free Greece, Grammos Headquarters.'

'I'm very proud of the "henceforth".' They laughed. He lifted her and swirled her around as if they had just been wed and were going on a honeymoon.

They joined the great migration to Pyrgos. Pascal was given a sawn-off shotgun by the pock-marked kapetanio who apologised for having nothing better.

'It suits you.' She examined him with a mock-critical eye.

They scaled the merciless rock, sweat pouring down their limbs.

'Kallistos will never climb again,' he said, puffing. 'I want to have money sent to him from France, get him prosthetic legs . . .'

'Goat-boy was marked.'

'What do you mean, marked?'

'He has the mark which distinguishes those who are the very first to die or get maimed.'

'You mean the mark of brilliance and bravery?'

'And something else, I'm not sure what to call it.'

'Desperation perhaps.'

'Perhaps. And I don't know that you can do anything for him. Once you leave us, there'll be no further contact.'

He stopped and turned. His skin glowed with sweat and sun, his eye was golden again. There was no one behind them, they were the last in the convoy. She found her hand gripping his shirt, his arms around her, her face against his sweaty neck, his hot mouth on her hot face.

'Daphne, my dawn, my flower, don't say this.' The familiar, terrible weakness spread down her legs again and they kissed as if this were the kiss to end all kisses, to drown the end of the kiss in the kiss itself. They were pressed so tightly against each other that she could no longer tell the landscapes of their bodies apart. And their landscapes fitted against each other perfectly, as if they had once been forcefully separated by an earthquake in a distant era of ice and sorrow and were now finally fitted back together. His face fitted perfectly against her breasts, which she let him bare by opening her sweat-soaked shirt, his hands on her flat stomach and bony hips, his mouth tasting her belly-button . . . But fear of being seen startled her back into reality. She urged him to get up from his knees. He looked the way she felt, drunk and capable of great madness.

'You could get executed for this, you know,' she whispered with what she could muster of her voice. 'If you weren't a foreigner.'

'I'd die a happy man.'

TWENTY-EIGHT

June 1998

They stopped in San Gimignano, at Véronique's insistence. An authentic medieval town, possessing many towers and fine Tuscan views from its hilltop, she explained. The reason why she wanted to stop there was a small restaurant in a small piazza. There was a waiter who performed tricks while serving and blabbering in a flurry of languages. She and her parents had laughed and marvelled all evening. The restaurant was still there, Ubu Re. The waiter was now the owner. At her request, he came out, fatter and balder than she remembered him. She explained in Franco-Italian about her first visit.

'Si si, I remember you. Your father, red frizzy hair. Your mother, very beautiful, young. You were the little girl with the cherry eyes. You've grown up very fast, I see!'

Véronique couldn't believe his memory, even if she hadn't been a little girl but a teenager. Her mother hadn't been that young. But still . . .

'I'll serve you,' the magician said. 'I don't normally serve any more, but I will, especially for you.'

And he did, in the hocus-pocus style she remembered. The entire restaurant watched from their tables. A white cotton serviette lay open in his palm. Véronique was asked to break a match and place it inside the serviette. His hand closed the serviette, shook it, opened it again, to reveal an intact match. Clapping. A coin in his palm. He flipped it on the back of his other hand. It showed the same side. That one she remembered clearly. Her father had called the waiter maestro for the rest of the evening. He dropped a glossy banknote between Véronique's fingers. Time after time, she failed to catch it. Theo too. Others tried, with the same frustrating effect. As she watched other diners try to grip the slippery note, she understood the mistake in the magician's recollection. He was describing her father with Nour and Justine.

'I'll leave you to your desserts.' The good maestro retired.

A coin in the palm. A broken match in a white serviette. The same magician, the same father. Different families. Different lives.

'Are you all right?'

She shook her head as if to brush the question away, and this restaurant, and the memory of it.

'We've come to the wrong restaurant for the right reasons. Or the right restaurant for the wrong reasons.'

He stroked her hand. She told him.

'Come on,' he said. 'It's a bit like feeling let down by the fact that your hotel bed has been used by others before you.'

'That's a hideous comparison.'

She pulled her hand out of his, scraping her chair against the floor to get up.

'Véronique, I wasn't serious.'

'You haven't lost anyone close to you, you don't understand.' She choked on her words and got up, knocking her chair over. Heads turned. The maestro had vanished. She stepped out of the ill-fated Ubu Re and into the deep Tuscan night. She almost ran. Tourists everywhere. Finally, she came to a small, quiet piazzetta with a well in the middle. She stopped to peer inside the well but there was an iron lid on top. She leant her elbows on the lid.

If memory was a country, this was its heart.

'Theo, do you know what you want?' she whispered that night.

'Yes.'

He turned on his side and embraced her.

The sliver of time in which his familiar lips pressed against hers was the flashing, deadly scythe that cut time in two. The same way her mother's phone-call in Istanbul had done a year ago. There was the half in which her father was alive, and the half in which he wasn't. The half in which she was in love with Theo and the half, freshly cut and beginning to bleed, in which she was out of love with him. And that would have been bearable, had they really been halves. But they were like the end of a snake's tail chopped off from the body, the two parts still writhing, trying to reconstitute themselves. The severance was irreversible.

Theo slept. She lay like a patient emerging from anaesthesia with the suspicion of an indefinite number of amputated limbs. She didn't dare move for fear of discovering the new, hideous boundaries of her life.

They stopped in Rome after all. At night, they tried to sleep above the hysterical orchestra of car-horns and hyperactive nocturnal crowds outside their window. During the day, they floated in a haze of heightened sights and sounds. Their lovemaking became viscously melancholic.

One hot morning, sitting listlessly with Theo in a café in the Piazza della Minerva, Véronique saw a tiny, clumsy figure in a corner of the piazza running after a pigeon. The child tripped several times until the pigeon, sensing the approaching danger, heaved itself obesely into the air. The tiny runner stopped, mystified by this sudden disappearance. A young man came over, picked her up effusively, covering the little face with kisses, and walked away. Véronique almost got up to follow them.

Because once, in a sunlit white piazza somewhere – she would never know where – Véronique, aged two or three, saw an attractive fat pigeon. The bird was mistrustful and ran faster than her, until it flapped its wings heavily and took off. She was upset. Her father turned her around and showed her a miracle: a piazza white with pigeons, all waiting for her. He showed her for the first time that there were no limits to what she could have. That nothing was ever lost. The Piazza della Minerva father didn't have the courage or the imagination to do that.

That was Véronique's father's gift to her, and his curse: the belief that everything was possible and within her reach. He tried to believe that himself until the end. He had been proven devastatingly wrong. Véronique couldn't reach out to these pigeons any more. She couldn't even reach out to the man sitting across the table who would respond instantly. There was no sense, no direction in all of this. All was lost before it had started.

Véronique suddenly lost control of her facial muscles and a shapeless sob came out of her throat, pushing two rivers of tears from her eyes. She covered her face with her hands, trying to muffle her sobs. Vaguely, she registered Theo get up and bend over her, put an arm around her convulsed shoulders.

'Véronique, Véronique.' Calling her out of a nightmare. She knew people were watching curiously. She got up and the pigeon-square spun. Theo kept an arm around her shoulders. As they stumbled away, he turned her drenched face to him, removing her sunglasses and wiping her tears. She could feel the fast beat of his heart. Rivers continued to flood her cheeks despite her best intentions. She wanted to say something to his bewildered face. That she loved him. That she was sorry but couldn't love him. That she didn't want to be here, that she didn't want to be anywhere, that she wanted him to go away but needed him never to leave her. That it was too late, too late, too late.

She cried on his shoulder for what felt to her like an absurdly long time, tears dripping inside his neck. In the hotel, she asked him to leave her and go to see the sights they had meant to see. He refused, angrily. She insisted.

'Véronique, I want to know.'

She told him.

He was silent. 'I'm sorry.' Then, after smoking in silence for a while, he said, 'At least you are facing it.'

'How do you mean?'

'You face your loss. Most people don't. I don't.'

'You have lost your grandfathers, both of them. I'd forgotten.'

'Not really. I never had them.' His voice became a staccato. 'But my family have lost so much that it has rubbed off on me and I keep ignoring it because I can't face it.'

She lay in the white linen of the bed where they hadn't slept for several nights now. She gripped his fingers with her ice-cold hand. He squeezed it and bent over her face. His neck was salty.

'I'm sorry I said you haven't lost anyone close to you,' she whispered. He kissed her eyes.

They didn't leave the room until the next morning. Holding each other behind closed curtains, they sank into the thick heat of the day like two millstones tied to the same drowning body.

TWENTY-NINE

July 1948

Markos was not in Pyrgos. But Illias was. As soon as they arrived, she saw him standing by the *vrisi* in the square, crouching next to some village women who were sitting by a case full of bullets, filling machine-gun bands.

'Illia!' She ran to his unshaven face lit up by the joy of surprise. He scooped her up, his bandolier digging into her chest. How could she tell him about Alexis . . .

'My little Dafinka, it's so good to see you! Where's Achilles?'

She waived her hand vaguely. 'I don't know. I'm not with the division. Are you moving on or staying?' She adjusted her cap over her fringe.

'We're staying. We have to set up positions on the peaks here.'

Pascal was behind her, waiting to be introduced. A few young men arrived with a message for the kapetanio, 'from the HQ'.

'This is Pascal Loublier, a French correspondent who's come to interview Markos. I was assigned as his guide.' She turned to Pascal. 'My brother Illias, known as Spithas because he's as quick as a spark.'

Illias shook Pascal's hand and his hard blue eyes rimmed with dark lashes examined the other man carefully. He smiled his beautiful smile, which made creases on the sides of his mouth. 'Welcome,' he said in

English and then switched to French: 'Malheureusement, Markos est parti. He goes away.'

'You speak French!'

Illias made a vague gesture – a trifle not worth mentioning. Daphne laughed and her laughter was somehow shrill. She was proud of Illias.

'He speaks Greek, Illia.'

'Oh!' Illias was impressed but preoccupied with his message. 'Excuse me a moment, I have to read this cable.' His face fell into a quick shadow.

'The government army attacked Smolikas six days ago. We have to start setting up our positions today.' He looked at Pascal. 'We must arrange for you to be taken up to Kastoria immediately and on to Thessaloniki. I'm afraid it's too late to look for Markos. God knows where he might be.'

'I'm staying.'

Daphne's triumphant pleasure equalled Illias's astonishment.

'I've come all this way, and I'm not going to sneak away at the mere sight of a gun.'

'But do you realise that we can't protect you here?' Daphne knew from the hue of Illias's eyes that he liked Pascal. 'This is war. It'll get ugly.'

'It's already ugly,' Pascal said. 'I know what war is.'

'Were you in the Résistance?'

'No,' Daphne chipped in, 'but he was at the same revolutionary newspaper as Camus!'

'You know Camus!'

'We were colleagues. I wanted to enlist in the Resistance, but they decided my health was too poor.'

'What's wrong with your health? You're tough as a mule!'

'I had tuberculosis when I was a child.'

'Like Camus,' Illias said dreamily, then snapped out of it. 'In any case, we'll have to make sure you don't get dragged into combat.' He paused in consternation – he knew this would be imposs-ible, everybody got dragged into combat, or hid in caves in the country.

'Illia,' Daphne said quietly, 'I have to tell you something.' His face suddenly knew.

'Illia . . .' She looked at him, hoping not to have to say it.

'Alexis, how is he?' he asked quickly.

'He . . . a few weeks ago they . . .'

'A mine?' Illias searched her face. She tossed her head back.

'Thank God.'

'They executed him.' She looked at the cobbled ground.

In his shock, Illias looked at Pascal. Daphne sat on the stone edge of the *vrisi* which gurgled joyfully, and unstrapped her rifle.

'He said that for every mule of foreign aid we get, the government army gets a shipload from America. But he died like a hero.'

Illias punched the low stone fence he had been leaning against. 'Why did he have to say that? Why?'

Pascal was washing his face in the *vrisi*, incidentally splashing cold water on her arms bared by rolled-up sleeves.

'I think the question you should be asking is why they executed him.' He straightened up, his face dripping.

'Were you there with him?' Illias asked, ignoring Pascal's comment.

'Yes. I buried him and put a mark on his grave.'

'Poor Alexaki. Poor Alexaki.' He crouched in front of Daphne who put her hands on his shoulders. He buried his head in her lap and, holding onto her, wept. She didn't weep. She just watched her tears fall heavily in his hair and stroked them away. Pascal went for a discreet stroll but a black dog leapt out at him furiously and he ran back to the *vrisi*. The village women with the machine-guns laughed and their laughter spilt on the cobblestones like bullets.

Illias showed them the headquarters in all their resourceful glory: barrels of salted lamb which they were never to taste; stacks of wool from which the village women would knit guerrilla socks for the winter; bottles of *mousto*, new wine; and literature for the education sessions: *The Communist Victory in the Chicago Strikes, The Ineffectiveness of the Atomic Bomb, Memories of the Spanish Civil War*, poetry by Mayakovski and Paul Éluard, Emil Zola's *Germinal*.

Daphne and Pascal worked beside the guerrillas and the peasants in the building of log-barricades for the machine-guns at the craggy tops, carrying boxes of ammunition and provisions up the hill. Exhaustion wiped them out before sunset and they collapsed at the foot of the hills.

'Now I know why they speak of Grammos as Slavo-communism's gravestone,' Pascal puffed.

'You don't have to do this, you know.'

'Do you suggest I sit in the shade and watch you labour up the hill?'

'Well, you could take notes!'

They fell into a happy though limited erotic tussle.

Illias would join them at the end of the day. The guerrillas slept inside the school and the church, but under Illias's orders, Pascal, as an honorary foreigner, was given a living room in a village house and Daphne, as his honorary guide, was given an adjoining room. The house was the mayor's. He had been shot by the guerrillas ('But not under my orders!' Illias stressed) for pro-government sympathies. Now only his wife and her daughter-in-law were living there. Her sons were in the government army. Her teenage grandsons and granddaughter were forcibly enlisted in the Democratic Army. The two women trod softly, dressed in black and somnambular with grief. Daphne and Pascal felt less than welcome. After the second night, Daphne moved to the church where she slept on the stone floor. Pascal moved there too.

'At least this way they can see we're not living in sin!' he explained unconvincingly.

'You could have moved to the school, at least.' But she was pleased. At night, when the last candle was blown out, they lay on their blankets, facing each other. His golden eye glowed like the gilded icons of saints above them. His hand looked for hers, his fingers stroked her palm and wrist. She was kept awake by this proximity. By the incredible suspicion that she alone might be the reason behind this strange Frenchman's sustained presence.

One night a few of them decided to sleep under the stars, on the hilly outskirts of the heavily patrolled village. They had eaten their meagre rations of bread and unsalted goat's cheese and drunk their tasteless mountain tea with a few crystals of sugar. Ouzo was sensibly kept for amputations and other emergencies. The fire was dying out. The rocky peaks enclosed them in a dubious, unpadded embrace. The air smelt of thyme. Daphne was drained from the sun and the exercise. Her head was on Alexis's shirt stuffed with fresh mountain herbs. Pascal sat beside Illias, sharing his few last Gauloises with him. Everybody else was sleeping, curled up or sprawled on jackets and blankets. Daphne was hypnotised by the twinkling of the stars, lulled by the presence of the two living people she most wanted to be with in the world. So much was missing from this night, so many. But even so, it was a strangely plentiful night. A night poised with inhuman grace between sensuality and sorrow. Pascal's gentle baritone and Illias's subdued bass played out a velvet, bilingual duet.

'In Camus's own definition, revolt is the only way to justice in a world where religious persecution has been replaced by political persecution,' Illias was saying. 'That's what we are doing. Notre révolte est une demande de justice, c'est tout.'

'But Camus also distinguished between revolt and revolution. The French Résistance was an instance of revolt. It was not well organised, it was based on a general liberal principle, not on ideology. It didn't achieve the overthrow of the pre-war social values. Whereas you have revolution here. It's based on some ideology, some dogma . . .'

'I don't know where revolt ends and revolution begins. Perhaps revolt grows into revolution when the society is ripe for it.'

'When the society admits extremes.'

'No, when the society has become conscious of a need for radical change.'

'Is Greek society conscious of that need?'

'Well, that's what the General Secretary Zachariadis says. He wants a revolution in the cities, not just in the mountains. And if there isn't enough consciousness, we must raise it. By an urban revolution.'

'It's too late. Or too early,' Daphne heard herself say from the depths of pleasant slumber. She was counting stars with closed eyes.

Two cigarette-lit faces turned to her, surprised.

'Dafinka, you're not sleeping?'

'It's too early because there's not enough urban proletariat for a socialist revolution,' she mumbled. 'And it's too late because the war is under way and it's a mountain war. The people are already polarised but not by social consciousness. By fear and desperation.'

She sensed them thinking and smiled contentedly.

'You're right,' Pascal agreed.

'No,' said Illias. 'There's no fear. The people are with us. The people want this revolution.'

'The people,' Daphne grumbled. 'Who are the people anyway . . .'

'Camus also warns against the dangers of revolution, what he calls its "prétension à l'éternel" – the tendency to sacrifice the individual to the ideal, to deny human realities in favour of an abstract idea.' Pascal's tongue groped for the right words. 'In other words, to become inhuman and, paradoxically, to become the thing itself that it fights against.'

Daphne and Illias thought about this.

'But surely the idea of justice will always keep revolutionary ideals in check,' Illias mused.

'If the idea of justice itself isn't turned into a dogma and becomes unjust,' Daphne said, thinking of Alexis.

Pascal nodded in the tiny, private fireplace of his cigarette.

Illias smoked in the moon-shadow of a brooding thought.

In the middle of the night she woke with a full bladder and stumbled up the hill behind some shrubs. She urinated upright in the black grass, as she had learnt to do in order not to expose herself to the dark probings of insects and snakes. A rustle startled her.

A male figure, familiar. She did up her trousers quickly.

'I thought you were a man,' Pascal whispered.

She was both relieved and embarrassed. 'That's the idea.'

'I'm impressed.'

'You just stood there watching me?'

'No, I kept you company.'

The grass was sharp, their bodies breathless, his smell intoxicating, his touch multiple and devastatingly precise, the night without end.

She would carry him with her from now on. This terrifying sensation flooded her, together with the first orgasm of her life. Inexplicable, slow tears dripped into her ears and she dug her teeth in his neck to staunch a sob. 'Mon amour. I can't believe I have met you,' he whispered.

Time was cut in two. She remained with him, on this side of a moonless July night, 1948.

She was still there when the new day struck them – a blow under which they reeled. When the desperate cry came 'Smolikas has fallen!', and then suddenly everybody including the peasants was rushing to the hills and the log-barricades and the machine-gun and shell-fire cut right through the days and nights until there were no days or nights, just a deluge of fire and the smell of phosphorus-burnt flesh and napalm-blackened rocks, just moon-bomb craters – their only cover. Until she learnt to sleep while firing at the waves upon waves of army soldiers sent up the hill straight to hell, because hell was where she was, up at the top where barricades collapsed and the Helldivers appeared, hungry and sleepless. She could no longer tell if she knew the limbs blown up on the rocks or the headless bodies, or the phosphorus-face which wailed at her until she ran, though there was nowhere to run, there wasn't even the shade of a tree. Cries came, 'Run to the north' and 'Run to Albania' and 'Die like heroes', and nobody knew which to do first, so some just leapt off the cliffs as in the times of the klephtic heroes. The people were victorious.

In the smoke nobody was Pascal or Illias, or anybody, except in a red flash she saw the surprise on the face of the French-speaking boy who gave his jacket to Pascal, the surprise when an explosion tossed him into the air and something landed that wasn't him. Daphne ran to Illias but Illias was far away like everything she had ever known, and she ran out of ammunition, *Would you rather talk about ammunition?*, and she ran out of life but she kept going, taking guns and bandoliers from the bodies which started to decompose in the sun because there was no time to bury them. And the sun which wasn't a sun but the god of war himself pounded them mercilessly, banging his shield against the white-hot worn-out anvil that was Greece and sparks flew, sparks,

Spithis, they were all crushed in between, banging, banging, with the planes pounding them from above. In the cacophony she heard a cry, 'Spithas is dead.' She ran so fast to wherever Spithas was that her heart fell out of her mouth but she had no time to pick it up, she didn't need a heart anyway, and she ran without legs and screamed without a voice. She tripped over and was kneeling in the gore of the open stomach of a girl guerrilla who had been lying there for days, and she retched though nothing came out, and she continued somehow though there was nowhere to continue. It was over.

People ran west towards Albania, people ran north towards Grammos, the people are with us, the people will be victorious. She ran towards Illias. Someone cried out 'Freeze!' and she realised everybody was lying on the ground with their faces pressed down because everybody was a dead body. But she couldn't freeze, no, she couldn't throw herself on the ground, no, it was too late, too early, even Camus would agree it was. So she stood at the top amidst the bodies and emptied at the plane overhead the magazine of a recently found Bren which made the plane rise and dive again at them, and then somebody cried 'Daphne, stop!', but she had no time to turn. Somebody ran towards her from an unknown place but she had no time for him, it was enough to know he could yell and run, so she emptied another magazine at the returning plane and another one, like in a dream from which nobody would wake up. And in that dream the plane went limp, a bird shot through the wing. It flew straight into the foot of the hill, bursting into brown flames and the corpses cheered. But Illias wasn't there to cheer. She ran to find him and someone ran behind her; she turned and Pascal crashed into her, his face black and ugly. 'Daphne, stop! You're wounded!', but she tore herself away because she couldn't stay in one place for more than a heartbeat of an absent heart. He ran after her but machine-gun fire cut between them and he remained on the other side to which she couldn't cross. She ran through the moonscape of bodies, they had all walked on the moon now, it had been a wondrous trip; down below the village was burning. Illias was lying on his back, a piece of shrapnel in his throat, his eyes open for he had had no time to close them, his eyes in which the blue sky of another summer had fallen. A summer

in which they went to Halkidiki for the first time and they jumped
from rocks and floated supine on the water warm like chicken soup,
and the sky shed two small but precious scales of itself into his eyes
where they were lodged ever since, rimmed in black, looking up now
at the sky which had gone quiet. She threw her gun away and lay next
to Illias who had been lying here by himself for some time and the
smell of his decomposing body was precious for it was the only thing
of his that lived on, and she found the medallion on his chest which
had their parents on one side – young, humourless and felicitously
retouched by the photographer, and on the other Daphne – long-
haired and inanely cherubic, a Daphne she didn't recognise . . .

Everything went quiet.

The chain was delicately broken on his hairy chest.

She fell into a dream in which she heard strange voices saying
strange things. The voices were coming from far away, perhaps from
the Albanian border, perhaps from the world of the living.

'Don't shoot,' one voice said, 'I'm a French journalist. I got trapped
in the battle.'

'Are you Pascal Loublier, the missing journalist? You're a lucky
bastard,' said a voice with an American accent.

'I'm looking for someone.'

'You're looking for someone! Everybody's dead, don't you see?
Have you been fighting along with the bandits?'

'I stayed behind because I'm looking for someone.'

'You've got friends among the bandits!'

'I have to find her and then I'll come with you.'

'Look buddy, you're coming with us now. We've been fighting
like dogs and lost a lot of men and you'd better go to Thessaloniki at
once or you'll stand trial.'

'Mind your own business. I'm looking for someone here.'

'He's shell-shocked. Get the doctor to give him an injection.'

'General, the doctor's busy with amputations.'

'Too bad. Shell-shocked or not, he's coming with us. This way,
Monsieur. You can get in my jeep.'

'I'm not going to follow anybody's fucking orders, least of all yours,
"General". As I said, I'm looking for . . .'

'March or I'll shoot you in the legs and you'll have to be carried on a stretcher!'

The voice was cut off by a manic laugh which blended into song:

Je suis tombé par terre,

C'est la faute de Voltaire . . .

'March!'

She wanted to say, 'I'm here, mon amour, agapi mou', but she couldn't – they were far away, at the Albanian border, over the hills, in the world of the living. He wouldn't hear.

Far below, truck engines started and a salvo was fired.

Time was cut in two. She remained with him, on this side of a moonless July night, 1948.

THIRTY

June 1998

One evening, in a street pizzeria in Naples, they were approached by a long-plaited woman with a scarf on her head. She simply came to their table and stared at Theo with her worn-out eyes. Then she stared at Véronique and said in Italian that she wanted to tell their fortuna.

'Non capisco, mi perdoni,' lied Véronique.

But the gypsy was resourceful: 'English.' She flashed a golden tooth.

'You.' She searched Theo's face, holding his hand. 'Big love.' He shifted uncomfortably. 'Big heart.'

A small audience was gathering around their table.

'Big . . .' A muffled laughter. Theo blushed. Véronique had a rush of something resembling love for him at that moment.

After inspecting Theo's face from an alcoholic close-up, the woman turned to Véronique with a less fond look. She pressed Véronique's fingers down to expose her long, narrow palm.

'You . . . Oooo' – the woman searched for the word, screwing up her face – 'mal, dolore . . .' – she gasped, pressing a hand to her monumental bosom. Véronique glanced at Theo. He was putting his sneering look back on, lighting a cigarette. The gypsy turned back to

him and, uncurling his hand, pressed her thumb over the soft flesh of
his palm. She did the same with Véronique's hand, using her other
hand. She closed her eyes. The audience held its breath. An inter-
minable moment passed before the mighty chest released its cargo of
divination. The eyes opened.

'Madonna Mia! Sangue!' She shook her head and put their wrists
across one another and rubbed them gently. Véronique and Theo
were startled despite themselves. Someone whistled feebly. The woman
pushed her chair back and got up with astonishing agility and a whiff
of urine. Theo put a 5000-lire note on the table. The woman cut the
air with her cracked hand and shook her head.

'No. No money per amore di sangue.'

She was then solicited by some of the onlookers whose payment
she promptly accepted. Theo and Véronique sat in front of their cold
pizzas.

'What a load of bullshit,' Theo said.

'She didn't take our money.'

'Yeah, for dramatic effect, to attract other customers.'

'She got some things right.'

'Like what?'

They left without finishing their dinner.

In the spacious, yellow-tiled bathroom of their hotel room,
Véronique contemplated the small heap of powder inside the carefully folded paper. She hadn't done it for at least a couple of weeks.
She rolled a piece of paper into a neat tube. Her nose tingled with
need.

Later, in the penumbra of their hotel room, she watched his face.
His nose, his cheeks, his lips were distorted fantastically by the
imminence of penetration. When he entered her smoothly, perfectly,
she didn't feel the usual shot of intense pleasure, but a distant stirring
as if her body were very long. He was still for a moment.

'What if I tell you that I take heroin?' she whispered.

His face was pressed against hers.

'What?'

She didn't reply. He resumed his movement at a slower pace and
whispered in her ear. 'So?'

'Would you snort it with me?'

'I'd swallow razor blades with you.'

'What was that about heroin?' he asked when he regained his speech. She hadn't come. She was floating dangerously close to telling the truth. He had the right to know. She had the right to unload herself.

'I was testing you.'

'Why do you need to test me?'

He peered into her face.

'Véronique, are you playing games with me?'

'No.'

'What are you doing with me?'

She said nothing.

'What are you doing with yourself?'

'You sound like the voice of conscience.'

'What is it that you want from . . . this trip?'

'I want to be surprised.'

'By what?'

'By myself. By you. By anything.'

'That's a lot of surprises.'

'I also want to forget.'

'What?'

'Maybe the same as you.'

He lay with his hands under his head. She lay on one side, her folded arm propping her head. The sea was far but impossible to forget.

'Where is love that with one stroke cuts time in two and stuns it?' Véronique quoted.

Theo didn't reply.

Capri hummed in the middle of the night like Naples' recurring dream. It was perhaps due to the proximity of the volcano that Naples always slept with one eye open.

Véronique just didn't have the nerves for Pompeii. The heat, the shadowless white dust, the screeching children from a local school, the

Americans dragging their pasty flesh around like luggage ('Jack, where is the actual Pompeii?') and, above all, the silent, eternally surprised dwellers of that moment two thousand years ago. The place was oppressive in every conceivable way. She longed for a cool hotel room in Capri with a view to the blue heat where she would be alone, far from everything, free to gather her straying thoughts like a dispersed flock and finally count them.

They parted company. Theo went looking for a wall inscription of an obscene poem by Catullus. She went looking for one particular wall with holes where the windows had once been. Standing in front of this wall, her father had said, 'Now imagine you slip your head through one of these holes, just for fun. When you want to move, you discover that you can't. You're stuck! Now, would they destroy a two thousand-year-old wall to retrieve your insignificant twentieth-century head?'

Véronique had to think about that. 'If you're in Greece they wouldn't,' she said. 'And in Australia, they wouldn't either, because they have no ruins there.' She was proud of her knowledge of other cultures.

'Correct, but you're in Italy.'

Her mother shook her head, dismissing the silly discussion altogether.

'So, would they instead cast you and add you to the human display? "And here, a person trying to escape through the window. Un-successful attempt."'

Even her mother laughed.

The wall with the two holes was still there. Fathers and daughters had died in this calamity. They were preserved for the centuries of voyeurs. Fathers and daughters, equally unconscious of their terrible plight, equally undead because so many walked past to scrutinise their death, the twisted jaws, the bent knees, the arms thrown in the air.

Theo's hands startled her. His breath on her neck.

'Did you find your wall?'

'Yes. It's right here. And did you find your obscene poem?'

'No. It's been censored.'

'Good. I wish I could censor my memory in the same way.'

'And I wish you'd cheer up.'

They had got to a stage where their sensitivity to each other's mood fluctuations had become unhealthy.

'We don't have to be always in the same mood, you know.'

'Oh, I wouldn't even dream of always! Just sometimes would be nice.'

'Nice! You're with the wrong person, mon petit.'

'Don't patronise me.'

'I'm going to look for shade. I might get the train back in fact.'

'Well, I want to see some more.'

'I'll see you at the hotel.'

Theo squinted at her, put his sunglasses on, hesitated for a moment, then kissed her lips laconically. His kiss stuck to her lips like flesh to ice.

She wanted to be somewhere else, someone else, to have never met Theo, to have never known Italy, to have never been the daughter of Alex Loublier and the granddaughter of Pascal Loublier.

'Tell me something about Alexander. Something interesting.'

It was mid-afternoon on Capri. She watched the heat make interesting shapes in the air and then unmake them like a child moulding forms from sand. They had stoically climbed the slanting, diminutive, perfect streets leading to the summit where Tiberius's Villa Jovis was. They were sitting outside the truncated walls of the giant square that had once been the imperial bathroom. The sea glittered through the flimsy trees.

'Everything about Alexander is interesting. This reminds me . . . my thesis, I've got to write it sometime. I just don't want to think about it.'

'You've got the rest of your life ahead of you to write it.'

'True.'

'Life is in front of us. We have all the time in the world. Etcetera. Actually, when you think about it, life is behind us. Before us, there is nothing. You are a scholar without a school. I am an Amazon without a bow.'

'Alas, Cassandra's prophecies were doomed to be scorned by her contemporaries.' Theo drained the remaining Coke. 'Do you know about the Gordian knot?'

'No,' she lied.

'Alexander was very ambitious. He was hell-bent on untying the famous Gordian knot in the city of Gordium, in Phrygia, where Midas had come after being exiled from the Precinct of the Nymphs – where we drove – and become king of the Phrygians. Midas had arrived in a sort of chariot which had a yoke tied to a pole with a knot of vine twig. Now, nobody could untie this knot, it didn't seem to have any ends, it was a mystery. Alexander had *pothos*, or yearning, to untie it. It was rumoured that whoever solved the Gordian problem would rule Asia. There are two versions of how Alexander dealt with this. One is that he pulled out the dowel to expose the ends of the rope and pull the knot apart. The other, more popular version is that, frustrated by the impossible task, he pulled out his sword and slashed the knot in two.'

'And did he rule all of Asia?'

'No.'

'Because he didn't solve the problem properly.'

'Because he drank himself to death.'

A swarm of young children flew past them, chirping, followed by a flock of bovine, sandwich-munching parents.

'Do you know that we're standing very close to the rock from which Tiberius liked to have people thrown into the sea?' Theo enquired.

'Yes.'

'Do you know about the fisherman who caught this huge fish and climbed all the way to the palace to present it to the emperor, who proceeded to have him dumped into the sea for having dared reach his palace?'

'No.'

Véronique was lying on the grass, looking at the flawless blue sky. When she sat here with her father, waiting for her mother who had gone for a pee, the sky suddenly packed up and a brisk, childish shower irrigated the island. A local man ran past them in search of shelter. 'Bruto tempo!' he shouted apologetically, as if he himself had botched up the weather. Véronique and her father exchanged puzzled looks before bursting into laughter. Bruto tempo! Now she couldn't see what had seemed so funny about it.

'You're so good at not being where you are, you know,' Theo said.

'Which means I'm very bad at being anywhere at all.'

'I don't know about that, but you're getting less good at being in the same place as me.'

'I think we need to spend some time apart. We've been together how long? Five, six, seven weeks?'

'It doesn't feel that long.'

She didn't reply.

'We're not together all the time, I mean we do our own thing sometimes . . .' he began.

She sat up.

'Are you bored with Italy?' he enquired.

'No.'

'You're bored with something else.'

'Theo, I am not bored.'

He got up with a heaviness unfamiliar to her and held out his hand for her, as if she was an old woman.

At night, Capri became a fantasy island with dark alleys where white washing hung outside peeling buildings and tourists in white T-shirts strolled in a heavy-lidded trance. Véronique and Theo exhausted the walks of the island in a few days and she left him to his own devices. She would have a snort in the hotel room and sit in the Giardini d'Augusto where she listened to the ever-approaching sea in a trance of heightened sound, in an infinity shattered with possibility like a mirror maze. She floated down its corridors and saw many Alexes, many Theos, many Michel Franchittis, many Paulines. Only Pascal was hiding his reflections behind one another, skilful bastard that he was. Everybody was looking for him but they all kept crashing into each other and their own multiple reflections. Finally, she realised with a shock of relief, like a tidal wave washing the shore of all the summer's impurities, that Pascal didn't exist.

Never had existed. He was the stranger in each one of those

wandering figures and they were really looking for the fiction of themselves. Pascal was the man who never disappeared because he never lived. Véronique wanted to yell to them to stop searching, but her voice was sticky like chewing-gum and however she kept pulling it and attaching it to invisible hooks in the warm air, it never reached them. Besides, after a while she realised with bewilderment that all she was saying was 'Stop Midas! Stop Midas!' She wasn't sure whether she meant it as an imperative to Midas or to those who ought to stop Midas.

When she returned to the hotel at night, she would leave the lights in the room out, so that Theo wouldn't see her unnaturally small pupils.

It happened unexpectedly on their second night in the Villa des Marées in Nice. After Theo went to sleep, Véronique had a snort outside on the balcony, in one of the old chaises longues Grandmother Pauline had loved. She yearned for Diane the Alsatian to trot her way, warm and lethargic. Down by the sea, a giant lit-up Ferris wheel turned slowly – or perhaps the night turned around it. Perhaps time wasn't chopped in two by the scythe, but rather fell onto the scythe and immolated its wholeness. Perhaps Pascal was still alive somewhere, breathing with his worn, white-haired chest in a sticky Levantine night, holding a cane or a whisky or a woman.

Suddenly she realised how hard it was to tell the alive from the dead, to see where one ended and the other began, to catch the moment in which the severance occurred and the two uneven parts forked from the whole. The moment in which the object froze under Midas's touch. The moment in which Pascal disappeared and her father died, and Theo tumbled out of her love. There must be a line which had to be overstepped in order to pass into that other dimension of non-life, non-love, non-future, non-language. She searched for the line, but the night was perfectly smooth and her fingers, far away from the rest of her, tingled with its absence.

When she finally went to bed and became a many-legged bug creeping somewhere along the edge of sleep, she felt a hand grope her breasts. This was odd. She heard a moan – this was odd too.

Then a light split her head in two.

'Sorry.' Theo was looking at her breasts with an odd urgency. He felt her breasts with relief, as if they might have run away while he was sleeping. He was breathing heavily. He looked at her. His face was covered in a thin film of sweat, his pupils were large and frantic, he actually had a squint. She could see his pulse beating madly under his naked skin. He stared at her.

'Your pupils . . . where've they gone?' He was leaning over her face. She covered her eyes with a hand.

'I had a nightmare,' he mumbled, 'I'm sorry to wake you up.' He wanted to say many things at once. He turned the light off. They lay in silence for a while.

'I had this nightmare,' he said. 'I was trying to find your breasts with my hands and couldn't. I opened my eyes to look for them, and they weren't there. There was a smooth surface, completely flat, where your breasts should be. I wanted to scream, but you know, in dreams you can't. You'd cut off your breasts. I asked why, why, why did you do it, but you just looked at me with this weird look, oh . . . God . . .' He shuddered and she felt him bury his head in a pillow.

The stroke that cut time in two. She suddenly knew why she had done it in his dream. Even in other people's dreams, she was so much more focused, so much more fearless than in reality. She actually *did* something in dreams.

She stroked the sweat from his brow, comforting a brother.

When they woke up, she felt sick. She had probably had too much heroin though normally there shouldn't be a hangover effect. Her stomach was upset, her head was leaden. Theo lay prostrate, staring at the ornate ceiling, his limbs all over Pauline's embroidered cream sheets, his face sweaty. Yet another glorious Riviera day reached through the blinds like fingers pushing through bars.

They lay at each end of the giant bed, a love-shaped gap between them.

'Véronique.'

'Yes.'

'I had a nightmare.'

'I know.'

'Your eyes had no pupils.'

'It wasn't a dream.'

'I know.'

Eventually, he got up with an effort and went out without a word. She didn't see him all day. She had another snort to dull the queasy panic and sat in the balcony chaise longue in the mute but loyal company of Diane the Alsatian, Grandmother Pauline, Pascal and Michel Franchitti. Her father would arrive any moment now. Everybody was pleasantly expectant.

When Michel Franchitti left and Grandmother Pauline retired to her bedroom, Véronique sneaked into the lounge, took a chocolate from the tray on the low table, fed another one to Diane, and looked at the xeroxed passport page. It had a man's face on it, pleasant-looking, kind of old, but not as old as a grandfather. This was Pascal. She touched it. And suddenly it wasn't. The name under the photograph wasn't Pascal Loublier. It was somehow the reverse of Pascal Loublier. She strained but couldn't read it. It was glazed over with afternoon heat.

She walked down the wide, affluent avenues with façades thrust forward like lavish, adorned bosoms. When she reached the Corniche, she got the elevator to the castle walls.

And there she was, the mad old woman in diamonds and gumboots, reaching into her slimy bucket, her head shaking uncontrollably, her greasy lipstick the colour of dead sunsets. She hadn't changed in twenty years. 'Come on, my little ones,' she croaked to the giant birds, ugly and bloodthirsty like vultures, 'eat up, eat up.'

Véronique sat on a bench facing the serpentine coast lined with palm trees and traffic. She finally understood the mad woman with the gulls.

THIRTY-ONE

August 1948–June 1949

For a few weeks, Pascal was treated for 'concussion and mild shell-shock' in Paris. His speech was slurred and his memory confused. He suffered from mouth-drying headaches.

He became a celebrity. Journalists came to the hospital. Communist figures, including Picasso and the poet Paul Éluard, came to shake his hand. Pascal faced the prospect of becoming an honorary communist. At first, he tried to explain that communism was quite beside the point, that something else fuelled the common Greek guerrilla, that it was much more complicated, that it went back to the world war, to the aftermath of the newly carved Europe, to the foreign queen, to unresolved ethnic tensions. But his thoughts were slurred like his words, leaving a humid trail that repulsed him. Then he refused to give interviews altogether. He was keeping everything for his book.

'But if you want to help the guerrillas, you should speak up,' Michel Franchitti pointed out, ever so slightly sceptical.

'Michel, don't patronise me. You know they're beyond help. They were vastly outnumbered by the army. The sooner it ends, the better. They have been fed too many deadly illusions as it is.'

'And so has the French Communist Party.'

'Whatever I say, the PCF's illusions will be intact.'

Michel brought the Greek news for Pascal. After eight weeks of kamikaze resistance against the government army, which outnumbered them by ten to one but which also perished en masse, the rebel survivors had crossed into Albania. Markos was among them and had been criticised by the General Secretary Zachariadis of the KKE who had 'differences' with him concerning strategies.

'I told you last year, didn't I. They were doomed from the start. This split in the leadership is fatal, quite apart from the superiority of the national army and Van Fleet.'

'And I never disagreed with that. It's just that . . . I saw the human face of doom.'

'I know.' Michel knew. Michel had seen that face too. But not *that* face, the pale face with coal eyes and a ruffled black fringe which shone at Pascal like a private, twenty-four-hour moon from the other side of a July night.

Pauline was not so much a stranger as an unaccountable part of what had evidently been his world until a few months ago. He couldn't account for finding her next to him in bed, red-haired and voluptuous in her satin top, for the mornings with croissants and café au lait, for the walks along the Seine, for the mellow autumn of Paris which she fitted with undeniable grace. She had just turned thirty and he had forgotten her birthday. She asked about Greece in a language that made him feel like someone with a mistaken identity pushed onto a stage to deliver a concerto on an instrument he had seen but never touched before. He would start telling her and then realise he was playing a jumble of notes that made no sense. He went to the places he had frequented before, made the habitual movements he had made before, even looked the same as before, only thinner. But he was not there.

At night, he lay next to Pauline, his nostrils invaded by her scent, looking at the moon, uncomprehending how this could be the same moon which had shed rust on the three of them and the two mules ahead braving the desolate crags, the moon under which he had made love to Daphne, under which so many had been butchered.

He gradually learnt to distinguish Pauline's anger from her pity, but not her love from her ignorance. If she knew truly how changed he was, she would perhaps stop loving him. That was perhaps what he hoped she would do. Because he could never tell her what he would have liked to tell her. He couldn't make love to her, though he tried, dutifully. She cried discreetly and unobtrusively, finally realising that he was unable to help her just as she was helpless in the face of his trauma. Alex was the only thing from his previous life which didn't seem absurd, though Alex didn't seem to be of the same opinion about the stranger who behaved as if he were his father. The child was attached to Michel Franchitti who had looked after him and Pauline as if they were his own. During his time in the hospital, they visited him together, the three of them, and one day Pascal was startled to see a perfect family – Pauline a red-haired, statuesque beauty, Alex her lookalike with his freckled, delicate features, Michel a guardian angel with protective hands and loving green eyes.

Le Monde had the grace not to fire Pascal after his embarrassing behaviour in Greece, but he left anyway and went to spend some time by himself in Marseilles. Le Vieux Port and the picturesque, once bustling and infamous suburb north of it had been defaced by the Germans in 1943. Reconstruction was under way. The central city was depressed and Pascal stayed within the relative idyll of the Maldormé area.

He began to assemble his notes for the future book. His headaches were like a mute companion who sat in a corner of his head and would have spoken to him if he could. He sat for hours, sometimes entire afternoons, by the window, watching the mistral rape the sea and assault le Château d'If on its rock island, the person in his head thinking of so much that Pascal had to go to sleep or alternatively go outside and be crushed against a wall by the wind. He looked at the photographs he had taken. Daphne was there too, among the guerrillas, dark and sharp like one of her quips. He sat on the ground himself and looked cross-eyed and vaguely Greek. Illias smiled his broad, devastating Jean Marais smile, his arm around his sister's shoulders, bandolier on his chest. He would have been a film-star in another life.

Pascal read and reread the undelivered blood-letter of Angelis Philipidis. After being taken by the army to Thessaloniki, Pascal was asked to leave Greece at once, under threat of arrest. Nobody seemed overjoyed to see him, except some of his reporter colleagues. The Minister of Order greeted him in Athens with an irony-free 'So, you are the French George Polk'. The French embassy, facing accusations of supporting the communists through its correspondents, was embarrassed and would rather pretend he didn't exist. He hadn't been able to make the trip to Edessa.

He cleaned Alexis's boots and polished them with the excessive fussiness of impotence. He glanced across at the rock islands and saw a ghostly Kallistos hopping on crutches, half a goat-boy. *Apollo, Apollo, don't run after Daphne for she will turn into a tree and you will mourn her forever.*

Pascal felt impoverished beyond endurance.

His mother dropped by regularly and, after pottering about anxiously and cooking for him, she would leave in despair, kissing him and saying, 'My boy, what has happened to you!' The editor-in-chief of *Le Monde* sent him a letter full of solicitude and expressing a strong desire to see him return to his post. Pascal replied that he needed another year away from the paper. Michel Franchitti came to visit him in the winter.

'I know something happened there which you don't want to tell anyone about. I know you are in a lot of pain. You need help, my friend, and you need to help yourself, not to shut yourself down here all alone like you're in the bloody Château d'If.'

Pascal was torn between telling him about Daphne and lying that he was fine. Instead, he surprised himself by saying: 'What I need is to go back and find what I lost.'

Michel shook his head. 'That's not funny. It's not funny at all.' He looked away from his friend and gazed out at the ruffled sea. 'What is it that you lost anyway, apart from your joie de vivre?'

'I don't know. It's difficult to know here, it's another world.' Pascal too was looking at the sea as if it would deliver an answer to all questions, ever.

'I was there myself, I know what it's like.'

'You weren't in the mountains, in the carnage.'

'I know that. I also know that you got caught in somebody else's

war and can't afford to fall apart because of it or because your
professional pride has been wounded by the fact that some guy from
the *New York Herald-Tribune* eventually managed to take an interview
with Markos and you didn't!'

'Michel, I don't give a damn about the Markos interview.'

'Well, I find it increasingly hard to know just what you give a
damn about. You have a life here, a family you didn't see for almost a
year, a country which also suffered a great tragedy and is slowly
picking itself up. I mean, look at Marseilles, look at the ruins! You
must begin to pick yourself up. Your prolonged despondency strikes
me as illogical and somehow . . . selfish. And, above all, you are
causing Pauline a lot of pain.'

Michel was so right. Pascal's head felt like an empty seashell on
one of Marseilles' desolate beaches, the mistral blowing through it,
the sea-swell never close enough to take it back.

Pascal followed closely the news from Greece. The rebels were
trickling back across the border, rebuilding their forces. There were
varyingly abortive rebel attacks on towns in the north. In December
and January, Naoussa was held by rebels for five days and Karditsa for
two weeks, the government army delayed by snowstorms. Was she
there, in the bitter blizzards, dynamiting bridges and building road-
barricades, her lips raw with cold and hunger? These were the last
battles in the mainland before the bulk of the rebel force withdrew
to their stronghold along the Albanian border. In January, Operation
Pigeon flushed the Peloponnese of over three thousand rebels with
an efficiency that won the government army general the nickname
'second Ibrahim Pasha'. Was she there, a frail captive prodded by
soldiers, or hiding in an icy cave, her boots disintegrating and her
feet frost-bitten beyond recognition? On 27 January, radio 'Free
Greece' broadcast a peace offer, its terms being the departure of the
American military mission, a general amnesty, the restoration of trade
unions and political freedom, and a new government of compromise.
The offer was immediately and contemptuously rejected. The
redoubtable Markos was announced by radio 'Free Greece' to be 'very
ill'. In February, there was a foolhardy attack on Florina in which

over a thousand rebels were killed or captured. Was she there, her corpse frozen on the hills, or sitting dejectedly in one of those cages they used for mass trials of guerrillas?

He knew that if he told Michel about Daphne, Michel would think for a while and then say, 'What makes you think she's alive in the first place?' and Pascal wouldn't have a sane answer to this. His hope was as frail as a flash of a girl guerrilla running down the craggy hill, her left arm limp from a wound, a rifle on her back, a brown cap on her cropped hair. It could have been a boy. It could have been someone else. But it was her. She had made it to Albania. She was alive and had all her limbs. She was not lying among the decomposing corpses on the hills.

Summer was the army's time, just as winter was the season of the guerrilla. The next major attack on the rebels could not be far away. It would be the last.

When, at the end of May, Paul Éluard and a couple of other French communists asked Pascal to be their guide to Greek guerrilla territory on their way to the Prague Congress, Pascal declined. He had his own agenda.

Arriving back in Paris and seeing Pauline check her joy at his return made his heart sink. She was ready to forgive him, if only he would let her. At dinnertime, Alex would ask after Michel. Pascal felt like a visitor. When he told Pauline that he was off on a trip to Sofia for the centenary of a Bulgarian national poet (which had in fact been celebrated the year before), he could see that she hesitated between sending him back to the hospital and hating his lie.

'Via Greece?' she enquired, lighting up a protective cigarette with a trembling hand.

'No. Via Prague.'

'Do whatever you like. I won't be expecting a telegram.'

Her pain was so palpable that Pascal sat next to her and took her hands.

'I will be gone no more than two weeks.'

'Whatever. But don't be surprised if Alex doesn't recognise you when you return.'

'What are you saying?' But he knew what she was saying. He kissed her knuckles and wondered about Michel.

The night before he left, elated by his imminent departure and touched by Pauline's beauty, he made love to her, with tenderness which was pity, with passion which was guilt. It was his apology, and the most eloquent way to avoid saying some truth or some lie. She responded with the generosity and fervour that she had kept intact for him, despite everything.

In the morning, Alex was huddled beside Pauline. Two luminous redheads, entire constellations of freckles sleeping on their faces. He was a stranger in this bed.

THIRTY-TWO

July 1998

Véronique started using every other day. She turned sex down. Theo pretended to act normally but his movements became stiff, as if a fine mechanism had been wound up inside him. His face became shuttered like their luxurious and stagnant bedroom, although the light still filtered through. They saw each other only at night, often eating separately, or rather he eating in town where he spent most of the time and she not eating at all. They spoke little. Véronique was surprised at his non-confrontational approach. After a week, though she didn't have a clear sense of the passing of time, he said he wanted to go to Monaco. Véronique wanted to head for Marseilles. They argued listlessly.

'Oh, I don't care where we go!' Theo finally shouted in exasperation. 'You're just as unhappy wherever we go. It doesn't matter where we go any more, does it!'

Véronique was making the bed, which had been unmade and loveless for days. She stopped, looked at him and had nothing to say.

'Your hair goes nicely with the sheets,' he said sadly.

'Theo, I know I haven't been much fun recently, and I –'

'No, you're fine. It'll be fine. I understand.' He raised his hands to ward off an unbearable confession. 'And we don't have to go to

Monte Carlo, I don't care. I'd much rather see Marseilles anyway.'

She sat on the edge of the bed. She knew she had lost weight, from using. She knew he was looking at her with a mixture of pity, panic and perplexity. He sat next to her and lit a cigarette.

'I know you're sniffing dope. You should've told me earlier. I mean you should've told me full stop.'

'I didn't want to upset you.'

'Upset me! I'm upset now!'

They sat next to each other on the edge of the bed, looking out at the distant stripe of blue framed by two robust palm trees outside the window. Véronique was reminded of the couple on the ferry – thigh by thigh, placid, sexless. Pleasantly dead. Is that what they were turning into? She put a hand on his thigh and squeezed it. He nuzzled at her ear.

'Tell me a story about your home-town.'

'Melbourne? I can't think of any stories about Melbourne. But I'll tell you one about Ohrid, where my grandmother lives.' He was relieved to have something to latch onto and so was she.

'Lake Ohrid shimmers in a peculiar way. According to one story, the shimmer dates back to the eleventh century when Tzar Samuil of Ohrid sent his troops to seize the much coveted Constantinople, but the Byzantine emperor Basil took them to task. He had the fifteen thousand prisoners blinded and left a single one-eyed man per hundred blinded men, to lead them home. When Tzar Samuil saw his returning army of fifteen thousand blinded soldiers, he died of heartbreak. But before he died, he sent back for the eyes to be collected, and had them placed in a golden casket which was then dropped in the lake.'

'So the lake isn't so good for swimming.'

He laughed shortly, nervously. It was the first laugh this house had heard in years and the last one it would hear for years to come.

She unlocked the heavy door of Villa Maldormé. It didn't creak, which was disappointing, but the rest of the house was suitably ghostly – dust coating every susceptible surface, the curtains and blinds shut tight, the smell of abeyance reaching that delicate point

where a house becomes a former house. No one had set foot here
for more years than Véronique could count. The water in the
bathroom sink had leaked in a rusty streak across the porcelain basin.
The tail of a dead mouse stuck out from under the sitting room
couch. But the view from the large windows was serenely unaffected
by rot, its blue simplicity specked with white.

The iron bed in the master bedroom upstairs was not comforting.
Some of the upstairs' windows were nailed shut and covered with
ugly brown lids. Weeds and cats infested the backyard, which was
delineated by a low whitewashed fence, although there was no need
to mark a boundary. There was a natural boundary – the cliff edge
below which there was simply the sea. The concrete steps leading
down to what had once been a landing but was now covered by
shallow water were eroded.

'I'd rather jump,' Theo said.

'You'll break your head, it's shallow.'

'I didn't say dive, I'm not brain-dead.'

There was a boulangerie on the main road, rocks to jump from
further down the coast, a tiny fishing boat harbour, Foreign Legion
barracks, and their lives curling ahead of them like endless rolls of
developed film left in the sun. What more could they want?

Véronique couldn't remember coming to this house at all. After
Pascal's disappearance, it was locked up and only her father might
have come once or twice in thirty years.

The novelty of the Villa Maldormé and Marseilles kept them in a
simulation of healthy liveliness for a week or so – especially Theo,
who was determined not to allow another descent into despondency
and gloom. Véronique had to find a reliable channel for good heroin
which she did at the Marché des Saracens. She had never done this.
In Istanbul, where she started half-heartedly on heroin, and in
Thessaloniki, where she continued, she had respectable contacts who
brought good-quality heroin to her apartment; consequently, she
didn't have the necessary know-how. When the fidgety Tunisian asked
her to come and collect it at night, in a shady central suburb, she said,
'How about I pay you a bit more and choose the place of meeting.
The Opera Square.'

'Are you kidding me, Mademoiselle? We may as well make it the police station. That place is crawling with cops. I don't know how you do it in Paris, but here . . .'

Véronique wasn't going to be intimidated.

'There's a café in the square, it's next to a brothel . . .'

'L'Opéra? Not my first choice but just for you, Mademoiselle.' He sighed dramatically. 'There was a shooting there last week, two cops were killed, chasing some Ukranian Mafia guys . . . And we'd better make it a grand.'

'I'll have to see the stuff first,' she said.

That night, she and Theo went to a restaurant in the Vieux Port, around the corner from the designated café. They had the thick and malodorous local bouillabaisse. She didn't tell him until five minutes before the rendezvous.

'What? A dealer?'

'Don't shout.'

Theo was lost for words.

'I . . . What are you doing to yourself? That's a fucking addiction you've got!'

People started to turn.

'Look, I'm only snorting, I'm not shooting up.'

'Oh yeah! So that's fine. But the way you're going, you'll be soon looking for veins. I can't believe you're doing this!'

'I've got to go.'

'I'm coming with you.'

'No, don't. I'll be back in a few minutes. Wait here, I'll be fine.'

Theo gripped her wrist painfully.

'Let me go, I'll be fine.'

'You're not going anywhere.' He shook his head, his eyes flaming with grim determination.

People were enjoying this. It looked as if she was trying to leave him. She kept pulling her wrist but he had an iron grip on it. She sat back in her chair.

'I'm sorry for hurting your wrist but that's a minor injury compared with what you're about to do.'

'You're just so bloody . . . righteous, Theo! Everything's so simple in your world! Healthy mind, healthy body, healthy bloody . . . everything.'

'Should I apologise? Watch you stuff your system with vile chemicals and kill your brain? And walk around with eyes like a zombie?'

'You don't understand.'

'I *do* fucking understand!' Her wrist was going numb. 'I'm not a retard. You're in pain, your father's death . . .'

'I don't want to hear that. I know that.'

'But I want you to hear it. Because you treat me like some half-wit, like I don't know what's going on, that –'

A large, imposing figure on crutches separated itself from the conspicuous group of fair young men sitting at the next table. They had soldiers' haircuts. The man had a striking face. He turned to Véronique and spoke in French: 'Mademoiselle, is he being a pain?' His accent was thick and she caught a whiff of heavy duty alcohol, perhaps vodka. His eyes were a pristine blue and he had a blond stubble. His short-sleeved shirt was neatly done up.

'No, it's fine.'

Theo released her wrist which had turned white under the pressure of his fingers. The man retired to his table. His brothers in arms, who had looked on, slapped him on the back approvingly. Theo and Véronique were alone face to face again. She got up and simply walked away. To her surprise, he didn't rush after her.

The Tunisian was waiting outside the Café Opéra. They went into a dark alley filled with the stench of an overdue rubbish bin. Her heart beat faster as she tasted the powder. It was good. She gave him the cash and stuffed the packet under her naked sole in the reliable sports shoe. He left without even coming on to her, weedy legs carrying him further into the putrid dark alley.

Theo was standing at the corner.

'Did you follow me?'

'Let's go home,' he said.

She felt responsible but wanted him just to go away. As they went past the restaurant, the crop-haired bunch were leaving. The giant with the crutches saw them.

'Ça va?' he enquired chivalrously.

'Ça va,' she smiled despite herself. Theo was not impressed. At that point, she identified the feature that made the soldier's face striking, apart from his glazed-over ultramarine eyes. His mouth: bright, almost feverish, its corners curling downwards in a failed attempt at scorn.

'Skinheads,' Theo mumbled.

'They're from the Foreign Legion. Our neighbours.'

'Great.'

They walked in silence. Drunks and strollers littered the Corniche. The sea was ruffled by the warm wind.

'When did you start taking . . . this stuff?' Theo asked.

'A year or so ago.'

'When your father died?'

'Just before.'

It was strange – he was the adult, she was the delinquent youth.

'Why do you do it?'

She thought about her answer carefully.

'It makes me less unhappy.'

'Okay, I understand.' The academic in him, systematic, rational.

'Will you please stop saying you understand?'

'You want me to say I don't understand? Okay, I don't understand but I'm trying to.' Exasperation leaked into his voice.

'I don't expect you to.'

He stopped and looked at her. There was violence lurking in his civilised body that she had never sensed before. But he suppressed it and lit a cigarette, leaning against the railing.

'Can't you think of something else to do to make yourself less unhappy?'

'Yes, of course.' She was surprised to hear her upbeat voice. 'I have. It doesn't work.'

'You're basically a dreamer, aren't you?'

Véronique thought about this. 'I'm a realist. Of alternative realities.'

'That's much of a muchness.'

The Slavic division from the restaurant trudged past them, sneering. The cavalier with the crutches nodded to her and limped on. She noticed that he was stepping on both legs.

'Your friend.'

She leant her elbows on the railing, facing the sea. A film of detritus had gathered in the shallow water by the promenade. Le Château d'If was fabulously lit up. Traffic flowed by incessantly, horns tooted. High-pitched, brittle laughter rang and shattered like a bottle smashed on the pavement.

'It's not the same,' Véronique said. 'The dreamer knows where he wants to be. And I . . . there is no place where I want to be.'

He shook his head and crushed the cigarette butt with more vigour than was necessary.

In the Gothic iron bed, Theo put his hand on Véronique's throat. She didn't budge.

'Do you know that when stranglers start strangling their victim, they can't stop. Even if they want to, they can't. It's a compulsion.' His fingers tightened their grip around her neck, just as they had around her wrist.

'Is this a threat?' She wasn't even curious. She just wanted him to go away. She wanted everything to go away.

He fell back on his pillow and punched the wall behind with a fist. His joints cracked.

'I can't threaten you. You're beyond threats. You're beyond . . . I don't know, just beyond.'

She didn't reply. She was quickly running out of words. She simply had nothing to say. In the night, he tasted her collar-bone, her ear, between her legs. She felt too indifferent even to repulse him.

In the morning, she heard him speaking on the phone downstairs, in Greek. He'd called Uncle Panayotis and disclosed the real nature of his trip. Panayotis wasn't shocked. He had expected it.

'All will be well,' Theo concluded vaguely and grinned. An intense pity flooded her. She put her arms around his waist. He pressed her to him. This was the convulsive grip of fear, the stiff-armed intelligence of doom.

In the early evening, she sat alone on the rocks outside the Foreign Legion camp, beside the sign 'Military grounds, nasty dog', hoping guiltily to hear the tap of crutches behind her. But he didn't come.

The next ten days trudged past. Eventually she met, exchanged awkward pleasantries and shook hands in ridiculous formality with the legionnaire. His name was Victor. His legs, from the thigh down, were prosthetic. A television crew was doing a documentary on the Foreign Legion and Victor was going to be the star. Véronique snorted only every second day – on the days when she didn't see him. Theo travelled out of Marseilles, by himself, on the bus. He went to unremarkably pretty towns nearby like Aix-en-Provence and Cassis, and returned sweaty, attractively tanned and confused.

Véronique began her modest and intermittent agony between guilt and insurmountable irritation, affection and annoyance, need and oversaturation.

One night, she went drinking with Victor at the Vieux Port. He had five shots of double vodka.

'When a legionnaire get malaria or other sickness, medical helicopter comes. But to land we must clear landing ground in jungle. Tough. We cut trees the size of room, then split them in two, like this, and lie them down next to each another, to make even surface for helicopter. Shit, what sweat! It must take six hours, but it take two days. When trees come down, all bugs livin' inside come out and fall on our heads. When they attack, you must freeze 'cause they love movement. If you move, whole team is fucked. Sorry. I swear too much.'

Véronique smiled, strangely delighted. His girlfriend was coming in a couple of weeks, to pick him up and take him back.

'If you're thirty percent disabled, you can go home or stay in legion, your choice. I stay in legion for three years after accident in Bosnia. But I'm hundred percent disabled. Now time to go home.'

They took a taxi on the way back, his crutches between them.

Theo was lying on the couch with the lights out, smoking. Without a word, he unrolled a white scroll and, in the darkness, the woman with the shapeless nose from the Capella dei Principi stared at her accusingly. 'Someone got lucky,' Theo said, cavernously.

Véronique watched the portrait curl on the floor like a body punched in the stomach.

She went to sit outside on the patio. At least three pairs of cats' eyes watched her from among the weeds. Le Château d'If was resplendent in its ruins. There was no point to all of this. No direction, no sense. They were supposed to be moving, travelling, experiencing the world and each other for the first time. She knew in her bones that they weren't going to make it any further. This was their final destination. This was the wall they would never climb. She would sit in the shadow of the wall. She would break Theo's heart despite herself.

Theo's steps crunched towards her. He stopped beside her and kicked the stone on which she was sitting. He gasped with pain.

'Just tell me what you want!' His words were bruises on the skin of the night. 'Just fucking tell me so that I know. Because I don't understand. It doesn't make any sense to me. You don't make any sense to me.' He kicked the stone again, with his other foot.

She got up unhurriedly and faced him. He reeked of tobacco, his face fierce with frustration. A wave of despair lapped at her. Her limbs felt limp, her heart too.

'I don't want anything. It doesn't make sense to me either.' She spoke in a calm, choked voice. She had to get it right this time – that was the least she could do for him. 'We're not going anywhere. This is it, Theo. We've arrived.' She gestured in the direction of the sea where le Château d'If winked at them. 'I've just realised. I wish it could be different. I'm sorry, I don't know what else to say.'

He paced towards the edge of the yard, peered down at the black water.

'Something's happening to my mind. It's like the world is shrinking around me, around us, like there's nowhere left to go and we can't move from here. It's like being frozen in a terrible spell.'

He walked back to her. He grabbed her shoulders, touched her face, peered into it as if it was black water. He punched the whitewashed wall. His fingers cracked. Whitewash crumbled. She closed her fingers over his fist. Peels of skin folded back painfully.

'Do you want me to leave?'

'You're free to leave if you want.'

She kissed the blood from his grazed knuckles. It was the Kiss

again, or some edited version of it. He sat on the much-kicked stone
and pulled her to him. She straddled him. For the first time in fifteen
days (he had counted them) they made love – with the crazed,
exaggerated movements that signal the mutation of passion into
desperation. He tore the zipper of her white linen trousers, ripped
the front of her T-shirt. She bit his neck. He cried into the hollow of
her neck. She cried out to the night without moon. He fell back
onto the ground with her on top, and they lay like this, his hands on
her back, her hands in his hair, pebbles and freshly crumbled
whitewash digging into their flesh.

Later that night a phone-call came from Melbourne. 'Your
grandmother's dying. You'd better go to Ohrid at once.'

Theo packed up in a daze. Véronique didn't. He had twelve hours
before his flight.

'Tell me the story about the Ohrid lake.'

'I've told you that story before.'

'Tell me again.'

'The surface of the lake shimmers. Here's why. Tzar Samuil sent
his troops to seize Constantinople, but the Byzantine emperor Basil
took them to task. He had the fifteen thousand prisoners blinded,
except he left a single one-eyed man per hundred blinded men, to
lead them back home. When Samuil saw his returning army of
blinded soldiers, he died of heartbreak.'

His voice was tangled like an old rope extracted from the sea,
overgrown with algae. He longed to look at her but he was a
disembodied voice. His voice talked while his eyes gazed at the
fabulous green surface. His fingers held a cigarette that was burning
fast in the wind. He felt like a raving tourist guide whose group had
long since sailed away from the island, behind his back.

'But before he died, he sent back for the eyes to be collected, and
had them placed in a golden casket which was dropped in the lake.
That's why it shimmers.'

Not a sound came from her. It was as though, like Orpheus, he
had been instructed not to look away, or behind, just keep going
until he left the underworld and found her next to him, restored,

corporeal. When he finally turned to her, she was looking at him from afar, from that hypothetical place which offered her a greater truth than these ruins – or greater than him at least. Euridice was gone and he couldn't even tell her this. No, the banality of myth couldn't do justice to how he felt. She was still in that breathless way she had when events surpassed her.

'Keep talking, Theo.' She barely opened her mouth. 'Please.'

They sat at the top of the If fortress, overlooking the blazing, polluted coast of Marseilles. There was no one else on the warm stone roof. The sea, seen through arrow-slits, was a mosaic of blue squares. The dusty whiteness of the salt island hurt their eyes. The island shed crystals of salt into the sea, shrinking by the minute. Soon, they would be sitting on a small mount of salt, paddling towards the shore. Or, more likely, waiting for the water to touch their backs, in an ultimate, unburdening embrace, and engulf them. Soon, they would cross back into town. He would fly low above Europe, east-bound, alone and caught like a bug in the hardening amber of his bafflement. She would stay on amid crumbling castles of salt, rocking in a chair next to a man with a soldier's cropped hair and artificial legs, and they would cradle vodka glasses in their hands, turned to the sea, light and quivering in the wind. Gulls squeaked over the castle, ugly and bloodthirsty like vultures.

She had something to say. He had been expecting it and fearing it for weeks. She gave him a slim book of poems in Greek and English, casually, as if it was a cigarette. The wind rushed between them, forcing them apart. He didn't accept the book, but didn't reject it either.

'Véronique,' he said.

'Yes.'

But he couldn't put it into words. He clutched her thigh. As if in a choreographed play, she lay back on the warm white stone. She was pale despite the heat – the deep-honeyed pallor he loved so much. He suddenly wanted to take her there, punishingly, to hammer his despair, his love inside her, to make her cry out, to remind her that she could cry out only with him. To cancel any other possibility involving another. To cancel separation. Gripped by the lightheadedness of despair, he pulled her top out of her jeans and up to her neck. Her nipples hardened instantly, as if retreating. He sucked the left one, then the right. He was running out of time. He had held back his feelings for too long. She lay still, soundless. Her hand stroked his head. This gesture said: do it but this is the last time. As if he had already left and she was remembering him doing this.

Some voices approached from the stairs, but neither of them cared to move. She cradled him in her arms, in her warm, mechanical body. He clutched her like an orphan clutching a kind stranger. People walked past them, at first shocked, then shaking their heads in pity or bemusement. Normally he wouldn't dream of doing something like this in public, but he wasn't his normal self and nothing mattered any more.

'Ça va pas, les amoureux?' yelled a young extrovert. An elderly English group turned their round backs in disapproval.

The boat horn sounded, muffling the gulls' croaks so they sounded as if coming from under the water.

THIRTY-THREE

June 1949

He flew to Prague and then over Yugoslavia. He hobbled along the punishing Albanian roads in an old Fiat truck, vomiting often. An American jeep, loot from the government army, took him across the border to a mountain villa overlooking the pointed part of the drop that was Lake Prespa. The rebels greeted him with enthusiasm and alcohol. They said that the poet Paul Éluard himself had arrived, only two days ago, and headed for Grammos.

At one point during the celebratory night of fires and songs, he enquired casually, 'Do you know anything about a commander called Illias Grigoriadis, or Spithas? He has a sister, Daphne, or Dawn.'

'Spithas? He was killed on Grammos last summer.'

Illias's dark-rimmed look by the fire, his confidence. *Notre révolte est une demande de justice, c'est tout.* C'est tout.

'And his sister?' Raki helped the nerves but not always. His sanity hinged on the answer.

'Daphne . . .'

Uncertainty prevailed. A pale young man recited a couplet from a Nikos Kavadias poem called 'Letter from Marseilles':

I ripped up lots of paper writing this;
it's made me dizzy being in Marseilles.
A moment doesn't pass, believe me, dear,
without my thinking, even here, of you.

Overwhelmed by a fierce sense of what he would have called fate and Daphne would have called fear, but for the moment remained unnamed, Pascal drank himself to a crispy mountain stupor and sang along to 'Night Without Moon'.

He moved south with a band of mules and guerrillas until eagles announced the naked grey and white granite of Grammos. Then suddenly it loomed before him in the full splendour of its nightmare, still breathtakingly inhuman. Icy waterfalls fell from the crags with deafening clarity, black pine forests beckoned from afar. The heroic mules climbed on, the adolescents around him cheered as if they were going to a feast. The silent person in Pascal's head was aching. Panic gripped him that he would never find her in this desolation of granite, under this gravestone.

After a few days that seemed like weeks, an echo rattled in the gully. The closer he got, the more its dreaded familiarity increased. Extravagant loudspeakers broadcast the soft French of Éluard, followed by a translation into sweetly accented Greek.

'. . . The French people are with the youth of Greece, with the *andartes* . . . The hour of the damned of the earth has come. Come join the fighters for freedom. The future is with them, with the people. Your generation is the future of Greece!'

'Peuple peuple peuple,' sighed the echo, and then 'Laos laos laos'.

In the eerie silence, massive cheers rushed down to the valley where the government army was silently massed. For Pascal and his companions, it was like listening to a recording; they couldn't see a thing. Not a gun was fired. And suddenly, as they reached the top, there they were, a sea of shabby guerrillas sitting and standing on the top of the next hill, and the army invisible below, on the other side. And a lone figure stood by a tree, holding a microphone, guerrilla cap on his head. He was picked up and raised on shoulders, carried off in the midst of cheers.

'It's the French poet!' someone behind Pascal said with awe.

'The world is with us! See, he's come all this way!' a gaunt one said, his voice cracked with emotion. 'Let's press on, synagonistes, we mustn't miss this occasion.'

They hurried on. Pascal surveyed the crowd. Impossible to tell women from men. If he didn't find her here, where would he find her? He was a fool to be looking for anything on this vast and hostile mountain. He walked down, his rucksack digging into his back. A few of the *andartes* noticed him and soon everybody cheered compulsively, thinking he was one of the illustrous French communists lagging behind. But as he climbed to them across a daisy-strewn slope, a kapetanio with a pock-marked face stepped forward. 'Pascal Loublier.'

'Kapetanio,' Pascal's heart contracted with hope. 'I'm happy to see you're alive.' They shook hands for a long moment.

'You can talk. When we crossed into Albania last summer, we thought you'd been killed. Then we heard you'd got back to Athens.'

They had a large audience now, though Pascal was not sure how friendly it was. He sat down on the grass, faking comfort, gaining time to think how to explain his being here. He glanced around. The faces were gaunt. Daphne was not among them.

'So you're back.' The kapetanio sat in the daisies next to Pascal and started rolling a tobacco leaf in a torn piece of paper. Pascal wondered if he wasn't a bad memory to the survivors of last summer.

'I'm back,' he said humbly. 'And you're back too.'

'We'll fight to the end.'

'Did you go back with the national army?' someone asked. Others sat around, thin in their baggy uniforms. This war had always looked like a school camp, except when it looked like hell. The kapetanio gave Pascal the rolled cigarette.

'Yes. At gunpoint,' Pascal replied.

'Come on,' another voice said, 'you stayed behind so you could go back with them.'

This was getting difficult. Pascal smiled to show that this assumption was wrong but that he wouldn't argue.

'He stayed behind to help me.'

The cigarette fell from his fingers.

His heart blossomed on his lips for everyone to see. The looks of others directed him.

She stood by a tree, only a few metres behind him. More frail than ever, clothes flapping on her frame, face somehow darker, almost a fifteen-year-old boy. But she had all her limbs and was so Daphne-like, unmistakable, precious beyond words, only flower of the rocks.

She didn't address anyone in particular; she squinted against the sun.

'He saw that I was wounded and disoriented. Then we saw the army soldiers climbing the hill and I pretended to be dead while they took him away. They warned they'd shoot him in the legs if he didn't move at once.'

Pascal watched her in a shock of bewildered ecstasy. The tired man in the corner of his head got up, tried to say something, then sat back down and crossed his legs. She was not looking at him.

A few youths came shyly to shake his hand; they had been among the fighters of Spithas's division. She didn't. She stood beside the tree, where Éluard had stood with a microphone. The crowd dispersed. Pascal took a deep breath and headed towards Daphne but then Éluard appeared.

'Pascal Loublier!' They shook hands. If the situation had been of the ordinary social kind, Pascal would have been mortified. But he didn't have a care in the world except the one standing darkly by the tree.

'So you made it.'

'So did you.' Paul Éluard smiled in his melancholy way.

'A fine speech.'

'A necessary speech.'

'I hope so, Paul.'

Pascal had tumbled into a valley of sun and déjà-vu. Was everybody mad or just him? The slender brown figure stood by the tree.

'Paul, let me introduce you to a brave fighter. Daphne Grigoriadis.'

The worst way to greet her. A shadow of a smile passed over her face as she extended her arm.

'I will take the image of your face with me back to France. The image of the future, the image of Greece, of freedom,' Éluard said in French, holding her hand. Pascal translated in an uncontrolled voice, drinking her in big, unsteady gulps – her battered uniform two sizes too big, her aliveness.

She smiled shyly.

Paul turned to Pascal. 'Did you know her before?'

'Yes.' A naked yes and all of Paris could know why Pascal Loublier from *Le Monde* had travelled back to Greece, after his terrible experience of the war, after being concussed and presumed murdered. He had to have a good reason, for it was clear (to him at least) that he was neither a soldier nor a communist.

The intoxicating energy she had exuded before was subdued now. She had folded her wings inwards to keep herself upright.

'I don't suppose you'll be coming to the Prague Congress with us.' Éluard gave Pascal's shoulder a discreet squeeze. He more than anyone knew what it meant to love a woman, and to lose her. Éluard waved with his red-starred cap to the clusters of guerrillas and, joined by his comrades, was gone over the hill.

'Markos is in Albania,' said Daphne in her defiant voice. 'You will miss him again, I'm afraid.' Pascal stepped towards her.

'And you are here.' He threw his rucksack on the ground.

And so they stood in a sudden world of granite and sun. They were clearly mad – no, everybody else was mad to imagine that they didn't belong together, that she should fight a giant with her bare body like an eagle fighting a Helldiver, and die on the crags and have her delicate flesh picked by vultures and her beautiful name rotten in the memory of the earth.

Then he was pressing her shaking, exquisite body in his arms and maybe he was saying something, maybe she was saying something, it was hard to tell because there was a storm of blood in his ears and the cymbals of the sun in his eyes, and he was holding his destiny. Whatever he was saying, he was saying it to the DAG badge on her cap, which he removed so he could say it to her hair, to the spiral of her ear, to the obsidian in her eyes, to her torn boots, to the feet inside them, and it was possible that all he was saying was Daphne, Daphne, Daphne. He was saying Daphne to the whole valley with

Paul Éluard and the kapetanios and the government army on the other side, and it made perfect sense. Daphne.

Then the slap came, sending him reeling off into the absurd field of daisies: 'Why have you come back?'

He searched her eyes, her mouth, her shaking body, to reassure himself that she didn't mean it. But she did.

'Because I enjoy so much riding in an old truck on the marvellous Albanian roads and I adore riding on mules along mountain passes and gazing at the gullies below. There's nothing like getting a nice bleeding saddle-burn.'

She smiled but there was something wrong with her smile.

'Tell me about that day last summer. Where were you really when I was looking for you?'

'I was dead.' There was something new in her, or rather something newly missing. He remembered the village house whose door was missing because it had been used for a stretcher. 'But I could hear you.'

'Illias, he . . .'

'Yes.'

'I'm sorry, Daphne. I didn't know until I got here. But all along, I knew you were alive.'

'That's funny because all along I was trying to die. But death isn't interested in our family any more.' She smiled and a chill ran through Pascal. 'How did you get here?'

'Through Albania and across to Lake Prespa. It was a lonely trek without my favourite guide.'

The old Daphne peeked out of her chap-lipped smile.

'How is France?' she enquired, refusing the cigarette he offered her. He put the cigarette between his scorched lips but then took it out. His knees were buckling with fatigue and nervous strain. He glanced around. A few eyes were on them curiously but she wasn't on edge about unwanted attention, as she had been last year. She had gone beyond such things.

'I don't know, I didn't notice.'

'And your family?' She wasn't cold, no, just . . . polite.

'Alex is well, growing fast.' Impulsively, he took a photo from his wallet and showed it to her.

She looked at the boy for a long while but said nothing. His panic grew.

'You were wounded.'

'Yes, but not seriously. Just my arm.' She rolled up her sleeve to reveal a still raw, messy scar on her slender left arm. 'It damaged some muscles so my fingers will remain stiff. They took the shrapnel out with a hot knife after I drank lots of raki. But that was nothing compared with others. I bet your friend the poet wouldn't be urging the army to join us if he knew this. I mean, they *have* anaesthetics. But we have nothing left to lose and that's the deadliest weapon.'

He ran the tips of his fingers over the scar. Her flesh. And he had got away with just severe sunburn and concussion. She was herself now – the Daphne he knew but not the Daphne he knew. Like the house without a door. Like someone sitting outside, not waiting, but not going anywhere either. His hope of dragging her away from here – or whatever his hope had been beyond simply finding her – was as sane as hoping to find Café Cyrano on Grammos. He struggled with the beast of that thought.

'And Kallistos, what happened with him?' he asked.

She rolled her sleeve down.

'Did he . . . get away?'

'I don't know. He was probably taken by the national army to the re-education camps somewhere on the islands . . .'

'Just what he most dreaded.'

She looked at him and his heart stopped with sorrow.

'And you, were you wounded?' she asked.

'Yes, but not seriously. Just my heart.'

Nobody importuned them, though there was the occasional jeer. Dusk fell. They would sleep under the stars. The crowd gathered around a fire that was never lit because of the proximity of the army. But no precautions were taken about noise, and for the third time, Pascal sang:

Night without moon, the darkness is deep,
But a brave lad cannot sleep.
What can he be waiting for, all night till morning

At the narrow window which lights his cell?
The door opens, the door closes but it's double-locked.
What's he done, that they've thrown the boy in jail?
The door opens and closes with a heavy sigh.
If only I could guess the sorrow of his heart.

Daphne sat next to him. The rules about sexual behaviour had loosened up – there was a girl nursing a pregnant belly and a couple leaning against each other. This army of dreamers, of Great Powers-bait, of starved inhabitants of the brave new world, was alone in the midst of the vast, arid, Grammos-like Cold War. Nobody was going to reach across this landscape of waste to save them. They had nothing to lose indeed. They weren't the future; no, Paul, not any more. They were the lost generation.

He gazed at Daphne's melted frame, her fevered, disconsolate eyes, her mechanically singing mouth. Everything about her seemed to say: 'Why have you come back?'

When everyone appeared to be asleep except the crickets in the field below, Pascal and Daphne sat on the fringes of the camp under a dry, broken tree – the last salient growth before the precipice hardened into rock. The only human noise was the typewriter at the other end of the camp, the political co-ordinator's endless reports to HQ.

'I brought you some new boots.' Pascal took them out of his rucksack. 'I hope they fit.' Daphne stroked the expensive leather but didn't put them on. He felt the heat of her face as she turned to him.

'Pascal, why have you come back?'

'To tell you a story. You see, for the last four months, I lived alone in my father's house in Marseilles. It's called Villa Maldormé, which approximately means bad sleep. From the windows, you can see le Château d'If where the Count of Monte Cristo was locked up, thanks to Alexandre Dumas's imagination. It's a bit like the Aegean islands, bare white rock. It's actually not a castle but a prison. The Man with the . . . masque de fer, iron mask, spent some time there too. His cell is still there. He was the brother of le Roi-Soleil, the Sun-King Louis XIV, and he looked too much like him. The king had him locked up and, as if that wasn't enough, he had him wear an iron mask.'

'A bit like this war really.'

'How?'

'It's a fratricidal war. The two camps are too much alike, and so we try to wipe each other out. A son killing his father. A brother killing his brother. Because one happens to be in the government army, and the other happens to be one of us. Every time you fire, you might be firing at your own. Except me. I'm out of danger now.'

She scraped at the dry soil and took a handful which she crumbled in her dirty, broken-nailed fingers. He brushed the remaining soil from her palm, then folded her fingers, as if they enclosed an invisible key, and held her hand. The crickets creaked madly in an optimistic crescendo. The orphaned stars twinkled like the eyes of small frightened animals in the dark. There was no moon. He let her talk.

'And it's still dry and barren, this soil. After all the blood it has soaked up. How much more does it want before it starts spitting it out?'

She spoke through gritted teeth. He squeezed her hand and brushed a strand of hair from her warm cheek.

'That's why I've come. So that your blood doesn't get spilled in this soil too.'

She pulled her hand from his grip. He took her by the arms and turned her to him.

'Daphne mou, listen to me . . .'

'No, you listen to me. I'm one of the many. So what if I die! What's left there to live for? Tell me, what's left? My brothers are dead. My parents are dead. You're married. What will you do with me in your France? Lock me up in your villa of bad sleep, while you go to your wife and play the good family man? And visit your little concubine from time to time . . .'

He scratched a violent match to light a cigarette.

'How can you say this!' He shook his head bitterly. 'I have come across Europe, across Albania, on mule-back, on foot, with splitting headaches from the concussion, to find you.'

She flicked her black fringe.

'Even last year, I said to you that if you come with me, I will get a divorce. But listen to us, it's ridiculous talking in this way when it's a matter of saving your life, for Christ's sake!'

Her eyes were enormous and feverish, pools of liquid tar.

'I can't desert. I'm too far down the track. What will I do in your France? I'll never be able to come back.'

'You won't be able to come back anyway, when the last of you get routed across the Albanian border!' He spoke with urgency, talking to himself, talking himself out of imminent defeat. 'You'll pick up the French language quickly. I know many people, I have many connections. You won't need to work, I have . . .'

He hated his voice; he wanted to pluck the coward out of his throat.

'Pascal.' She put a hand on his knee. A slender young hand, unwashed for days, with grazed knuckles and nails full of soil. 'During the Nazi occupation, my father said to us – we were together, the whole family, for the last time – "My children," he said, "if we die, we'll die free. If we stay at home, we'll die unfree. We're making the right choice in a time of bad choices. And if enough of us make this choice, we'll live to be free."'

She paused, breathless with words. He waited with a dry throat.

'They all died free. Alexis, Illias, mother, father, my cousins, my uncles. If I desert now, it would be like spitting on the graves they don't even have. Like pretending none of this happened. I can't believe that you've come back. I knew you were alive and that was enough, even if I couldn't stop thinking about you. But I must see this through to the end. Perhaps I have no future here, but I have no future in your France either. Besides, how do you imagine me getting out of here? Captain Paleologos will have me shot, or, if he doesn't, someone on the way to the border will.'

Pascal's heart pounded his chest like an angry fist.

'You know there's a way around these things. Bribes.'

She clicked her tongue. 'Forget it. The Democratic Army is beyond bribes.'

'There *is* a way, I'm sure.'

'That's beside the point, actually.'

'Daphne, I respect and admire your dedication. But this war is a mistake and you don't deserve to pay for it.'

She snorted. 'It doesn't work that way.'

'How *does* it work, tell me!'

She shushed him.

'Don't shush me. I don't care if someone hears. I came for you.'

Tears filled his eyes. 'I . . . I simply can't stand to lose you, to know I'm leaving you to get blown up on these fucking rocks.'

'You have no choice.' She touched his cheek with cold fingers, the tar of her eyes boiling. 'Like me.'

He threw the cigarette butt on the ground. Not knowing what he was doing, he pressed her in his arms, the tight knot of nerves and steel, and broken youth that she was. He pressed his face against her sticky neck and wept like a child while she held him. Then he buried his face in the smelly scramble of black hair, feeling her bony back under the thin cotton shirt, suffocating with bewilderment. It wasn't possible to lose her so completely, no. She shook slightly and took gulps of air like a fish flung on a beach.

They tumbled on the ground and their mouths not so much kissed as clashed, knocking the breath out of each other. The typewriter went quiet. The crickets scuttled away. With a frantic hand, he unbuttoned her shirt and her grimy trousers. Her legs and hips were white against the black grass, and the strains of malnutrition and combat hadn't managed to completely erase her feminine lines. He slipped his jacket underneath her. He pressed his face against her flat stomach, against her breasts, breathing in the fragrance of her skin fiercely as if it were the oxygen on which his lungs would depend from now on. When he returned to face her, she propped her outstretched arm against his chest and unbuttoned his trousers. Pascal's insides contorted wildly with grief and desire until he could bear it no longer. She folded her arm to let him in and sealed his mouth with her silence.

They lay in the black grass, his hand stroking her cheek, her hand stroking his chest, sticky and floating in the vast mountain summer. Time was pieced back together, and the scraps of human flesh and the dead faces with eyes open in surprise, and the body parts scattered down napalm-blackened hills, and the artillery thunder and buzzing planes overhead, and the stench of rotten flesh and ouzo-soaked bandages, and the endless march under a withering sun and in skin-stripping blizzards, and the youths leaping from cliffs, and all the miscarried shadows of Hades retreated into the dark womb of the great, carnivorous myth-maker that was history. Their hearts returned to their original places. Everything else was back where it belonged. They were together and nothing could sever them, so long as this night without moon lasted forever.

'Tell me again about the Castle of If and your Villa of Bad Sleep,' she breathed in his ear.

He kissed her smooth cheek and whispered in her hair:

'From the Villa Maldormé you can see the Castle of If where . . . where I will take you so that we can look back at the coast and see the Villa Maldormé. Daphne mou . . .'

'And we'll dynamite the Castle of If to mark the end of all prison islands!'

'And we'll live in the Villa Maldormé so that we don't sleep and we make love all night.'

'And there'll be no guards around, and we'll eat croissants and café au lait and sleep in every morning . . .'

'Every morning, mon amour.'

When she had taken Angelis's still undelivered letter to pass on to someone going to Edessa, they said goodbye and he left. Then returned five minutes later, unable to leave, shaking her by the shoulders as if to awaken her from a trance, while she stood rigid, touched by the hand of Midas. He walked away again and forever, along the ridge of the mountain.

When he reached the next hill and looked back, she was unbearably small and frozen against the backdrop of granite.

Grammos swallowed him. His teenage guides whistled a tune. The mules scuttled along on thin legs. Mountain streams pounded rivers. Every step he took away from her was a betrayal of his destiny. A hundred times, he thought of turning back. But he felt in the roots of his hair that she was irrevocably lost to him. Grammos shook its white head and as he walked on he wished he could turn into granite himself so that his agony would be frozen and he could remain, unfeeling and eternal, here in the land of Midas.

PART THREE

*The
Castle
of If*

THIRTY-FOUR

July 1998, Marseilles

Véronique sat in a corner of the seedy legionnaire haunt Le Matelot, watching a film crew interview Victor. He was only slightly drunk. The film crew were used to it now. Very romantic – the Ukrainian inebriate, handsome and tragically legless. Véronique had had two shots of vodka herself. Flies buzzed overhead, sweat gathered on her brow and back.

'Do you regret what happened in Bosnia?'

'Regret? I sometime have dreams of those people running from bombs, homeless at railway stations, crying, wounded children . . . I, I . . . did what I can. I was there to help and I'm . . . glad I helped.'

His fair face glistened with sweat.

'Would you say it was worth the sacrifice?'

She got up, scraping her chair against the floor. The TV crew's heads turned towards her. 'Pardon.' She walked out as if stepping in cotton.

In the blinding sunshine the television van glistened like an extravagant and repugnant bug. A couple of swarthy legionnaires stood in the shade of the green canvas awning, chatting in an approximate language. She walked up the steep street. Sweat trickled down her back and legs, tickling her. She just needed shade – that's all she needed. And Victor to sit next to her, silent and drunk, married to his glass. Or Theo. No, not Theo. He was flying now, no, he had arrived already. It was better this way. No, it wasn't better at all. It was awful. It was a disaster.

All the streets in the Maldormé area were white and listless cul-de-sacs, reptiles ancient with sun. Instead of worming her way to the villa, she found herself in front of the green awning again. The TV van had gone, and so had the two swarthy legionnaires. But Victor hadn't. He sat alone, folded over his glass.

'Where did you go to?'

'I went for a stroll but didn't get very far.'

'I know what you mean, I got the same problem. Let's get outa here. I'm sick of this place. It's so dark.'

He picked up the half-empty bottle of Stolichnaya and they went to his other haunt up on the promenade, Les Dauphins.

'When is the last interview going to be?'

'When my girlfriend arrives.'

He sipped his beer. She sipped her lemonade. He smiled in that self-conscious, shy way that he had the first time they spoke. The sun gold-sprayed his cropped hair and eyebrows, the hairs on his arms. His blue eyes were veined with gold. He squinted painfully against the sun.

She put on her sunglasses.

'The first time I saw you, you know what I thought? What a couple, what fucking . . . perfect couple. Fuck, I felt . . . sorry . . . so jealous. Not because I wanted nothing. Just jealous. Because me and my girlfriend were like that, once . . .'

'We're not a perfect couple.'

'That's why you didn't went with him?'

She shrugged.

'Maybe you should go with him.'

'Your French gets better when you drink. That's one good thing about drinking.'

'Ah! No, no. There are many good things about drinking.'

'I drink therefore I am.'

'No no, that's you, French, with your wine. We Ukranians, we are, how do you say, we are, thereafter . . . we drink.'

They raised their glasses. His lips were chapped and puffy from sunburn.

'The first time I saw you in that pub in the Vieux Port, I didn't realise . . . I mean, you know, you were with a bunch of other legionnaires, and you looked . . . just like them.'

His smile was gone. She had made a blunder. He ordered another beer and asked what she would like. Nothing. Too much. Silence.

'They looked after me real well when this happened.' He nodded at his legs. 'They fit me with best prosthetics available in West.'

'But why didn't they do it earlier? I mean, you've been, you were . . . like this for a long time.'

'I didn't want fucking artificial legs. I was stubborn. For two years they tried to talk me into it.'

'Why didn't you want them?'

'It was like, what difference does it make if I've got fucking prosthetics? I still don't have my legs. I don't want to be walking on fucking stilts like some clown. What's the point in pretending. I just stayed away from people, I didn't want to see or talk to anyone, not even Katya. I didn't care where I was, here or back home. I just kept to myself, got into drinking . . .'

She put her feet up on a canvas chair, then put them back down, fearing it might be insensitive. He stretched.

'Habib!' he called. The Tunisian waiter arrived at once, sleek and gracious in his leather pants.

'The bill please.'

'Is that all for today! Are you on a detox programme or something?' Habib winked at Véronique.

'Ta mère.' Victor waved him away affectionately. 'I never think I can be friendly with Arab. But some of them are okay, you know. That's one good thing about the legion, you learn to mix with all sorts.'

'It's just unfortunate then that you all look like skinheads.'

He grinned.

'Some are. Especially Poles. We got banned from some bars 'cause of them, 'cause they're looking for trouble with locals. There's this bloke, a Pole, bit of a Nazi, he got pushed over rail-tracks by bunch of Arabs. His leg was cut off by passing train. He hadn't no insurance so he's fucked. Anyway, we all get along but I rather hang out with . . . Actually, I rather not hang out with nobody.'

'What about me?'

'You are . . . different. You're like gift from sky. But too late.'

He fumbled with some banknotes and left too much in the little saucer.

'Do you have to go?' she asked.

'Go where?'

'I don't know, back to HQ?'

'I'm invalid, remember? I don't have to report to no one no more.'

They walked by the sea. Slowly, so slowly. His crutches tapped on the pavement. People watched them.

'And you?' he asked. 'Do you have to go?'

'Where?'

'Home.'

'You mean the dilapidated yellow house overrun with weed and stray cats?'

They trudged on. Teenagers leapt from white cliffs along the promenade. Below, on the white terrace of a restaurant overlooking the sea, a fleet of brown oiled breasts bobbed in the light wind, their nipples staring up like so many dumb, mouthless faces. Victor stopped and pointed with his crutch at something across the road – a sprawling spray graffiti decorating the wall of a derelict house: *But I could have been elsewhere*. In his eyes Véronique found bloodshot glitter.

That night, Véronique lay in the giant iron bed upstairs, listening to the gramophone play Edith Piaf's 'Mon Légionnaire'. She had found a collection of Piaf records in a dusty filing cabinet. Despite the fluffy cover of dust on the gramophone, the needle was intact and the characteristic, juicy r's rolled off Piaf's tongue and spilt inside the hollow house. 'Happiness lost, happiness vanished, always I think of that night . . . They found him in the desert, his beautiful eyes open, clouds passing across the sky . . . Happiness lost, happiness vanished, always I think of that night . . . '

The moon stared at her and she stared back. The sea splashed below. Theo's side of the bed still bore his smell, his shape, his sculpted body, an odd-eyed flash of accusation.

THIRTY-FIVE

September 1967, Paris/Thessaloniki

'Better than the real thing.'

Michel Franchitti handed Pascal Loublier his forged passport and shook the cold rain from his lush, greying hair. His shoes left wet prints on the carpet. The lounge smelt of coffee and Pauline's perfume, a present from Michel. A recording of Joe Dassin was playing. 'If you didn't exist, tell me, how would I exist . . . In this world that comes and goes, I would have felt lost . . .'

'Whisky?' Pauline enquired absently. 'I suppose it's a superfluous question.'

'Now, now,' Michel said with exaggerated playfulness. 'I don't need hints.' He took the glass and rattled the ice-cubes inside. He paced around the room while Pascal inspected his new passport. Pauline came over to look at it over her glasses. Her perfume struck Pascal with a forgotten familiarity. He had been away in Marseilles for over four months.

'Ludovic Pêcheur? You're using your nom-de-guerre from the days of the Resistance!'

'Well, it makes sense, doesn't it?' He was often defensive with her, as if he expected her to pounce at him, for he knew she would have every right to, though he also knew she never would.

'Does it?'

'Just in case somebody there remembered unfavourably my real name from '48.'

'Is this actually necessary, Pascal?' Pauline sat on the plush couch and crossed her shapely legs. Michel stood at the window, glass in hand.

'It's just a precaution,' Pascal said.

'You told me it was safe to go. Why do you need to take precautions like this? I mean, as precautions go, this is fairly extensive, don't you think?'

Michel stepped forward. 'Pauline, it is safe to go, come on, the place is full of Americans!' Pascal snorted sarcastically and Michel joined him. Pauline didn't.

'But you can never be too cautious in Greece,' Michel continued. 'All the more that he'll be in contact with people who have records from the civil war and you know, in the current situation . . .'

'Darling, can you pour me some whisky?' Pauline turned to Pascal who was standing by the glass cabinet. In the autumnal morning light oozing through the lace curtains, Pauline's paleness was framed by the blaze of her hair.

'Don't forget he's an old fox,' Michel said. 'He knows his way around. How's your Greek by the way?'

'I'm curious to find out myself.' Pascal chuckled nervously. 'It's been a few years. Remember, when I first arrived in Athens in '47, you asked me the same thing?'

'And you said "etsi-ketsi".'

The two men laughed. 'Means so-so,' Michel explained to Pauline, seeing her blank look. 'Of course I didn't know that. I'd been in Athens for two years and still didn't know how to say "so-so" in Greek!'

'Yes, but you knew the word for mines and I didn't!' Pascal put an arm round his friend's shoulders. 'Ah, Michel. You knew when to call it a day. And I was so naïve.'

'Now, now. You turned out this terrific book as a result and became a *writer*. And I've just been languishing at the paper, an ordinary journalist.'

'You know you're just being generous now. I'm the one who quit.'

Pascal fidgeted with the bottle tops of various liqueurs in the cabinet.

'I want you to call me every other day.' Pauline got up and looked around, searching for something to hold on to, brushing invisible fluff from an armchair, straightening the leaves of a pot-plant. 'Just to say you're okay.'

'Look, Pauline, let's not exaggerate. I'll be safe.'

'That's what you said in '47 too!'

'And I was right, wasn't I? I came back.'

Pauline turned to Pascal. There was nothing in her face except a tired reproach. Or perhaps he didn't want to see anything else.

'All right, Pauline, relax. He'll be fine.' Michel put his hands on her shoulders.

'And make sure you're back for the birth of Alex's baby.'

Pascal looked at her as if to say 'Are you saying I'm irresponsible?'

At the airport, Pascal hugged Alex and his wife Lucile whose dark elegance was undiminished by the indignities of advanced pregnancy, kissed Pauline on a corner of the mouth, and finally squeezed Michel.

'My friend,' he said to him quietly, 'you know the real reason I'm going.'

'Tell me anyway.'

'Because there's only one thing that can liberate Pascal from Pascal. I think you know.'

Michel gave him an inquisitive look but Pascal raised his palm in a prohibitive farewell and was off.

'Pascal!' Pauline called anxiously.

He turned round. She took a step forward. Everybody looked at them expectantly.

'Nothing,' she said and waved her already age-spotted hand as if dispersing an unpleasant thought. 'Nothing, go on.'

He stumbled into somebody's luggage. 'Pardon,' he mumbled but there was no one there. It occurred to him that this heap of luggage was like his life in the last eighteen years – unchecked, unattended, only neatly labelled. He often stumbled into it himself and for a second wondered what it was. This trip was an attempt to take his baggage along with him and somehow put it to use.

'What is the purpose of your visit?' The officer at Athens airport looked at Pascal with a glimmer of interest which was quickly drowned in the immensity of his habitual apathy. Pascal pretended not to understand Greek. The man repeated the question in approximate English.

'Tourism,' said Pascal. 'I'm a writer for a travel magazine in Paris and I was commissioned to write about tourist attractions in Greece. She's becoming very popular as a tourist destination in France.'

The clerk handed Ludovic Pêcheur his passport. 'Very good. Tell to the French people about the beauties of Greece.'

By the time he came out on the other side, his shirt was sticking to his back with sweat. He didn't really want to make a nostalgic detour to the city, all the more so because there was nobody he wanted to see there. Nobody? Almost.

He took a taxi to the Protonecrotafio, the First Cemetery. At the gate, he faced the immutable, crouching Parthenon up on its hill. He bought some pink carnations and walked into the stone city overseen by another stone-city, between endless rows of life-size statues, photographs, burning and burnt candles, women in black bending over to straighten some flowers or brush the dust from name plaques. He didn't know where the tomb was. After forty minutes of wandering among the cruel eccentricities the living inflict upon their dead, he spotted the Latin script. It was a humble grave, unpampered by frequent visitors. He placed the carnations over the words '8 May 1948, Thessaloniki'.

A sun veiled in cloud like a poached egg greeted him outside Thessaloniki airport. Driving in a taxi along Via Egnatia, an absurd reflex flooded forth from 1948: mines. He almost chuckled nervously.

The familiar low hills pressed the newly sprawling city down towards the sea. He checked into the Hotel Mediterranée which held onto its Renaissance charm in the midst of sporadic urban ugliness. Wandering around the city, he tried to hold the soup of his emotions under a lid and simply observe. In this city of graffiti, he looked instinctively for writing on the walls and found one, not only whitewashed but unfinished, though the name of the dictator from

the thirties was unmistakable: 'The colonels are the stooges of
Metax . . .' On the wall of a street kiosk, the torn remnants of anti-
junta posters stirred in the wind. He could make out: 'Down with
the junta' and 'Democracy'.

The White Tower, the Byzantine Parthenon of Thessaloniki, sat
plump and inscrutable at the waterfront as it had done nineteen years
ago, the blue and white flag flapping in the warm breeze, brightly
signalling a free Greece. It was closed, but Pascal would climb to the
top the next day. The dubious waters lapped at the cement promenade
as if all had always been well in the bay.

Pascal bought a couple of newspapers and sat at a pleasant
waterfront café with a cup of intensely sweet coffee, struggling with
the Greek script of which he had lost the habit. '"Greece is an
important country in the Mediterranean region and a keystone
NATO member in the South," said the US defence minister yesterday.
"We will continue to support its new government . . ."' 'Colonel
Papadopoulos: "Man's life is a struggle. We must persevere in our
sacred struggle to present the truth. We have a patient here, and we
must strap him down for an operation; failing that, he may die."'

He had followed the unfolding of events since April that year.
Little reliable information was reaching the West about the severity
of the junta repression. But a few weeks before he left France, there
was a visit to the offices of *Le Monde* from a Greek émigré journalist
who pleaded for column space in the paper to expose the outrages
that were allegedly taking place in Greece. The assistant editor had
called Pascal, who was still regarded at the paper as an expert on
Greek affairs. Pascal was in favour but said that caution was advisable
in the absence of verifiable information. It turned out that the
journalist was closely associated with Democratic Defence, an
underground anti-junta organisation – consisting of a handful of
members in Greece and half a handful of supporters abroad – which
was increasingly militant and even allegedly involved in small-scale
smuggling of explosives. The editor decided it was not wise to get
involved with amateur liberals but gave the desperate journalist
Pascal's address in Marseilles, thinking that the man would be put off
by the fact that it was at the other end of France. Pascal was in the

Villa Maldormé at the time, with his mistress Sophie.

When the journalist turned up, Sophie was sitting outside in a chaise longue, barefoot and in déshabillé, leafing through a magazine. Pascal was sitting next to her, reading the grim, freshly published memoirs of Soviet Gulag prisoner Evgenia Ginzburg. The journalist was drenched in sweat. He'd taken a train from Paris because he couldn't afford the airfare. Pascal attempted to revive his Greek but gave up after realising that the young man's French was more alive.

'Monsieur Loublier, I know your book on the civil war. That's why I came to see you.'

Nikitas was breathless with excitement as he gulped down the grapefruit juice. Sophie took a moderate interest in him.

'I came to Paris in April, just after the coup. I was afraid they'd arrest me. I've been involved in Democratic Defence ever since. I want to set things straight, though. The movement is still very young, the risks are high, which is why it's hard to recruit new members and, above all, we need support abroad. It's essential to have the backing of influential people. That's why I came to you.'

Pascal frowned. 'I'm not influential! But I hear what you're saying.' Nikitas's face lit up. 'Of course I need to know more about your aims, your strategies, and more about what's been happening since April.'

'I have brought you some materials to look through. The beginnings of a compilation of evidence for torture and imprisonment. It's early days yet – it's hard to get people to testify, mainly because they're in jail. Or because they're afraid.' He handed Pascal a manila folder. Sophie nudged Pascal and shook her head with a discreet pout of disapproval.

'Tell me, is there anything happening in Thessaloniki, in terms of your . . . movement?' Pascal patted Sophie's hand reassuringly.

'Yes, we have a cell there too. Why?'

'I'm heading that way in a couple of weeks.'

Nikitas's face lit up again. 'That's an extraordinary stroke of luck.'

'For who, though?' Sophie said ironically and was ignored.

'It's a private trip,' Pascal said.

'Perhaps the best thing to do is to just give you a contact name there. There are a couple of prominent figures, and we have some links between Athens and Thessaloniki.'

He opened the folder and wrote down a name.

'You can contact this man, Odysseos Varda, he's a lawyer. This isn't his real name, though. For safety reasons, when they deal with newcomers, they use pseudonyms. Now, because phone lines may be tapped, you won't . . .'

'Wait a minute,' Sophie interrupted. 'Pascal, you're not going to get involved in this, are you?'

Pascal squeezed her hand again and smiled insouciantly. 'It's okay. I'm an old fox.'

'So,' the journalist continued, 'you won't call him. He'll know when to expect you and he'll send someone to meet you at a designated place and pass on a message about where you would be meeting. I'll give you the details. I can't believe how lucky we are to have you with us.'

He shook Pascal's hand.

'I can't promise anything, though,' Pascal warned.

Sophie's mood had already been soured, but when Pascal, upon hearing that Nikitas was going to spend the night in one of the foul establishments near the railway station, offered him a bed in the house, it became positively rotten. Nikitas, who never stopped sweating bucketfuls of excitement, spent the rest of the day sipping gin and tonic in the company of a menacing, semi-naked Sophie and a benevolent Pascal.

Listening to the earnest Nikitas in the declining Mediterranean blaze, clutching his warm gin and tonic, pinned down like an extinct species by the August sun, holding the hand of a spoilt, pretty woman, Pascal made a resolution. He would do something for Nikitas, for whoever needed his help.

For himself perhaps.

For anyone spellbound in the Land of Midas, the place that had broken his heart.

THIRTY-SIX

July 1998, Ohrid

Dafina was fully absorbed in the act of dying. He held her hand, the one paralysed by an old shrapnel wound. His mother, fresh off the plane from Australia, kissed him absently. Her arresting irises bloomed in the extraordinary, troubled burst of violet that Theo had seen in moments when events had surpassed her intelligence. He was late.

In one of her few clear moments, the old woman said: 'You know, darling, now I know that the best way to get you to come and see me is to be on my deathbed. Pity I can't do it more often!' And she smiled with golden teeth, shaking her head with tired affection. Finally, this fierce woman was tired. She knew why he hadn't come earlier. Families are like secret police. She even found the strength to ask: 'Is it love? Is she the one?'

It punched him with such brutality that he almost doubled over. 'Grandma, what do you mean?'

'The French girl, is she the one for you?'

Yes, she is the one for me. The tip of his tongue was stuck to his palate, painfully. The silence fattened suspiciously. His mother looked at him, tense with unspoken reproach for his being so late, for having been so difficult to locate, for roaming around Europe, evading reality and indulging in impractical pleasures.

Dafina closed her eyes, as if her last hope for fulfilment had been shattered. He felt betrayed by Véronique. But he had also betrayed her by being an attendant to her despair. For not being the one for her.

The morphine travelled feebly upstream in Dafina's silenced body. They listened to it, a stagnant river amidst the crumbling ruins of cells. The hospital fan buzzed over them. The summer trickled inside the dirty windows. Nobody knew the cancer was so advanced. She hadn't told them until the last moment. This was the last moment, Theo thought. Last moments feel just like any other moments, except more stale. They are the aftertaste of themselves. The dilated pupil of disaster. He didn't know how to handle death. Or was it the waiting that he couldn't handle, the infinity of the last moment?

At one point in her delirium, Dafina muttered: 'The watermelons are all split, everybody's dead, we're all dead, nobody left – nobody except the Frenchman.'

'Who?' Theo and his mother leant into her mouth, a mossy well hiding a buried treasure. But she wouldn't make another attempt at articulation. She drifted out of reach. Was it because death was her natural habitat now? Because death threw light on her, showing her to them in her unknowable essence? Or maybe it was the act of taking her secrets with her, an almost physical act, a wrenching of memory from the organism of life.

Periodically, Dafina's old friend Stamatis would appear in the door, noiselessly, take off his tatty straw hat and approach in frightened, uneven strides. Theo remembered him vaguely from his childhood – a pleasant man with a semi-closed eye, two symmetrical bays of receding grey hair, and fidgety hands that constantly probed the depths of his pockets and patted searchingly all available surfaces. He was a man afflicted by the chronic loss of small objects. Stamatis sat with them, hat in shaking hands, and they exchanged a few trivialities. How's the boat? Good – needs a paint job though. And how is Australia? Good. Many crocodiles? Smiles, condescending. Stamatis looked smaller than Theo remembered him; he had melted away as some strong men do in old age. His nose was veined – perhaps he drank too much. Dafina didn't emerge from her coma to acknowledge the visitor and he would leave with uncertain strides, even smaller than when he arrived.

Latinka, another friend of Dafina's, came regularly and brought food which Dafina naturally couldn't eat.

Sitting by the wasted body of this once indestructible woman, Theo tried to imagine her as a twenty-four-year-old guerrilla, fighting high in the rocky mountains of Northern Greece, under the scorching sun and in the crippling winter. She would have called him a petty bourgeois element then, with no ideals or readiness for sacrifice. Acting solely out of self-interest. Obsessed with a woman of the old blood-sucking European aristocracy. She would've had him shot as a traitor perhaps. Such things happened and perhaps she wasn't as innocent as the benign status of grandmother had made her. But who was that 'Frenchman'?

From the other side of the bed two troubled violet irises smiled at him wearily.

The funeral was surreal in the Sunday summer haze of the Ohrid lake. The lavishly bearded priest swung a golden chain and chanted in his disconsolate bass. Women in black bent over the coffin and wailed, their voices ricocheting against the hard hills, lamenting their own dead. Theo's mother stood with her lips pressed together and a deep furrow between her brows, the violet bursts of her eyes darkened by incomprehension. A few friends of Dafina's were there, including Stamatis with his purple nose and dazzlingly white hair in the bright sun. He didn't weep – he seemed to be in a shock, fixated on an invisible point. Theo wore sunglasses, dutifully held his mother who didn't need holding, and wished he could wake up somewhere familiar where everything was as it should be. A place where he could just crawl into his thesis and never have to come out.

Dafina's house was empty and overflowing. Empty of Dafina, overflowing with her misunderstood life which made no sense without her. Theo's mother had to go back to Melbourne. At Skopje airport, she kissed him and said, 'Theo, there are no more of the Grigoriadis left now. She was the last one. Take care and come home soon.'

Theo had the vague impression that she was in fact saying something altogether different, something that came like a gurgle from a faraway mountain gully. Her skin moved him with its softness, the way he remembered it from his childhood.

'Your skin is so soft.'

'Because I'm old.' And suddenly, in a shock of flabby skin, she did look old, as if her mother's death had doubled her own age.

'Nonsense, you're young,' he said helplessly.

A flash of moist violet and his mother disappeared behind harassed-looking migrants on their way to better places. Theo waved with forced cheerfulness and was surprised to feel his throat tighten in a spasm. From here, Australia and the Pacific seemed like the extravagant fantasies of a bored brain. He had been sucked into a regressive current of time and couldn't stop walking backwards, until his back hit a damp wall and the dim lights went out.

Theo was perhaps five or six. It was his first time in Greece and Europe. A Frenchman came to Uncle Panayotis's apartment and they shook hands. Theo sat shyly in the corner, in one of his uncle's giant armchairs, mesmerised by the Frenchman's flaming, frizzy hair. The Frenchman wanted something from Uncle Panayotis who kept shaking his head sadly. Sadly, he shook his head and Grandmother Hrisoula sat immobile in her great, iconic indifference. Then Auntie Paraskevas whisked Theo off to the market where ensanguined animal members hung forlornly in dingy streets and candied fruit of improbable colours swam slowly in barrels of its own blood. Theo forgot about the strange man's red hair.

Theo needed to make sense of something but didn't know what it was. He felt like a melancholy archaeologist in search of coded meanings who kept stumbling on scribblings left behind by the mocking hand of an extinct civilisation.

THIRTY-SEVEN

September 1967, Thessaloniki

I n his hotel room, Pascal went over his list of names and addresses. His heartbeat faltered at the thought of the address across the border in Yugoslavia, the one he didn't have but was going to visit anyway. It was absurd to think of it as a visit, of course, but then it was more absurd that he had not done it earlier.

She had changed her name, naturally, Slavicised it. She had a teenage daughter. She lived in a town near the Greek border called Ohrid. She had only moved to Yugoslavia recently. He remembered how his heart had stopped when he learnt that she was alive and had been in Tashkent since 1950. Then he had wondered about her child, who the father was, but then decided that these speculations were unsuited to the magnitude of the fact that she was alive, somewhere in the vast Soviet desert. After more than three years of writing letters to her and waiting in vain for a reply, it occurred to him that something was perhaps wrong and he should just pack up and go to Tashkent to look for her. On reflection, though, he admitted that she was most probably married – thus the child – and simply did not want to be reminded of him. How dreadful it would be to go all that way only to see her turn away in vague repulsion, or not even want to recognise him. The humiliation of rejection, the wasted hopes of reunion, the unredeemed, ten-year-long agony of not knowing whether she was alive, unable to find out. Was it worth it? Was he delusional to imagine, even for a second, that it wasn't too late, clearly, clearly too late?

And why would he assume that he deserved Daphne anyway, after all these years of living the good life, of sitting on the laurels of his literary success extracted from the tragedy of so many thousands, Daphne among them? For just as action, not intention, defines the man, so his protracted, low-intensity agony about his marriage with Pauline, his profession, his beliefs, his sedentary search for Daphne, was of no value because it had amounted to nothing palpable. Until now, anyway. He could only hope for a brief recognition, a few words exchanged in remembrance of what had been. A hug perhaps, or even hearing her story about the final days, the crossing of the border, life in Tashkent. To shake her husband's reliable hand, meet her teen-age daughter who was no doubt a beauty. To tell her in laconic, matter-of-fact sentences about his book, his retirement from *Le Monde*, his failure to divorce his wife. Of the eighteen terrible years between them, years of treated, then sublimated depression and indecision. Of sifting the real from the unreal and starting all over again because they were inextricable. Of reading his own book and wondering how all this could have happened, with him on the periphery of it, with her right in the middle of it. Of wanting to abandon everything and go in search of her, across the world. Of being cajoled, time after time, by the inexhaustible attentions of Pauline. Of following the growth of his unusual and gifted son Alex. Of seeing his book translated into other languages. Of the string of varyingly unsatisfactory mistresses, the latest of whom was Sophie. Of being trapped in the hardened inertia of his life. And the years rolled over like the destinations on the departure boards at airports. And every now and then he would trip over a pile of abandoned luggage, wondering what it was until he would see it was his: neatly labelled, disowned, going nowhere. His life.

The first people to see were the Philipidis father and son. They had given no phone number, only an address in Thessaloniki. He had written them a note saying he would come around the end of September. He wondered how they were placed in the current situation, with Angelis's incriminating past as a recent prisoner. Had their two abducted children come back from abroad? The son of Angelis Philipidis had sent a typed, formal letter dictated by his father to *Le Monde*. It had been forwarded to Pascal at the beginning of the year.

Dear Mister,

You may remember me from our brief encounter in Piraeus Harbour. I gave you a letter to my wife, Hrisoula. I was released from prison in 1964, three years ago. I have since written, with the help of my son, a memoir of my years on the island camp. Seeing that it is not possible to publish it here, would you be interested in having it translated and published in France? The truth must be known, at least somewhere if not here where it is most needed. I will look forward to your reply with much hope. Forgive me for not addressing you by your name, but you never introduced yourself.

This was why Pascal decided to go to Greece in the first place. He owed something to Angelis.

He had taken several copies of his own book, the French and Italian editions, to give away. But now it occurred to him that this might not be such a good idea, as far as the Philipidis were concerned. It would be somehow awkward to show that he had used Angelis's idea about Midas. It was better to keep it that way, at least for the moment.

He also had to meet a woman in a designated place, the church of Saint Dimitrios, who would tell him where to meet the Odysseos Varda man.

On a hot, still Saturday afternoon, he climbed the labyrinth of steep streets in the Old Town on his way to the suburb of Nea Varna. The dust settled on his shoes. There wasn't a soul about. Not even the distant noise of traffic. Only a grey, limping dog followed him sadly some of the way. The City Walls snaked up the hill to the Eptapirgio, the prison of the Seven Towers which must be out of use by now, he thought. Even during the civil war it had the reputation of being inhuman.

The Philipidis lived on the top floor of a three-storey house. The doorman was startled from his afternoon slumber.

'Where are you going?' he said stroppily, wiping dribble from his chin.

'To see some friends.'

'Who?' Pascal went up the stairs, ignoring him. 'Hey, young man! You can't just enter a building like that! I'll call the police!'

This wouldn't be good. Softened a little by the 'young man', Pascal went back a few steps and said: 'The Philipidis.'

'That's better,' said the doorman and settled back in his gutted armchair.

A large, hirsute young man opened the chained door a few inches and gazed at Pascal suspiciously.

'How can I help?' he said without a trace of helpfulness.

'I'm Pascal Loublier, from France. I apolgise for the impromptu visit –'

'Pascal Loublier!' The man undid the chain and pulled Pascal inside urgently, shutting the door and bolting it as if Pascal were being chased by wild dogs.

'I'm Panayotis Philipidis.'

They shook hands.

'Was there anyone outside the building when you came?' Panayotis enquired breezily, as if asking 'tea or coffee'?

'No, not that I noticed. Just the doorman. He asked who I was after.'

'That's all right, he's senile; he probably forgot it instantly. Do you know that we're the unwitting participants in a very funny coincidence? Do come in first.'

Panayotis showed him in. The curtains in the sitting room were drawn but the late summer heat still managed to filter through.

'You haven't seen Irini yet, at Saint Dimitrios?'

'How do you know?' Pascal was startled.

'I know because she is supposed to give you a time and place to meet with Odysseos Varda, right?'

'I . . . I can't really say.'

'It's good to be cautious, yes. These days one never knows.'

They sat in plush armchairs. 'Let me get you a drink first. Brandy?' He opened a small, modestly equipped cabinet.

'You see, I'm Odysseos Varda.'

His throat unfolded into a hearty, padded laughter. Pascal felt his mouth hang open and closed it with an effort.

'It wasn't the safest thing for you to come here, but you can't know this, of course. Let's just hope that nobody saw you. Cheers.'

As they clinked glasses, Hrisoula Philipidis walked in.

'Mother, this is Pascal Loublier, the French journalist who . . .'

'Yes, I know.' Her features were prohibitively stony.

Pascal sprang up and kissed her hand. Something about her imposed a need for dignified formality. He didn't know whether Angelis's letter had ever reached her.

'It is good to see you, Monsieur Loublier,' she said with what in her terms must have been warmth and then made a smooth exit to get coffee. Panayotis smiled.

'We've been waiting for you. But the coincidence was unexpected – and most welcome, of course. Nikitas sent me a message from Paris that I was to meet this writer and journalist . . .'

'Well, former journalist.'

'Right. He told me your pseudonym. I made the connection. But then it makes sense, doesn't it, that you would be willing to support the movement. I got the impression, from what Father told me about your brief meeting in '48, that you were on the side of justice, as it were.'

'I was trying to see things from both sides. I ended up staying with the partisans for several weeks, through some of the battle in the summer of '48.'

'But no other Western journalist has done that! You must have gathered a lot of material for your reportages.'

'Yes. In fact . . .'

Hrisoula entered again with a tray. Behind her came Angelis. At least Pasacal assumed it was him, for there was no resemblance between the stooped old man in the doorway and the fiery-eyed giant at Piraeus harbour.

'Father,' said Panayotis and there was something careful in his voice, 'this is Pascal Loublier, the man to whom we wrote about your memoirs.'

Pascal stepped forward as Angelis trudged across the room like an octogenerian. He couldn't be more than early fifties since he was in his early thirties back in '48. Only his voice was the same.

'Pascal.' They shook hands extensively. 'You didn't tell me your name. But I never forgot your kindness.'

Pascal put his other hand on top of Angelis's, not finding the right words. What could he say?

'I knew you would pull through,' he said, unsatisfactorily.

Angelis probed his soul with a brief look and Pascal's chest felt hollow.

'When they released Father, in 1964, he was one of the remaining thousand prisoners from the civil war.'

Pascal still held Angelis's hand. Like old friends.

'I often thought about you,' Pascal said.

'Thank you.'

Hrisoula served olives, fried meatballs, tomatoes and coffee.

'What about your other kids?' Pascal ventured onto dangerous territory.

After a moment of silence Panayotis said, 'Kostas and Sophia haven't been back. They ended up in Tashkent with many other refugees. Sophia went to Australia with her husband two years ago. Kostas . . . well, he's still in Tashkent but going to Yugoslavia. He has this girlfriend who is Macedonian and has recently moved to Yugoslavia, and he wants to marry her and go to Australia too.'

'So you haven't seen your brother and sister at all?'

'I did. Mother and I went across to the USSR, to Baku, a few years ago. We met halfway.'

'And . . . they haven't seen their father.'

'Of course not. How could they? He was in prison until a few years ago. They're not allowed back. And he's not allowed out of the country.'

The emptiness inside Pascal's chest was expanding. Hrisoula was looking at him expressionlessly, adding to his malaise. Angelis wiped a tear with a palsied hand.

'But anyway,' Panayotis continued with absurd brightness, like putting on a party hat to cover a head-wound, 'tell us about France.'

They spoke of De Gaulle, of the Americans and, inevitably, of the junta.

'It's like a replay of the civil war,' said Panayotis. 'Except this time they're roasting us on a low fire.'

'And the same people are getting arrested.' Angelis smiled with the out-of-place insouciance of those who have crossed some boundary and remained beyond. 'I'm really surprised they haven't knocked on our door yet.'

'We don't keep anything "suspect" here any more,' said Panayotis. 'I moved most of my books and records to an underground apartment since two of my friends were arrested for having *Zorba the Greek*. The junta has banned over a thousand books, even classic Greek authors like Euripides and Sophocles! Of course I had just about all of the banned books.'

'By the way,' Pascal said, 'I brought the printing machine, but of course I didn't know to bring it today.'

'It's much appreciated. We need it in the office where we do the printing. It's a basement, rather.' Panayotis glanced at his parents. 'Mum, Dad, could you leave us two to discuss some boring matters?'

Hrisoula helped Angelis up. He looked like her father. He smiled at Pascal with his wrecked teeth and waved towards Panayotis: 'Don't let him bug you too much.'

As soon as they were gone, Panayotis took off his party hat.

'My father . . . you remember how he looked before he went to the islands? He's fifty-two. Look at him. He has what are known as the three illnesses of Greek jails: spinal arthritis, duodenal ulcer and tuberculosis. He's a mess. I typed his memoir and helped him structure it. It's two years worth of work.'

'Can I see it?'

'We don't keep any suspect printed materials here, for fear of raids. A few people from Democratic Defence have already been jailed and tortured. My parents don't actually know the extent of my involvement and how much danger I'm exposing myself to. You see, there's no real information here except from the Greek Service of the BBC which I listen to. I don't want to worry them.'

'Do you have a family?'

'Wife and kid. They're with the in-laws at the moment. I want them to be as safe as possible in the circumstances. The manuscript. I keep one copy with a friend who's a doctor in the 401 Military Hospital. They don't search there so much. Go to him. I'll let him know. The manuscript is signed with a nom–de–plume, of course. If there's a possibility to publish it in France, it must be under that nom–de–plume – otherwise it's too dangerous, you see, because the KYP – the Intelligence service – will sniff it as far as France. Unless things change here in the meantime.'

Pascal nodded. 'Can I be of help in any other way?'

'You are an influential man in France . . .'

Pascal laughed tensely. 'I'm not. I've retired.'

'But people know your name. You've written a book on the civil war, I'm told.'

He nodded.

'Democratic Defence needs the support of people like you, so that the world learns what's happening here.'

'I'm happy to help.'

'The danger for you is small, since you're a foreigner. But you mustn't come here again because they are probably monitoring the house. Oh, and you don't need to go to Saint Dimitrios tomorrow, obviously.'

Panayotis smiled. He was an ameliorated version of the younger Angelis, with fire in his black, offset eyes and an expansive forehead.

'I didn't intend to stay here longer than a week,' Pascal said as he was leaving, 'but if I can be of any use, I will.'

'I suggest you change your hotel in a couple of days. Just to be on the safe side.'

'Why, is the Mediterranée unsafe?'

'No, just so that they don't become suspicious. Move to the Astoria.'

'Where George Polk was last seen . . .' Pascal lifted his eyebrows. 'I do need to get out of here, eventually. I have other people to see in the north. I want to do some research on survivors of the civil war.'

Panayotis smiled almost patronisingly.

'The civil war, yes . . . But you see, what's happening now is a direct consequence of the way the civil war ended. In a way, it never did end. It has burnt and disfigured Greek society like acid over the years. It's a never-ending civil war sponsored by the Americans in their noble crusade against the red threat! Nothing else matters as long as the government is anti-communist, that's the rudimentary logic. And so we must live in a rudimentary world, you see, governed by idiots like Papadopoulos and Pattakos.'

'I believe that most of Europe will have a different opinion, once the evidence is out. This is the decade of hope, after all.'

'Yes. After all.'

Before Pascal left the apartment, Panayotis had a good look at the street, to make sure nobody was watching. Downstairs, the doorman was still frozen in catatonic repose. No one was observing the building as far as Pascal could see. Panayotis was exaggerating in his eagerness to convey the seriousness of the situation.

Pascal didn't move to the Astoria. He made a phone call to a contact in Kozani, a former partisan, and was told by his wife that the man had been arrested in April. He phoned another partisan, in Edessa, to the same effect. Perhaps he would have to shift the focus of his visit.

The manuscript, strapped inside an inconspicuous folder, was lying between other inconspicuous folders in a filing cabinet. Dr Nikolau handed it to Pascal. *Sisyphus: A Memoir of a Political Prisoner 1948–1964*, by Ikaros and Odysseos Varda. A knock on the door startled them both. 'Dr Nikolau' – it was a nurse – 'routine check of the premises. The police are just down the corridor.' Dr Nikolau stared at Pascal who rushed to the window, to see if there was any way out. There was the tin roof of another building a couple of metres below the window.

'Take off your jacket and shirt and put them over there. Quick.' Dr Nikolau suddenly snapped into action.

Pascal did as he was told. They placed the manuscript under his clothes on the examination bed. The doctor grabbed his stethoscope and smacked it on his ears. As he placed the round rubber on Pascal's chest, the door burst open and three men from KYP stepped in.

'Security check.'

'Sure,' said Dr Nikolau. Pascal breathed in and out.

They flung open the doors of the filing cabinet, looked on shelves, pushed some folders, looked behind the curtains. The dark spot of Pascal's clothes in the whiteness of the room hurt his eyes. It was just asking to be lifted.

'Anything serious?' One of the men nodded at Pascal who shrugged ignorantly.

'About to find out,' Nikolau smiled benignly.

'Good luck.' And they closed the door behind them. Sweat beaded on the large, deforested forehead of Dr Nikolau as he took off the stethoscope.

'Now I might really need a cardiac check-up.' Pascal laughed. Nikolau didn't.

'For small misdemeanours, such as having a pen or pencil in one's possession, a prisoner is punished with a "bath" – being tied into a sack with a cat and thrown into the sea. Those who dare hide their pencil, hide it up their anus. One of them is found out. They shove a steel rod where the pencil had been . . .

'One of the guards, Trayanis, is homosexual. He picks his victims among the young – no more than sixteen or seventeen. For months, a beautiful boy from the Peloponnese, Dinos, is abducted from his bed at night, every few days, and returned, stumbling in the pitch darkness, breathing like a wounded animal, sometimes crying quietly. One morning, we wake up to a horrifying sight: Dinos is lying in a pool of coagulated blood, his throat cut open and black – he has used a rusty, jagged tin-lid that he has somehow smuggled from the kitchen. We bury him in the sea, as we did with all the others . . .

'We break rocks for ten hours a day, without food or water. Nobody needs these rocks. They are just giving us something to do, in order to break us. We break them and then carry them down to the beach. On the way back to the hill, we take sand. And so, month after month, under the withering sun, we move like somnambulists in our universe of rock . . .'

From his small balcony, Pascal looked out to the beguiling blue of the Aegean and in the far, hazy distance to the outline of the unreal Olympus, a gateway to a world of wonder and horror. Pascal thought of his son – what it would be like not to see him for eighteen years, as Angelis didn't see Panayotis. Or worse, to never see him again, to wave to him across some border. To never see his grandchild. To live in the hazy realm of the unknown, as Panayotis had lived, surrounded by harsh blue and white. To lose everything except hope. To lose hope as well. To have nothing but his bare life.

In a flurry of emotion, he lifted the receiver and dialled the Philipidis' number. Just to tell them that the manuscript was so powerful it had to see the light of print and he would make sure it did, though it was imprudent to make promises at this stage. There was no reply. In any case, he was meeting Panayotis at an appointed place the next morning to give him the printing machine.

THIRTY-EIGHT

July 1998, Marseilles

The most beautiful prostitutes were to be found in Brazil. But, failing that, you got a taxi from Paramaribo across the border into British Guyana in the west. It cost 300 francs per head. There were some good quality whores in Guyana. In Brazil they were more expensive but worth it.

In the dimly lit, cavernous restaurant the waiter's moon-face was glowingly black and strewn with pox-craters. Through the crescent window Véronique glimpsed the harbour rocking the boats to a disquieting dream of other seas. They were attacking a second bottle of cheap Amour de Provence red. Victor hadn't touched his poulet à la confiture de songe. Songe means dream, Véronique explained. No, songe is a plant on the Réunion Island, explained the crater-faced waiter.

'What about your experiences with the prostitutes?'

'There isn't nothing to tell.' He was suddenly embarrassed. 'I had nice time. Nice girls, understanding, simple. Not like French girls.'

Three jazz musicians popped the bubble of intimacy with their saxophones. A picturesque trio arrived at the next table – a colossal black man with a mesmeric golden chain over his hairy chest and two pale young women with heads weighed down by waterfalls of blonde hair and shoulder-long earrings. The man poured the wine, flashing his rings. His cowboy hat cast a giant shadow onto Véronique's and Victor's table. Something propelled her over the boundary that she had never crossed and she spoke into Victor's willing ear over the metallic blues of the saxophones.

'I spent a year in Istanbul. One night, I was having dinner at a restaurant in a poor part of the city. I saw this boy behind the counter. A teenager. He had the most beautiful face I'd ever seen. But it wasn't just that, there was something about him . . . Something beguiling . . . I couldn't take my eyes off him. I sat there, drinking cup after cup of apple tea. I went back two days later. Then, I did something really stupid. When I got up to leave, I managed to slip a note to him.'

'What did you write in note?'

'I wrote the name of a hotel, a time, and my name – except that I gave a false name. And I wrote "this weekend" in Turkish. I chose a nice hotel that wasn't too expensive so I wouldn't scare him. I checked in the next day and waited. I knew he'd be working in the restaurant until late. I've never been so nervous in my life. I didn't even know what I would do if he turned up. I almost hoped he wouldn't.'

The trio at the next table exploded in a triple wave of laughter, and to Véronique's ears the bass thunder and the two girls' high-pitched whining had a damning sound, as if they had been listening and this was their verdict. The man pinched a glowing cheek with black pudding fingers.

'And?' Victor prompted.

'And just before midnight on Sunday, there was a call from the reception. I knew I'd made a horrible mistake. But it was too late. He stood at the door and he was so young in his worn-out clothes, I was stunned. He smelt of fried meat and onions. He looked lost. I let him in. I'd imagined this moment many times, but now it didn't feel real. I offered him a fizzy drink. He spoke a few words of English. I spoke a few words of Turkish. His name was Ahmed. He looked like a captured animal. I asked how old he was. Fourteen. He was fourteen! I offered him another drink. I tried to convey that I liked him and wanted to meet him, that's why I had invited him. He blushed. I wanted to weep with shame. I wanted to protect him from myself. He lived at the other end of town. He followed me downstairs. I gave the taxi driver money and told him to drive Ahmed home. I wanted to say sorry but I knew that would only make it worse. I stood in the harsh light of the hotel lobby. When the taxi took off, he turned to look at me until they drove out of sight. I felt like I'd just sold my soul . . . For a bit of a thrill, for a bit of innocence, for . . . I don't know for what.'

Véronique filled her cheeks with air and exhaled, hanging her head.

'It's not so bad. You were lonely, you wanted some love. Don't take it so hard, you didn't do nothing in the end.'

He ordered another bottle. He was completely sober.

'Actually, something like that happen to me once.'

'Really?'

'In Brazil. I smoke some local grass, strong stuff. We were in bar with few friends from legion. There were prostitutes. One's sitting next to me, real stunner, you know, black eyes, great tits . . . So we start talking, and we end up in hotel room.'

Under the neighbouring table, the man was fondling the two girls' rounded knees with his bejewelled, padded paws.

'We do what we do, you know. Suddenly, I notice bulge in wrong place. Because I'm stoned, I don't click. The girl, Felice, tries to tell me something. Then – bang! Felice is not Felice. Felice has dick. Er, sorry. I can't believe my eyes. But it's real. He expects me to hit. But I don't hit. I just say, "Get your arse our of here." I start swearing. In Russian, in Ukrainian, in French, whatever. I go to bed and cry, and think of my girlfriend, this shitty life. I think how I never should be in legion, in fucking jungle in Brazil, if only I can stay at home, live normal life in normal country, have someone to love. I didn't have nobody in the world. Nobody to wait. Nobody to love. It was the most worst fucking night of my life. Sorry for swearing.'

The three musicians sweated rivers of emotion. Their faces were polished ebony carvings in the velvet case of the night. Véronique's foot touched Victor's. He didn't feel it. The man at the next table whipped a thick wad of banknotes out of his breast pocket and put it on the white tablecloth between the two girls. But their bloodshot, smudged mascara-eyes were on the strange white-haired woman and the soldier with crutches.

It was a night that should not end. It was a night that would end and Véronique could see nothing beyond it.

In the Villa Maldormé, they sat on the couch by the panorama windows, looking out to the sea with its flashing lighthouses. Victor's crutches were parked by the couch. Véronique knew it would be better if they didn't touch. She rested her head on his shoulder. He smelt of wine and cheap after-shave. The night was vast and liquid. They sank noiselessly inside it like two long silver spoons in a vat of clear honey. He put an arm around her shoulders and kissed her hair.

'I wish I can stay with you. But my girlfriend arrives tomorrow and we're going back to Odessa. And she loves me.'

'Do you love her?'

A pause.

'I don't know. I must. But in any case, she loves for both of us.'

'What does she do?'

'She is nurse.' He rested his face in her hair. 'Why is your hair white?'

'Because I washed it with bleach once, by mistake.'

He smiled and buried his head in her lap. She stroked the sun out of his sweaty hair. Le Château d'If had long been extinguished and was now a slumping silhouette. Her palm found a thinning patch in his hair. She smoothed it away, replanting it with the stream of lost years. They slept like this on the couch or imagined sleeping. *There was sun on his forehead, light in his hair, they put him under the sand, my légionnaire* . . . This was all happening in a song from the 1930s, it was a record turning under the old needle. They were the dated, ridiculous characters of an Edith Piaf song. They didn't have to feel.

They remained turned to the sea which, like a giant blank film screen, promised at least a white gliding ferry. Or simply the dawn, the night's small ruptures bleeding into a blue-veined morning.

In the morning, they walked down to the rocks outside the legion's HQ and sat facing the pale, placid water. A gentle gurgling below them rippled the silence. Véronique spotted a dark blotch moving under the water, bubbles coming out.

'Look, someone snorkelling down there.'

Victor scoffed. 'Edi the Georgian. Fishing hedgehogs for breakfast.' His freckled face was tired.

'Have you seen film *Papillon*?' he asked.

'I've read the book.'

'I was in Devil's Island in French Guyana.'

'What is it like?'

'Like nothing. There is nothing. You know story of Papillon's escape?'

'Yes.'

'I wish sometime to do that. I wish to stand on cliff waiting for seventh wave. When seventh wave comes, jump in sea with coconut raft. Maybe live. Maybe die. But not wait. Not limp. Be free man. You jump with me?'

'Perhaps.'

Two hours later, she left him at the main gates of the HQ. The TV van was already waiting. Some of the crew were watching them. Véronique felt a rush of sickening panic – that she hadn't told him the most important things, that she hadn't asked him the most important things, that it was too late for those things, too late for him to have a life, for her to have a life . . . His face was angelically sun-struck and already retreating into memory.

'Good luck with everything. Have a good trip home,' she said.

'Have good trip away from home.'

And after an unbearable look that said 'Yes, it's too late for everything, and we're fucked but we must pretend it's going to be okay', he made his way to the TV van.

In the cool kitchen of the Villa Maldormé, she rang a rental car number, regarding her dialling hand with a numb curiosity, as if it was a prosthetic she had believed to be a real hand all this time.

With the same intractable hand, she opened her chequebook and wrote the curious ornamental shapes of 20,000 francs. Why exactly these shapes? She added another zero and crossed out the comma. Her brain reminded her that she didn't have this amount in her current account, only in other, frozen accounts. She wasn't too sure in fact. Her hand crumpled the paper and stopped over a fresh one. 100,000. An envelope extracted from a musty drawer of a desk with a red leather folder in the corner. Licked, sealed.

The gates of the legion's HQ were open like arms. In the main office, a fat-bellied man in a green tracksuit with surprise for a face and sausages for fingers took the envelope with Victor's name. 'Merci, Mademoiselle.'

She drove the rented BMW to the beach where she knew Victor and Katya were to be filmed. Stark limestone shimmered over burnt grass.

Victor hobbled along the beach while a girl hopped excitedly beside him. The ballerina and the lead soldier – followed by the cameramen. They laughed. Later, from closer up, Katya appeared as a lively, plain girl in a printed floral dress and bright lipstick. She was interviewed while Victor sat in the passenger seat of an old Renault to be driven by her. The TV crew were only a few metres away from the bench where Véronique sat. She heard the French interpreter's fragmented speech as Katya brightly answered the camera's questions in soft, wise Slavic sounds: 'This may sound bad, but in a way it's good that he lost his legs.'

Victor spotted Véronique in a shock of recognition. He put his arm out of the open window, not reaching out to her, not waving, just an arm stuck out of a car window, as if to say 'Here I am, and there you are. Strange.' She wanted to touch his hand but he was being looked after by a nurse, after all. She frantically thought of what more she could give him, in this very last moment. The gold ring with de la Martinière's coat of arms on her little finger? But what would he do with it?

'Before, we were never really together, he was too involved with the legion. Now it's like . . . we're finally truly together, we finally belong together and I'm going to look after him.' Katya giggled.

Véronique got up from the stained bench on which someone had engraved, with a pocket-knife, 'This bench belongs to Leila and Momo. That's all', and got into the car. Victor had buried his head in his hands. Katya, glowing with post-interview jubilation, sat in the driver's seat and tried to hug him. He pushed her away. The intrepid camera watched them. She tried again, tireless, nurse-like. He pushed her away again. Véronique's hand turned the key in the ignition, her teeth clenched. When she looked again at the Renault, there was a happy end for the camera: Victor had succumbed to his girlfriend's embrace. She stroked his head.

A silver BMW glided between burnt-out hills and white-hot rocks. The sea below furrowed and raw like a throat that had been screaming for a long time and had finally gone quiet.

THIRTY-NINE

September 1967, Thessaloniki

Pascal waited for half an hour in the Evangelistria Cemetery. If he had been local, he wouldn't have exposed himself by hanging around for so long. But he felt he had nothing to lose. He had the case with the dismembered Gestetner. A few blocks down the alley a woman in black – the eternal woman in black – was putting fresh flowers in a decapitated plastic bottle. Eventually, unable to find a taxi anywhere along the way, he walked back to his hotel, struggling with the heavy case, drenched in sweat.

No sooner had he walked into his hotel room than the phone rang aggressively.

'Pêcheur Ludo?' a male voice said.

'Speaking.'

'You are strongly advised to leave Greece immediately. You will not receive a second warning,' the voice said in American-accented and correct but unpleasant English. 'Otherwise someone might get hurt.'

'Who are you?' But the caller had hung up.

Startled, Pascal looked around the room for traces of a search but everything was as he'd left it earlier that morning. Panayotis had been right about moving to Hotel Astoria. Someone had sniffed something. He dialled the Philipidis number. Nobody answered. He packed his few possessions, checked out and moved to the Astoria. The characteristic façade with its nineteenth-century tower at the corner was unchanged since '48. Even the street kiosk was still there, and so were the trees lining the other side of the street. Pascal checked into a room on the third floor with a view to the sea and immediately dialled Nikitas's number in Paris. At least he could be sure that his phone wasn't tapped, so soon after moving in. He was the only other contact of the Democratic Defence Pascal had aside from Panayotis-Odysseos.

'I haven't actually been in touch with the Thessaloniki cell for a while,' Nikitas said. 'I've been working with the European contacts, organising traffic to and from Athens. But it doesn't sound good. I suggest you leave at this point.'

'Come on, I'm a foreigner, they won't dare.'

'In principle no, but they're thugs and I wouldn't push their patience too much.'

'But what do I do with the Gestetner? And what about Panayotis, I mean, Odysseos?'

'If you're prepared to stay, you should move to one of the safe houses there, just out of Thessaloniki. I can't give you the address over the phone but you'll get a message from someone in the next twelve hours. Someone will take you there. And please be extra careful. Now that they're watching you, you could put others at risk.'

Pascal decided he wasn't going to take the ridiculous anonymous ultimatum seriously. He wasn't sure exactly what he would do, but to leave now would be somehow ignominious, especially if Panayotis had been arrested by the secret police, and especially if he himself had unwittingly contributed to it with his uninformed behaviour. He tried the Philipidis number again. No reply. He would go to their house, regardless of the risk. Maybe the secret police were waiting for him there. What the hell. They couldn't do anything to him.

Nobody was following him or hanging about in the street outside the Philipidis' building – just the usual passers-by. The doorman nodded at Pascal. The doorbell rang like an alarm. He heard some shuffling inside. The door opened cautiously, the chain still across.

Hrisoula's face peered through and he knew something was wrong.

'Kyria Philipidis, I've come to see Panayotis.'

'They took them away.'

'Who?'

'Panayotis and Angelis.'

'Who took them away?'

'Please speak quietly.'

'Who?' Pascal whispered.

'KYP.'

'When?'

'Yesterday.'

'Where to?'

'I don't know. You should go now. They'll arrest you too.'

'Don't worry about me.'

He didn't know what else to say. Hrisoula was not about to invite him in. Her face betrayed no emotion except the perennial grief of stone.

'I'll do everything I can to get them out,' Pascal said thoughtlessly.

'They have seized the memoirs,' Hrisoula whispered.

'Where?'

'I don't know. There was one more copy hidden away.'

Pascal realised that he hadn't checked for his copy when he moved hotels. He wanted to comfort Hrisoula but she didn't yield to comforting.

'Angelis can't take it, they'll kill him,' she said in a stony but fractured voice.

'Hrisoula,' Pascal said, putting his fingers against the door chain, as if she were behind bars, 'I'll try to get them out. I . . .' He took a breath.

'They're probably keeping them in the military base near the airport while the interrogation lasts, but they'll likely transfer them to a prison soon. Now go. Go back to Paris. You can't do anything for them here.' And she shut the door.

Pascal stumbled down the cool stairs. Task number one: call his lawyer in Paris. Task number two: call *Le Monde* and ask them to make space for Nikitas, as well as for a story Pascal was going to write straight away – the first in many years. A voice startled him from his anxiety.

'Last visit to the Philipidis?' It was the doorman. Pascal tried to read his expression and saw nothing reassuring there.

'Mind your own business,' he said.

'I am,' chuckled the man, 'I am.' And he chuckled again. Pascal slammed the heavy door, realising with angry astonishment that the doorman was not exactly senile. Even Angelis hadn't picked him as a spy.

As he stepped inside the hotel lift, he became conscious of a malodorous presence behind him. Two clean-shaven men in suits shared his uncomfortable ascent to the third floor, staring at him interestedly in a way which left no doubt about the nature of their interest. There was something about their faces, their crudely chiselled jaws perhaps, and the way they held their hands in front of their crotches, which brutally crushed Pascal's momentary hope that they might be contacts with news about the safe house Nikitas had mentioned. He stepped out of the lift coolly, followed by his unpleasant companions, and stopped in front of his door, key in hand. They followed him closely.

'May I help you, Messieurs?' He turned to them, speaking in French. They looked at each other, momentarily confused.

'Doesn't he speak Greek?' said the one who seemed to exude the BO.

'We know you speak Greek, Mister Pêcheur,' said the one without the BO. 'And we wouldn't mind if you invited us in.'

'Who are you?' Pascal continued in French obtusely, knowing it was ultimately pointless but wanting to prolong their confusion and give himself time to decide on his strategy.

'Stop speaking bloody French at us!' The smelly one raised his voice. 'And get in.'

'Get in!' said the other one in English.

'You're two awful, ugly, unwashed thugs.' Pascal took childish delight in the insult.

'What is he saying?'

'No idea,' said the one who seemed to be senior on account of his better hygiene and more understated jaw, if nothing else.

'Right.' The junior one took a hand-pistol from inside his grey raincoat and pointed it casually at Pascal. 'Now open the door.'

Pascal followed the succinct instructions while putting on his best look of bewildered indignation – which wasn't too far from how he felt anyway.

'It's better for you if you co-operate,' said the senior thug, while the other one poked through Pascal's unpacked luggage with the barrel of his gun.

'Let's go, Monsieur Pêcheur. You'll feel more at home at the station. They speak French there. They speak a lot of languages there.' He gave in to an acute fit of mirth, then blew his nose in a large checked handkerchief.

Pascal decided not to provoke them.

'Can I make a phone-call?' he asked in Greek.

'Be my guest,' said the mirthful one, folding his handkerchief carefully. 'You know why?' – and he unfolded the soiled material again for another emergency – 'Because your phone is being tapped.' Now both of them laughed. Pascal was beginning to feel concerned. 'So, whoever you call will be keeping you company in a cell next door to yours.'

'I don't understand what's going on,' Pascal said indignantly. 'I'm a tourist.'

'Yes, writing for a travel magazine, right? I think you need to have a look at our jails for a fuller picture.'

They accompanied him in the lift again. He carried his bags, including the luckless Gestetner. At reception, they watched him closely pay his bill (for the night he hadn't spent there), pick up his passport and hand over his key. The receptionist displayed a marked lack of curiosity about Pascal's premature departure and his companions. The men steered Pascal discreetly down the street and around the corner where a black sedan was waiting.

'Where are we going?' Pascal protested. 'I don't understand.'

Once they were inside the car, the younger one handcuffed his hands and sat next to him.

'You're arresting me now?'

'You're going to have a chat with Inspector Voulgaris,' he said sooth-ingly, as if it could have been a lot worse. 'And I suggest you keep your voice for Inspector Voulgaris later on. You'll need it. He looks forward to talking to you so much that you mustn't disappoint him.'

During the long ride in the direction of the airport, Pascal cursed himself for getting involved so lightly in something he didn't know enough about. Had Panayotis told them about him? Or had he led them to Panayotis? How was he going to get access to a telephone? Were there enough witnesses to his arrest? How could he help the Philipidis if he was detained himself?

'Monsieur Pêcheur, it's an honour to have you among us.' Inspector Voulgaris grinned manically, revealing a chipped tooth, and then yapped at the guards, 'Take off his handcuffs. How am I supposed to shake his hand?'

'I can't say the same.' Pascal didn't shake the outstretched hand. 'You owe me an explanation.'

'I understand,' Voulgaris said intelligently, almost compassionately. 'You see, Monsieur Pêcheur,' – he went around a desk laid with folders and sat down, pointing to a chair for Pascal – 'it's exceedingly simple. I want you to understand our motives. We are democrats. We are struggling for a democratic, modern society, for fundamental Greek values: order, Orthodoxy, loyalty to the fatherland. It is a tough struggle. We have many enemies. We are surrounded by enemies, within and without. Fortunately, we also have very powerful friends: the Americans. In today's difficult world, we have aligned ourselves with them, with the only just cause.'

He offered Pascal a cigarette from a gilded case. Though dying for a smoke, Pascal declined.

'What do I have to do with this?' he asked.

'Right. Pertinent question but I suspect you can answer it yourself. You see, we are concerned for you. We have reason to suspect that you are misled in your views and have been hanging out with the wrong crowd, so to speak. We are eager for you to revise your opinions in order not to inflict further harm on anyone, especially yourself.' He paused and looked concerned for a moment. 'Do you follow me?'

'No.'

'I'll speak more slowly.'

'No, I don't follow your ideas.'

'Oh.' The inspector opened a thick folder. Pascal could hear the two guards breathing a few metres behind him. '*Sisyphus: A Memoir of a Political Prisoner*. Now, what were you intending to do with this piece of execrable communist propaganda?'

'There is no propaganda inside, just facts. It's a memoir. I have an interest in the subject of political imprisonment and I wanted to collect material from various sources, not just in Greece.' He was being foolish. Was this his copy or the other hidden copy?

'Yes, in fact you have a very neat system of listing your sources.' Voulgaris flicked the pages of Pascal's address book, as if fanning himself. 'All of them foul communists. Fortunately, most of them have been dealt with appropriately. We pride ourselves on our efficiency. Our methods always work, as in all true democracies. All our enemies finish by agreeing with us and telling us what we need to know.'

He glared at Pascal and his angular features were naked without the veneer of false friendliness.

'I am not an enemy of the Greek state,' Pascal said and hated himself. 'I have no ideological or political motives. I am a writer.'

'Writer, yes . . .' Voulgaris suddenly slipped into a romantic mode. 'I love French writers. *The Three Musketeers*. You know why? Because it's about loyalty, serving one's country no matter at what cost. Oh, and *The Count of Monte Cristo*. The Castle of If. The perfect prison and the perfect escape. It makes me dream you know. It must interest you too, I imagine. We have our own Castle of If, I'm sure you know it, though only from the outside of course. It sits on top of Thessaloniki, by the city walls. Except you can't escape from Eptapirgio like from the Castle of If because, well, there's no water around!' He burst into a brittle laugh. The chairs of the two guards behind Pascal creaked. Pascal's back crawled. With typical abruptness, Voulgaris wiped the laughter from his face like spittle. He picked up a book from the folder.

'*La Terre de Midas: la catastrophe de la guerre civile grecque.* Do you like my pronunciation? Now, I already see a mistake in the title. We don't say "civil war" but *andartopolemo* or *simoritopolemo* – it was a war of the kingdom of Greece against the aggression of dangerous criminals who wanted to destroy Greece. I'm surprised you didn't know this. After all, you spent an exceedingly long time among them, Monsieur Loublier. Your wife must have been very worried indeed at the time. People, even foreign journalists, were killed for much less.'

'I was only doing my job – reporting from the front line.' Already Pascal was defending himself.

'Yes, of course. But you were lucky the bandits didn't bump you off. But then why would they? You were defending their cause in the eyes of the world, after all.'

Pascal cursed himself again for underestimating the Greek intelligence service – for years they had worked hand in glove with the CIA.

'Now, I want to share with you the cause of my anguish. We have here the passport of one Ludo Pêcheur. Now, what is the reason for this deplorable forgery?' Voulgaris looked at Pascal with a falsely beseeching sadness. It occurred to Pascal that he was dealing with a high quality psychopath.

'I wasn't sure if I would be admitted under my real name. I didn't know much about the situation in Greece.'

'The situation? The *situation*? The situation is normal. Democratic. Friendly.'

'Is that why I'm under arrest?'

'Secondly,' Voulgaris pursued, 'we have here a disassembled printing machine which you were going to hand over to Panayotis Philipidis, an activist in a terrorist organisation working against the Greek state and whose father, Angelis Philipidis, has long been in the black books of the state . . .'

'I have never associated with terrorists and never will.' Pascal hoped that black-and-white statements would make an impression on this black-and-white mind. 'The Philipidis are good people who . . .'

'That's what you think.' Voulgaris was shedding his courtesy. 'You are mistaken. The Philipidis are monsters. They, and all the others you will tell us about, endeavour to overthrow the order. Their activities are aimed at undermining the Greek state. It is unforgivable for a Western writer and journalist to be so misinformed.' He stared at Pascal.

'No, *you* are mistaken if you think you can imprison and interrogate people at your whim. My lawyer . . .'

Voulgaris barked with hilarity. His chipped tooth strangely bothered Pascal – it was the ultimate mark of untrustworthiness. The two guards chuckled.

'Your lawyer!' he gawked in a worrying falsetto. 'I can wipe my behind with your lawyer. I am your lawyer here, and your judge, and your prosecutor.'

'You can't get away with a second George Polk.'

'George Polk? Why? We're not going to give you over to the commies – you're safe with us. We are the Americans, remember? Not the Russians. We just need you to tell us what you know and not a hair will fall from your head, Mister French Writer.'

Pascal had a withering craving for a smoke. He took out his cigarettes and lit one without asking. Voulgaris didn't object.

'I want to know where the Philipidis are,' Pascal said assertively, blowing rings of smoke. He was refusing to be a character in a Kafka story.

'Your friends the Philipidis are here, with us. You may hear their melodious voices later on. They need to have their tongues untied because they're like mules.'

'You have no right to torture civilians! Angelis is very sick . . .' Pascal's pulse was fast and he felt a sickness at the core of his being.

'Monsieur Loublier, we have all the rights here. Besides, I am not interested in your opinion regarding human rights. You're a pitiful communist and I have shown the good will to talk to you which, please note, is not inexhaustible.'

It was so grotesque Pascal could have laughed if his sense of humour hadn't vacated him in the last few minutes. 'I'm not a communist and you know this,' he said instead. 'I care about people. That's why I'm in Greece.'

'Is this your care?' Voulgaris kicked the bag with the printing machine. 'If you really care about this country, you will tell us the names of other terrorists from this organisation. We know they are trying to infiltrate Europe too, so that they can smuggle their poisonous propaganda – and worse – back into Greece, and those emasculated, so-called liberal European governments aren't doing what's necessary to stop them. We need to know who is snooping around, say, in France. We need to protect our country.'

This time Pascal laughed, his nerves giving in. All this was so clearly a mistake. The two guards scraped their chairs and he felt their iron grip on his arms.

'I'll give you some time to reflect, to gather your memory as it were. I very much hope that you won't disappoint us. Because I simply won't be able to take it.'

'If you think you can keep me here and blackmail me, you're tragically mistaken. You'll cause an international scandal.'

'Ha!' Voulgaris exclaimed theatrically. 'Ha! and again ha! What would your evidence be? We won't do anything to you that will leave marks. Besides, you may not be going home as soon as you think. When you went to bandit territory in '48, everybody thought you'd been abducted or killed. Was there a scandal? No. Then it turned out you were there voluntarily. Well, you might just happen to disappear once more, voluntarily. And you flatter yourself if you think that your government will mess up its relations with the Greek state over you. I think that old fool De Gaulle has other things to worry about. Unfortunately for you, and fortunately for us, you're not American. Think about it, my dear Pascal, show that you are a thinker.'

Pascal was rewarded with another psychopathic grin, lifted from his chair with brutal precision and escorted to a damp, sepulchral cell with a concrete floor which immediately reminded him that he had claustrophobia. There was a bunk and no toilet or windows. He lit another cigarette and noticed his fingers were trembling. He lay on the bunk and stared at the naked bright bulb hanging from a cable.

They wouldn't touch him, it was all just manipulation. He could only give them one name – Nikitas, and the name of the woman contact he never met. Of course Nikitas's name was in his address book anyway. And the street where the basement used for printing was, though he'd never been there. In the pocket of his trousers he patted his wallet which, miraculously, they hadn't taken. He kept all his cash there, which was otherwise unintelligent but in the present situation a godsend. He had 2500 drachmae which was about 100 US dollars and plenty to bribe a guard or even two, depending on their greed. Bribe a guard to let him make a call, for example. He tried to remember the phone number of his lawyer. They would surely take his cash during the next interrogation. He thought of *Papillon*, where prisoners rolled their cash in tiny metal cylinders and inserted them in their anuses. He brushed away the offensive thought.

He cursed himself for having been such an obedient arrestee, for not having made a fuss during his arrest. He'd thought he could explain. He'd thought it wasn't that bad. He had been a fool. Yes, Voulgaris was right – it was unforgivable to be so misinformed. He could be held here for weeks before anyone in France was startled into setting up an inquiry. The only witnesses of his arrest were the receptionist at the Astoria and possibly the staff at the Mediterranée, if the secret police had snooped around there too, and those people had probably been bribed or terrorised into silence. Then there was the doorman who was an informer anyway. But even so, was the French government going to quarrel with the junta on account of one missing ex-journalist and not particularly fashionable writer with left-wing credentials? The only way to go about it would be through the Council of Europe. The investigation would last months, in which time they could do anything with him in this dungeon. Voulgaris's logic wasn't as brittle as his grin, but it was as sinister.

Pascal closed his eyes and for some reason saw Daphne hold out her arm for the field doctor to dig out the shrapnel with a hot knife. He wondered if her fingers were still stiff.

Or was he still in his bed in Villa Maldormé, with the shutters down and the Mediterranean summer rotting sweetly outside? The two fetid men in the lift, the grimace of the maniac, the febrile Panayotis and the ghost of Angelis, and the mesmeric blue gloom of

Thessaloniki, all that was a dream. It was the effect of the traumatic Evgenia Ginzburg memoirs. Any moment now he would remember who and where he really was and grope for the lovely curves of a semi-naked Sophie next to him. Or even the less lovely but statuesque shape of Pauline, breathing anxiously under cream satin sheets. He would wake up and Greece would ache dully inside him the way it always had, petrified and unreachable.

Muffled screams travelled through the porous substance of Pascal's dream and he found himself in a damp place exactly the opposite of the Villa Maldormé: the unblinking eye of a bulb staring at him; multiple, hard steps echoing closer; and what ached dully inside him was the unfamiliar and surprising sensation of fear.

FORTY

July 1998, Ohrid

People whispered with benign curiosity. They just didn't know what the Australian was still doing there, a week after Dafina's funeral. The Australian didn't know either. The voluble newsagent called him 'Dundee', and his underage daughter eyed him up wishfully. Pallid northern tourists unloaded from shiny buses. Dusty, extenuated Albanians leaked across the border. He expected the town to crumble any moment, proving that what was happening was indeed unreal.

He walked past the *chinar*, the giant plane-tree that used to house an entire café and was struck by lightning a few years ago.

He almost collided with Stamatis who was stumbling out of a bar.

'Uncle Stamatis, are you okay?'

The old man looked up at him through a thick haze of alcoholic meaningfulness and waved. 'Splendid,' he spluttered and grabbed Theo's arm.

'They thought they were waging the third world war!' he muttered. 'The beginning of a world revolution! But they were alone on the mountain – we were alone! Alone while the bastards pounded us from the air . . . Greece was their laboratory experiment. Do you understand?'

Theo didn't understand. Stamatis let go of his arm and slumped under a tree, still muttering, pointing an eloquent finger at an invisible listener. Old guerrillas die hard. Theo hesitated, then shrugged and continued his aimless stroll, thinking how sad Europe was. But even amid ruins of hideousness, he couldn't hate Europe so long as Véronique inhabited it. He couldn't leave this continent while she was on it. On the same piece of land, in the same hemisphere, only a couple of Greenwich hours away.

He sat at the kitchen table and opened his laptop. His prose was substandard and his ideas unfocused. His reference books hadn't been opened for weeks. He picked up the phone with a sweaty hand and dialled the Marseilles number. It rang twenty times. The doorbell rang too.

Purple-nosed Stamatis was at the door, stinking of alcohol, with a loaf of fresh bread.

'Thought you might be starving yourself, son. Dafina gave me instructions to look after you.'

Theo invited him in but the old man was on his way to the harbour, to give his boat a new paint job. Theo went along with him, not sure why. Stamatis's boat had a new name as of today: Dafina. Theo passed the second coating over the white letters.

'Did you and Grandma . . . I mean, did you . . . um, have a close relationship?'

Stamatis took a puff from his pipe, examining the work. 'Yes.'

'How long did you know her for?'

'Long.' He wasn't the talkative type.

'And did you . . . ever go back to Greece?'

Stamatis puffed his pipe inscrutably.

'Yes.'

'Why didn't you stay?'

'It turned out I had nothing to go back to after all.'

'Because of the war?'

He nodded indefinitely and wiped non-existent saliva from his pipe.

Stamatis had an appointment with Dafina's notary, to pick up something she had apparently left for him. But Theo suspected the old man just wanted to get back to his drink. They shook hands. Stamatis's bad eye had closed almost completely. His good eye was a smudged blue. He was one of those people who either had a great mystery or pain buried at the core of their being like a treasure, or were simply overwhelmingly vacant like a barren, rocky island.

Lake Ohrid turned slowly in the fading late afternoon. Theo walked along the jagged top of Samuil's Walls, overlooking the old town.

Cronos ate all his children except one, and that one created the universe. Atlas propped the sky on his mighty shoulders. But what titan, what god, would bend the universe, shape it in such a way that Véronique would come back to him? Not physically – that was easy. After all, he was the one who left, physically speaking. The book she gave him was thin, but it weighed his jacket pocket down. He opened it and her dense voice slipped from the page.

Where is love that with one stroke cuts time in two and
    stuns it?

He clapped it closed with a shudder. Her voice stopped. Like her face which wasn't simply a face, her voice wasn't simply a voice. She had recited this hateful couplet ad nauseam. He was spellbound by the words, but only because they came from her mouth, in her voice. She had recited this one night in Naples. They lay still in the sticky night, the angular hills edging towards their balcony, and he felt a chill come from her. For the first time, he sensed that inside her there could be a glacier, a place of such desolation that no Mediterranean nights of passion could thaw it into a lake.

The horror of Véronique's season. She was inside it now. But he was there too, in the season of no heat or cold, no hope or faith. A season to forget all seasons.

Suddenly, surprising himself, he flung the book sideways with a flick of the wrist. Its wings fluttered helplessly in the still air before it hit the dry grass. It would rot there, in the naked summer sun of Ohrid. Veronique loved Greek poetry in a way she couldn't love people. Living people.

Sometimes, when he looked at her, he wondered whether she really was extraordinarily beautiful or whether there was something else totally irregular about her. Something a bit unreal, perhaps, which

was an inexhaustible source of fascination. Something like the dream
of Europe converging into her face and body, Europe with its ravines,
deserts, lakes, reflections, eerie dawns and macabre nights, ravages,
violences, desires, perversions and discoveries. In her converged the
myth of Europe. He merged with her and with much more than her.
He held her and was perhaps holding the key to a locked, esoteric
world. He entered her before he understood her. But he could
understand her only by entering her. And once he was inside, it was
too late to understand – he was too love-stricken. Véronique was a
moment petrified into eternity – and he had remained there. That
was all. He was there yesterday, he would be there tonight and
tomorrow. It was pointless to keep up the pretence that he had left. It
was impossible for her to empty herself of him, she must feel him
still, tonight, tomorrow, always, as she stirred under the damp sheets
alone, her nose tingling from last night's snort. 'Blood love,' the
misfortune-teller in Naples said. They would never part.

A gunshot ripped his slumber. Theo sat up and looked around but in
the dark he saw only the distant flickers of houses below and the
discreet outlines of pines. He waited for another shot. But the night
healed over the rip so gently that it had never existed. It could have
been at the other end of town; sound travelled with crisp definition
here. The humidity of the wall had seeped into his body. He climbed
down and picked up the ruffled book lying on the grass, forgetting it
was meant to stay and rot there. He walked past the cardboard-cut
houses sleeping like poultry, their heads tucked inside their necks.
The sharp rusty moon hung over the lake. He wanted to cry out but
something was gagging him. When he stopped and looked back to
the ghostly walls, he saw the Balkan night keeping vigil, armed and
delirious with exhaustion. Like Midas, like Theo, it desperately
wanted everything to be undone.

His steps echoed in the labyrinth of narrow cobbled streets.

In the moonlit kitchen of Dafina's house, he contemplated the
phone for a while. He decided that writing always had a more
devastating effect. So he took a sheet of paper, sat at the kitchen
table, and wrote in large, uncontrolled letters:

28 June

I am Midas, lurking in the gardens, drinking the diluted wine of knowledge, waiting for some obscure revelation. Enter Silenius. Silenius is a woman. Thirty years old, white hair, the face of Helen that launched a thousand heartbreaks, and Amazon breasts (two). I know she can whisper to me something I've been waiting for. Instead, she offers to take me away and show me, in full colour as it were, the answer. We travel. I touch the world and it touches me. Silenius and I cross golden cities and coasts. I have everything, except soon I realise that she has slipped away. And I am stuck with the world which is poor of her. Gold is no use to the starving Midas. Midas is poor beyond endurance.

But before she left, she wispered to me in my sleep the secret of life: life is full of grief. That's all. And I am alone with this knowledge.

No, it's not all. We buried Grandmother Dafina a week ago. I'll be here for another week or so, if you want to contact me. Write c/o Dafina Grigorova, Illinden St, Ohrid. After that I'll be going back to Melbourne.

Theo.

FORTY-ONE

September 1967, Thessaloniki

'We don't like hurting foreigners but you are special. For you, we might have to make an exception,' Voulgaris said thoughtfully, sizing Pascal up as if to assess him for the most suitable form of torture. For an hour, Pascal had sat in an interrogation room filled with fetid smoke, in a chair that creaked with the slightest movement, repeating: 'I don't know anyone in Paris, or here. I don't even know what the movement is called. I didn't know what the printing machine was for.'

Voulgaris's colour changed several times, but he was making a visible effort to control himself. 'Your statements are full of contradictions. How could you not know anyone in Paris when they gave you instructions to bring the machine? There's a Nikitas in your address book, snooping around in Paris. Who is he? And how did you know to meet the Philipidis? And what about the manuscript? And all these other reactionary elements in your address book? And the forged passport. And the move to Hotel Astoria. And the stopover in Athens. What were you up to in Athens? Every scrap of evidence is incriminatory and you tell me you're innocent as a new-born! And my patience, like everything in life, is only finite. Especially since yesterday there was an explosion in a street rubbish bin in Athens and anti-government leaflets were dropped on the city.'

Pascal was tired, too tired to protest any more, too tired even to be afraid. Voulgaris nodded to the two men by the wall. Hands tied behind his back, they dragged Pascal to another interrogation room where the chief hangman waited. Pascal knew it simply from the shape of the man's head – squashed at the back as if he had been dropped as a baby, the forehead protruding over his sunken eyes – and the way he was slapping his palm with some wire. All Pascal could think was, 'Kafka, pure Kafka.' Now what? Were they going to flash out their knives and stab him to death, whispering cryptically, 'Like a dog'?

'Do you know an old Greek method of inducing cooperation, called falanga?' the hangman asked joyfully. Another man, short and weedy, was leaning against a rifle behind him.

'Yes,' Pascal said, almost curious. So finally he was confronting the famous falanga at first hand. The hangman was visibly disappointed: he was deprived of the pleasure of detailing the agonies of feet-beating.

'We have instructions not to leave too many marks on you,' he said. 'So we'll have to perform a limited version of it.'

Pascal was puzzled by this introduction – he felt quite detached from the process, almost to the point of looking around for the subject of torture. But he was soon reminded. Two men pushed him up on a solid wooden table and immobilised his ankles with the strap of the rifle on which the weedy man in the corner had been leaning. They didn't take off his shoes before they proceeded to pound his soles with an iron bar. Pascal's shoes were of good quality, the soles were reliable, but the first major wave of pain that flooded his body was mixed with the terrible thought of what it would be like to have this done to naked feet. He tried to drive the pain back inside but it burst from every pore. He tried to think of his feet as separate from his body, so that the pain wouldn't reach his brain. He tried to remember that he was dreaming and so he couldn't possibly be in real pain. Cold water was splashed on his face. He tried to think again of what he could say that they would like to hear.

The door opened and what sounded like Voulgaris walked in. He blocked the shards of light coming from the bulb. He was holding something.

'This is very disagreeable to us,' he said. Pascal disagreed; some of those present visibly enjoyed it. 'But I've just had a confirmation of your guilt. Philipidis Junior has signed a declaration saying that you are indeed involved in their illegal activities.'

'What did you do to him first?' Pascal managed to gurgle. Even his voice felt as if it had been beaten.

'What was necessary.'

'Will you release them?'

'Oh no, of course not. They're dangerous anarchists. We'll just move them to somewhere more comfortable because, as I already pointed out, we are humane.'

'I will get you for this,' Pascal growled. 'You will pay dearly, thug.'

'You will first have to get out of here, Mister Writer. And convince others that you have been here at all.' He turned on his heels and mumbled to the hangman, 'That's enough for today.'

In his cell, Pascal was visited by a man with a fascinatingly large nose and distant, myopic eyes behind thick glasses. Without a word, he set about removing Pascal's tattered shoes and cleaning his bleeding feet, which to Pascal seemed an act of premeditated cruelty since it only aggravated the pain.

'Do they always look after their victims like this?' He spoke slowly, so that he wouldn't gasp.

'No. You're treated as a special guest.'

'Is that why I didn't have to take off my shoes before coming in?'

The officer was impassive.

'Do you work here?' Pascal continued his absurd small talk while the man daubed his feet with something that looked like iodine. A thought nibbled at the back of his clouded mind.

'Sort of.'

'As a guard?'

'No.'

'As a . . . doctor?'

The man was not talkative.

'Is it night or day?'

'It's midday.'

'I've been here twenty-four hours. And it already feels like weeks.'

There was no expression on the man's face. Pascal had to act quickly, for he didn't know when he would see him again.

'I need you to help me,' Pascal said. There was no reaction.

'I'm here by mistake. I'm a writer from France and I got arrested yesterday in my hotel . . .'

'I know.'

'What are they going to do with me?'

'I am not in a position to say.'

'Look, I need you to help me. Take me to the 401 Military Hospital. I . . .' He checked himself before he managed to make the mistake of mentioning his contact there.

The doctor had finished his job. Pascal's feet felt as if they had been stripped from their skin.

'Look,' the man said and pushed up his glasses, 'I was moved here from 401 as a demotion. I'm nobody here.'

This made him even dearer to Pascal.

'But you can take me to the hospital, can't you? Say that I'm gravely injured, which I am . . .'

'My friend, you don't know what gravely injured means. Your bones aren't even shattered.'

'Still. Just . . .'

'Nobody takes orders from me here,' the man whispered. 'I'm on my way out anyway. They're bringing new people in, their people.'

The man looked at him with the eyes of a drowning puppy.

'I have a lot of money.' Pascal had never supposed he was capable of uttering something so vulgar. 'I could have money sent to you from France in a matter of weeks. Days!'

'Keep your voice down.'

'My wife is from the aristocracy,' Pascal whispered, resigned to the vulgarity of it. 'She's very wealthy. Do you know what I'm saying?'

'I'm sorry. I can't help you. They'll skin me alive.'

Pascal fell back with a sunken heart. The demoted doctor strode out in his matter-of-fact, broken way. Pascal lifted the tattered mattress to make sure the cash he had hidden between the planks of the bed was still there. His wallet had been taken before the interrogation, as he'd expected. There was a buzzing noise inside the bulb. He wondered if he would ever walk again, then marvelled again at his own miscalculations. He had advised the editor of *Le Monde* to be cautious about Nikitas. He had thought they wouldn't touch him. He had thought Greece couldn't take any more terror after '49. Perhaps he wasn't a thinker, after all.

The punch to his left eye sent him flying to the nearest wall. The world lost its credibility. He *was* a Kafka character after all, despite his resistance. Pain and blood fell like a curtain over his vision. Had he lost his eye?

'Don't make things worse for yourself, Frenchman.' The hangman crossed his arms and watched Pascal scramble up. 'Or we'll have to rough you up.'

'I'd say it's you who is making things worse for me.' Pascal wiped the blood from his face.

'Don't answer back.' Everything looked like a red, liquid oil-painting. Pain thickened inside him.

'I can give you one name,' he said, 'in Paris.'

He could sense a sudden mood of happy animation in the room. The rustle of paper. He was surrounded by people who lived under the tyranny of paranoia.

'Yes?'

'Patrocles Vartholomaiou.' He prayed there wasn't a real person by that improbable name in Paris.

'He was the one who put you in touch with Philipidis?' Voulgaris chirped.

'Yes. Late forties, balding, tall, with tinted glasses.' Someone scribbled furiously.

'And he told you to bring a printing machine?'

'Yes.'

'What else did he tell you?'

'He gave me some information about human rights . . . about what's been happening here since April.' He figured he had nothing more to lose – except his other eye, of course.

'Any other contacts? Names?'

'No. I'd tell you if I knew.'

'What were you doing in Athens?'

'Nothing. Visiting the cemetery.'

'Why?'

'I went to a friend's grave.'

There was a moment of uncertainty in the room. Pascal needed to sit down. His feet were padded with pain, his eye throbbed.

'You're lying.'

'I don't know anyone in Athens.'

'Call Yannis,' Voulgaris ordered, and a minute later the doctor appeared.

'Have a look at his eye.'

Yannis had a look. Pascal was leaning against some surface. The blood was still dripping; there were trails on the concrete floor. Yannis daubed his eye with a cloth.

'He needs some stitches. In the hospital.'

'Can't you do it yourself?' Voulgaris's intonation told Pascal that Yannis's days here were indeed numbered.

'No sir, I don't have anaesthetics.'

The hangman laughed.

'And no stitching thread,' Yannis hastened to add.

'Stop bloody laughing, you animal.' Voulgaris yapped at the hangman. 'You could be more careful. All right.' He was headed out of the door. 'Take him to 401. Yannis, you go with him. I'll send another man with you.'

'Yes sir.'

Bastard, thought Pascal. Then he noticed his own shirt was splattered with blood.

'I need my jacket, I'm cold,' he said.

Someone nodded and he was escorted to his cell where he asked to be left alone for a moment, to pray. He reached under the mattress and extracted the banknotes which he put inside his underwear. He then asked the guard if he could have a change of clothes from his bag.

'This isn't the Astoria,' the guard grumbled and led him down stale-smelling, depressing corridors where screams emanated from behind a door. Pascal prayed it wasn't Angelis or Panayotis. When Pascal was passed over to another guard, he repeated his request. He was allowed to change his shirt. This simple act filled him with hope, as if he was preparing for freedom.

In the jeep, Yannis sat uncomfortably next to him, the guard next to the driver. Pascal's hands were untied so that he could hold a cloth against his brow to staunch the blood. On the way into town, the two men at the front engaged in a frivolous conversation. Pascal pulled out the banknotes and put them on the seat between himself and Yannis. Yannis glanced at the money sideways.

'Two thousand and five hundred,' Pascal whispered. 'Give me your address and I'll send you more.'

'Monsieur, I'm afraid this is impossible,' Yannis said in perfect French.

Pascal stared at him in surprise. 'But you speak French!'

'I studied at the Sorbonne,' Yannis said impassively, as if it were the most natural thing.

Overjoyed, Pascal continued in French. 'Listen to me. Put me in the care of Dr Nikolau, let him do the stitches, and I'll manage the rest.'

'You'll be sewed up by whoever is available, I'm afraid.'

'Hey, what's going on back there?' The guard turned around.

'I'm practising my French,' Yannis said sweetly and the guard returned to his conversation with the driver, feeling out of his depth.

'But I must . . . we must go to the south wing of the hospital, second floor.' Pascal had a plan – not a very good one, but a plan.

'I can't promise anything.'

'And in any case, if I suddenly disappear, try to delay the search. Leave me in the doctor's room and go for a stroll down the corridor with the guard. Slow things down.'

'I can't promise anything.' Yannis's fleshy face was atremble with fright, which was a good sign – he was considering it.

'Please take this.' Pascal nodded at the cash.

'I haven't done anything for you.'

'I insist.'

'Please do not insist.' Yannis's politeness was an expression of his permanent distress.

'Tell me your address so I can send you . . .'

'I can't, it's too dangerous.'

'I will find a way to thank you.'

'As I said, I haven't done anything.'

Yet, Pascal wanted him to add, but Yannis sank into an anguished silence for the rest of the trip.

He was taken to the south wing, second floor – a good start. A doctor prepared to attend silently to his eye, without anaesthetic but no doubt with ample stitching thread. It occurred to Pascal that he could even attack the doctor, smack him on the head with something and flee. But he couldn't attack the person who was caring for him, even if it was without anaesthetic.

'Could you go and get Dr Yannis? I'd like him to do it. Please.'

The doctor looked at him with surprised annoyance.

'Please. He's been treating all my other wounds.' He hoped his foreign accent would work in his favour. He could see hesitation on the doctor's face.

'Nurse!' The doctor called out, phlegmatically. Oh merde, merde! there goes the plan. Mercifully, the nurse was taking her time.

'She's hopeless. Just when one needs them, they vanish.' The doctor disappeared through a side door. Bless you, nurse.

Pascal unlatched the double-plated window feverishly and yanked it open. He perched on the sill and surveyed the terrain below. It was as he'd seen it from Dr Nikolau's room. He closed the window behind him and jumped. As he fell agonisingly, and noisily, onto the tin roof, he had the strange sensation that his life suddenly changed. Or that, in hindsight, this was the point at which his life would be changed. As if someone else jumped onto the roof, with raw feet, a throbbing eye and trembling insides. Without getting up, for fear of being seen from the windows on the first floor, he crawled to the edge of the roof and jumped again, onto the pavement, praying that he wasn't, by some nasty twist, going to find himself outside the main gate where the jeep was parked with the driver hanging about. And again, he felt as if someone else fell in the middle of a quiet side street lined with plane trees. As if that someone walked away as fast as he could without running. There were two things he had to do urgently: first, get to the railway station, which was miles away at the west end of the city, without attracting attention and without using any form of transport, and second, vomit. Or perhaps in reverse order. The nausea that had been building inside him since the blow to his eye suddenly rose to his face and he retched on the side of the street while a bedraggled dog looked on sympathetically.

He couldn't know from which direction they were most likely to pursue him. He looked around before ducking into the doorway of a building to catch his breath. He wasn't actually convinced that he had to be cautious any more. It was hard to believe that the interrogation rooms, the cell, Voulgaris and his shadow entourage had existed at all. One day he would look back in amusement, telling his grandchild about his crazy stint in Greece. The lobby of the building was semi-dark and musty, and fortunately had no doorman. He had to get to the railway station as soon as possible, before they placed a patrol there to catch him on his way out of town.

He emerged back on the street and started walking west. If he went onto Egnatia Street, just one block up, and kept walking, he would end up at the station. But Egnatia was too obvious, so he turned down Tsimiski Street. His laborious limp and swollen eye (he presumed it was swollen since he couldn't see with it) were attracting looks. Only two days ago he had found the crowds sparse, now it seemed that the entire city had poured outside. What day was it? Saturday? Friday? It wasn't difficult to project an image of a disoriented drunkard emerging from a brawl. He did his jacket up, to cover any new blood stains on his shirt, and limped on with clenched teeth. Wherever he could, he took side streets. At one point, he went past the bookshop in Tsimiski Street – where he had bought his *Thessaloniki Through the Ages* in '48. It was an endless trudge. The city spread like cancerous cells. He was sure his feet were pulped by now – or rather, the feet of the person who was trudging along with his absurdly closed eye. He wanted to laugh this away and go back to his life. But he had wanted to escape from his life, hadn't he? He had escaped. Why was he rushing to get back now? Or was he just rushing? The surreality of being beaten and treated in ways that did not fit with his vision of himself had somehow chipped away at his sense of self, of being Pascal Loublier.

He aimed straight for the platforms. Sneaking around wagons, he was at his most suspect and vulnerable. Any train going north would do, but especially if it was going to Yugoslavia, because that was his ultimate destination. He was completely out of his depth and somewhere in a remote part of himself he felt that what he was doing was doomed. He kept crossing tracks to get to the next platform. He was surprised each time that nobody yelled out at him. He looked for Belgrade on the metal plates but the international trains probably ran at night. Perhaps there wasn't a train to Yugoslavia at all – he knew nothing of the relations between the two countries. The trains were going to Edessa, Larissa/Athena, Alexandroupolis, Gevgelija . . . Of all these, Gevgelija was the non-Greek sounding one which, if he was lucky, could be a border town (but which border – Yugoslav, Bulgarian or Turkish?).

The train consisted of three empty wagons. Perhaps they were going to the border and then back. How would he do the transfer then? Or were these wagons going to be attached to local ones at the border? There were a couple of benches on the platform and no people. But there were people on the other platforms. He scanned them quickly for the distinctive civilan-clad figures of the secret police. He was exhausted. A sudden wave of self-pity engulfed him. How had he deserved to be a Kafka character, to be a fugitive with no sight in his left eye, not daring to ask anyone anything, fretting about wagons and borders and police, unable to even sit on one of these benches and rest?

Sullenly, he got on the middle wagon of the modest train and walked down the grim corridor to the front; he didn't quite know why. In the driver's cabin, there was a small, neat pile which he unfolded into a sudden railway uniform – dark blue trousers, light blue shirt with the SEK logo of the Greek railways on its left breast pocket, dark blue jacket with buttons bearing the same symbol. Even a dark blue cap. With thoughtless movements, he began to take off his clothes and put on the uniform, as if working under orders. The trousers were a bit baggy but otherwise the right length – as if it mattered. The shirt, short-sleeved, was just right and so was the jacket. In one of the breast pockets there was an ID card with a photo but he had no time to examine it. Now what?

He put on the cap but felt silly and took it off. Something in the trouser pocket prodded his leg. He took it out. It was sharp and made of metal and it looked like a . . . His heart leapt, unbelieving, like a starving man finding a roast duck on a park bench. Oh how beautiful it was, how perfectly square and smelling of impersonal metal and of the dear hand of the absent-minded railway worker who had left it behind. But he had to be sure that he had a door for his key.

He bundled up his clothes and limped to the lavatory area. He inspected the ceiling for the precious hatch that every self-respecting wagon should have. And there it was – the lock, square-shaped as the key. Be blessed, nurses and train conductors of Thessaloniki, and all other gentle promoters of public service incompetence! He had planned to rely on bribes for the conductors, and suddenly here was providence. He would just lie there for a couple of hours and it would be all over when he came out. Here was his chance to re-enact something he had read about in the memoirs of a Resistance fighter who sabotaged a German train.

A few people were beginning to appear on the platform. With the square key, he unlocked the manhole and had a look inside. Plenty of room and abominably filthy but hygiene clearly couldn't be a priority. He tossed his clothes up first. He didn't need the uniform any more but suddenly the wagon shook, indicating that someone was getting on. He mustered his strength and lifted himself up, closing the hatch and locking the light out with the precious square key.

'Hey, Trayani,' thundered a voice, 'have you seen my uniform? It's not in the cabin.'

'I told you not to drink so much last night!'

'I'm not kidding, the uniform's not here.'

'Didn't you leave it at the office?'

'I don't think so.'

'Someone must've been in a rush to get on duty and snatched it.'

'Don't joke, Trayani, I need my uniform.'

'Go get another one from the office.'

'Go fuck yourself.'

'Oh come on, Stamati, it's not my fault you drank like a trooper and can't remember where you left it!'

The wagon shook with the weight of more people, though it was hard to say if it was the weight of one large, hairy, angry person – like Stamatis – or that of several smaller ones. Someone ran down the corridor. Whistles ripped the day to shreds inside Pascal's head. Trains thundered off in mysterious directions – slowly like giant aged birds flapping their wings before a graceless take-off. A non-eventful eternity passed before someone shouted angrily, 'Pame!', going. A whistle went off and the wagon shook with imminent departure like a beast awakening from a stupor.

He felt the dirt he was lying in and prayed there were no rats inside or other sizeable undesirables. For the moment nothing moved around him except the giant Tectonic plates of his existence which rotated slowly, readjusting themselves in unfamiliar configurations. He had to lie very still, breathless, in order not be crushed in the great grind. He wanted to think of what he was going to do when he got out, but for some reason his brain refused to offer him a believable version of the immediate future, of how he would be regarded by the locals, of his lawyer's and Michel's reaction at the other end of the line when he told them. He couldn't imagine what would happen after that, how the Greek KYP would be charged with human rights abuse – the scandal, the confusion, perhaps even the eventual overthrow of the junta! Hugging Panayotis and Angelis, while stone-faced Hrisoula looked on as if nothing had happened. Panayotis's brother and sister would be finally allowed to come back to Greece. Reunion of the Philipidis. Pascal would write a moving book about it, achieving world fame overnight. *Night Without Moon*. He would divorce Pauline, finally – oh, but he loved her in a way; he loved her once! He would separate from Sophie before she dumped him – oh, but he loved her too, in another way! He would find Daphne-Dafina of course. He would become the man he should have always been and briefly was, in '48 and '49 . . . It was absurd and tacky. It was someone else's life.

The train rocked for what seemed like hours before stopping at what sounded like a border, if borders could have a sound. He gripped the bundle of his clothes. His heart started thumping in his chest. Wait or jump out? The train could go back into Greece or move on across whatever border they had arrived at. He turned the square key in the lock and opened the hatch just a fraction, peeking out. Out of the smudged window he saw a deserted platform and a sign in Greek, 'Idomeni'.

'Half an hour before departure!' someone shouted who sounded like Stamatis. People laughed outside and no doubt smoked and drank coffee. Pascal's mouth watered constantly. The stuffiness was unbearable. He wished he was Stamatis, in somebody else's uniform, hungover, but smoking and drinking coffee, and filling his eyes with the melancholy September sky . . . But he had been lucky to take the right train.

At the next station, on the other side of the unnamed border, Pascal waited with an equally deranged heartbeat before peeking out. He couldn't see a sign. People weren't getting off. The wagon started to shake after a while, as if someone were tampering with it. Good, let them tamper away, attach it to a local train.

He decided to wait for a larger station at which to clamber out. He tried to imagine the geography of the three countries he could be in, their big cities. If only he had a map of the Balkans and a torch!

After several small stations, he despaired of ever hearing the bustle indicating a larger station. Then at the next one, he assured himself there was nobody around, let the hatch fall and jumped out as softly as possible. It was night-time and his feet hurt less, both facts confirming that he had indeed been entombed for an eternity. He headed for the door, feeling a strange emptiness about him and realising he'd left his clothes behind. He couldn't risk going back so he prepared to get off. Two railway staff were standing outside the station, smoking and chatting, facing the train. The other side might be safer.

He pushed the door open. Being in a vertical position after lying down for so long caused a rush of blood to his head. He stumbled blindly down the three metal steps and blacked out. At that very moment a sword of light pierced his darkness and a violent blast of air created by a fast passing train smashed his head against the metal steps as he caught the wagon door in full flight, slammed from the pressure of a double current.

FORTY-TWO

July 1998, Marseilles

The sun rose at six but the night lingered, needy and obsessed like an abandoned lover hanging around the old places. Véronique lay on the roof of Villa Maldormé, on a white bedspread. Last night, she had a near overdose. For many hours she lay on the roof, floating in a blue, deflated world until the gentle gurgling of the morning's transfusion woke her. The arteries of the sky, which only a few hours before unwillingly poured their blood into the vague, moody sea, were now being refilled, slowly swelling with light pumped from the luminous water. A gull lunged towards Véronique with a homicidal screech. She covered her head but was only brushed by the gull's vulture-shadow.

Véronique knew where she was, if not why. Yet again she awoke in a familiar and unloved world. Without her father. Without Theo. Without Victor. And, worst, without herself. She rolled over on her stomach to check up on the chief excrescence of the town: the Notre Dame de la Garde, a virgin in solid gold topping the Sailors' Church on the highest hill, which shone with fake reassurance in that endearing way popular gold virgins have. The whitewashed houses of the exquisite fishering village huddled around the minuscule bay. The diving school, cheerfully blue and white, with its flag the colour of faded sun. The low, fenced-off HQ of the Foreign Legion, with a sign 'Military grounds. Nasty dog.' Victor must be sleeping there with his small, triumphant girlfriend.

Véronique would have liked to howl but she was too inhibited. The small rocky islands off the rocky coast slowly came into focus. There was the Rocher des Pendus, Rock of the Hanged. Further away, the ruins of the old hospital where the plague-stricken were neatly shipped off to die. And, yet further away, the barren islands of Frioul, and of course le Château d'If, a grey slump of a fiction. Standing on top with Theo some ten days ago, she had felt as if she was remembering being there with him.

From this roof, she waved to two distant, god-like figures standing on a Mount Olympus peak in 1979, and hoped that they saw her and would wave back with divine politeness, naturally without recognising her.

The terror of freedom spread all around her like a once-fertile plain devastated by locusts. Only one voice still spoke to her, in a pointlessly eloquent repetition:

Where is love that with one stroke cuts time in two and
*   stuns it?*

The severance was irreversible and the two unequal parts had stopped twitching.

She had read all the Greek poetry. She had read all the graffiti in the world. The last ones she had read in Marseilles:

Arabs, go home
Algeria, I love you
This street/bench/wall belongs to Leila and Momo, that's all
Here rests the Lie

And Victor's one: *But I could have been elsewhere . . .*

Véronique surveyed the flat roofs around her. A few roofs away, two black workers sprang up, dazzling in white overalls and baseball caps, carrying heavy buckets and long brushes. One of them whistled a tune from a Céline Dion song. They dipped their brushes in the buckets and began to paint the balustrade a faint yellow. They had a life. She wanted to be them.

On another roof, there was a black cat, perfectly still, its back arched and tense like a question. A seagull sat on an aerial fixing its yellow eyes on the cat – or vice versa. A tall thin woman in black tights, shiny pointed black shoes and a black wig in the style of singer Mireille Mathieu, suddenly appeared on a sloping roof and started fixing a satellite dish.

Véronique watched the woman in surprise and found that she had zoomed up to her face, which was perfect and dead like a still life – her black eyelashes were painted on, with delicate flourish, her eyes were of glass, her exquisite cheeks waxen. Zoom out and Véronique noticed that the woman's position was awkward. How could she stand on the sloping roof at this angle without slipping? How did she retain the grace of her movements? But as she focused on the woman's movements, she realised that there were none. The woman wasn't moving at all. She wasn't fixing the satellite dish – she had merely assumed a frozen, dish-fixing pose. Véronique searched for the gull and the cat and found them frozen in the same mutually predatory poses as a moment ago. And suddenly she saw that the closed, pleasantly blue and peach shutters of that same house were painted on. And so was the satellite dish, against the pale blue wash of the sky. She sharpened her hearing to catch the splash of the sea and couldn't. The sea had gone mute. It too was a daub of thick paint. And the silence . . . An odd, erosive silence, as if a white city were crumbling into dust in some old, mute footage. As if silence was the very tissue of deterioration.

Véronique was standing among props. She was standing in a nightmare of inanimation.

In the space of a missed heartbeat, she looked down at her bare feet. She begged them to move, to prove that at least she was animate. But her feet – or any other part of her body – were incapable of making the slightest movement. She concentrated on feeling the roughness of the floor under her bare feet. But her feet didn't feel a thing. She wanted to touch herself, but it was too late.

A new but ancient terror spread its rot inside her. She wanted to scream but a scream would crack the whitewashed silence, and the balustrade she was leaning against, and her ceramic Midas body whose pieces would lie in the sun uncollected until one day someone came up to this roof and, with a mildly surprised indifference, found them and swept them into a dustbin.

She wanted to cry but Midas's tears would turn to something solid as soon as they were shed.

She wanted to speak, but Midas had nothing to say except to beg for the curse to be lifted.

Please, please give me my humanity back. I will make better use of it. Give me the world back, with its seagulls, satellite dishes and lovers for whom it is too late, the world of magnificently predictable sunsets and sunrises, and dog-shit hardening and crumbling in the sun. Give me back my childhood Riviera, Dad's lost Greece, Theo's Ancient Macedonia, Victor's Devil's Island, Pascal's no-man's-land, Monte Cristo's Château d'If. Give me the finality of the moment, the frustrated magic of the familiar, the imponderable depths of these flat Mediterranean surfaces – and I'll never ask for more. Give me back my empty future – and I'll populate it with this seagull, with these painters on the roof, with my body which will sag soon, with ruins, with dog-shit, with anything that is real. Anything. I will take anything.

Then Midas could do nothing but wait.

Everything she had touched had turned to something else: gold, shit, dust. Touch was the instinctive gesture of love, wasn't it? Wasn't it? She couldn't love without touching, and her loving touch eroded everything. She applied that same touch to everything – to Theo, to the boy in Istanbul, to Victor, to the memory of her father, perhaps even to the memory of Pascal. Now, finally, when everyone was gone, she had touched herself.

Véronique stood on the roof for an eternity. She grew old, then simply continued to grow older, and older, but without approaching a resolution. She stood like a stone column through the ebb and flow of her unstoppable age. She became smoothly ancient like a salamander inside an ever-burning flame. She watched her petrified ceramic body from another place, with a calm and unsurprised understanding, with a sorrow so profound she didn't feel it – because she was it. She became the ruins of Europe herself.

Time ripened, became distended, multiplied . . . and popped. What hatched out of it?

A soft radio-voice announced from another roof: 'It is midnight.' Véronique's petrified Midas brain started playing backwards.

Descent of the Mediterranean night, reclining, hooded and soaked with the rippling, multiple stench of summer – almond, sewage, fish, petrol, coffee, salt. Like Silenius, it knew everything and it was jaded and sad.

Sunset – a slashing of the sky's veins, a putting down of the day's vanquished hours, a massacre of what had just been.

Afternoon – shimmering and endless.

Morning – gull, cat, woman in black, satellite dish. Feet of clay, feet of ceramic, feet of gold, feet with no feeling, Midas feet. Please, please give me back my feet.

Véronique moved a toe, then another one. Then the other foot. Silenius watched from under a vine. She lifted a hand, carefully, as if animating a puppet, and placed it on the balustrade. It felt warm and corporeal.

The arch-backed cat stirred indistinctly in the darkness. The white gull took off with harsh wings and glided towards the islands. The woman walked down the roof with giddy grace in her shiny pointed shoes and disappeared into an attic room. Father was alive on Mount Olympus, 1979. Pascal was alive in the uncertainty of his death. She was alive, here. Nothing was lost.

Not everything was lost. She felt trickles down her cheeks, tickling her chin and crashing heavily on her feet. When she looked down, she found the glitter of water between her toes. She smiled.

FORTY-THREE

Summer 1978, Ohrid

Over the roar of the sewing machine, Dafina hummed along to an Edith Piaf radio song. Hearing that language stabbed her inadvertently. She lifted her foot from the pedal, turned up the volume and Edith Piaf spilled into the room. 'Happiness lost, happiness vanished, always I think of that night . . . They found him in the desert, his beautiful eyes open, clouds passing across the sky . . .'

Dafina sat back in her chair and listened to the drawn, languorous vowels of that unreachable language, faintly guilty for letting her guard down. The afternoon light oozed through the gauze curtains, heating up her left cheek. Soon the town would fall into the beatific coma of high summer. Soon, Maria and her family would come from Australia – finally, finally. The phone rang just as Piaf entered the refrain again.

'Hi Mum!'

'Maria!'

'It's Theo's fifth birthday today.'

'I know. I'm so glad you remembered to call me.'

'Mum, don't be like that, of course we remembered. Hold on, he wants to say something to you.'

The child breathed on the phone. He had nothing to say to her – he'd never met her.

'Theo, you're a big boy now,' she helped him.

'Grandma, we are coming to visit you soon.'

'That's wonderful, I can't wait. I send you a big kiss.'

'Mum, we're coming in two months. Kostas will be going to Thessaloniki with Theo. We hope.'

'Will they let him in?'

'We hope so. It's out of the question for me, of course.'

'Of course. I'm here and I'm waiting. Kiss Kostas for me.'

Dafina put the phone down and looked out of the window, dazed. The chipped walls of Samuil snaked over the hill, over the pretty red roofs. Nothing ever changed here. Edith Piaf was gone. It would be nice to have a gramophone and play her records, but she couldn't have everything now, could she.

The doorbell rang. She straightened her trousers and tucked loose strands of hair under her hair band. Her friend Latinka stood at the door with a shopping bag. Her face flushed with excitement, she marched straight in.

'Have you heard about the new man in town?'

'What new man?' Dafina put a pot of coffee on the stove.

'The Greek. He's been here a couple of weeks and I only just learnt about it now!'

'You're so behind the times!'

'He's about sixty, nice silver hair, blue eyes although one is half-closed for some reason. He speaks the language, speaks Greek too, naturally. Unattached. Mysterious. He was a train conductor for a few years. But!' She paused dramatically. 'He has a drinking problem.'

'I see. What does he do?'

'Nothing at the moment, as far as I know. He's on an invalid's pension.'

'What's his name?'

'Stamatis Argirov. Some say he's a refugee from the Greek war.'

'Oh well. Could be.'

'But some reckon he's a fugitive from the junta.'

THE CASTLE OF IF

'Could be as well.'

'Yet others reckon he has something to hide.'

'Who doesn't.'

Dafina poured the coffee into tiny cups.

'Is everything okay with you?' Latinka enquired, sipping the coffee and immediately screwing up her foxy face. 'You made it too sweet.'

'It'll last you longer. Maria is coming with Theo and Kostas.'

'You're serious! Mind you, it was about time. You haven't seen her for how long? Six years?'

'It's a long way to come.'

'She's only got one mother.'

'They wanted to combine it with a visit to Thessaloniki but it's been impossible.'

'A mother's a mother, Thessaloniki or not.'

'I'm just trying to be rational about it. Kostas hasn't seen his father since he was a small child. His father died in '67, at the hands of the junta, and I remember Kostas and Maria going to the border to see his coffin. He hasn't seen his mother and brother either. Maria was crying when they came from the border. She hugged me and said, "Mum, at least I've got you." ' Dafina swirled her coffee in the cup – something that everybody knows shouldn't be done with Turkish coffee – and lit a cigarette.

'And then off they went to Australia,' Latinka quipped.

'I don't blame them. They needed a better life. They were never at home here.' Dafina looked out at the hills again.

'You could've gone with them, you know.'

'I know.'

'You still could.'

'I still could.'

Dafina got up and rattled the cups away.

'Oh well, I'd better leave you to your sewing.'

And Latinka was gone, her shopping bag in tow, bursting with red peppers.

Dafina sat at the sewing machine again and pushed the slippery fabric under the needle. She would not go to Australia but she was going to buy a gramophone.

Two weeks passed before she saw the new man in town. She had forgotten about him. She was at the market, buying a watermelon and thinking of how little Theo would enjoy the watermelons, when she heard the distinctive soft Greek accent at a nearby stall.

'This one. With the brown strap. I like this one. How much?'

He had an air of unbelonging about him. Silver hair receding inconspicuously in two neat bays, corduroy trousers, an unmatching jacket, battered shoes. And the profile of a ruined nobleman. He was buying a watch from a stall selling leather products, kitsch jewellery and miscellaneous junk.

She paid quickly for her watermelon and walked away. The sun was ripening and the town, having stirred joyfully in the spring sun, was now entering a slow decline into summer torpor. She walked past the *chinar* in the square – a giant oak tree inside which there was a tiny café. The usual suspects lounged about in the sun, gossiping, puffing cigarettes. She exchanged greetings with them.

She set out to make lunch for herself – a humble tomato salad with bread and cheese, and watermelon. She realised she had forgotten to buy tomatoes from the market and bread from the bakery, as well as coffee from the grocer's. She had rushed to come home. No, she had rushed to get away from the market.

She turned on the cold water tap over the watermelon and sat at the empty table. She didn't feel like eating. She felt unusual. *This one. With the brown strap. I like this one. How much?* The accented voice buzzed in her head maddeningly, like an invisible fat fly in a hot room. She wanted to swat it but she couldn't locate it.

She sat at the sewing machine, without lunch, and worked the afternoon away, putting the final touches to an elegant linen suit. The radio blasted away over the roar of the Singer: Italian pop music, then the local pop variety, then news – 'Comrade Josip Tito received the President of Such and Such African Republic' – always the same, then a folk music programme. In the evening, her head throbbing, she turned on the TV and left it on, filling the small apartment with the gaudy dialogue and soaring music of yet another episode of the Brazilian soap opera that had the entire country glued tearfully to their screens. She sat on the small balcony, smoking. Youths walked past on their way to the lake waterfront, for the evening promenade. At the foot of the street, the Saint Sophia church, the colour of salamander, was lit up.

Stamatis meant 'stopper'. Argirov, from *argiros*, meant 'silver' – like his hair.

The beautiful slave-girl is alone with her enamoured owner. 'But I am not free,' she pleads. 'I will make you free. Because I love you.' Swelling music, he clasps her in his democratic arms and gives her back her freedom through a passionate kiss.

This one. With the brown strap. I like this one. How much? She only saw his profile. Not his face, not his eyes. She went inside and extracted a box full of banknotes which she counted. Enough for a gramophone. Plus she was expecting some money from two clients. She looked at the TV. The couple were gazing at each other with erotic coffee-bean abandon across the battlefields of vanquished colonialism. She turned them off.

She went to bed and put a pillow over her face to stifle the voice. But she couldn't stifle her dreams.

She stands on top of a mountain. Someone is waiting at the foot. But she must first find someone among the decomposing bodies on the slope. She can't remember who she is looking for but if she sees him, she'll recognise him. The faces are all the same – horrifying in their anonymous rot, the bodies twisted and broken. She and the person who is waiting down below are the only survivors. She can't remember what has gone on here and why. She can't remember anything. She looks down and sees that there is a sea of watermelons instead of a field, all of them open and bleeding, and among this green and red sea, a man is standing, waving at her, beckoning her. She can't recognise him. The sweet, watermelon round r's of Edith Piaf roll from loudspeakers as she intones 'Partisans, partisans', flooding the watermelon valley, and she realises that the watermelons are the government army and they are beckoning her – in French – to desert. She is surprised: isn't it too late to desert? It is all over, the watermelons are all split, everybody is dead.

The countdown to Maria's arrival began and Dafina guessed that was the cause of her palpitations at night. That must also be the cause of her irrational expectation of a knock on the door at odd times. A friendly knock from someone she had forgotten, and yet she lay in bed on the increasingly warm nights, terrorised by bizarre possibilities, pressing a pillow over her face.

Latinka and a few other professional neighbourhood snoopers kept her up to date with the strange movements of the stranger.

'Do you know that he's just moved into the derelict house at the bottom of the street and he's doing it up? He's working on it like a possessed man. He sleeps on the floor, he's doing everything by himself. Mind you, he's made a few friends among the local folk, but of course he's Greek . . . and, you know . . . And do you know that Apostol the Aegean recognised him from the civil war? But he can't say where he knew him from, he just recognised his face.'

Dafina walked down the winding cobbled street, past the Saint Sophia church and into the narrow cul-de-sac. He was inside, hammering away. She stood, her heart pounding, unsure whether to walk in or walk away. The hammering stopped. His head popped out of a hole in the second floor. A lock of hair fell over his eye.

'Good afternoon,' he said.

'Hello. Are you Stamatis Argirov?'

'Yes.'

'I live up the street.' She gestured vaguely towards the church and the old town beyond it.

'You must have a nice view there,' he said and coughed from the dust.

'Yes, it's lovely. Look, I won't hold you up, I just came to say welcome to Ohrid. I know what it's like to be a stranger in town, I was one myself not so long ago. The people are wary at first, it's provincial, but . . . they're good people.'

'Thank you,' he said. 'You're very kind.' Something beneath him started shaking and she realised he was on top of a ladder. She cried out as he gripped the window frame to steady himself, dropping the hammer which hit the wooden floor with a dull thud.

He grinned and for some inexplicable reason a blade pierced her from end to end. She walked inside to pick up the hammer and hand it up to him. But he was coming down the ladder already. He was covered in dust the colour of his hair. Inside, there was a small camp stove, a few pots, a couple of bags, an old mattress, a Grundig transistor and a faded print of Thessaloniki's White Tower at the waterfront propped against the peeling wall.

'Pleased to meet you.' He wiped his hand on his jeans and stretched it out. It was warm and nicely shaped. She looked at his face. His semi-closed eye was of an unusual colour – if indeed it had a colour. His good eye was blue. His grey stubble gave him a melancholy air, like a once stately house overgrown with weeds. She had to search for her voice.

'If ever you want a place to eat, you know, a table, or a bed to sleep, you're welcome to come to my house, there's room there if . . . ever . . . Or if you just want to watch TV.'

'You are very kind indeed, Missus . . .'

'Grigorova. Dafina.'

'Very kind indeed.' She handed him the hammer which she had been holding in her sweaty hands. He took it with care as if he was taking a glass of water. The blade twisted inside her, like one of those bayonets with teeth, used to pull out the enemy's guts. She nodded and fled.

The hammering resumed, echoing in the acoustic, soporific streets of the old town closed in by the hills, calling her wherever she went, knocking the breath out of her.

A few days later, the knock on the door came. Not a ring on the bell, but a knock, as if he knew. Getting up from her Singer, the blood rushing from her head, she opened the door. He was holding a plastic bag with something heavy inside.

'Good evening. I catch a trout in the lake. Maybe you put it to better use than me.' He handed her the bag with another of his lacerating smiles. His teeth were ruined. His blue eye was luminous, his bad eye was dull, hooded.

'Please come in.'

'I don't want to disturb you.'

'You're not disturbing me.' She smiled to prove that she wasn't disturbed and tucked loose strands of hair under her band. He stepped in diffidently.

'It won't take long to cook. I've got some lemon and olive oil, and some fresh herbs. In fact, I'll make the traditional Ohrid trout, why not, stuffed with rice and peppers.' She became talkative in her febrility. 'Have you tried it this way?'

'No. I haven't tried it any way.'

He stepped inside the lounge.

'Someone told me that you speak Greek,' he said, while she was busying herself in the kitchen.

'I used to.'

'You used to live in Greece?'

'Yes.'

'Where?'

'Edessa. And you're from Thessaloniki.'

'Yes. How do you know?'

'I saw a picture in your . . . in the house.'

'Do you mind if I smoke?'

'Sure.'

'Would you like one?' He held out a packet of cheap local cigarettes and she took one.

'Please sit down.'

He sat on the edge of the lace-covered divan like a child in a dentist's waiting room. She poured some rakia into small tumblers and handed one to him. The briefest of silences opened up and Dafina, terrified beyond reason, rushed to cover it up.

'Yes, it's difficult for a newcomer to be accepted by the locals, it's a provincial town, the mentality is . . . you know, you come from a big city, you know how it is . . . I myself spent many years in Tashkent which is larger but it's still difficult when you're a stranger. Of course there were many of us, we stuck together although that wasn't easy either, whereas you're by yourself. Or . . .'

Meaning to appear inquisitive, she looked at him with something approximating fear. He didn't understand and just smiled, waiting for her to continue which she did.

'Ohrid has a mild climate, although in the winter it can be cold and the summer gets pretty hot . . .' He smiled again and she realised what she had just said. 'I mean, it's quite pleasant.'

'Yes.'

She placed a small plate of pickles on the table.

'Please.'

'Thank you.'

'You're obviously quite a capable builder.'

'Not at all. I help a friend some years ago to fix his house. Otherwise not.'

'In Greece?'

'No. Here in Yugoslavia.'

'I see.'

The gap of silence widened until it was big enough to fall in. These bays of receding hair, these eyes that were not the same, not the same . . . colour, this dimple in the cheek, these hands with dirty nails and scratches . . . She bounced back from the edge of the gap.

'I think the trout is ready to be stuffed.' She got up.

'Can you speak some Greek with me?' The voice stabbed her again, as it had at the market. Whenever she wasn't looking at him, it stabbed her in the back, insidious. She reeled in front of the gaping trout. The knife struck and detached its head.

'Sorry?' She turned to him, seeing red blotches.

'Only if you want to,' he said apologetically.

'Greek. I haven't spoken it for years.'

He seemed confused. He shuffled in his chair.

'I'm sorry. I have disturbed you,' he said, fingering the tablecloth and glancing around as if he'd suddenly realised he had lost something.

'No, not at all. Let's see,' she said in Greek and his face lit up.

'Oh, you speak well, better than me,' he said in accented Greek.

She laughed and her laughter sounded somehow shrill.

'But you're Greek,' she said and tore off the black thread with which she had sewn up the trout.

'Yes, yes,' he mumbled, 'I'm Greek. But sometimes you forget your language.'

'Do you have a family?'

'Well . . . ' He avoided her eyes. 'Not really. No, as a matter of fact. And you?'

'I have a daughter. She's in Australia with her husband and son but they're coming to visit me soon.'

'Nice.'

Dafina didn't want to sit face to face with him with no food to separate them and continued to hover in the kitchen.

'I heard you worked on the railways.'

'That's right.'

'Here in Yugoslavia?'

'Yes.'

'And I suppose that's what you did in Greece too.'

'Yes, yes, I was a train conductor in Greece.' His accent was unusual. It must be from years of not speaking the language. The smell of trout began to permeate the air.

'How long have you been here then?'

'Me?' He looked around as if there were other people at the table. 'Since '67. That's right, '67. I came in '67.' He frowned.

She took the dish from the oven. The trout was a success. She put it in the middle of the table and proceeded to cut it. It was absurd. What she was experiencing was simply impossible. It was impossible to be sitting here with this man, with this Stamatis, this Stopper, eating trout and making small talk. Her hands shook. She looked at him and he looked up at her, his good eye blue, his bad eye murky in the dusk-struck lounge, his stubble frosty with silver . . . A shudder went through her, almost making her teeth chatter and her bones rattle inside her skin. She gripped the knife as if her life depended on it. The knife cut the tender flesh, the thread, the stuffing. It scraped the bottom of the baking tray, but she kept pressing as if something still remained to be severed.

'It looks like a dream,' he said. He was right. It was all a dream. She placed a piece on each plate. Aromatic steam rose to their faces. He lifted his rakia tumbler which she had refilled three times already. She lifted hers.

'Cheers.' He smiled timidly with his bad teeth. 'To the

Ohrid trout. To you.'

The first sip burnt her lips.

'I hope I can do the same for you when the house is done,' he said, tasting the fish. He was getting talkative. 'It will be beautiful when it's ready. Right on the lake, with a view to that church up on the hill, what do you call it?'

'Saint Kaneo,' she whispered.

'With the cypresses. Like Greece. And the mountains in the distance.'

'Do you miss Greece?'

He stopped chewing and thought.

'I guess. Yes, of course. Of course I miss Greece.'

'So do I,' she said from the depth of her dream.

'When did you leave?'

'In '49.'

'Me too.' A frown appeared between his eyebrows.

'You left in '49?' She looked at him.

'Yes, I left in '49. No, I mean . . . I left in . . . in '67, didn't I? That's when I left. Yes, of course.'

'Were you in the war?'

'Yes, yes, I was. I was in the war. In '49. In the civil war. *Andartopolemo* they call it, guerrilla war, some call it. But it was a civil war, wasn't it?' He stopped chewing again.

She wasn't going to pour any more rakia for him.

'I'm sorry, Daphne,' he said and looked around again, apologising to the whole table. Her left hand dropped the fork but her right one clutched the knife. 'I mean, Dafina.' He smiled helplessly and joylessly.

'Daphne?' she said from afar.

'Daphne. Like the legend. What was the legend? I've forgotten the legend.'

'Daphne and Apollo.'

Apollo, Apollo, don't chase Daphne for she will turn into a tree and you will mourn her forever.

She gathered her voice patiently, like rainwater in a tumbler, and said, 'Apollo, Apollo, don't chase Daphne for she will turn into a tree and you will mourn her forever.'

Stamatis seemed to think about this. 'Of course. Apollo, Apollo. And Daphne. Apollo and Daphne. Of course.' His smile was unbearable. Everything was unbearable.

'You were in the mountains in '48?' She sent small talk to hell.

'Yes. In '48, '49, in the civil war. In *andartopolemo*. Some even call it *simoritopolemo*, gangster war, don't they.'

Something was very wrong with Stamatis but she was terrified of finding out what it was.

'Yes. Because we were *simorites*, gangsters.'

'Were we? Were we gangsters?'

He wasn't provocative. He was simply asking. Like asking: 'What is the climate of Ohrid?' or 'Could I have some more trout?'

'Don't you remember what we were, Stamati?' His name felt strange. Wrong.

'Of course. Of course I remember. We were not gangsters. We were . . . losers.'

The word slapped her.

'We weren't losers. We lost. We were overpowered.'

'Yes, yes, we lost, that's right. A terrible loss. But we weren't gangsters.'

She took a cigarette to stop her nerves from snapping completely. He struck a match for her and reached across the table to light her cigarette.

'You don't like the fish?' he asked.

'It's lovely. But I've had enough.'

'I've had enough too. You cook like a dream.' He lit a cigarette.

She realised they were sitting in the dark; the only light came from houses across the street and the moon.

'Night without moon, the darkness is deep,' she said and bit her lip.

'Night without moon, the darkness is deep,' he repeated thoughtfully, as if straining to remember. 'But a brave lad cannot sleep. I remember it!' He was pleased. 'It's a poem. Where was this poem from?'

'It's a song. A rebetiko.'

'That's right, a rebetiko. "Night without moon, the darkness is deep, but a brave lad cannot sleep."' He laughed contentedly in the semi-darkness. The accented Greek in the husky voice. The fire casting shadows over his unshaven cheeks. There was no doubt and yet it was impossible.

'It's impossible,' she said, not meaning to.

'It's impossible,' he repeated. 'What's impossible?'

'This. You remind me of someone. Terribly.'

'Someone,' he said and looked about in that chilling, apologetic way he had. 'Sometimes I remind myself of someone too.'

'Of who?'

'I can't remember.'

'I can. The worst thing is, I can.'

'Who do I remind you of?'

'Doesn't matter. Doesn't matter. Someone I knew in the war.'

'Well, I was in the war.'

'Yes, yes. You were.' The ashtray was full. Automatically, she got up and emptied it in the bin.

'Would you like some watermelon?'

'If you are having some.'

Under the knife, the watermelon cracked open like a burst skull, startling her from another dream. Sweet redness leaked from it.

'Watermelon. I love it,' he said. 'It reminds me of . . . of . . . something.'

They ate the cold slices with a fork and a knife. It was delicious. She swallowed too many seeds.

He bid her goodbye by kissing her hand. 'Kyria Daphne,' he said, 'thank you for a wonderful dinner and company.' *Kyria, I will never forget your hospitality. May your husband and your son return safely when this is over.*

She listened to his steps down the cobbled street. They were uneven and inconclusive, as if he were looking for a street number or was unsure of the way to his house that wasn't his.

That night, she didn't sleep. Or if she had been sleeping all along, she didn't wake up. The pillow over her face was no good. The moon looked down on her pitilessly. She thought of Stamatis sleeping on his gutted mattress, next to his faded picture of Thessaloniki and his tiny stove. What did he dream of?

All these years she had somehow managed not to lose her mind. Finally, it was happening.

Only Maria's arrival could save her.

FORTY-FOUR

August 1998, Ohrid

From the wall, Dafina's young portrait stared at Theo with her undeciphered eyes. He had found the portrait in her bedroom, in a locked coffer, the key to which was nowhere to be found. He had to break the lock. It was a realist portrait of a young woman with large, hard obsidian eyes, her mouth tightly shut like a closing bracket that would never open again, her black hair so thick it seemed to weigh her head down. Looking at the portrait now, Theo's back started to crawl. It seemed to him that she was nodding, slowly, imperceptibly. In a shadowy lounge, in a drowsy Balkan town, this was time's microcephalous nod, coming from a place he hadn't visited and never wanted to. An invitation to investigate further? A warning? Simply a greeting? Uneasily, he turned away and climbed the creaking stairs to the attic.

At her deathbed, Dafina had said to him and his mother, 'You must burn everything in the attic, everything, all the boxes, all the junk. It must all go with me.'

Rummaging through junk in the musty semi-darkness, he found some typewritten pages in Greek. One text, or at least what he could make out of it, read: 'Greece is situated at a crossroads in the British Empire's communication network. As long as there is a British

Empire this artery will exist and Britain will do everything in its power to preserve it . . .'

And so on. He also found what looked like a cable, folded in four and perfectly flattened.

'Dimitri died like a hero on 19 February on Ikaria. Comrade G.'

It bore the date 28 February 1947.

Theo's grandfather Dimitri died on the prison island of Ikaria some months before the end of the civil war, his mother had told him. Of course his mother only ever had Dafina as a source of information, since no other member of the Grigoriadis family survived. Uncle Panayotis, on the other hand, always questioned this. He asked how it was possible for an active guerrilla to be deported to an island at the end of the war, rather than executed straight away. But after all, Dafina knew best what had happened. She had paid the highest price.

'And *we* haven't paid a price? Our family is scattered like a body hit by a grenade!' Theo's father pounded his fist on the table and the cutlery rang musically. But he never managed to be as threatening as he was distraught. 'I never saw my father again! I don't even remember him. My sister never saw him either. My father was broken on the islands. And then some bloody foreigner takes his memoir away, never to be seen again! And my brother is locked away in the dismal jails of the colonels for three years! You don't call that a price?'

Theo's mother shook her head bitterly, and bit her lip.

'I know, I know. I was just saying that Panayotis is wrong to question my mother's recollection. She lost everything. Her family wasn't just scattered, her husband wasn't just interned on the islands! She didn't just have her house confiscated. I never even knew my father. Therefore, nobody has the right to question her recollection of the past. Not even I.'

Theo sat at the dinner table in front of an unfinished dessert, cursing his 'heritage', vowing never to be sucked back into that quagmire.

'I'm not questioning it! Nobody's questioning it.'

Theo's father's hand tic appeared – the twitch at the wrist, the agitated thumb like an animal awaking from hibernation. The three of them stared at it for a moment, then his mother put her hand over the twitch, like someone closing the eyes on a dead face. His father rubbed his thumb on the reconciling hand in silent apology. Nobody ate dessert. Once into his teens, Theo stopped asking questions. Perhaps his parents were waiting to be asked, to be dragged out of the shipwreck.

Now that his parents were beginning to age visibly, Theo noticed that they were shrinking into a terrible loneliness. Whatever had happened to the Philipidis and the Grigoriadis families was still freshly sore for them, but only rank history for him. He now began to see that by slamming the door to stop the chilly draught of those histories, he had also slammed it in his parents' faces. His mother's moist violet eyes, his father's midnight pacing around the house . . . But wasn't it their fault for being so difficult, his father saying when he first questioned him, 'Some things are too terrible to tell. Some things need time.' The time had never come.

He dug for more documents and a photograph of Dimitri. He found a group photograph of partisans, sitting and standing, a few women among them. The photo looked very familiar. Had he in fact seen it before?

He had. On a dusty shelf, in French. Exactly the same one. Theo held his breath. Here was the face that caught his eye then: the man sitting in the front row. His hair sleeked back, two streaks of white or perhaps blond hair running back from his temples. His eyes gentle, his features those of a musician, not a guerrilla. There was something odd about his face, in fact; he seemed slightly cross-eyed, looking both straight at the camera and sideways, the way Theo sometimes looked in photographs, not quite a squint but almost. And here was Dafina-Daphne: sombre, short-haired in a brown cap, boyish in her baggy fatigues. Theo hadn't recognised her in the book. He remembered the caption under the photograph: 'The author with guerrillas in the Grammos mountains'. No names. *The watermelons are all split, everybody's dead, we're all dead, nobody left except the Frenchman.*

Theo sat on the floor in a daze. His hands got caught in cobwebs. When he flicked through Pascal Loublier's book in the Marseilles house, he was in a state of controlled madness. He hadn't recognised his grandmother in a book because he wasn't seeing anything apart from Véronique. But also because he wasn't prepared to recognise her. Don't we only see what we can conceive of?

The men were all hollow-cheeked, with fever in their eyes, unshaven.

The day Theo looked at Pascal Loublier's book, he meant to ask Véronique if by any chance her grandfather had known any of the Grigoriadis in the civil war. Not that Véronique would know. But when she came back late that evening, they had a fight. She was tormenting him. Taking that poison that made her pupils disappear and her eyes harden like amber, inhuman. Spending the evenings with that crippled skinhead. He shouted, kicked that stone, nearly broke his toes. Véronique told him, in a calm but choked voice, that something was happening to her mind. That the world was shrinking around her as if there was nowhere left to go, as if they couldn't move . . .

He scrutinised the cable again, vaguely bothered by something. And then he registered the date: February 1947 – two and a half years before the end of the civil war. Plus the year and a half Dimitri spent on the island before he died. This meant that, technically speaking, Dafina was pregnant with Theo's mother for about four years. He was clearly missing something. Perhaps she visited Dimitri in jail, on the island – but surely they didn't allow visitors. Unless she too, was imprisoned with him, and then released? But then she would've told them so. How many ways were there to conceive a child when she was high in the mountains and he in the middle of the Aegean nowhere? And why would Dafina choose to mislead her daughter, construct a lie? She had to have a very good reason.

Dafina brought nothing with her when she crossed the Albanian border in the summer of 1949. She was a pregnant partisan, she had her bundle, an empty bandolier and her bare life.

From his three visits to her, Theo knew Dafina as a handsome, still, contained woman. When the family offered to take her with them to Australia, she said, 'I left two countries, I'm not leaving this one.'

But what about Dimitri? Theo's knowledge of the Greek Civil War was too poor to help him in this amateur investigation.

On his second visit, Dafina told him that there was a precise spot in the Grammos where you could enter a time-loop and suddenly find yourself in the heart of the combat, or trekking with the guerrilla army up the goat tracks, sweat pouring down your face, hunger in your gut, large like a saucer and turning, always turning. Theo asked where exactly that place was. She said, 'I would have to take you there myself.' 'Why don't we go?' he asked, excitedly. She sat at the kitchen table where she'd been bottling raspberry syrup and suddenly started to cry, her heavy hair shaking, her apron smeared with raspberry blood, her hands covering her face as if he had said something monstrous. It was the most terrifying thing Theo had seen in his life – this indestructible woman crying. He never asked again.

Her Greece was not the Greece Theo knew. Dafina too, in the end, was not the woman he knew.

Theo was groping his way through a damp labyrinth permeated with a stench he couldn't identify. Water dripped from the ceiling, distant moans echoed across the vaults and he knew that running would no longer save him.

The dust made him sneeze. He went down the creaky stairs, warily leaving the labyrinth. He stared at Dafina's portrait. She had stopped being his grandmother. She was now the icon of unknown circumstance, the record of the untold, the woman he never knew and perhaps nobody did. The gate through which he could step into a time-loop if he wasn't so wary.

He lay on the lace-covered couch and put his feet up after removing his shoes. Dafina was strict about shoes. The lace was made by her.

Sleek boats glided on the smooth lake. The neighbour's parrot launched an offensive of garbled curses at an invisible visitor.

Véronique runs to him across the dissonant faraway orchestra of gulls and traffic, she runs dishevelled and he opens his arms to catch her, to stop her – just in case she isn't running towards him, to love her again, still, forever . . .

And there he sees, standing on a bare hill scorched by napalm, a ghastly apparition. She stands, one foot set on a stone, in the classic guerrilla pose, holding a gun in the classic sentinel pose. The ground is burnt, her brown uniform is dusty and faded by the sun. The sky is low and black, without a trace of sun or moon. He doesn't want to look at the head but he has to. The head is thrust forward through a frame – and the frame is what was once Dafina's portrait by the anonymous artist. It's the back of a head. Short-haired, the hair messy and ashen. He knows it's Véronique but also not Véronique. He is struck by terror. There are no signs that it's a woman, but he knows it's Véronique, and also Dafina at twenty-four, and also someone else . . . He vaguely tells himself that he must go round and see the face, but he can't move. Besides, he knows there is no face. He wants to howl at the black sky with no moon, but he has no voice.

The phone rang distantly and he let it ring ten times before he dragged himself across the room and picked it up, suppressing the surge of hope in his heart.

'Alo? Theo?' An obnoxious, local female voice, doubly odious for not being Véronique's.

'Yeah.'

'I'm Latinka, your neighbour. He tried to shoot himself.'

'What? Who?'

'With this old pistol, last night. He's alive though. Thought I'd let you know though, because of, well, Dafina. He tried to shoot himself in the head but fortunately he was very drunk and the bullet only scratched his temple. He's in the hospital if you want to visit him later on. It's just that you know, he's got nobody.'

'Sure. But . . . how . . .'

'I don't know. I don't know anything. He must've lost it, too much to drink or something. Loneliness gets to a man, you know . . . Now that Dafinka is gone.' Latinka sniffed.

He wandered over to Stamatis's house, at the foot of the street, past the Saint Sophia church. Hairy-faced, well-meaning Latinka was snuffling around.

'Everything's as he left it, I haven't touched a thing.' She followed him inside. The air was stale, the curtains closed, the bed unmade.

Scraps of food were left on the table. There was also a torn, empty envelope on the table, addressed to Stamatis although it bore no stamp.

'There were pages scattered all over the floor,' Latinka jumped in helpfully. 'I picked them up and put them together. Here.' She reached for a bundle of sheets. Theo scanned the first page. A letter from Dafina, scribbled with a desperate, barely controlled hand, full of crossed-out words. 'Stamati, my only love', it began. Theo cleared his throat, folded the curious bundle and put it in his back pocket to read later, feigning inconsequence in front of Latinka who was watering Stamatis's plants given to him by Dafina. She had of course read the letter already, and probably discussed it with all the neighbours and their pets.

He walked back through the summer-stupor of the old town, thinking confusedly about the gunshot last night, and the notary, and the red boat, and that certain disquieting *je ne sais quoi* about Stamatis.

FORTY-FIVE

Summer 1978, Ohrid

Dafina saw Stamatis several times before Maria's arrival. He worked on the house without a break. Sometimes she brought him vegetables from the market, a loaf of bread, fresh yoghurt. The residents in the Saint Sophia area kept a skewed eye on Stamatis at first but gradually reassured themselves that he was harmless. Some even came to have a look at the evolving house, clicked their tongues, exchanged a few words with the builder and scuttled off. A man who had recently built a house brought him leftover building materials in a truck. The speculations about him, after reaching boiling point without coming to a resolution, continued to simmer on the low fire of provincial ennui. Dafina overheard a conversation in the *chinar* square among a cluster of men as she sat outside the tiny café with her shopping bags. She was soon joined by Latinka.

'A Greek spy, it's clear!' Mitre was saying.

'Come on, they wouldn't let him snoop about without checking him up thoroughly!'

'There are ways, you know. Especially for the Greeks.'

'Not under Tito there aren't. Security is immaculate. Moreover, they had the junta in Greece.'

'I heard he has a Yugoslav passport!'

'You're joking.'

'Nope. Maybe he's a spy for another country posing as a dropout Greek train conductor.'

'Don't be daft! He wouldn't be living like a pauper, doing up old houses with his bare hands.'

'But why isn't he going back to Greece? The border's open now.'

'He's probably a criminal.'

'He doesn't look like one.'

'He doesn't look like a train conductor either.'

'What are you saying!'

Laughter. Mitre had worked for the railways.

'Hey, Mitre, you could check up with the railways.'

'I did. He was working for them all right. For six odd years. Which doesn't mean he wasn't a spy.'

'Bizarre.'

'Really bizarre.'

'And he doesn't talk much.'

Dafina exclaimed angrily, 'Do you talk to him?'

All heads turned to her in shock but nobody answered.

Latinka nudged her. 'Don't give them food for gossip.'

'I don't care,' Dafina said and got up. 'You only think of yourselves. You don't know what this man could have been through. Has anybody helped him with the building so that he doesn't have to sleep on the floor? Has anybody invited him to their house? He's got nobody here. And he's a foreigner. He has learnt our language. The least we could do is to make him feel less homeless by showing a bit of kindness. It's not as though he's been given accommodation by the state like the rest of us Aegeans. It's not as though he's taking skin off anybody's nose by doing up a burnt-out house and improving the look of the town.'

She walked past the stunned men. Latinka shook her head reproachfully and followed her like a puppy, half-admiring, half-terrified.

Dafina buried herself in work. Ohrid buried itself in a deep, sheltering, blue summer. Boats appeared on the lake and bathers at the beaches on the eastern side where the haze of the Albanian mountains began to thicken. Stamatis's house was more or less ready. He had no furniture, but some people donated old pieces that had been sitting in their attics.

Dafina made curtains for his windows, sheets for his bed and gave him a mirror. Somebody had given it to her when they arrived ten years ago. It had a kitsch mock-baroque gilded frame and she didn't like it but she had nothing else to spare.

'Not bad for a refugee, though,' Stamatis commented on her house one evening over pastry and fresh yoghurt.

'I'm not a refugee.' She was piqued.

'Oh?'

'I'm . . . living in exile.'

'Isn't that the same?'

She thought for a moment. He smiled for no reason with his wrecked teeth which she didn't mind. The afternoon sun splashed its soft heat on the lace-covered divan where he sat with a cup of coffee, his back to the balcony, his face and upper body drenched with liquid gold, the receding hair, the blue eye . . . He had aged so well. Whoever his younger self had been, he had aged well. She smiled for no reason too, as if they were saying sweet nothings.

'What about you?' she said, inhaling from her cigarette. 'What are you?'

The sun of his smile set slowly over the hill of a pained effort. He looked inside his cup and swirled his coffee unwisely.

'I mean,' she helped him, 'how do you see yourself in this . . . scheme of things?'

'I don't know,' he said with appalling simplicity.

She got up to empty the ashtray.

'I suppose,' he said slowly, listening to his own voice, 'I suppose I'm living in exile from myself.'

She nodded and smiled again, though she didn't mean to. She didn't avert her eyes from his, though she meant to. For the first time since Maria had left for Australia, Dafina felt that there might be some twisted harmony in the world after all, some dizzying circularity, some bitter contentment.

'I know I'll probably die without having seen Greece again, but I still live with the feeling that I have somewhere to return to. It's probably an illusion but . . .'

'What about Tashkent?'

'It was never my home. We felt we were there temporarily.'

'And here? You should feel at home here.'

'I'm different from them. They call us "the Aegeans". Some resent us because, when we came back from our countries of exile, the government gave us apartments and jobs. The people complained we were appropriating what was rightfully theirs.'

'That's what my friend from Prilep said. He's also an Aegean.'

'How did you meet him?'

This seemed to require some thought.

'He works in the railways. He was the first person I met here.'

Dafina did not prod further. She let the dense, ever-receding truth of Stamatis elude her. Being with him was somehow sufficient, his mere presence fed her need for explanation.

Often, when she was with him, she fell under a spell, as if time had stopped at some distant point in the past, and she was gazing at him – and at herself – from that point. As if she was suddenly back on the other side of the impenetrable night that were the last twenty-nine years. On the right side. She had no strength or desire to extract herself from that spell. Suddenly, the disfigurement of chance became life's very flavour, as it had been on the other side of that night when she was young and feared nothing and lost everything. She still had no fear – she had nothing left to lose.

Stamatis drank no more than the local men. He drank without falling over. Only his speech became slightly slurred and his expression opaque. He drank with the locals, sometimes by himself, and the locals were not above attempts at inebriating him in order to untie his tongue. He proved immune to these and stumbled down the narrow streets with cobblestones so white they shone in the dark and showed him the way. Dafina was not there to see this but she was duly filled in by those who were. He didn't have much of informative value to say. Whenever asked a question about Greece or how he came to be here, he would say simply, 'I don't remember', thus feeding wild speculations. Sometimes his speech fell into a jumble of Greek, Slavic, French and English and he had to be reminded. This never happened when he was with Dafina, though – they spoke in Greek. She had initially found this idea unappealing because of the memories, but gradually discovered that the sharp stab of his accented Greek became pleasurable, as if her young self were listening to it.

The hard certainty of accumulated loss was shaken like a charred tree from which the surprising birds of possibility fell.

Maria and her family arrived and Stamatis was obscured by their busy presence. Theo was shy and culture-shocked. It took Dafina days to get used to Theo's odd eyes. Dark blue and light brown, almost speckled. Maria had told her about the child's eyes but to see them was something else.

Kostas had obtained a Greek visa and left for Thessaloniki with Theo. As Dafina and Maria went for strolls around the town, people greeted them and asked about Australia. They sat in the fragrant shade of long afternoons and talked about Melbourne, about Theo, ordinary conversations between mother and daughter who live at opposite sides of the world.

'Have you thought about, you know, coming to Australia?'

'Yes. I might come to visit.'

'Mum, we want you to come and stay.'

'You know how I feel about this, Maria. Why do you press me?'

Maria tossed her fringe in that nervous girlish way she had.

'I don't want you to be lonely here.'

'I'm not. I've got my work, I've got . . . friends. Look, Mimi, I left my country once. Then I left Tashkent. I can't leave again. Especially now, after the junta, when things in Greece are loosening up. See, Kostas got a visa. You never know . . .'

Maria's eyes filled. Dafina hugged her and held her for a while, trying to be the strong one. Then a knock downstairs startled her – intimate, unique, an instant giveaway. He never rang the bell, as if it were only for those not in the know, for the common visitor. Dafina didn't move.

'Is that someone knocking?' Maria mumbled, sniffing.

'You stay here, I'll get it. It's a neighbour from down the road.'

Stamatis smiled and handed her the bag. 'Almost alive. I know you love them twitching.'

But she didn't laugh. She dithered on the doorstep. Maria was coming down the stairs.

'It's for your guests, to make them dinner.'

'Come in for a coffee.' It was a half-hearted invitation.

'Oh no, I must go.'

'Hello,' Maria said brightly.

'Maria, this is Stamatis, my neighbour.'

Maria smiled radiantly and Stamatis took her hand warmly.

'Why doesn't he come in for a coffee?'

'He will.'

Stamatis stepped in, happily vanquished. Dafina trod the stairs as if ascending a gibbet, Maria before her, Stamatis behind. She was climbing to the second floor of her own house but wasn't at all sure that was where she would find herself.

She set about making coffee.

'She looks just like you,' he said to Dafina, following her to the stove like a child, not looking at Maria.

'Doesn't she.'

'And where is the little one?'

'Kostas and Theo went to Thessaloniki to see his family.'

'Oh.'

'You are obviously Greek.' Maria enquired amiably, sitting on the divan where, years ago, she had read in the twilight.

'Yes.'

Dafina sensed Maria's reluctance to delve further into his origins – she knew people were sensitive about these things and Stamatis was exile on legs.

'Do you live in the neighbourhood?'

'I do.'

'He did up the old burnt-out house on the shore, down by Saint Sophia, remember?'

'It must be nice down there. But damp.'

'I don't mind dampness. I like boats.'

'Stamatis used to work for the railways.'

'I see. How interesting.' Maria was polite as always.

Stamatis stood next to Dafina and conversed with Maria from a distance. Dafina wanted him to move away; they looked too much like a couple.

'In fact,' he began, remembering something, 'weren't you on the train from . . . I can't remember where, on the train once, that's right, mother and daughter with lots of luggage, from . . . Belgrade? A few years ago.'

Dafina and Maria exchanged surprised looks.

'Actually, we were. You remember us from ten years ago?'

'Was it ten years ago?'

'It was in January '67. We were moving here from Tashkent.'

'From Tashkent. On the Belgrade train, '67. That's right – '67. And the girl had pig-tails. No man. I noticed that. I don't know why.'

'Phenomenal memory.' Maria nodded with wonder.

Dafina frowned. 'Maria never had pig-tails.'

'Could have been another mother and daughter,' Maria said brightly.

'No.' Stamatis threw his head back in the Greek way. 'It was you. It came to me now, when I saw you together. Ten years! How the time goes. And yet nothing really changes.'

The moment froze. Dafina stood in the middle of the kitchen, coffee pot in hand. Maria sat on her divan, bathed in dusk. Stamatis looked at Dafina askew, his clothes crumpled.

'Well, it was a big journey from Tashkent.' Maria broke the spell. 'We didn't know what we were coming to. Mum had this distant relative in Ohrid . . .'

They drank their coffee. Maria talked about Melbourne, how Theo was learning three languages at once, how they were happy there although they worked hard, how Sophia, Kostas's sister, had two kids Theo's age . . . Maria had changed, had become less guarded, somehow uninhibited. She would never talk to a stranger like this five, seven years ago. It must be Australia. They had too much space

there, didn't need to erect protective walls, didn't have borders . . .
But Maria had a life of quality. That at least, Dafina had successfully
seen through. She looked at her talkative daughter with pride. She
looked at Stamatis, who had relaxed into his characteristic air of
solicitous interest – an air which wanted to convey that everything
was fine with him and he was here simply to enhance others' lives. It
was this look that made him friends and alleviated the grossest
suspicions of the locals.

It was an ordinary afternoon over ordinary coffee. Stamatis was
an ordinary Greek neighbour. Maria was her lovely daughter from
Australia. There was no need to dig. Dafina smiled indulgently at the
overly sweet Turkish coffee and the waffles, at Maria's dimples and
surprised violet eyes, at Stamatis's unironed clothes, at the way the
last rays of sun broke softly against the cheap vinyl cover on the
kitchen table, at nothing in particular. She suddenly gripped her life
with fierce joy, as if finding a long-lost possession.

Kostas and Theo came back. Theo had got over his culture shock
and was more assertive now, poking his curly head everywhere.

'It's all been a bit too much for Theo,' Kostas said. He looked as if
it had been too much for him. Because of his ulcer, he smoked more
than he ate. Everybody was fine in Thessaloniki – Panayotis, his wife,
their kids, his mother Hrisoula. He was positive in an exaggerated,
brittle way. Maria probed him for a few days and finally, one day
before they were due to leave, he confessed.

'While I was there, Panayotis had a visit, this French guy who . . .
well, he's living in Thessaloniki temporarily. He was looking for . . .
He was trying to trace his father who disappeared at the end of '67
in Greece.'

'Disappeared?' Dafina was making dinner by the stove.

'Yeah. Apparently. Just vanished. This guy, his name is Alex, was
trying to find out as much about him as possible. And you see, it
appears that his father actually met Panayotis and Dad in '67, just
before they were arrested. Of course Panayotis had no idea . . .'

'What was the name of the missing man?' Dafina asked.

Kostas thought for a moment. 'I can't remember actually. He was a former journalist, I think. You see, he was interested in Dad's memoirs from the islands. He took one copy with him. Panayotis wrote to the address he'd given him in France a year ago, but naturally there was no reply – except from Alex who went to Thessaloniki to try and set up a private inquiry. The Greek police have just released the journalist's passport, you see. Hold on, I think I remember the name because I looked at the passport. Pêcheur. Ludo Pêcheur.'

Dafina sat down and crossed her knees and arms, her hands wet, her brain trying to work. Another French journalist, obviously.

'How did he know Panayotis and Angelis?' she said carefully.

'From the civil war, apparently.'

'Was he in Greece at that time?'

'I think so.'

Kostas was confused as well. Maria was packing their luggage. Tomorrow, Dafina would be alone with their shadows again.

'Why, did you know someone like that in the war?' Kostas asked, stubbing out his tenth cigarette for the morning and getting up.

'No, not really.'

Dafina got up too and went back to making dinner.

She farewelled them with a heavy, sick heart. Maria had been given to her as a gift. She sprouted from the thick sorrow of one fumbling night of passion, the only such night in her life. She sprouted from her famished body which had not menstruated for months. Maria had stayed with her for nineteen years, injecting her mother's amputated life with the morphine of hope, before she had vanished into the imaginary blue of the Pacific, receding further into the future with her child, with her Australian ways.

Over long dinners, multiple tumblers of rakia and packets of cigarettes, Stamatis listened to Dafina recall things she had not told anyone else. She hurled herself into the last, apocalyptic battle on Grammos in the stone-melting heat of August '49, pursuing death but never catching up with it.

She crossed the Albanian border with thousands of others and wept with them in Korca where they had to hand over their empty guns which meant this time it was really over and although she wanted it to be over, she cried, for what felt like the first time in years.

She cried day and night, crouching in the Albanian summer dust, and she knew she would never stop crying and she wished someone would shoot her. She cried for her gun, for Alexis, for Illias, for Pascal, for her mother before the execution squad and her father, chained and whipped in the deadly heat of an Aegean island, for Kallistos and for the pock-marked kapetanio who was eviscerated in the last days of Grammos, for the mad woman in the rags, for the French-speaking boy with the Russian jacket, for all the others she had known, and even for her enemies. She wept for the boys of the government army who didn't have a choice and for the pilot she had shot down in that duel, for the mothers orphaned by their children and for the orphaned children scattered around the Eastern bloc, for the partisans with phosphorus burns who lay around in the listless Albanian shade, inconsolable in their agony, for those who wanted to die but couldn't. She wept for her boots which had fallen apart so she had walked barefoot the last few days until her feet too had fallen apart, for her dowry, for her stiff arm, for Edessa of the fresh waterfalls. For the land of Midas.

She stopped crying only because they had to board a nightmare ship and spend fifteen days without daylight, buried deep inside the entrails of the vessel below stacks of wheat-bags amid the squalor and despair of many weeping others, past the Peloponnese and Crete, leaving behind Greece which they wouldn't see for who knew how long, and even though she was vomiting more than the others, she thought it was just seasickness.

Once they entered Soviet territorial waters in the Black Sea, they were allowed out and she went delirious with sun.

She then gazed at the shimmering yellow desert of the Azerbaijan Plains, convinced she had finally died and was in Hades.

She waited with great impatience to miscarry in between more vomiting bouts on the impossible voyage to Tashkent across the Caspian Sea.

She reeled with the shock of the wild Soviet East where she would have to make a new life, the child her only reason not to hang herself on the nearest street lamp. She called her Maria, after her mother.

Maria grew up with the parentless Kostas Philipidis and his sister

Sophia who had both been taken from their mother in Edessa in the 1948 *pedomasoma*. Maria and Kostas became inseparable. When mother and daughter moved to Ohrid in '67, Kostas followed in their footsteps. The young couple emigrated to Australia soon afterwards where Sophia had already gone with her husband.

But, for reasons unbeknown to her, her story always began after the last farewell with Pascal. After they had waved to each other across the granite desert of Grammos, she had looked at the edge of the cliff where they had lain the night before. She couldn't say to this day what stopped her from simply stepping into the abyss.

Her story always began on the other side of a moonless July night in 1948, the side where she was not.

FORTY-SIX

August 1998, Marseilles

A lighthouse flashed to the east. She must kick heroin. She must find Theo. She must change her life. In the moonlit house, she stumbled against objects suddenly so precious she wanted to stroke them, but mustn't, for fear of freezing them. Everything had been restored to her and now she had the new talent, not of possession, not of owning but of beholding. She could have without touching now. She could experience *jouissance*. She could treasure without wrecking.

She didn't have a watch and the clock in the corridor had probably frozen on three forty in '67, when Pascal walked out of here for the last time. With somnambular precision she went straight to the study. She flicked the switch and the crystal chips of the chandelier dripped with viscous light. On the shelves, books dark not so much from age as from neglect. The desk with the red leather folder by the window.

Here, Pascal must have sat, writing his Greek tragedy forty, almost fifty years ago. She sat in the leather armchair, crossed her legs and placed her hands on the arm-rests. An obsolete smell of old pipes, dust and leather hung in the air, as it should in a place like this. She had avoided this room since they arrived a few weeks ago. Theo had asked her something about her grandfather's book but now she couldn't remember what it was.

She pulled open one of the desk drawers. Rusty scissors, blank sheets. In another drawer a box full of old coins, and a ruffled pile of postcards and letters. Thirty years old, even older, addressed to Pascal Loublier, *Le Monde*, Paris. But not all of them. A couple were addressed to Villa Maldormé, Marseilles. She opened one from the Federal Republic of Yugoslavia, dated 12/5/58, in Greek and two pages long. Véronique switched on the shaky desk-lamp and strained to decipher the words. *Pashanko died at Grammos, Perycles is in Latvia with his brother, Slava in Hungary, all his family died, Daphne Grigoriadis in Tashkent, with her child, Mitre lost both his eyes but is alive in Czechoslovakia, Alexandros lost his hand and his sweetheart Magdalena was . . . by a . . . before his eyes, I saw it too – he is here, Georgi is in a psychiatric hospital, the Dimitriades brothers . . . themselves when they were surrounded by the army . . . My friend, we went through hell, I still can't sleep at night . . .* And so on. There were also sentences she couldn't make out. Something about *la belle France* at the end, followed by an illegibly baroque signature.

Another letter from the same person dated from May '67 was a spare few lines conveying that a certain Dafina Grigorova had now moved to Ohrid, Macedonia, Yugoslavia.

She ran upstairs and searched for the five photocopied pages in her bag; they lay, crumpled and abandoned at the bottom, smudged with shampoo. Daphne Grigoriadis. Dafina Grigorova. Not quite different enough. But were they similar enough? She returned to the study. Her eye caught the battered red leather folder again. She leant over and opened it. Disaster! More Greek. At least it was typewritten. She sat on top of the desk to read against the tentative dawn light. The title page announced: *Sisyphus: A Memoir of a Political Prisoner 1948-1964 written by Ikaros and Odysseos Varda*. Screwing her eyes, she scanned the pages for familiar words. Then she realised. The manuscript! *Really harrowing stuff.* The manuscript whose author was never found. Or rather was found but . . . What was the story again? The manuscript which caused Pauline's breakdown and which she burnt, together with all of Pascal's papers. A fire-proof manuscript, obviously. Her father must have known. He must have scrutinised every single scrap of paper in this room. Her eyes bored holes in the sheets. Someone had underlined words and sentences with a red pen and scribbled their French translations in the margins. Possibly her father's handwriting, though it was hard to tell. With the help of the translated words, she put the difficult sentences together. 'If you ever come out of here alive, you will have the three illnesses of Greek jails: duodenal ulcer, spinal arthritis, tuberculosis . . . All communists have them. He was right, when I came out, I had all three of them, without even having been a communist . . . For small misdemeanours, such as having a pen or pencil in one's possession, a prisoner is punished with a "bath" – being tied into a sack with a cat and thrown into the sea. Those who dare hide their pencil, hide it up their anus. One of them is found out. They shove a steel rod where the pencil had been . . .'

Blood rushed to her head; she put the manuscript down. She spotted a piece of paper tucked into an inside pocket of the magic folder. It was folded in two. Greek again, sharply handwritten. The ink was a bright, caustic blue. 'Dear Pascal, After you left that day, the police took Father and he died in prison a week later. I was imprisoned for three years. I still had one copy. You understand why it is even more important to me now. We never heard from you. I will wait for your reply. Yours, P.' Date: 12/5/76.

When Michel Franchitti was gone and Grandmother Pauline retired to her bedroom, Véronique took a chocolate from the tray on the low table, fed another one to Diane, and looked at the xeroxed passport page. It had a man's face on it, pleasant-looking, kind of old, but not as old as a grandfather. This was Pascal. She touched it. And suddenly it wasn't. The name under the photograph was not Pascal Loublier. It was somehow the reverse of Pascal Loublier. Ludovic Pêcheur. The opposite of her grandfather somehow. Disappointed, she went back to the balcony where Diane fell asleep and Véronique poured melted raspberry ice-cream into her parched, bored mouth . . .

Pascal was multiple. Was she missing something? Had she

entirely misunderstood the world all her life?

He went to look for his partisan sweetheart. He must've found her since he never made it back. That's what Pauline believed.

Calamity is when the man you love leaves you. And he never returns. And you never find out why.

What was her name?

I don't know. But I think she made a deep impression on Pascal.

Her drugged heart was suddenly beating so fast that questions stumbled into each other and fell collectively down the gutter of her logic. But still no reason for her father's last trip to Greece.

Her father: *I've got something that might be interesting to follow up.* Michel Franchitti: *This woman is most likely not in Greece – if she is alive at all.* The bureaucrat with the walrus moustache: *Don't worry your pretty head with it. It's a non-starter.*

She opened her eyes and it was morning.

The doorbell exploded inside her head. She trod the air with soft animal paws. She opened the door and in the square of light there stood an ageing postman with wistful rat-whiskers who handed her a courier letter. She heard her own voice offer him a glass of water. He stepped inside. His moustache needed a trim.

'I haven't seen a living soul in this house for thirty odd years now, except for the Monsieur who was here last year. People say it's haunted, with all the cats around . . .'

'What Monsieur?'

'The Monsieur who came last year.'

'How did he look?'

'Oh, let's see. He had frizzy hair, what he had left of it anyway, and glasses, I think.'

'When was he here?'

'Oh, I couldn't say. I couldn't say. Hold on, it was . . . summertime because I remember climbing this streets in the blimmin' heat and the Monsieur was there, at the desk downstairs, and he waved at me a couple of times.'

'How long was he here?'

'Oh, I couldn't say. Are you related?'

'We are . . . in fact, yes.'

The postman gulped the water, wetting his whiskers in the process, and was wearily gone.

Véronique fingered the thin paper, stunned by the sudden speed of events after the catatonia of the days and nights before. She was too used to nothing happening inside her life – except the past. She didn't know her father had come to this house last year – of course she couldn't, she was in Istanbul. But she didn't know other things too. The truth was, these last years they hadn't been as close as they used to be. Her gypsy lifestyle ensured that she couldn't keep up with her father's life. For a whole year she didn't know about his girlfriend, for example, not to mention his girlfriend's child from a previous marriage. Her father's guilt? Her indifference? But then, even earlier, when she was still with her parents and they nominally with each other, she didn't know about her father's infidelities. Her father had the gift of concealment and, accordingly, she had the gift of selective knowledge. She forgave him everything because she had nothing to forgive him for.

She saw with a terrible, sudden clarity that their closeness had no current value; it had expired years ago. Theirs was a closeness sitting on the laurels of the past. The result was here, in this house, in this study. Pascal was the missing link that could have bound them together but instead stood between them implacably like a phantom Berlin Wall quietly building itself, until they found themselves inhabiting different countries, living different lives. She had done nothing to prevent it. Pascal was the father Alex had died for. And Véronique hadn't even read Pascal's book.

Sitting on the doorstep in the merciless morning heat, in the queasy upside-down swing of hindsight, she fingered the letter in her hand. Why hadn't Theo called instead? She ripped the envelope open.

'Write c/o Dafina Grigorova.' With a heartbeat difficult to contain within a body her size, she walked back to the study and checked, unnecessarily, the name in the letter from '67. And through the straight and unblinking funnel of time she stared at this name. She stared like an astronomer spotting a new galaxy in her telescope, spinning with the known and unknown universes, travelling back at the speed of light to some other, dishevelled, suddenly local time where everything was possible – and dead simple. Deadly simple.

She checked timetables and packed with precise, deliberate movements. She called Theo. His voice was thick with morning sleepiness – or something worse.

'Theo, I got your letter.'

'Good.'

'I'm coming over. Do you know something. Your grandmother knew my grandfather.'

'I know.'

'Are you okay?'

'Yeah. I mean, I'm not sure. Weird things are happening. Are *you* okay?'

'I'm not sure either. Weird things are happening here too. I've missed you.'

'I've missed you too.'

'Shall we meet in Thessaloniki?'

'No, come to Ohrid first, there's someone here you must meet.'

With the heavy key, Véronique locked all bad sleep back inside the Villa Maldormé. Perhaps she would be back, perhaps not. Anything could happen from now on.

She drove in the rented BMW along the waterfront, the Island of If growing sharply from the shimmering water into its midday delirium. She left it behind. She followed her new, her only itinerary.

FORTY-SEVEN

Summer 1978 – summer 1998, Ohrid

Dafina and Stamatis had dinner together every second night. The town was abuzz with ribald joy. The two Aegeans hooking up – the strange Dafina with the even stranger Stamatis. It was somehow right and yet it disturbed people for a while, for perhaps neither of them was entirely to be trusted after all. But gossip had a finite life and since Dafina and Stamatis did nothing to either alleviate or feed it, it reached a saturation point after which they were left alone.

They became lovers in a spontaneous, inevitable way. It had been a long and sensual Indian summer day. They sailed across the lake in his boat to the Saint Naum church at the southern end of the lake. They had a delicious picnic of bread, boiled eggs, olives, smoked chicken, tomatoes and white wine on the grassy banks of the lake. The Albanian mountains shimmered elusively. The ash-coloured church stood lone and narrow on its rise. They talked about their childhood. Their conversation once again stumbled into the Chinese wall of Stamatis's memory – impossible to cross it or reach its end or beginning.

'I remember a stone fortress on an Aegean island in the distance. My father's drunken leer, my mother's silences. But I can't remember anything anyone said. Perhaps I was deaf as a child, or mute. Perhaps my father beat me too much and so I've forgotten everything.'

'What was the fortress called?'

'I can't remember. But I was afraid of it and fascinated by it. I wanted to go there but I knew that if I did, I would enter a fiction and never come back.'

'Perhaps you did go there.'

'Perhaps I did.'

The sun declined gracefully. The moment was perfect in the fragile, unprecedented and never-to-be-repeated way that the slightest wrong movement or word could topple like a sandcastle decorated with one shell too many. Stamatis stroked her cheek with the back of his fingers. She smiled. Their kiss was slow and ripe, undemanding, unquestioning, just happy to be. He looked around.

'If there were flowers here, I would put some in your hair,' he said.

Her heart stopped. She whispered, 'But all of Greece is rock.'

'What?'

'Nothing.'

'You are the only flower here. Daphne. Dafina. Flower of the many names.'

He took a handful of her still black hair threaded with rough strands of silver, and rubbed it against his face, inhaling.

On the way back, gliding across the fading blue, cormorants quaking hoarsely on the shores behind them, they were bound by the intimate knowledge that physical love was now a mere technicality. They had bypassed lust in the process of holding each other up, being each other's mirror, and whatever happened from now on – disfigurement, sex, the absence of sex, natural disasters – nothing would sever their bond.

And so, without a word, they moored the boat, stepped into his house, and pulled the curtains made by her. In the penumbral hum of the lake, they undressed and lay in his humble single bed with sheets made by her. They held each other with hands from which everything had slipped away. Except this.

Her bad left hand stroked his bad left eye. They held the

inexpressible fullness of each other, the final, ecstatic immobility of being here in this town of petrified beauty, the certainty of having each other indefinitely. Like two great, ancient, depredated cities, they were thrown together by a seismic blessing that killed everything on its way except them, because they had already died. They gazed into the steep, eroded terror at each other's core and smoothed it away. They drew lovingly the unloved creases on each other's faces. Their monastic bodies unfolded into exquisite patterns of passion. Dafina's body forgot its age. Stamatis's body loved it as if it had no age. He kissed the breasts that were no longer perky, the veined insides of her flabby thighs, the inexplicable tears that pooled into her ears, the sweat in her still raven hair, the sleepless eyelids, the stiff arm with its five stiff fingers. He didn't ask questions. She didn't need answers.

She drank from the spring of his still powerful, grey-haired chest, from his mouth with its wrecked teeth, from the alcohol-burst capillaries on his cheeks, from the receding bays of his temples, from his palms, gentle and endless like the plains where the fresh waterfalls of Edessa had rushed with the youthful violence of spring.

And although they didn't need to say anything, they said it – or perhaps she thought it simultaneously with him. My love, agapi mou, mon amour, as in a dream of something done before which didn't yield to interpretation or even memory.

And in that first afternoon of complete love Dafina understood that although time was everything to a human being, ultimately it could do nothing. Time was a stone fortress that held her prisoner but never her soul. She understood that, after dying so many times, she had become invulnerable to the common ravages of mortality. Nothing more could befall her, or him, so long as she could hold what was left of this man against what had remained of her, every declining afternoon of her life from now on. And she did.

In 1982, when former civil war partisans of Greek ethnicity were allowed back, Stamatis, with many misgivings, went to Greece on his Yugoslav passport – the only one he had, as Stamatis Argirov. Dafina was still not allowed back. She became sick with the terror of Stamatis never returning, discovering his previous life there, or discovering something that would prevent him from coming back. She didn't know and didn't want to know the nature of her fear, only its impact, which was devastating. She lost her sleep, stopped eating and waited incessantly, with every particle of herself, for news from him, which came irregularly. The talk of the people did not help her. 'He won't come back.' 'You can't turn blood into water. The wolf can't become a lamb.' Others wished for his return. 'He only needs to take a look at Greece to realise how much better it is here,' they said. 'We gave him a passport, we gave him a roof.' Dafina fled from people and retreated behind walls of fortified torment, not answering the door, furiously pressing down on the pedal of her Singer day and night, the radio blasting.

After a few unendurable weeks, he returned. They fell into each other's arms and, before she gathered the courage to ask any questions, she reassured herself in the declining afternoon that the way he loved her was unchanged.

Then he said, 'It would appear that I don't exist.'

Dafina laughed but her laughter was hollow.

'No, don't laugh. It's very odd. There was a Stamatis Argiris in Thessaloniki, and he did work for the Greek railways in the sixties and seventies, but . . . he died in an accident two years ago.'

They were entering territory the mere idea of which chilled her to the marrow. She didn't want to hear anything about his trip, and yet she had to know.

'What kind of an accident?'

'He fell off the train. He had an alcohol problem.'

'Two years ago?'

'Yes.'

'And you had your accident in '67.'

'Yes.'

'But there could easily be two people of the same name.'

'Yes of course, but you see, the Greek railways only ever had one employee by that name.'

'Did you go to the Intelligence Service?'

'Are you joking! In fact, some people at the railways started getting really suspicious when I was asking too many questions and I was told that I would be dealt with by the police. I couldn't risk getting detained. What if they stopped me from going back across the border? What was there for me anyway? A secret file from the civil war and the junta, if that.'

He smoked, looking at her. She put her cheek against his, speechless, and held him, and felt her life stir in him thickly, immutably. He had come back because of her. He stroked her hair.

One day, he dug out his notebooks filled with illegible notes he'd taken while working on the trains. He was going to write a book with the recorded stories passengers had told him about themselves and others.

'You see,' he explained to Dafina, 'the stories of people on trains are always somehow . . . fabulous. Because they always travel towards some place that exists in their minds in a certain shape or form, not necessarily the way it is in reality. They construct castles with their stories, if you like, and with their stories I want to construct my own castle, in the form of a book, you see. It's that fortress that fascinated me as a child.'

He didn't know what to call his book. But Dafina did. *From the Villa Maldormé you can see the Castle of If where . . . where I will take you so that we can look back at the coast and see the Villa Maldormé. Daphne mou . . . And we'll dynamite the Castle of If to mark the end of all prison islands. And we'll live in the Villa Maldormé so that we don't sleep and we make love all night. And there'll be no guards around, and we'll eat croissants and café au lait and sleep in every morning . . . Every morning, mon amour.*

All it had taken was thirty years.

Maria, Kostas and Theo came twice more. Each time, all three of them went to Thessaloniki. Each time, Dafina looked at her gracefully ageing daughter and wondered if she didn't owe her the truth. But how was the truth to be told from the lie?

A lie was an affirmative statement about something that wasn't true. The war had been a lie, for example; they had believed in it and died believing, and sent others to their deaths. Alexis's execution was a lie. A lie was also something that had happened but couldn't have possibly happened, a monstrosity bigger than our capacity to live with it. To see fourteen-year-old children ripped to pieces by mines. To lose not just what we have, but what we don't have – hope and the right to be loved. To be broken with exhaustion and grief, unable to carry on. To carry on. To carry on until we mutate into someone else. That was a lie.

Waving to Pascal on Grammos was a lie. Killing systematically her love for him, on the wrong side of that moonless July night, was a lie. But this man who sounded like him and perhaps looked like him and who stood in front of her, groping for a self – any self, a lost one or one he never had – was the truth. Stamatis was the truth, whoever he was. And to speak of Pascal Loublier now, after a lifetime of silence, would be to force herself and her daughter into a violence of knowledge that could annihilate them.

Dafina went to Australia once, in between Maria's visits, and was relieved to return a few weeks later – there was too much space there, too much sky, too many people who didn't speak to each other, too many of her countrymen living in bitter exile. And she could not bear to be without Stamatis.

In '94, Dafina was diagnosed with breast cancer. She lost a breast and was given a year or two to live. 'Don't listen to them,' Stamatis said. 'You've got as long as you want to live. And I love you no matter how many breasts you have.' She didn't tell Maria until the summer of '98 when her condition deteriorated rapidly and she only had weeks left. Theo, whom she knew from photos as an intense young man with arrestingly odd eyes, went to Thessaloniki in early '98 for his studies, but took a long time to get to Ohrid. Dafina and Stamatis waited for him every day. Dafina fretted that she would die before he made it.

Through the semi-conscious haze of pain and morphine that finally vanquished her, she heard a hospital fan buzzing overhead. She perceived her daughter's moist violet eyes, calling her from afar and a young man moving like a foreigner. Theo had come after all. He had met a French woman and Dafina managed to smile and ask if she was the one for him, but of course Theo didn't know; the young just didn't know anything in these times of doubt. She had known, always.

She wanted to tell Maria and Theo many things, but they kept floating further into the world of the living and she could only perceive them from her island of pain, unable to speak or even wave to them.

Through her agony, she saw them: Alexis, Illias, her mother and father, the entire Grigoriadis family. They rose from the rocks where they had been lying unburied. They descended the sharp, bespattered hills of Grammos, wind in their hair, rags on their bodies, disarmed, barefoot and bloodied, but happy to see their Dafina finally, after fifty years. You haven't changed a bit, they said, and she said you haven't changed either, and she understood that separation had been a momentary cough-inducing draught that was staunched as soon as the windows and doors were slammed shut in the face of life. That time meant nothing and her soul was intact, after all. That she had done what she could.

Stamatis came and went. She heard his voice, the accent of his voice, the love of his voice, the silver of his voice. His voice lulled her in a red boat called *Daphne* that was going nowhere because it had arrived, because Stamatis had stopped beside her forever. His voice rocked her in a swing of sunshine suspended over the lake. His voice rushed to the plains of Edessa with the youthful violence of spring. His voice rustled on this side of a moonless July night, 1948, the side where she had remained. His voice echoed through the limestone pot-holes of his unremembered childhood. His voice beckoned her from the white, crumbling Castle of If.

EPILOGUE

With largely somnambular but hyper-lucid gestures, they arranged the interlocking fantasies of their two destinies. Then they contemplated the improbable work, alternating between profound belief and a profound sense of insanity.

They touched each other's bodies with strangers' hands and lips, incredulous and detached. No money for blood love. They could not love each other after all. Not the way they needed to.

On the second day, before they went to see Stamatis in the hospital, Theo gave her Dafina's letter. She read it and her reaction was the same as Theo's a few days ago.

'No,' she said, then failed to laugh. She read the letter again. She looked at him for help.

'But . . .' she said.

'I know,' he said.

'But . . .' And she read the letter again.

He waited patiently, if nervously, while she tried to make sense of it. 'It's ambiguous,' she concluded, her hands shaking, her laughter hollow. 'It's totally ambiguous. I mean this for example: "Wasn't I seeing what I had hoped against any hope to see, ever since I waved to him from the crags of Grammos? Weren't you an impersonation of my longing for him? Weren't you someone entirely different, a lost Greek who had stumbled across the border and just happened to look like him, twenty something years older? What is a person without his memory? Who does he become? Who would I, Dafina, be if I suddenly lost my memory? If I didn't remember the war, my brothers and my parents, my friends, Tashkent, Pascal . . . I have in fact tried to forget for so long, I changed my name, I tried to crush my love for him, I never told my own daughter. Haven't I too become someone else?" Theo, I don't think she knew either, until the end, whether it was him.'

'Maybe you can tell if it's him.'

'Theo.' She took his hand feverishly as never before. 'I didn't know I could be this scared. I'm terrified.'

'Me too,' he said simply. This wasn't a time for false bravado.

'We must talk to your Uncle Panayotis and to Michel Franchitti.'

'Maybe. We must first of all see Stamatis.'

They shared an unspoken mutual gratitude for firmly sticking with the name Stamatis, for never mentioning the other name.

On the way to the hospital, in the dusty bus, Theo explained to Véronique why Stamatis was a mess. He had developed Korsakoff's alcoholic syndrome. He had suddenly crumbled like a dry sandcastle. He was on anti-depressants. The doctors believed he was also suicidal, something unusual for Korsakoffs, which was why they kept him under surveillance.

Véronique and Theo entered his room, hearing each other's heartbeats. They sat by his bed. Theo said in Greek, 'Stamati, this is my friend Véronique.'

Véronique shook the old man's hand, began to say something in Greek, then in French – she didn't even know what it was – choked on her words and, to her own shock, started to cry. She cried for the three weeks without Theo and without her sanity. For the fifteen-hour-Midas ordeal. For the year without her father. For a lifetime without Pascal. For everything that came too late.

'Miss,' Stamatis said tenderly, 'you are so beautiful I hope you have a damn good reason to cry.'

Theo tried to be the balancing factor, although the white room spun around him. He was crouching beside Véronique, trying to hold her.

'Is it him?'

Véronique shook her head, nodded, shrugged her shoulders and eventually said pathetically, 'I don't know. I don't know. I've never met him. How can I know?'

'But the eyes, look at the eyes. The bad one is speckled.'

She nodded again and shook her head, covering her face as if not to look at Stamatis, then taking her hands away and staring at him uncomprehendingly.

Two curious nurses peeked inside. Véronique pressed herself against Theo. She smelt of salt, but not of his future.

'I never took her there,' Stamatis said casually, looking at them, as if continuing a conversation from which they had impolitely tried to sidetrack him.

'Who, Stamati?'

'Dafina, who. I promised to take her there. I mean, she promised to take me there but . . . I can't remember where it is any more. It's too late.' He fixed his worried blue eye on Véronique.

'What is he talking about?' she whispered.

'Stamati, can you tell Véronique about the Castle of If?'

'The Castle of If is a place, somewhere, far back in time. It's white and crumbling, on an island. All the people on my train were going there. It's a very popular destination. I have been writing this book, I have many notes, but the closer I get, the more the castle recedes. The train never took me there so I got off the train. Then I got a boat, it's red. But the boat won't take me there either. She knew. I promised her but . . .' He waved his hand despondently and his head fell back on the pillows. Then his eye sparked with a brilliant new thought.

'Miss,' he turned to Véronique, 'do you know where it is, incidentally?'

Theo and Véronique looked at each other.

'He asked me this too,' Theo said.

'What did you say?'

'What could I say? I'm not sure if he means the same thing I mean. But I suspect it doesn't matter anyway.'

Stamatis was anxiously waiting for an answer.

'Yes.' Véronique had no idea what she was doing or saying and yet she was quite sure of it. 'I know where it is. I think we all know where it is. Pascal and Daphne, you and Dafina, me and Theo.'

'And the Count of Monte Cristo,' Theo added seriously. Véronique raised her eyebrows.

'I suspected that all along,' Stamatis muttered, nodding pensively. 'So she's already waiting for me . . .'

He threw off the covers, sat up shakily and put his livid feet inside his tattered slippers.

'Come on, children,' he said. 'Time is ticking away. Take me there.'

RECONNAISSANCE

Kapka Kassabova

A powerful and sensual début novel.

Nadejda is backpacking around New Zealand, in the surreal haze of summer. Her encounters are comic and revealing – and often sexual. But Nadejda's tour is a deep and personal one; it is a journey into memory and family myth.

Faded memories of happy times conflict with more disturbing pictures as her determination to uncover the truth is diffused with an immigrant's yearning to belong and a young woman's longing for love. And who is the mystery narrator who 'talks' to Nadejda as her travels lead her to him?

Set against the turmoil of present-day Bulgaria and the sweet simplicity of her new country, *Reconnaissance* is a grand, sweeping novel of family secrets, dislocation and ultimate reconciliation.

Winner of the Best First Book category in the South-East Asia and South Pacific region of the 2000 Commonwealth Writers Prize, and finalist in the 1999 Montana New Zealand Book Awards.

Classical
Music

JOY COWLEY

We dive together and come up, our clothes floating around us. The water is surprisingly warm and it occurs to me that this is the first time we've been in the sea together since her near-drowning incident.

Delia and Bea, sisters, but never close. Delia lives a glamorous life in New York and Bea lives thousands of miles away in New Zealand, looking after elderly parents and playing the role of dutiful daughter. Delia and Bea both long for the warmth and intimacy of sisterhood, but it always eludes them.

When Delia rushes home for their father's funeral there is an opportunity to spend some time together, but Delia and Bea move in orbit around each other, both recalling grievances and hurts, neither prepared to admit their need for each other. But as the day of the funeral passes, memories are unlocked: memories of their mother and her passion for music, memories of their father and memories of a magical summer and a man they had all loved.

Joy Cowley is one of New Zealand's most loved children's writers. She is also famous all over North America for her wonderful children's readers. *Classical Music* is her second adult novel.

THE CURATIVE

Charlotte Randall

The narrator of this compelling and unusual novel is an inmate of Bedlam, the London mental asylum. He is living chained to a wall in unspeakably horrible conditions, yet he is witty, urbane and seemingly sane. He reflects on freedom, on love and on love lost, and on the fleeting nature of happiness.

As this beautifully constructed story unfolds we learn about the bizarre treatments he has endured under the asylum's curative regimen, his life before Bedlam, and the answers to the critical questions: *Why is this man here? What has he done?*

This novel deftly explores the devious in human affairs and the intricacies of language to create a brilliant and utterly memorable book.

Charlotte Randall's first novel, *Dead Sea Fruit* (1995), won both the Reed Fiction Award and Best First Book in the South-East Asia and South Pacific region of the Commonwealth Writers Prize.